Laotion
Highway Patrol

A Novel By

James A. White, Jr.

 www.trafford.com

North America & international
toll-free: 844-688-6899 (USA & Canada)
fax: 812 355 4082

Dedication

A book was written after World War II about the PT Boat crews plying the vast seas, in their small plywood craft, called "They Were Expendable." It reminds us that in all wars there are the "expendables." During the second Indo-China War, or Southeastern Asian Conflict, or Vietnam War, or Our War, we helicopter crews became this generations "expendable." Not dashing in atop large white steeds, or in battle weary supply ladened tanks, or aboard sleek fast moving boats. NO! We arrived with much noise and fanfare from the heavens in awkward shaped vehicles painted with strange hieroglyphics to signify our individuality. As in wars past, and surely in future wars, there will be those like us, a few considered "expendable."

On a cold granite wall are the names of over 58,000 who made the ultimate sacrifice. The names, of which 4% are helicopter pilots and over 7% are helicopter crew chiefs and/or door gunners, are those who we toiled beside to get the green rotary-winged aircraft mission ready, flying, and then home safely. Men who spent, as we, their Vietnam lives waking up in darkness and falling asleep again in darkness, trying to keep the beat of the blades thumping in a far distant land.

Carved carefully in black upon the wall, for millennia to come, is the testament that those who wore Silver or Gold; Air Crew, Combat Air Crew, or Aviator Wings, are not forgotten. This book is dedicated to you, who wore and will always wear those WINGS. Wings that remind us that on some days, individually or collectively, we rose to heights of warriors in centuries past. Thank

i

you, for letting me have the honor to be one of Vietnam's expendable.

This is also dedicated to the men of MAC-V-SOG's Op Plan 34A and 35. Your story will never be fully revealed through the few of us who had the distinct pleasure to serve you. This assignment, in my life, is the highlight of years of a mediocre military experience. Your confidence and professionalism meant that in over 2675 cross border high risk missions we lost only 103 men. I think of and pray for you and for CCN's 59 MIAs everyday.

A motto of one of the associations I belong to reads:

YOU HAVE NEVER LIVED UNTIL YOU HAVE ALMOST DIED. FOR THOSE WHO HAVE, LIFE HAS A SPECIAL FLAVOR THE PROTECTED WILL NEVER KNOW.

This says it all.

TO MY BROTHERS:

Captain KIA/MIA	KEITH ALLEN BRANDT 18 March 1971 Body Returned 19 July 1980 D/101st AVN 101st ABN DIV
Warrant Officer 1 KIA	RALPH RICHARD QUICK, JR. 27 April 1970 Headquarters & Headquarters Company 108th Arty Group

Sergeant Major   FREDERICK B. DOUGLASS
KIA   23 October 1983
                      (Beirut, Lebanon)
                      Headquarters &
                      Headquarters Company
                      23rd MAF
                      Vietnam: Gunnery Sergeant
                      HMM-262

Staff Sergeant   MADISON A. STROHLEIN
MIA   2 June 1971
                      MLT-2 CCN MAC-V-SOG

Corporal   JAMES MICHAEL AKSTIN
KIA   12 May 1967
                      HMM-262, MAG-36,
                      1st MAW

Acknowledgements

This would not have been written without reading Layne Heath's (C/158AVN 101st ABN & D/1st/10th CAV); Ron Winter's (HMM-161); and Marion Sturkey's (HMM-265) writings about helicopter operations in Vietnam. Their stories told me that Vietnam helicopter operations were of interest and should be told so others might understand the gallantry and unselfish giving of so few, and yes to even preserve some history for future generations. Though I have never served with Layne, Ron, or Marion, we all served and I would have been honored to have flown with them - ANYTIME, ANYWHERE!

To Norm "Frenchy" LaFountainne (HML-167); MGySgt (USMC Rtd.) E. R. Smith (HMM-262); Major (USMC Rtd.) Jerry Piatt (HMM-262 & HMM 265 & Air America); and Jimmy Akstin (Cpl. USMC KIA 12 May 1967, HMM-262) who all went off to war as Marine helicopter crewmen and returned so differently, but also so much the same.

When the title Green Berets is spoken images appear within one's mind and for many of us that image is of Billy Waugh, Sergeant Major (USA Rtd.). Around Billy you performed at a higher level and this surely saved lives, both of his Recon Teams and us, the many novices flying helicopters for his Mission Launch Team (MLT). In the military there is a much overused cliche which says: One should lead by example. Billy was our example and the results of CCN's Mission Launch Team 2's missions are testament to his leadership. I am alive today because of two men, and one is Billy.

Thank You Sir!!!

To John Garrison (CWO-3, USA Rtd.) and Richard "Rick" Freeman, who for over 30 years have remained friends during the ups and downs of our lives. John, who's tours with Special Forces on the ground in Laos led him to decide to become a helicopter pilot. In his last Vietnam tour flying for the GRIFFINS, led him to once again be "on the ground" in Laos, for a few days after being shot down during LOM SOM 719. I'll never be able to repay him for the small things, such as bringing home "Fred" my dog, rather than let him end up in a large soup bowl, which was something neither Fred nor I will ever forget. To Rick, GRIFFIN IP and ARA Section Leader extraordinaire, who in my darkest hours arrived "Back On Station," and in typical GRIFFIN fashion reached out with a hand. Decades ago you taught me that friendship under fire leads to bonding for life, and you remind me of this each and every day. As a combat pilot, when the mission was over you could have crawled back into your cubical - like most of us did - awaiting another call, but NO, you never distanced yourself. All the GRIFFINS thank you for this. I am sure this is the one reason why we never lost a GRIFFIN while you were with us, as your IP training continued in and out of the cockpit. We've spent many hours together and though not much has been spoken, we have been able to communicate in volumes. If there is a "SWEET GRIFFIN," and only we GRIFFINS know, I am satisfied in knowing you and he are one and the same.

To Rory Folsom, big Jim Stockman, and Paul Thomas: Two Marines and a sailor who through conspiracy and superior planning, or maybe just plain dumb luck, kept me working on this project without distractions. Not only without distraction but with a gentle nudge when I would decide to give up or throw away an idea. These three kept a daily vigil to insure I moved forward and did not wallow in the mire of what was right, or wrong, about the War. Though not serving with you, I would have welcomed the chance.

After pages upon pages of rough manuscript were written, Sheryl Gottesman and Art Blomker (USN Sub Service) revised and edited, and returned for re-write after re-write, and finely turned it over to Steve Prefontaine for its final layout.

The cover is based on a painting by Joe Kline (B/101st AHB, 101st ABN DIV), a noted combat artist who painted from his memories of the Khe Sanh plains while flying in the area in 1969-1970.

All of this gathering of resources, laying out the cover design, and the countless number of small "projects" that never get done without a person who commits to a project like this is because of G.L. "Red" Logan (GySgt, USMC Rtd., HMM-262 & HMM 265). Red is not only a dear friend, but a fellow warrior whose meaning of friendship is a model for all. I am honored to call him my friend. Even though at times during this project our friendship was tested, he kept at it, and it would never have been completed without him, he is as much the author as I.

A final thank you goes to Nancy, who has had to struggle through the Vietnam experience as a wife, and though a peace loving soul, is one of the most patriotic people I have ever known. Nancy: There once was a tune in my heart, then I met you; and for the first time I hear the words. Lady, these words say it all.

Dau Tranh,

Sneaky

Chapter 1

"Quang Tri Tower, Griffin over."

"Griffin, this is Quang Tri," immediately came back through my headset.

"Roger Quang Tri, Griffin Nine-Two Gulf with a flight of four to the southeast for landing at CCN."

"Roger Griffin, your flight is cleared direct to CCN. The winds are three-two at four, altimeter two-niner-niner-four, DA three-one-five."

The clipped reply from the Air Force air traffic controller signals just how busy this small airfield is already this morning. To our two o'clock, the air over the airfield is full of black specks of helicopters on the move.

My wingmen acknowledge hearing our landing instructions on their UHF radio by squelch breaks on the VHF. Our flight has now stretched out into a staggered trail formation to allow landing on the tiny south to north pad. I glance to my ten o'clock to see where I'm going to set down and enter a dogleg base to a final approach. I have to wait for the UHF radio to quiet down because of the heavy traffic in the local area. Quang Tri Tower not only controls the main airfield, but the dozen or so small pads used for the many units stationed around Quang Tri Combat Base's perimeter, as well as what is left flying out of Dong Ha Combat Base.

"Quang Tri, Griffin flight is turning final to CCN, weapons cold."

For this flight we haven't armed our weapons systems since

take-off, less than 15 minutes ago. We flew here via IFR (not the FAA interpretation "Instrument Flight Rules", but mine, "I Follow Railroads, Rivers, and, in this case, Roads.")

Cutting off the tower's response, I switch to the VHF radio, or Victor as we call this radio, "Let's keep it tight. The slicks aren't here yet."

Again, the VHF radio lights up with squelch breaks.

At the same time, on the FM radio, Doc calls the MLT to notify them we're landing. "MLT-Two, Griffin inbound with a flight of four."

"Roger Griffin, go ahead and shut down," a voice I've gotten to know over the years replies. It's hard to picture the man behind this high, almost soprano, tone as a Special Forces Sergeant First Class, but there's no doubt it's Milo.

I ease my heavily armed helicopter to the far northern end of the PSP matting serving as the MLT landing zone. Located within a large secure fire base, across QL-1 from Quang Tri Airfield, the LZ isn't on any map and doesn't invite one to land to ask for information or directions. From the air, the average helicopter pilot would miss it. There is no wind sock fluttering in the wind, no bright numbers painted on the PSP, no landing lights sticking up around the PSP, nor revetments laid out in neat rows. The PSP has been in place long enough for the weeds to have grown through and, in some spots, high enough to easily rub against our helicopters' bellies. There are no signs welcoming you here or, for that matter, telling you who is here.

Encircling the compound are rows of concertina wire layered high enough to keep out most people, except maybe highly trained NVA sappers. They would love to get into this compound at any cost. On the east side of the PSP are the hootches that the compound's inhabitants live in and work out of. Three hootches are lined up with their ends facing the weed covered matting. Between these three and the eastern rows of concertina are four other hootches, a bit longer, and set 90 degrees to the smaller three. The four appear to be more run-down than the others.

Between the three hootches, and the four waiting to launch team hootches, is a long bunker, three smaller MLT team hooches, and a pair of wooden buildings that serve as a shower and a latrine. Each of the twelve hootches has the rusted roof and unpainted exteriors common in Vietnam which give the hint of a wild west ghost town from the turn of the century. Speckled here and there are signs of life, usually in the forms of brightly colored clothes hanging from the many scattered lines between the buildings. On close inspection, one can also see the olive drab clothing that confirms the residents are Americans.

Not visible from the air, even on short final, is a gate on the southeastern flank of the compound. On further inspection, a small dark-skinned boy is sitting on a folding chair next to the gate. He's shirtless with a floppy hat and dirty yellow-colored boxer shorts, like the ones seen hanging between the huts. As I hover past him, its obvious he's really not a boy, at least by Asian standards, and he's armed to the teeth. There's a CAR-15 slung over the chair's back. He's wearing a .45 caliber pistol hanging at his side on a heavily laden pistol belt .

As I ease the skids to the ground and roll off the throttle, I look back at him again. Now he's holding his hat with one hand and waving frantically with the other. Though he can't speak English, he does understand some of it and, more important, he's been in enemy held territory enough to know to wave and be nice to an armed helicopter. I'm sure that there have been numerous occasions that an aircraft like this has proven to be a lifesaver. I give him a salute, then turn back to the business at hand, shutting down the Lycoming engine. Letting the engine cool the Army's required three minutes, I watch as the first of the four Hueys land in the open area between our aircraft and the hootches. As they land, I close my window rather than have all the dust, sand, and other garbage blow into my cockpit.

After shutting down, Hunt gets out and ties the main rotor down. I climb out and walk straight for the far northern hootch which has numerous large antennae jutting along its side. In the plywood structure, I come face to face with Captain Stanton, who is Mission Launch Team 2 Commander. Though the MLT is made up of a small group of men, only ten Americans, it's a highly skilled and very efficient group.

"What's up *Dai Uy*?" I ask, knowing that he will refer me to Sergeant Major Washburn who in fact really runs the operations as the Senior Operations NCO as well as the number two man in charge as far as paperwork goes. The Sergeant Major really is the executive officer, if one needs a title.

"How's it going Sneaky?" without waiting for a reply, he slips by me and adds, "Billy's not here so Milo will give you the run down once everybody's inside." He steps out and lets the screen door slam.

"Sneaky!" From the back of the building comes Milo's high pitched voice.

"Yo Milo. What's the word?"

"I'm your man for the day. Billy had to go down to Da Nang for some bullshit briefing. You know how those Headquarters types are about briefings." He chuckles. He knows my feelings for any Headquarters types.

Sergeant First Class Stanley 'The Man' Milo is the Assistant Operations Sergeant for MLT-2. He's been in the Army almost twenty years and probably weighs the same as he did when he entered. He once told me he stayed in because the Army gave him three squares a day and a new pair of shoes every so often. He wasn't sure he could get that back in southern West Virginia if he got discharged. His Korean War record marks him as what most would call a warrior. His appearance though doesn't bear evidence of his record. He's thin as a rail, wiry, but I wouldn't want to tangle with him in some darkened alley. His black hair is flecked with grey where it's clipped neatly to frame his bald pate.

"You want all the pilots in for a briefing?"

I know the answer. SFC Milo likes to hold briefings as if he were giving them to General Westmoreland. Everyone there, sitting up straight, note pads and pencils in hand. He'll cover everything at least twice if there is time. He ensures all questions get answered. Though usually I shine a lot of briefing material on, I attend CCN briefings with the attention of a very hungry bear opening a camp cooler. Where we're going one cannot afford to miss some small detail. It's better to ask a stupid question than get killed by a stupid bullet.

"Don't worry, *Dai Uy* went out to gather them up."

Without another word, he turns back though the rear doorway into the small radio room. As he does, I hear the random crackling of radios accompanied by squelch breaks and static from some far off location.

Grabbing a chair in the front row, I listen as the pilots filter noisily into the room. Without being told, they quiet down.

CWO-2 Loften slides into the seat next to me and whispers, "Shit, I ought to be down at China Beach getting a tan."

He volunteered to fly with us today, even though he only has five days left in-country.

"Fuck you Tex, the Army needs your valuable expertise today."

I play along with him though I know I would do the same thing. I would fly the last possible flight I could. While I'm laughing with Tex's answering grin, Milo slips back into the room holding a hand full of stabo rigs. He moves stealthily as a matter of course.

"Any of you guys need these?" he asks, while I shake my head no in anticipation of his question. Today's Griffin crew is made up of all regular CCN pilots, therefore have our own stabo rigs already on.

"My flight needs them," someone from behind me says, probably the slick's lead aircraft commander.

All Hueys should be set up for strings and every crew member flying should have a stabo rig on. The nylon webbed harness, called a stabo rig, has several D-rings attached to it. If you're shot down and not able to be picked up by a landing Huey, a hovering Huey equipped with strings can get you out. The crew-chief and gunner throw several strings down and you hook onto them. The ride is sickening, scary, and gut-wrenching.

The Huey must hover straight up to get you clear of the trees. Sometimes it's over one hundred feet. Then you're dragged through and knocked around tree limbs and branches as you're lifted. Hopefully, the Huey doesn't come under fire to make the pilot decide that being there is not in his best interest, because moving horizontally means interaction with non-moveable trees. It takes a gutsy pilot to climb vertically especially if he's taking gunfire. The temptation to fly away is there. At least with me, it would be.

After all this is completed, you're left dangling a hundred feet below the slick on this string. Then they, with you below, fly to a secure spot to land — which might take forty-five minutes. During the ride, at fifty to sixty knots, you're spinning around and getting dizzier at each revolution. It helps to hold on to the others swinging beneath the slick with you to try to stabilize your twisting. You become an airfoil, though a poor one, and stablize, if you have several guys all linked up.

On landing, you have another problem. The rig is so tight around your legs the circulation is completely cut off. My two rides ended with me not able to stand. Both times the crew-chief had to carry me, and my co-pilot, to the Huey and deposit us unceremoniously on the floor. Humiliating, to say the least, but I lived to fly another day.

"Listen up gentlemen," Milo says as he hands the rigs to one of the Phoenix pilots. "We have a team in trouble and will have to extract them this morning."

Turning around, he takes his dog tag chain from around his neck and using a large key hanging off it unlocks the large plywood box built onto the interior wall. After unlocking it, he swings open its large double doors and pulls back a thick, but faded, purple cloth revealing a six-foot square map. I've always found this whole process very melodramatic, but it sends a quick message to the new pilot.

"All right, here's what we have."

This pronouncement brings a hush broken only by the shuffling of pads on the pilots' knee boards. The men await the mission details that will take them into harm's way and, hopefully, back home again.

"At this location," Milo points with a long stick at a grid on the uncovered map. "Xray Delta three-five-nine. . . five-zero-four, we have RT Coral."

I, like everyone else, am writing down the coordinates, when Randy Hunt taps me on the shoulder and shoves his map toward me. He's marked the area in with his black grease pencil. I grab it and glance closely at the terrain we will be flying over and into.

"They were inserted here," moving his hand a bit to the northwest of their present location, "four days ago. Their objective is classified."

This is the standard statement with MAC-V-SOG operations. Everything is classified so we don't have a need to know what they were doing; just where they are and how many. I've gotten to know a lot of the team members, at least the Americans, so I usually find out what the team is trying to do, or more likely, what they were trying to do.

"The team is made up of three Americans and three 'yards, and one of the 'yards has sustained wounds from a firefight at zero-two-three-zero hours. Since then, the team has been on the move trying to break contact," he moves his pointer to the LZ, "and are now trying to reach this LZ. This was not the original or secondary pickup LZ, but things have changed quite quickly in the past couple hours. We expect them to make it to this new LZ within the hour. Gentlemen, I don't have to remind you, this will probably be a hot one."

With this news, the two groups of pilots take a different tack to the final part of the briefing. The Huey drivers will hope that things will calm down, as they are the ones that will have to enter the LZ, hover while the beleaguered team climbs onboard, then slowly (much too slowly for their taste) exit the LZ. We Cobra pilots listen up with the knowledge that not only are we going into Indian country where we can shoot at will, but with the team in contact they'll provide us some targets of opportunity. Plus, the slick pilots will draw out a few targets for us while they waddle into and out of the area.

"Coral's call sign is Papa Alpha Kilo and they are up thirty-six point one-five. Covey is presently on station, he's reporting the weather as clear. His call sign is Straight Arrow One-Three and he's up two-forty-one point two-zero. Covey can get fast movers if needed and Hillsborough has been alerted." Looking directly at me, "You'll use Dancing Bear," then looking over my head, "and the slicks will be Silver Fox."

Milo stops to let everyone catch up with their note taking, "Lead slick will carry one *bac si*, and the other will be in Chalk Three."

Before he can continue, the NCO who's been monitoring the radios enters and whispers in Milo's ear.

"Gentlemen, you'll launch right away, things are getting tight out there. Before you leave, one last thing. If you go down. . ., stay with your aircraft for as long as possible. Then if, and I mean this, if you must E&E head north or northeast toward QL-9. Understand?"

As the gravity of his last few words sinks into the audience, he turns and, in a quick jerk, snatches the cloth back over the map, snaps shut the two wooden doors, and slaps the padlock back on. Everyone recognizes the closing snap of the pad lock as a sign of dismissal.

Quickly, before any of us move, he turns around and looks each of us in the eye, for just a brief moment. His eyes are icy, I don't think anyone knows the color. Milo has made the past ten minutes very personal to each of us.

"If there are no questions, let's get airborne."

There is almost a rush for the door as sixteen men move at

the same speed to get to their aircraft. No telling what is going through their minds, especially the Lead and Chalk Two Huey pilots. They will be the ones experiencing this mission up close and personal.

I step out of the hootch into the bright morning sun. A mission like this before seven could set the tone of a very busy and long day. I catch up to Randy before he goes to the tail and unhooks the rotor blade.

"Here's your map."

I really don't need it now. I know where we are going and how to get there and back. Plus, my map is in my lower left pant leg pocket. It's easy, you leave Quang Tri headed almost due west, fly over Camp J.J. Carroll, then past the Rockpile and a southern dogleg past Vandy, then follow the abandoned QL-9 and it's westerly heading out to Khe Sanh. Once at Khe Sanh, we'll have plenty of altitude as we cross out of the war zone of South Vietnam and enter neutral Laos. Though QL-9 meanders like a snake, generally it's almost a due east/west dirt track, called a road on the maps we've been issued. About forty clicks west of the border is Tchepone, which was a thriving small city long before the war. While in Laos, QL-9 is bordered at times with the Song Ba or as some call it, the Tchepone River to the south. This river rages during monsoons and becomes almost nonexistent during the dry season. To the south of the Song Ba is a large escarpment that overlooks both the river and QL-9. That is where our recon team is presently perched. On the map it looks like a fairly easy mission, though we are all aware this trip will take us to the limit of our range. We know that it's not going to be just a simple trip out and back.

I quickly start my aircraft. As soon as the gauges head for the green, I come up on VHF, "Griffins, you ready?" They will all have set our unit frequency on the VHF radio. Without waiting for replies to my query, I switch to UHF and wait for the Air Force controller to finish his sentence.

"Quang Tri Tower, this is Griffin Nine-Two Gulf with a flight of four at CCN with a scramble to POL, over."

The tower operator knows who we are and can probably guess what we do or where we go, so I get an immediate, "Griffin Nine-Two Gulf, your flight is cleared from CCN directly to three-six with a turn off at POL." Then as an afterthought, "Winds are three-six at ten, altimeter two-niner-niner-three, DA three-thirty."

"Roger, Griffins lifting." I have already started my slow takeoff as I call that we are lifting. Gathering speed, I turn into an elongated left three-sixty degree turn headed for the Quang Tri active runway. Doc calls that he's off so I know my flight is up and moving.

"Quang Tri, Griffin flight is on extended base for three-six, weapons cold."

"Roger Griffin, I have you in sight, you're flight cleared direct POL." Then, he responds to Phoenix Lead's request to take off and head west.

As I nose into the POL point, I'm called on FM. "Dancing Bear Lead, this is Silver Fox Lead, over."

"Go Silver Fox."

"Roger Dancing Bear Lead, we're off at this time and will orbit Carroll."

"Roger, we'll call when we're off Silver Fox." This is a good idea as it will give the Hueys a bit of time to start their climb to altitude, while we top off with fuel.

While topping off, I've marked my map with all the call signs, frequencies, and the LZ, so I have it all handy. Randy has put the call signs on his window so I can see them. His writing is as terrible as mine. I tune the FM to the recon team's frequency and, as soon as we're airborne, I'll tune in the UHF. I'm ready to go.

"Dancing Bear Lead, Sundance Halo, over." Milo's on the radio for me already.

"Go Sundance."

"Ah... Lead what is your estimated departure, Straight Arrow has notified us another Whiskey India Alpha with Papa

Alpha Kilo, over."

"Roger that, we'll be off in two. Silver Fox is enroute now, over." I acknowledge the urgency of this question. We've got another man wounded in RT Coral.

"You guys ready?" I ask, while looking over to see all the co-pilots have re-entered their aircraft. The aircraft commanders give me a thumbs up. Immediately, I pull up to a hover, while calling the tower, "Quang Tri, this is Griffin flight at POL with a scramble to the west." Without waiting for an answer to my call, I continue my hover toward the active runway.

"Roger Griffin, your flight is cleared to the active. The winds......"

Without listening to the rest of the tower's clearance as it's just weather related data, I change over to FM to tell the slicks we're on the way. While doing this, I arm the weapons system for the first time today. I pull the four-way seat belt restraints a bit tighter. Taking a couple of deep breaths, I put myself into the mission mind set. When flying in Laos, one's mind must focus on the mission, but also on the area one's flying through. This dual focus is second nature to me after crossing the fence so many times. Still, I mentally go through the paces of getting ready for. . . God knows what.

Chapter 2

Our flight to Camp J.J. Carroll lasts just a few minutes, and after we join up with the Hueys, we become a package and head west. The slicks lead us and are at a higher altitude. We trail them, like a coon dog with its nose to the ground, sniffing, looking, hoping for trouble. Though the slicks are in an orderly, but loose formation, we are not. If our flight school instructors could see us now they would surely flunk us and recommend for us to go before a flight evaluation board. We are below the prescribed flight level for helicopters flying in Vietnam and for flying to and from a mission. We are not flying in any formation but rather flying in individual weaving patterns that sometimes cross each other. No one out here will get a grade for what they do. Only the chance to come back home in one piece. For us, this is as good a grade as one could hope for.

As we overfly the old Khe Sanh fire base, I call, "Straight Arrow One-Three, Dancing Bear Lead, over."

There's no answer, but I really didn't expect one this far out. There is no doubt that the Air Force O-2A FAC aircraft is diving in and out of the hills to our west. Not only is he trying to keep an eye on the recon team, but I am sure he's trying to stay out of the gunsights of the many anti-aircraft weapons that make their home in Laos. Also, when you're on the ground and seventy-five to one hundred miles from any, and I mean any, friendly troops, then having the Covey FAC flying overhead has to give you some inspiration, no matter how gloomy things look. Plus, the Covey FAC has told the team we're on the way. I continue to make several calls trying to raise the FAC, when the Phoenix Lead calls.

"Dancing Bear, Silver Fox Lead, over."

"Go Lead."

"Bear Lead, if you want I'll try calling One-Three as I've got a bit more altitude..... ah.... if you want?"

I'm not sure this is some regular Army Captain's way of saying he doesn't like my method of escorting his flight, or if he really is trying to be helpful. This Phoenix Captain is one I do not know. Though Phoenix warrants fly, most of their commissioned officers do not fly CCN missions. Ah, what the hell, I'll let him try. "Fox Lead, go ahead and try. If you make contact, relay we'll be there in one-five or so."

I have thought about the best place to keep the slicks orbiting and hopefully out of danger while we go over and get the team ready for extraction. Common sense would have them in a high orbit over the Song Ba, which flows three clicks or so to the north of the team. Though every NVA within five miles will see them, and therefore, where they are going, at least they will be a bit safer than flying near the large escarpment that the team is presently sitting on.

"Dancing Bear, Dancing Bear Lead, Straight Arrow One-Three, over." The loud voices surprise me as I wasn't prepared for it.

"Go One-Three." I answer before the slick lead can interject.

"Roger Bear Lead, ah.... I've been busy getting Papa Alpha Kilo ready. Ahhhhh.... what's your location, over?"

"One-Three, we have the package... and are one-zero out of your location along the blue. We are ready as soon as Kilo is in position, over."

Turning to either side, I see that the other Griffins have tightened up into a semi-formation. We are no longer hunting as we now are almost to the fox's lair. Within a few minutes, we will go from a coon dog style of hunter to the police german shepherd, bearing our teeth if need be. Each of us knows what we must do.

"Bear Lead, if you would come in and do a quick prep, ah...

they have some active enemy small arms, ah... the Lima Zulu will be hot. Then bring the package in. I think we might get them out quickly and without further damage, over."

"Tally Ho, little bird at eleven... he's in a dive." CWO-2 Marty St. Claire on VHF says. I know that if anyone would spot the O-2 it would be E'Clair for his eyesight, especially his night vision, is legendary within the Griffins. I've not been able to see the little high-wing aircraft, but I'm sure E'Clair will keep him in sight.

Before switching to VHF, I have Randy turn its volume up a bit. Marty's voice was too soft, even for Marty. Then only giving Randy a thumbs up for a thank you, I lay out the plan to the Griffins. "Alright, here's how we'll handle it. E'Clair and I will go over and find the team, and see if we have to prep the Lima Zulu. Then Tex will lead the two slicks into the Lima Zulu, with Doc trailing. We'll leave Chalk Three and Four either over the blue or to the east of the team in a very high orbit. Ah.... any questions?" It's taken just a few minutes to formulate a plan for the extraction. Though I've not told the slicks yet, I'll wait till I physically see the LZ before I tell them. For now, it seems the safest plan for all concerned, though telling this to the two unescorted Huey crews might draw a totally different response. To me, having four Hueys, four Cobras and a Covey FAC all in a small tight area would not only add to the confusion but also might cause a mid-air. And dying in a mid-air in Laos is really the last thing any of us wants.

In the next few minutes I lay out my thoughts on the plans to the Phoenix and the Covey. The Covey immediately tells me that whatever I feel would be the quickest and safest is fine with him, but he does remind me several times that he feels we should not overfly west of the team, as along the escarpment there are surely many anti-aircraft gun emplacements. I'm sure on the Phoenix VHF frequency there is some discussion with regard to my plan, but these missions are not run by a group vote but rather by direct command by men, regardless of rank, who have the expertise. Today, this means it's me.

Commands of this nature tell you to do things that you

know you would never do, except in the rush of adrenalin that sweeps you into the frenzy of madness engulfing you and those around you. You seem, at times, to feed upon each other. Daring each other, though not through words but by your actions. So you push your wingmen harder and harder, and they in turn push you harder and harder. Then, once the mission is over, it's a time to sit down and reflect. This reflection is not in an analytical way, but more of a child-like fascination of what you and your wingman just accomplished. Then after a few beers, immersed in one's own thoughts, you see just how stupid it was and you quiz yourself as to why you would ever try anything like this. As friends of mine have said after some really crazy missions, "I just got carried away with things." The real answer that you refuse to think about or admit, even to yourself, is that for the one instant you were not in charge of your own senses, but rather you were swept up into some type of euphoric trance. If you think about it, you understand how mobs form and then do what they do. But in the end, it's all justified by how you remember the mission. It's always in slow-motion, even though you lived it in real time and it moved like a bat out of hell. You can close your eyes and see everything vividly in very slow-motion.

"Ah... One-Three, Bear Lead is on the way over. We'll hold the package with two Bear aircraft over the blue to your November Echo, over." While telling him this, I've peeled off toward the southwest and E'Clair is closing up next to me, on my left. Before the Covey can answer, I add, "Tex, you start your high orbit here until we call for you."

The only replies from Tex and the Hueys, are numerous squelch breaks. For the first time I see the small white and grey fixed-wing climbing sharply in front of me. Though still over a mile away, he's not hard to miss. He flies without armor or any defensive weapons on board. His ability to move quickly keeps him from taking too many hits. In something that small, any hit could prove to be disastrous.

"Bear Lead, I'm going to roll out to the south then turn back on a November heading. When I pass them, I'll call a mark."

The Covey is now getting ready to mark Coral's location. I look off to my seven o'clock and see E'Clair has started to lag back from his tight echelon position. He's done this not only to allow me more maneuvering room, but also to give him a clear view. As the O-2 makes a sweeping turn back toward us, he calls on FM, "Alpha Kilo, Alpha Kilo, One-Three inbound with a low pass to mark your position. Get your panels out."

The next thing I hear is a muffled sound. I can only bet that the radioman is whispering into his headset, not only from fear the NVA will hear him, but from the fear surfacing from close calls with death. Once he sees the Hueys on final, his voice will raise with the elation that comes from knowing he's about to get his ass out of the frying pan.

"All right, keep an eye out for any AA from the western crest of the escarpment. They could really eat out our ass up here today." said to no one in particular, though everyone not only heard it, they are now acknowledging it.

We are flying due east of the indent in the long east-west escarpment. The Covey will fly right down the draw. We still will not get a good pinpoint of the team until we overfly them. Out here we are safe as we have over a thousand feet below us, but once we turn in to the team, we'll go down to less than a couple hundred feet. When this happens, things escalate in a hurry.

Just as Covey seems to be skimming a few low trees, or maybe those are high growth bushes, he calls "Mark! Mark!" Then he breaks into a sharp upward spiral that surprises me. As he climbs up through five hundred or so feet, a stream of red, then yellow, shoots up after him. Before anyone can yell for him to get out of there he says, and not too calmly either, "Shit! Taking fire...... Ah....Ah.... heavy fire from nine o'clock."

Without thinking about it, I jerk the cyclic to the right and shove my foot hard on the pedal trying to bring the aircraft, and therefore my gunsight, around to the heart of this stream of poison. Though I'm getting into position, I'm not fast enough and the red stream abruptly stops before I can line the pipper up on what I feel is the AA gun emplacement.

"Sneaky, I'm at your seven."

Marty is surely thinking I'm going to look for this .50 caliber before we bring the slicks over. But if, and only a quick fly-over exposing myself will prove this to be true, the NVA gunners are on the back side of this escarpment then maybe, just maybe, we can get the slicks in and out using the crest of the ridge to hide behind. We'll know in less than a minute, as I continue my charge toward what I feel is the emplacement.

"Bear Lead, if you give me a few minutes, I'll get some fast movers down here to take care of that problem." Covey says, his voice calmer now. It's amazing how a few moments can change the octave at which you speak. But then, this is an everyday occurrence.

"Ah... One-Three, if you give me a minute, I think we might be able to avoid this guy." Then switching to VHF, " E'Clair, I'll try to draw him into firing at me. You stay low and see if he misses seeing you. I'll be breaking right into a one-eighty once he fires..... ah... then head back into the valley."

Though some would call this trolling, or looking for an NVA gunner to open up on me, I really am not trying to do this. What I want, though I wouldn't admit it, is for the gunner to expose his exact location and give me enough time to duck down and scamper out of here. So here goes.

"Randy, if you see anything, open up!" Talking as I look up at the small mirror over Hunt's right forehead. Though we usually don't shoot our nose turrets, this would be an appropriate time.

Crossing over the crest, I look down to the right side and see not only the rough stone landscape, but also the vegetation that isn't thick. Right away I see a well worn path, which means not only enemy activity but plenty of it. When a path gets this wide and void of vegetation, it means that the foot traffic is often and heavy. Otherwise, small growth would quickly engulf it.

"Dancing Bear, Dancing Bear, Papa Alpha Kilo, you're to our

November, over."

The whisper seems to be getting louder, though it's not because I'm flying closer to him, but rather from the confidence that salvation is just a few minutes away. I ignore him, but not because I'm bothered. It's the focus thing. My mind set is before me, looking, no... waiting for the instant surprise that surely awaits me as the NVA gunners send up their surprise.

BANG! BANG! Sudden fire from somewhere has hit us, which causes a reaction. My hand and foot both move, with my right hand, arm, and shoulder throwing the cyclic to its right hand stops. The right leg shoots out pushing the pedal to the end of its throw. Then I notice my ass has puckered, the nerves in my sweaty skin tingle all over, my stomach knots up and then... relief!! I feel the coolness as adrenalin rushes throughout my body. During the next few seconds, my mind, my spirit, and even my body functions without my control. It's reaction. The hits, the shock, the adrenalin, the movement to correct the problem. It's the same every time. The hits, the shock, ..., the same every time.

"Taking fire We're taking fire"

At least Randy had the sense to get a radio call off. Before he finished I interject "Ah.... Bear Lead, just took some small arms.... November Whiskey of Kilo." Trying to be calm, though everyone knows my voice. "Everything's in the green." I try to continue to project the calm leadership role that I am supposed to, though I still feel the adrenalin effects. I quickly scan the gauges while trying to think of how many pounds of torque I pulled getting the bird turned around.

Once we break back over the valley, I've regained complete control. The adrenalin has subsided and goes back to wherever. Now I only feel the sweat on my body. To make matters worse with my air-conditioner being broken, the cockpit seems like an oven as the sun bakes through the overhead windows. For the past several weeks I've had to put up with this and I am going to raise hell about it when I get back tonight. I've had enough of our maintenance officer's excuses as to why he can't fix it.

"Papa Alpha Kilo, Dancing Bear Lead, over."

"Bear Lead, be advised that you took a lot of small arms fire when you passed by our location."

"Roger that Kilo. I'll be doing a low level pass from the Sierra. Put out your panels so I can get a tally."

While telling him this, I've already started my flight to the south of his location. I'll do a quick one-eighty and fly along the spine of the ridge just like the Covey did, but lower, then when I spot the team, I'll call a mark. Not only is this for my benefit, but for all the pilots to see.

"E'Clair if I take any fire, I'll break east so lay off my tail."

I'll also get a good feel of the LZ so when the slicks come in, I can forewarn them of any possible surprises. This is a lesson learned once when a team said they were in a clear area and the slicks could land with no trouble. When the slicks came to a hover over the team, the pilots found themselves looking down the throat of a .51 caliber. Needless to say, they not only got the hell out of there, but from then on, when the team said things were just perfect, we all remembered how lucky the Huey crew was that day.

"Breaking right!" While making my sharp one-eighty, I turn back to the north. I roll out so I fly just a bit to the east of the ridge line. Then quickly switching to FM, "Kilo, Alpha Kilo, Bear Lead inbound.... put your panel out."

Now as we race along the crest, I slowly edge us closer and closer to the west. We're no more than a couple hundred feet from the crest, but at least seven hundred feet to the valley floor. Any gunfire we will receive will be from my left. No NVA will try shooting at us from the valley floor. One thing about the NVA in this area, or for that matter in Laos, is they do practice very good fire control. For some reason whoever started the myth that Asians, whether North Vietnamese or the Japs in World War II, were small people with thick eye glasses and weren't smart fighters never had a chance to meet them on the fields of combat. These guys are tough and they practice fire discipline as good as any troops there are.

"Bear Lead, you're to our Sierra, you're .... Mark! Mark!" then a rush of squelch in my headset, "Bear, you just passed us."

"I got 'em Sneaky, they're on the north side of the clearing."

"I got 'em!" I didn't need to acknowledge Randy as he could see me through the mirror and we had made eye contact. I continue my pass up the ridge crest for a few more seconds then peel off to the right heading east toward the orbiting package.

On VHF, and not using formal call signs, I lay out the plan to the other Griffins. "Tex, get ready to bring the package over. I want you to take the package to the Echo till you hit the blue running Sierra. Then, follow it to the Sierra into the draw, till you are due Echo of me. Then we'll bring in the slicks one at a time. I think we might have to use strings as there are a couple trees in the way and I don't think we have the time to move the team." The problem with strings is it takes time for the team to get hooked up to them. The quickest way is for the aircraft to land, the team pile on, and the aircraft to leave, but with the trees in the area, it may not work today.

I get a squelch break while I'm turning the radio selector back to UHF. "Everyone up Uniform?" I ask, then before there's time to reply, I continue, "Straight Arrow, we're ready to get them out. I'll bring the package to the small blue to our Echo. Then with forty-second intervals will bring Silver Fox in. Be advised Fox, you may have to use your strings. I'm not sure you'll be able to get on the ground. There's a few trees in the area and I don't want to waste any more time moving them. Questions?"

This is it, this is the best they are going to get for a plan. In flight school we would have had a twenty minute discussion with how to enter, how to leave, and what to load. But here, we might not have all the facts so we play a lot of it by ear. We'll go with what we have and be prepared to make some quick and probably drastic changes if we have to.

"Dancing Bear Lead, Silver Fox Lead, over."

The Captain leading the Phoenix flight today is far too formal for flying out here. All he's got to do is say what is on his mind. "Go."

"Bear Lead, do you have a positive on Kilo and are they ready for extraction?"

For Christ sake, these guys have been ready for extraction since they were hit early this AM, and he must have heard my confirmation of their location. Where's this guy's head, up his ass? "Ah... Fox Lead, ah... and flight.... I've got the team marked and will direct each of you straight in. They are ready for you. Once you are there.... and remember Chalk One you will have three on board... three on board. Chalk Two will have three on board as well .... Any more questions?" I gruffly add.

My orbit has been a tight counter-clockwise rotation northeast of the team, but now I stretch it further out so we will be in position with the slicks at the proper time.

The Covey, flying his orbit to the west of us, has been high and out of the way. I'm sure he's not only observing us, but looking for targets for his fast movers once we get the team out of the area. If we are going to take any AA fire, it will be from this area, so he's going to have a good perch. My goal is for us to be below any big stuff and just deal with the small arms fire. And I bet the slicks will agree with me on this one.

"Okay Kilo," now on FM. "The package is about five out. Your ready?"

Though I know they are ready, telling them to get ready will ensure the slicks are ready. It's something that I've found funny in the military. If you are told to be ready, you sort of take your time from years of the hurry up and wait syndrome. But when you hear the other part of the mission, in this case the team is now ready, then you know it's the real thing this time. As we all know, the most dangerous part of Coral's mission now will be the extraction. Not just because it's an extraction, but because the NVA know about where they are and they hear the helicopters and in some cases have had a shot at me. Many times I've heard a team member say he could not wait to get away from the helicopter as it drew too much fire. Infantry and helicopters don't mix.

Faintly I hear the team, but it's too faint to understand what's being said. I repeat my question, this time after turning up the volume.

Louder, "Bear Lead, we're ready. Be advised we're taking some small arms from the Sierra of the Lima Zulu... and... ah.... hold it... ah..... we've got a lot of movement to our Whiskey and November. You copy?"

"Roger Kilo," then as an after thought, "Fox flight copy that?" Then without regard to any answers I continue, "Kilo, what is the Lima Zulu like, over?"

Knowing the type of LZ will have a major bearing on how quickly we get the Hueys in and out. My fly-over wasn't good enough for me to see if there was a spot the Hueys could set down on, and I did see several trees scattered throughout the clearing that we are now calling an LZ. I know if we have to use strings it will be a turkey shoot for the NVA gunners and it will at least double the time we need to complete this extraction.

"Bear Lead, we are in the November Whiskey of the Lima Zulu," which I knew as I saw the green shapes with the two panels out when I flew over them, "with a touch down possible. Just watch the trees to the west. Shit..... we're taking fire from our November." We can hear the gunfire, though I am not sure if it's NVA incoming or the teams outgoing. It doesn't matter, things are getting hot.

Well, another typical CCN mission. As time marches on, things get worse and worse. Just our luck, but then we wouldn't expect it any other way. I switch to UHF as the package with Tex leading arrives. Without being told, they join into Marty's and my loose daisy chain. "Okay, here's how it goes..... I'll head directly toward Kilo, break over them in a tight two-seventy to the right. I'll then nail the Sierra portion of the Lima Zulu, then turn Echo. When I do this, Fox Lead will head toward the Lima Zulu, with all four Bears on you. You'll go in, pick up, and do a three-sixty and come out the same way. Do not... do not... do not overfly the Lima Zulu."

"Chalk Two will start heading for the Lima Zulu after a forty-second separation, understand?" I wait for a reply, there's none. "Chalk Two will enter and leave the same way as Lead. I don't think we'll need strings but be careful of the scattered trees to your nine and twelve o'clock. Chalk Three and Four will hold a high orbit here and Lead will return here after the pick-up. Questions?"

There's silence on the radios. I know they are talking on the unit VHF, but it will only last a minute.

"Bear Lead, Fox Lead, ah.... let's do it."

So much for questions. "Roger, Fox Lead, I'll go in and nail the Charlie." Then I let the Griffins know what we're going to do. Though still on UHF, I disregard the formal radio etiquette. "Marty, get on me and Tex and Doc, bring the Lead in when I call. We'll work a double daisy pattern on each side of him. But don't fly past the team. It's big guns out there." The replies are given on VHF.

I turned away from the package and head due west towards the team. They are in the highest corner of the clearing and close to the tree line. But with a little luck, we'll be able to get the Hueys in to them without much trouble.

"Kilo, Dancing Bear is inbound your location, be ready in three mikes for pick-up."

Then I check my airspeed as I don't want to overfly the team. Randy points to the clearing as if reminding me where to go. I can almost hear my heart beating and the adrenalin is starting its charge again. Strange but even without the air-conditioner, I don't feel hot.

Just as I leave the valley floor, I call, "Kilo, get your heads down", then I start my tight right hand turn.

While doing so, I look down and I see I'm right over the team. They are in a circle around two panels laid out that can only be seen from the air. Pulling the Cobra in such a tight turn, I can feel the G forces on my body, until I complete the turn and roll out to a one-eight-zero heading. Then quickly I look at my torque and adjust it to thirty pounds, all the while I'm using the pedals to try to keep the aircraft in trim. Without a target really before me, but clearly with the southern end of the clearing in view, I fire pair after pair of rockets. After each stroke of the little red button, I push on one of the foot pedals to allow my rockets to spray the area. Then, just as sharply as my turn toward the target, I break hard to the left. It's then when I see Marty has been along to my east waiting to see if I took any gunfire.

Before I finish the turn, "Fox Lead, come on in." Then I quickly switch to FM. "Kilo, Bear Lead. Your ride is on the way. Call sign Silver Fox, over."

At less than a quarter mile away from the sheer drop, I turn back toward the team and pull back on the cyclic while reducing the collective. This will slow me down as I am now waiting for the lead Huey.

"Papa Alpha Kilo, Silver Fox Lead is in-bound."

Louder now than any time today, "Roger Fox Lead, we're ready. Be advised some small arms to the November, over."

I interject, "Kilo, Bear will try to fix that problem, over."

I've got my airspeed down to sixty knots, which really is dumb, when the first Phoenix passes me and the door gunner gives a thumbs up. Before the Phoenix breaks over the escarpment, he starts his flare and then I hear what is good news.

"Fox, we're at your twelve o'clock."

"Got you in sight." as the Huey noses up, though more to do with the tail dropping sharply down. This aircraft commander is trying to set down on a dime, but then I don't blame him. Then the helicopter settles down.

I fire a couple pair of rockets to the north of the squatting bird then call my break, "Sneaky breaking right."

Almost at the same time, Marty on the south side of Fox Lead calls his break to the left. We've each been on either side of the Huey firing our rockets.

"Fox Lead is down."

I meet Tex as he has started his run toward the LZ and

Marty has met Doc as well. I can see, much further to the east, the three slicks orbiting. Then, as if reading my mind, one breaks away and turns directly toward me. Chalk Two has waited a bit longer to start his approach, but I'm sure this was the lead Phoenix's call. What is taking the first aircraft so long? If it's this long for me, it must be forever for the Huey crew and the recon team. But so far he's not called out with any difficulties.

Then, to everyone's relief, "Lead's out with three on board." The voice is almost at a yell as if trying to out scream the noise of the rotor blades.

"Taking fire! Taking fire....weee're hit!" a screaming voice yells.

A steadier, more controlled, voice comes from the Huey, "Ah... fire from nine o'clock ah.... think it's AK.... ah....."

Tex has started firing his rockets, but like mine, they are impacting a bit too far to the north. If anything, we might be driving the NVA toward the team, or at least what's left of the team. If the Huey was within gunfire range while doing his one-eighty, or as he left the LZ, it means the enemy is a lot closer than we thought. Looking back over my right shoulder, as I turn back toward the LZ, I see a steady stream of red tracers leaving the Huey. The crew-chief, who's on the left side of the aircraft, must have a good target as the stream is not wandering all over the area, but is concentrated at the same spot. Then abruptly it stops.

"We've been hit, we're hit!" is all we hear for a few seconds.

Again, a much lower, calmer voice says, "Chalk Two is on final.... ah..... taking fire from two .... ah... three..... o'clock."

The two Hueys pass by each other and though not as close as they appear, they do look like they almost touch.

"Romeo's breaking."

As Tex makes his call, I roll toward the LZ and the Huey on final. Then as Doc makes his breaking call, Marty calls inbound. We've kept the two Hueys under constant coverage.

"Kilo," with rotor blades popping in the background, "Chalk Two is flaring ah.... pop some smoke, over."

Pop smoke! Hell, these guys are not ready to pop smoke. What is this guy asking for? Maybe a red flag to show the NVA where he's going to land. Why wasn't he watching where the first aircraft landed anyway?

"Tally ho Kilo... we have you.... Chalk Two is down...."

While he talks, we can hear machine gun fire. I put my pipper to an area to the north of the helicopter along the tree line. I am able to see the Huey's main rotor blades spinning as one of them has been painted white on its top. This was done for easy spotting from above and it works this time. I keep pushing the red button and pair after pair leave my aircraft. Then I break hard to the right and make the call.

No sooner than I make the call, Tex calls inbound, then Marty calls his left break with Doc calling his coverage.

"Two's lifting with three, repeat three on board."

I'm not in position to watch him come out of the LZ, but I know it must be a hot one as the sound of gunfire is heard across the radio.

Covey, who's had a ring side seat to the extraction, calls to ensure all are aboard. "Fox Lead, give me a count."

It's not that Covey doesn't believe the count that was called out as the aircraft were leaving the LZ, but it's a double check. My experience has been that when in a hot LZ, and this one was surely what I'd call a hot LZ, things sometimes get missed. Without thinking about it you could count the same man twice, then finding out that you have four on board and not five, you realize there's a huge error. So we always make a second count once we are away from the LZ when things are calmer and, if possible, more relaxed. Adrenalin, for some reason does wonders to your strength, your nerve, your ability to react to unplanned events. But at the same time it sure plays havoc with your ability to perform analytical processes, i.e., your ability to count.

"Silver Fox two with three, repeat three on board."

"Silver Fox Lead with three on board, ah... two are Whiskey-India-Able, over." The Captain seems to have found his calm voice.

"Roger Fox Lead, we have three and three." The radio goes dead, then, "Dancing Bear lead, it's your flight to take home. I'll stick around and run some fast movers on our friends down there." This draws more than squelch breaks as several pilots voice their happiness with this bit of news. One of them, I know is Randy, who says something like shit hot. "I'll contact Sundance Halo with the extract info." Then, before the Covey clears the UHF frequency, he adds, "Good Job! I'll be up TAC Two." Then I'm sure he has changed over to the fighters tactical frequency.

"Bear Lead, Fox Lead, over."

Damn, doesn't this guy get it. Conversations are relaxed out here. "Go!." I answer with a short tone.

"Bear Lead, my Charlie-Charlie has been Whiskey-India-Able and after leaving him off at 18th Surg., I'll need to RTB to get another aircraft, over."

Well, that explains why the crew-chief's machine gun quit putting out fire as they were leaving the LZ. But at least this Phoenix crew member has a Special Forces medic on board. There's no one, including our unit flight surgeon, who I'd rather work on me than an SF medic. Here at the MLT, we have two of the best and they're twins to boot. These guys ought to be doctors rather than medics, but they wear the title *Bac Si* with pride. After all, they surely have earned it over and over.

"Straight Arrow, did you copy that last transmission, over?"

Knowing that the O-2 has two UHF radios, he's now climbed up to at least ten thousand feet so that he can have a line of sight transmission to the MLT and therefore notify them of the successful, though costly, extraction. To me, this is our biggest problem. The helicopters don't have direct contact with the MLT. Things have to be retransmitted and this means precious time and sometimes erroneous information being sent. What I'd give for one great radio.

"Roger, Bear Lead, I've got Sundance Halo. I'll relay the info and they'll be waiting for you at 18th Surg."

Our flight, with it's four Hueys and four Cobras, now starts back home. Maybe, but hopefully not, it might be the start of the way home for the Phoenix crew-chief. We are climbing up to two thousand feet above the terrain. It's not that we're scared but with the fuel running low and the injured aboard, the two and possible three aircraft with unknown battle damage, we're really not in fighting shape. We need to go home and lick our wounds. We always have this afternoon, tomorrow, or next week to come back and avenge today's actions. Yes, tonight, and for the slick crews I'm sure many more nights, there will be the war stories of how men cheated death today on the side of a sheer drop that was deep in enemy held territory. For us, getting back to the MLT is just the start of it. There will be the inspection, and a close one at that, of the aircraft, the debriefing and possibly, very possibly, another mission or two. Looking down at the eight-day clock, I see it's only going on nine AM. Yes, today will be another long day, there's no doubt about it. For me, in this hot unair-conditioned cockpit, it will mean I will be drained when I finally get back to Camp Evans tonight. Oh well, a small sacrifice to pay for flying the hottest missions in this war. Plus, I know I'll be drunk within an hour after returning to Camp Evans, so really all I have to worry about is getting up tomorrow.

For the recon team members, they know it's over for them. They will have some R&R, given to them after each mission, then a few weeks of getting ready before they're fragged with another op-order. But that's the nature of the beast and here in Laos, the beast is one mean son-of-a-bitch.

Now, as I listen to the idle chatter on our unit Victor frequency, I start to relax. I notice that the four way seat restraints are a bit tight, so I loosen them up. I know that just as we Griffins are shooting the breeze, so are the slicks on their unit Victor. The radios, even with the ADF playing rock and roll and the Griffins talking, are really quiet. There is no straining to hear the whispered words on the recon team's FM or the interplay between all the aircraft on UHF.

"Randy, you've got it."

Looking into the mirror, Randy's and my eyes met, and without words further spoken he nods and I feel his input onto the flight controls. He has taken over the flying of the aircraft. I'll sit and relax for the first time since take off. Not the resting kind, but one that lets your heart pump a bit less and you breathe a bit slower and deeper. With Zero-Two-Seven's inoperable air-conditioner, it's becoming a sweat box in here. The large plexiglass windows, great to look out at targets with, let a lot of bright sun light in. With no cool air circulating and with Randy's body heat as well, it's feeling like a Japanese steam room in Okinawa. Fucking maintenance officer. He just doesn't know how hot it is in one of these. Maybe, if he'd fly a mission or two without one, he'd learn what I've been telling him for the past week. I reach down and turn up the ADF. Might as well listen to the latest tunes. War is hell, isn't it!

Several times on our trip back, Randy has closed in on the slicks so the crew-chief and door gunners can take pictures. In the third Phoenix, I notice that as we passed by, the co-pilot put a camera to his face. Must be his first CCN mission. I am able to look at the sprawling green forms on the floor of the first two Hueys. These Hueys have their seats stripped out so it allows men to enter and exit quicker, giving more room and what all helicopters flying in Vietnam need--less weight to carry. The wind really whips around and causes anything loose to flap, at times stingingly, on Coral's faces. But you can see they are relaxed and less than twenty minutes ago this was not something they could do.

As we cross over the Rockpile, long ago abandoned by the Marines, I take control of the aircraft. Immediately, I start to let down as we approach Quang Tri. "Let's go to Quang Tri." Then, before I hear any reply, I turn the UHF radio selector to the tower frequency. The first to make a call is the Phoenix lead.

"Quang Tri Tower, Phoenix Two-Six, three miles to the west for a straight in to 18th Surg. with three, this is an emergency, over."

The controller answers with a new tone of authority, "Phoenix Two-Six, you're cleared direct to Surg. The winds are zero-four at six, altimeter two-niner-niner-three." After a moments pause, "Six, we're on the land line with Surg., they know you're inbound."

"Roger, Quang Tri, and thank you." The lead Phoenix breaks off to the left as he sets up for an extended base. I then call, "Quang Tri, Griffin Nine-Two Gulf, with a flight of three Phoenix and four Griffins entering an extended downwind for landing, POL." I pull into the lead as we Cobras will need a bit faster approach speed. Plus, we'll first go past the POL points to the rearm area.

"Roger Griffin, I have your flight in sight, call base, your number two for landing behind the Pachyderm turning final."

As I make the turn to the base leg, I once again call the tower telling them of our location, that our weapons are cold, and that we Griffins will head to rearm while the Phoenix will go straight to POL. After the Phoenix top off with fuel, they relocate to the MLT. During the time while we Griffins were moving south from the rearm to the POL points, I heard the Phoenix Lead call his lift off from 18th Surg. and his departure to the south toward Camp Evans. He'll either get a new aircraft or send a replacement one with crew. We Cobras don't load up with fuel as the DA is climbing. So, after a half load, we too reposition to the MLT pad on the other side of the combat base.

After shutting down, both Randy and I search for any hits to Zero-Two-Seven. Helping us is CWO-2 Jeff 'Scoop' Winston, the newest Chief Warrant Officer 2 in the Griffins. Today he's flying with E'Clair as a copilot, but he's due to make aircraft commander within the week if Sweet Griffin can find the time to give him a flight test. Right away, Scoop calls that he's found a couple of bullet holes. Randy, who's climbed up on top by the rotor head, starts to get down. I make my way to the kneeling CWO and see he has put his finger in one of the holes, as if I won't be able to see it without his graphic demonstration. I see the two holes that are low in the tail boom and, after looking at the exit holes higher up on the other side, I pronounce that these will have no bearing to us being flight ready. They clearly are T&T's. They have hit nothing structural, only punctured the thin skin. They have gone 'through and through' so we'll not return for another aircraft, just put some blade tape over them and have them fixed tonight when we get home.

After making the proper entries into the log book, I walk to the operations hootch for my debriefing. Walking past Phoenix's Chalk Two, who now has become, if only temporarily, Phoenix Lead, I watch as the crew-chief is vigorously sweeping out the floor of his aircraft with a cut down broom. The door gunner is going over one of the machine guns, probably oiling it, and making sure the ammo belts are untangled. The brass, mud, dirt, and general mess from the extraction is now in a heap along the Huey's skid. This filth seems to really bother the crew-chief, who really looks far too young to be crewing, never mind being in a war zone or for that matter even being in the Army. But from my experience, the best crew-chiefs are the younger ones. Maybe it's because they don't have the wisdom to know that besides all the work you have to do to keep it flying, the helicopter really wants to kill you. Then, when you toss in the NVA, well, it could and far too many times is, the ending of a lot of very young lives.

I let the door slam behind me and squint my eyes to adjust to the darkened room. There are several chairs now set up facing each other. This is not a formal debriefing like one would have gone through with the Air Force and to be honest, it's not even a regular debriefing that we would get from Sergeant Major Washburn. But today, Billy's not here and 'Stan the Man' is in charge and he does go for the formal and as he says, the proper military way.

I quickly sit down, grab the soda that's handed to me and gulp half of it down, then quickly go over what I saw and when, where and how many. Then I answer a couple of questions that, in this case, are redundant because I've just told Milo what he's asking. Maybe he ought to listen or believe me when I tell him the first time. But I'm through within five minutes or so and, in general, its painless. Milo tells one of the other NCO's sitting and listening to what happened that he has to go over to 18th Surg. and check on the 'yards, who have been wounded.

As I leave, he says to me, "Our 'yards will be back tonight but I think the crew-chief will be medevac'd." Then, with no expression of emotion, "He got gut shot."

Milo isn't cold hearted but this wounded American has gone from being a crew-chief to another statistic in the war. Though I'm sure that to him, his Mother, his family, and maybe his high school sweetheart, he's not a statistic but their loved one. But in tomorrow's briefings at battalion, group, division, corps, MAC-V, and even at the Pentagon, he'll be one of the numbers that are called out. The problem is, as the higher it goes up the chain, the less anyone thinks or for that matter cares, about him. Just another day in the office for the mass of paper pushers who seem to dominate the running of the war.

Milo, before he can take a break, will go over and ensure that everyone is properly cared for at 18th Surg., that we are all debriefed, that the recon team is on its way back to CCN Headquarters in Da Nang, and he makes his formal report to CCN. That report, once reworded, edited, and shortened, will snake its way up the same chain as the wounded crew-chief's status. Captain Stanton will go over it before it goes out, then to Da Nang and CCN HQ, then to MAC-V-SOG Headquarters at 137 Rue Pasteur in Saigon, then onto a very private briefing to MAC-V Commanding General, and on to Washington. Once again, those that read, hear, and in some cases ignore the report will have no idea just how hard it was on the 30 or so personnel involved with the team, the pilots, and the air crews.

The first step is the MLT-2 Detachment Commander. Stanton, unlike Billy and Milo, doesn't get involved with the crews that fly the missions. But because the Griffins have become his regular Cobra unit, he has made friends with some of us, though it's been a strained friendship at best.

After a half hour or so, and several sodas in cans that are well on their way to rusting through, I'm relaxed enough for a short nap. If I weren't so sticky with my unclean flight suit and the lack of a shower this morning, I probably could sit anywhere and pass out. But what strength I had was sapped out of me with both the mission and lack of cool air that I should have had pouring over me during the flight. So, rather than joining the pilots playing cards and with nothing to read, I go to one of the hootches in the back where the 'yards stay, and find an open cot. After stripping off my flight suit shirt and the damp OD green tinted t-shirt, I lay down. I let my mind wander in hopes that I just might fall asleep.

Chapter 3

"Sneaky! Sneaky! Let's go!"

It's Doc Holiday, who has brought me out of my nap. Looking up at him, while shielding my eyes to the bright light in my face now that the t-shirt is removed from my eyes, I see him turning his finger in a circle.

"Time to earn our pay."

"As if we haven't earned it yet," I say in spite of the rancid taste in my mouth. I raise up and stretch, grab my shirt and chase after Doc leaving the t-shirt. "What's up?" knowing he'll know the reason for the flight.

"We've got an insert they want to do around six but we have to brief now," he says as he opens the Ops back door for me.

Quickly we step through the radio room and into the briefing room. It appears that everyone has been waiting for me as the chairs are full with impatient looking faces. Several give me an icy stare, including the Phoenix Captain who must have returned with another aircraft. I sit in the first chair I come to then turn to see if all the Griffins are here. As I make the quick head count, Randy nudges me with my knee pad and my map, which he's already marked with info. He's a good co-pilot, eager, but not too eager. They say the sign of an intelligent man is one who thinks like you. Today, Randy has been thinking like me.

"Gentlemen, and you too Sneaky," which gathers chuckles from the pilots, though strained ones from the slick drivers, "our mission for this afternoon, well really late this afternoon, is to insert a seven man team into this area." Then he turns and bends toward the large map, running his finger along the Song Ba till he stops at a blackened dot, "Xray Delta three-seven-five, five-seven-five."

"Not bad," I say under my breath. It's only six miles or so into Laos along the abandoned QL-9 and in an area of low rolling hills. It's an area that is lush with vegetation and scenic views.

"As you see, it's right where QL-9 passes through this dry stream bed, which should make for an easy touch down. The mission will require a couple of false inserts along QL-9 as you return back to the border. We want you to overfly the LZ by a couple of klicks then turn back to it. There will be no secondary LZs. It's a one time try. Understand?" Looking around I watch Milo scan the room waiting for everyone to finish writing down the info. "The team, Bull Snake, will use Delta Tango Xray for a call sign and they will be up thirty-two point six-zero. Covey is on the way out there now and will give us a weather report before takeoff, but I don't expect anything but blue skies. Covey's call sign will be the same as this morning, Straight Arrow One-Three. He'll be up two-thirty-nine point five-five. He'll have Sandys on call and fast movers if needed. He'll notify Hillsborough when you launch."

I look down at my overly expensive watch, the typical style pilots wear with all the small dials we never use, and see it's a little after two. Hell, I got a good nap, almost five hours, but I still feel like shit.

Without any noise, an American enters the room through the back door. He's dressed in a sterile uniform so there's no doubt that he's the one who's going out on this mission. Milo turns to him after realizing that the pilots attention has shifted behind him. He turns back to us, smiling now, "Phoenix, your call sign will be Able Dart and Griffins will be Red Scarf. Lead will carry four, Chalk Two will carry the other three. The team is four Americans, three 'yards. There will be no nightingales used in the dummy LZs. " Then, purposely lowering his voice, "If you go down, stay with the aircraft. If, and only if you have to leave the aircraft, try to go southeast down the stream bed till you get to the Song Ba.

Other than that," once again eyeing the pilots, "any questions?" For a moment, there seems to be none. It's deathly quiet.

The CWO who's the AC for Chalk Two, and briefly the Phoenix Lead, raises his hand. Then, before any acknowledgement, "About the false inserts—how many and where?"

Good question. I forgot about asking that myself.

Milo, without turning toward him, asks the camouflaged SF team member, "Don, it's your call."

Whoever this Don is, starts to talk, which brings a smile to our faces as we all try not to laugh. Don's problem is he has a very large mouth with neatly placed white teeth. So as he talks, with all the green, brown and black camouflaged paint around his mouth, and being in the darkened end of the room, he looks like a set of suspended teeth chattering away.

"Well, I really don't care where you do it, it's the pilots call. But make your landing on QL-9 in at least three different spots to our east. Also, have them at least a klick apart. Anyone see any problems with that?" Upon closing his mouth, he seems to have disappeared back into the shadows again.

There are no responses from the slick pilots nor any questions. "We'll take a look at some possible areas when we fly over on the way out," I say as I turn to look past the Phoenix Captain and lock my eyes on the CWO. No doubt this is the senior pilot of the Phoenix flight, but the Captain is in charge.

After a few minutes of what seems to be getting uncomfortable silence, "Gentlemen, I'd like to get you airborne by eighteen-thirty or so." Milo has spoken over his shoulder as he now closes the map box.

One of the Phoenix pilots whispers a bit too loud, "I sure as hell hate to have to Prairie Fire after dark."

True statement. Prairie Fire missions are hot anyway, but to do them in the dark is pure bullshit. At least I'd be flying a Cobra and not trying to land a Huey.

As I join some of the other Griffins outside, I see that one of the *bac si's* has brought several cases of LURPS for us to eat.

Normally, I would grab one or two and enjoy. But I'm sure the 'yards have something cooking in the back hootch and I'm always welcome there. We've got almost four hours of laying around, as long as there's not a Prairie Fire anywhere else, before we have to get back to work. Though I'd like to eat and sleep some more, I know that the chances of me falling back to sleep again are nil.

"You ready Sneaky?" Milo has found me, shirt off, laying on a cot pulled out of the hootch getting the last of the sun's rays.

"Yeah, I'm ready."

Though I don't look up at him, I know that he's come to me about something else. I get up, put on a t-shirt I took off one of the clothes lines, and the flight shirt, then grab the cot and struggle getting it through the 'yard's hootch door. For some reason, it's harder getting it back into the hootch than it was getting it out. When I walk back out, Milo stops me.

"Sneaky, about the dummy LZs. Ah... I think you should make sure they stay on the ground for ten seconds. I know they don't want to spend all that time on the ground, and really I don't blame them, but...." he lowers his head as if searching for the right way to put it, "... shit, we need them to think we put the team somewhere else."

"No fucking problem.... you want ten seconds, that's what you'll get." I say this knowing I have really no control on how long the slick pilots stay on the ground. Milo should know this but he has to ask anyway.

We walk in between the hootches and out past the Hueys that now are buzzing with activity. Not only the air crews are getting ready, but the team members are also loading up.

As we walk up to Zero-Two-Seven, Milo says softly , to keep Randy from hearing it. "You might not get this team in, I think it's going to be a shit sandwich."

I stop in my tracks. Milo is not what I would call a pessimist, even in a business where half our inserts are blown out before we get them on the ground.

"What aren't you telling us?"

"It's not what I'm not telling you. Really I mean this." 'Stan the Man' looks deeply into my eyes. "But there's been a whole lot of truck and foot activity in that area. This is why we're going in there. Plus, last week Coveys spotted a couple of tracked vehicles there. We think they were bulldozers but... ah... they could have been tanks. If they were tanks, you can bet they'll have a lot of ground troops... so take it easy and careful."

Why the tanks, or if we have any good luck, bulldozers, were not mentioned during the briefing I don't know. But I'm sure it would have made the Phoenix Captain a bit more cautious. Where we are going, caution is a good thing, but being too cautious can also be deadly. Sometimes you need to just go in and do it and damn the possible outcome. Well fuck that, it's too late now. We'll go out there and see what surprises the NVA have for us or, if Lady Luck is with us, get the insert done and be back in the club with a cold beer in a couple hours.

I strap in and get cranked up. While waiting for the temps to rise, the co-pilot, a WO from the Lead Phoenix, comes over and tells me they will take off after us and meet us at Carroll. With that said, I get us airborne and around to the POL. Landing at the POL we have to wait as a heavy red team from the Condors, of C Troop of the 2nd/17th Cav, are filling up. Plus there are several CH-47's filling up, so our wait is longer than I expected.

Once we are topped off, I make the call for take off, again calling for a scramble. With the sun dying down, and the cool breezes coming in off the South China Sea, the DA has dropped to under one-hundred. This allows us to take a full load of fuel, along with our seventy-six rockets. The flight out to Carroll goes quickly and we join up with the slicks. From there, it's the same trip we always make, all the while heading to the west.

Looking down, I see that the sun's rays cannot reach into the many valleys and draws below us. This gives the bright green hills a different look than they had nine hours ago. Now the tops are green but along the sides and at the bases are dark areas as the day fades to an end. The sun is low in the sky and the heat and humidity seem to have fallen off sharply. It's become tolerable in the cockpit at long last.

"Straight Arrow One-Three, Straight Arrow One-Three, Red Scarf Lead, over." We're crossing over Khe Sanh and are ready to start our let down and the insertion.

"Roger Scarf Lead, I'm to the November and will be at the Lima Zulu within ten. Lead, what's your location?"

It seems the Covey is flying in an area we usually don't go to. Either he's looking for targets or he's working one of our teams that has been inserted from NKP. Whatever it is, he'll not tell us.

"One-Three, we're within one-five of the Lima Zulu and are starting our let down." Saying this, I hope, sends the message to the slicks to come on down.

"Roger Scarf, we'll meet Echo of the Lima Zulu in five or so."

For the next five minutes our flight starts its let down, doing slow turns rather than going directly toward the LZ. When the Hueys get within a thousand feet of the ground, I tell them to hold up. No use getting blasted before we even get to the LZ.

"Red Scarf Lead, One-Three, over."

"Go One-Three."

"Roger, got you in sight at my eleven. Take your flight to the Sierra of the blue and continue Whiskey. Start Able Dart's let down..... and ..... keep the three and four Dart's high."

"You copy that Dart flight?" asking though I know they have heard. The squelch breaks are not only from the Hueys, but also from my wingmen.

"We'll fly along the blue until I give you a mark. Then go about a klick before you turn back and go for the Lima Zulu. I'll give you some possible dummies as well, copy?" Once again, squelch breaks.

We Griffins are now low, maybe five hundred feet or so, and have all our power pulled trying to keep our airspeed up. No use getting shot down in this area.

"Randy, get a good spot on the dummies." It's all I've got to say and, in each cockpit, the same message is repeated.

For the next few minutes, as we travel along the river, Covey calls out possible LZs for the dummy insertions. After the third one, he gives us a mark on the primary LZ. It's a bit too far away to see, but it looks like it will be a straight in and out for the slicks. As soon as he's marked it for me, I lay out the plan for the next few minutes.

"Listen up. Dart flight get some separation. Three and Four will hold present altitude until Two goes in. At that time, Three and Four will come on down and land in dummy one and two. Then Lead and Two will land in dummy three. At least ten on the ground, understand?"

Then quickly switching to VHF, I continue with "E'Clair and I will cover the insert to the November. Tex and Doc cover the Sierra. We'll do a daisy wheel on each side of the aircraft. Might as well do it all the way, including the dummies."

After switching back to UHF, I remember one other thing, so on UHF I add, "Use only nails on the Lima Zulus." Then I call out to the Hueys, "Ready to turn back in fifteen secs, and let's do a twenty sec separation. Go in headed to the Echo and exit straight out to the Echo. Do the same with all Lima Zulus. Copy?" While the plan is set for the insertion, I know that this will not only be a quick run, it could really get fucked if we lose a plane.

"Breaking right ah....." The lead Huey makes a sharp one-eighty degree turn and dives for the deck as it heads back for the tentative landing zone, "... Two give me twenty seconds." This must be the co-pilot calling as he's more relaxed sounding.

"Breaking right!"

I cut in before the turning Huey in order to get to his northern side. While doing this, I look around and see that all the aircraft are in position. There is no need to tell them what to do. They know how we are going to do it, so it's just execution now. CWO-2 Lofton makes his breaking call, though he's turning to the left and south. I check down at the gauges and see we are in trim with about thirty-five pounds of torque, so I lower the collective to get it to the proper thirty pounds, then look through the rocket sight and the bright red pipper is lit up but not on target yet.

We're skimming along a couple hundred feet off the ground, doing one hundred and fifty knots, and once again today the adrenalin has flushed my body with courage. Then as the LZ comes into view, I start massaging the button, sending pair after pair of 2.75 folding fin aerial rockets toward the ground. After ten or so strokes and the red dye floating in the air from the exploding rocket heads as it sends the nails into the air, I start my break to the left at the same time calling it.

"Dart Two breaking right."

Right after that call, Tex makes his call. As I climb up and back to the west, I see that E'Clair is still behind the lead Huey but gaining fast.

"Dart Lead, your Lima Zulu is at your twelve. Ah... start your flare..... ah you see it?" Though I'm not in the right position to lead him in to the Lima Zulu, I will be as soon as E'Clair makes his break and I turn black into the LZ.

"Roger Scarf at my twelve...... I doooo nnnnooootttt...." the pilot has left his mike on while trying to look for the LZ. "Taking fire! Taking fire!" Then dead silence. Who was that?

I look back over my left shoulder just as E'Clair says. "Lead's in trouble. Two break away and climb out."

I see the tracers from the lead Huey's door gunners' spraying out either side of the aircraft. They're firing close in. The enemy must be on the road.

"Break right Lead...... Break right, I'm on your ass!"

E'Clair is firing rockets to the north of the Huey. Then, as if the pilot got the word, he changes to a nose low attitude and we can see the Huey try to gather speed and slowly start a drift to the right.

"We're hit! Hit hard! Ahhhhh...... We've got to put it down right now." I still can't recognize this voice.

I've turned us around and now see E'Clair pull out to the left of the Huey, which seems to be slowing down while still flying a nose up attitude. It's obvious that it can't climb and the rear starts to sway back and forth. This guy's in trouble.

"Lead, go for the blue.... the blue.... and put it down. We're on you," is all I can say.

"AC's hit bad.... I'm going to the water." There is sheer panic in the voice of the young co-pilot, though as I roll in on the road I can see both gunners are firing. At least they're still flying.

In no time, it was only a klick or so, the Huey has waddled its way to the blue. Without calling, or even a good flare, it crashes on the south side of what there is of the river. During monsoon season, this would be under many feet of water. But now it's a sand bar with no vegetation near it. The rotor blades come to rest before there's any movement from the aircraft. It slid forty or fifty feet, rocked its nose into the sand, then back, and settled into the sand. Still there was no movement from the body of the aircraft nor was there any tell tale red tracer fire coming from its sides. As I overfly, I look down and then see green shaped forms scrambling out on both sides.

"Lead's on the ground. Get Chalk Three over here right away."

"Roger Sneaky, we're on the way. Three, break away now." Tex has answered.

"Scarf Lead, Delta Tango Xray, over." The recon team is calling me.

After I switch to the FM radio, I say "Go Xray."

"Roger, we're down and need an extract. We're taking some small arms from the November..... across the blue. We've got three Whiskey-India-Alpha. Do you copy, over?"

"Roger Xray, I copy. Dart Three is on final, your position. Put four, I repeat four, on board. Chalk Four will pick up the rest, you copy?"

Then back on the UHF I tell Chalk Four to follow Three to the blue and for Chalk Two to climb up and stay clear. After telling them this, I tell Doc he's to stay on Four and Tex to bring in Three while E'Clair and I start working over the area to the north of the downed bird.

What should have taken fifteen minutes is now taking less than five, as E'Clair and I have started gun run after gun run along the northern side of the river. With the river as a natural boundary, we're able to put our rockets along the waters edge without fear of friendly fire on our guys. Twice Covey has asked if we wanted to wait for Sandys. Though I would like to use the A1-E's, we're really running out of time as the sun has started falling.

"Sneaky, we're on final...... ah.... Dart Three, you have the downed bird in sight?" Tex asks.

"Roger Red Scarf. Break! Break! Xray, Xray, Dart Three on final, mark your location, over." The Phoenix AC must be an old timer. He's not at all rattled.

"Roger Dart, land at the one-eighty of Lead. We'll be there." In the background you can hear the gun fire. Though they haven't said it, I think things are a bit tighter down there than they are letting on.

E'Clair and I keep making our round robin passes to the north of the river laying down three or four pair each time then break to the south over the river.

"Sneaky, run your breaks to the left."

Tex is now running the slick in for the pickup. I do not answer. Why confuse things? As I break, on VHF, I call a left break. As I start my climb in the tight left hand turn, I hear the small arms coming up at me.

"Marty, we're taking fire at our three." There's nothing I can do about it. Our first mission is to get the crew and team out of the downed bird and back into the air.

"Roger Sneaky, from your three."

"Three's down!"

"I'm breaking right.... you got it Doc."

"I'm on him." Doc has now joined in behind Tex, providing cover for the slick on the ground.

"Four's on short final."

"Roger Four, come on. We're lifting with four on board."

Though he sounds calm, the sound of machine gun fire, as well as the large rotor blades popping, adds to what must be pure confusion.

I look over and it seems as if these guys have planned this operation for months. As the Phoenix aircraft is lifting off the ground and starting its climb out of the river bed, the second one's landing in the same spot. The sand, blowing from the first one's rotor wash, hasn't settled as it envelops the next Huey. The time on the ground seemed like only seconds but it was long enough for me to make several passes and each time as I pulled out, we could hear the fire coming up at us. It's a wonder we haven't taken a hit.

"Four's out with four, repeat four. Ah.... we're taking fire.... ah.... five o'clock heavy fire. Heavy Fire!"

Doc has started putting rockets down toward the area before calling, "Roger at your five.... rockets inbound!"

"Let's get the hell out of here Sneaky." E'Clair is pulling out of his rocket run about half way through it. There's no reason to keep firing rockets now.

"Able Dart flight, this is One-Three. I need a count, over."

"Roger One-Three, Dart Three with four, repeat four, on board. Three are Whiskey-India-Alpha, do you copy?"

"Roger Dart Three."

"One-Three, Dart Four with four on board."

"Roger Four, you have four on board. Break, break! Red Scarf Lead, you've got a total of eight. Am I correct?"

"Roger, One-Three, that's what I hear."

"Roger Scarf Lead, take the package home. I'll notify Sundance Halo and I'll bring in Sandy to burn up Dart Lead."

Well, so much for that Huey. One thing about getting shot down out here, you just walk away and leave the aircraft. No use in risking a lot of lives trying to get out an aircraft that is already full of holes and after one night will be booby trapped. I guess it's been a rough day for the Phoenix Lead, one crew-chief hit, now his second aircraft lost.

"Dart Three, One-Three." then without waiting for an

answer, "give me the wounded, over.

"Ah....." the Hueys blades are the only thing we hear for a moment. "Phoenix Lead AC, ah.... one Uniform Sierra and one soap bubble from Tango Xray plus the Dart AC, over."

The Covey then asks for a repeat of the injured and then tells us he'll have 18th Surg. ready.

It's getting dark, but still light enough for us to see. I think we'll all be back in time to land before darkness. I wonder if the Captain is hit bad enough that he might be going back to the States with the crew-chief. It happens this way. I've seen it before, especially in Aero-Scouts. When you lose one, you seem to lose two or three. Never just one, it runs in cycles.

The flight back is made in total silence, even on our VHF. I'm sure that it's the same way on the Phoenix push as well. Well, I think we can call it a day. Unless there is a Prairie Fire, we'll be released when we get back.

Over the Rockpile, the same usual calls are made to Quang Tri tower. Just this time a different Phoenix will be going to the Surg. I call the MLT and ask if we'll have another mission. We're told no, that once we rearm, refuel and debrief, we'll be released. The slicks will have to turn in their stabo rigs and they are probably in a hurry to return to Camp Evans as they will have maintenance to do. For us, we'll land and head for the club, though I will come down to see Willie and see how long before the battle damage is repaired. Plus, I usually bring him a case of beer and with the two holes, maybe two cases of beer.

After we rearm and refuel, we fly over to the MLT pad and land. As we're shutting down, I watch as the three remaining Hueys are left at flight idle while the pilots do a quick debrief beside their aircraft. Milo and a couple of other NCO's go to each bird and talk to the crews. Nice touch on Milo's part. Rather than have them shut down and go through a formal process, he just rushes them through it, collects the stabos, and sends them home.

"Sneaky, you want us to shut down?" a slow Texas drawl says.

"Roger."

I now start my shut down that will take about five minutes all together. I have shut the engine down and am sitting filling out the log book when one of the 'yards, who has been running to each of the Hueys, runs up to my side of the aircraft. From the ruck sack he's carrying, he pulls out a beer and hands it up to me. Randy comes around the front of the aircraft and gets one as well, then the short brown-skinned man, grinning broadly, takes off to E'Clair's plane. Before I open the beer, I put it against my forehead and rub it back and forth. Hoping I can get some relief from it before I drink it down. Trying to calm down, I take several deep breaths. Screw it, let's go outside and see what the damage is.

As I climb out of the seat and down the side of the aircraft, Randy yells from the back of the tail boom, "Sneaky, we've got holes in the main blades."

"Fuck!" If I need new blades, Zero-Two-Seven will be down for a week or so. One thing that is at a premium here in Vietnam is main rotor blades. I walk back while looking up. The one blade that's not directly above the tail boom has three holes in it, though all near the trailing edge. For sure none of these three hit a spar, which would mean major damage. "Randy, go over the whole aircraft and let me know the damage." I spin angrily toward Milo and holler, "We'll be inside," then walk toward the Ops hootch.

Fifteen minutes later, after Randy has reported that besides the three hits in the one blade, we have another in the other blade. Plus, we have another hit in the tail boom, unless we missed seeing this one from this morning. Milo enters. Our debriefing with Milo and his NCO'S goes slowly as he wants to know what we saw. I almost lose my temper twice when I think back to his remark about the enemy activity that he didn't tell the rest of the flight. Yes, we all should expect anything and everything when going out there, but still, he could have said something to everyone. Though I am sure we still would have lost the aircraft and probably had the three wounded even if he had told us this. The count is all three wounded are going to be medevaced. The

Phoenix Captain was hit in the left shoulder and bled really bad, while the other two had leg wounds that were T&T's.

We all sit around after Milo has gone into the back room. We could rush back into our aircraft and head back to Evans, but we don't. We have another beer, then slowly stand up and start milling around. When Milo comes back from making his report to Da Nang, he gives us a release for the night.

Before I climb back in, I look at the other rotor blade to ensure it's not spar damage. I'd hate to be flying back from a day like this and lose a rotor blade. It sure would ruin my day, and my life. But then, my wife would finally get to collect my insurance policy.

The flight back is done directly without any practice GCA's. We fly directly into the Griffin pit and park our aircraft. As we are shutting down, I call to Griffin Three, the Operations Officer, and tell him that Zero-Two-Seven is Red X'd until maintenance clears it. I give him our flight times and then finish the shut down. All the while, I watch as Wee Willie is lead to the rear of the aircraft by Randy. Once the blades come to a stop, Willie climbs up on the side of the aircraft with a cold beer.

"Well, once again, you've cheated death." He's smiling even though this battle damage will cost him hours of labor.

Our relationship is a close one, though it's more to do with my past than who I am now. Wee Willie really is a friend. Many a night we've sat up working on something that was either broken or battle damaged. He knows I'll get my hands dirty to help him. After all, we're all a team —Willie, Zero-Two-Seven, and me, and to get this team to work at its best, we have to work together.

"I'll be down here to help you after chow and a few beers." I say.

I gulp the beer down without stopping, hand him back the can, and unstrap. It's then I notice that my seat is wet. I wasn't that hot during the last mission, so this is 'fear water', which I seem to sweat out when I get in a tight jam. Fuck it, I need a shower first. I start my walk up the hill to my hootch.

Chapter 4

Slowly I stir from a hot sticky sleep, now being accelerated by the taste of rancid beer. It's dark, except for occasional rays of light gently dancing through windows and cracks in the plywood hootch. Half-heard disturbances of far off mortar tubes belch out sporadic flares and punctuate the stillness. My Rolex's luminous dial shows four thirty-five a.m.

"Another day," I say to no one in particular. Trying to get a few more minutes of peace, I lie still. But pulsating shots to my head remind me that I drank too much. "Hell with it! Maybe the heater was left on and I'll get a hot shower for a change."

Sitting up, I put on the new pair of Ho Chi Minh tire sandals our overpaid hootch maid bought me. Fred jumps up from the foot of our bed. Yeah our bed, because when in the hootch the bed is his domain and he shares it only begrudgingly. His long skinny brown tail is already wagging, awaiting needed attention that was missed during last night's drunken party that apparently wasn't for dogs. Scanning across the hootch I look into darkened cubicles, each with sleeping forms secured in dreams of places far, far away from the DMZ of South Vietnam.

"What's indicated Fred? Who was here and how long did it last?" Fred's overly large ears perk up at the sound of his name and he snuggles his moist nose into my armpit.

"It's already hot. God, it's going to be a long, rough day," I gripe, thinking about my aircraft's inoperable air-conditioner. "Damn spineless Sherrily doesn't know priorities does he? We gotta get moving, no matter how bad I hurt." Slowly I stand up.

While pulling an OD green towel off one of the many rusted nails scattered across the plywood wall, my tan dog bounds off our bunk and races to the back door, nails clawing at the floor. Soap and towel in hand I follow Fred, but only after I've stooped down to the small refrigerator under the foot of my bunk. Opening the small wood grained door, I feel around for the coldest can then close the door quietly. I open the Korean-made Crown beer with the church key suspended by safety wire next to the door. The noise causes stirring among the cubicles.

Stepping outside and pausing on the porch, I enjoy the placid feeling and take a needed gulp from the rusted can. Laid out before me, in the wavering parachuted light rays, are the unit hootches. On my left, the 3rd Platoon hootch is still pitch-black and lifeless. Twenty meters before me are the enlisted men's hootches lined up in typical military manner. At the bottom of a natural ravine, behind the enlisted men's hootches, are revetments holding the tools of our trade: AH-1Gs, Cobras, Snakes, Gunships. These are the aircraft that bring 'Death From Above'. We are the Griffins; C Battery, 4th of the 77th ARA (Aerial Rocket Artillery), of the 101st Airborne (Airmobile) Division.

Across the ravine through the early morning mist, in faint silhouette, the image of our maintenance hanger appears. Dark this morning because Griffin critical maintenance is caught up for a change, except for my Snake's air-conditioner.

Stepping off the porch, I spot Fred to the right taking a piss against the 1st Platoon hootch wall.

"Good thing you know 2nd Platoon is home," I remind him.

We pass 1st Platoon's hootch as another flare hurtles skyward and starts its lazy drift back toward our bunker lines. The wavering light of the flare creates shadows of murky forms, which in my drunkenness, become NVA infiltrators trying to penetrate our perimeter.

Passing the 1st Platoon bunker, I hear a rat scurry back into the cool black recess built between the hootch and maintenance road.

"Fred, you're no fucking gunny," I say to my floppy-eared companion for the past seven months. He's lost several, almost fatal, battles with the ever present rodents.

As I cross the road, the pungent aroma of the four-hole

latrine next to the Officers' showers hits me. In Vietnam, one can't go too far without walking through the lingering smell of ever-present piss tubes, or the burning of latrine "honey buckets." Opening a broken screen door, the dim red overhead light adds to the shower's eeriness. After the many baths Fred's been forced to endure, he refuses my offer to come in.

I put the half-finished beer can on the ledge, peel off clammy boxer shorts, and twist the rusted valve to the hot water. Immediately it tells me the water heater was turned off, and long ago. I need to wake up and the invigorating cold water will quickly rescue me from my stupor and get me ready for another day's flight deep into Laos. As water pours on me, I find the only way to warm up is by rubbing my skin roughly. Trying to lather up in the cold water is futile, but I keep at it.

My mind wanders to last month and to my thirty-day leave back to the States. While washing my lean body, I remind myself that I should have called it quits. If it wasn't for the kids it would have been nothing at all. "Yeah, nothing at all." Saying to whatever creatures inhabit the mildewed ceiling.

I'm sending money to a blonde North Carolina bimbo, whose only interest in me is a government insurance policy she hopes is currently paid up. Should have done something, but what? It didn't help to arrive unannounced, especially when I knew what to expect. After calling my sister-in-law, Kathy, for a ride from Wilmington Airport to Sneads Ferry, she delayed me at her house on some small pretense. Kathy was stalling for time and this should have signaled that something wasn't kosher.

Hell, all I want is to stay in Nam and fly. The best I can ask for is here. Cheap booze. Great friends. Shit-hot missions. What more could I want?

Voices drifting down the hill, and Fred growling, signal that others are starting their day. Peering out the window slit, I see hootches now lit up as young warriors start their daily ritual.

"Fred," I yell, "you'd better be quiet or the Old Man will have my ass."

Shadowy movements warn me of someone coming toward the shower. 3rd Platoon's Captain Crane and Lieutenant Stahel are striding down the hill. Just what I need to start my day.

"Bastards are too goddamn cheerful in the morning," I mumble.

Quickly I step out of the shower and guzzle down the last of the Crown before their arrival. I want the chit-chat kept to a minimum with these prima donnas. Rather than dry off, I tug the same boxers on and they now cling like a rubber glove. Grabbing the soap and throwing the useless towel over my shoulder, I open the door.

"Good morning, Mr. White." Crane says, awaiting a formal reply.

"Good morning, gentlemen."

Forcing a smile, I stand there like a hotel doorman. After they pass, I slam the door shut before starting to move up the path.

Crossing the maintenance road, my feet and ankles are already powdered with the never ending dust of Camp Evans. The only time there is no dust is when the monsoons hit, and it turns to a mud that sticks to everything.

"Fred, I'm flying today so you're restricted to the hootch."

Ignoring me, he darts ahead, head down and sniffing the ground for a scent that may lead him to a new adventure. He stops to leave his calling card, again, on the stained wall of the 1st Platoon hootch.

"Good Boy." He looks up at me with a sparkle in his eyes.

To my right, the crew-chiefs' and mechanics' tape players are blasting a tune from The Doors. A faint marijuana scent drifts up from the bowels of the enlisted hootches. I feel sorry for them — helicopter crew-chiefs, getting no flight pay or flight time. I remember flying with my plane when I was a crew-chief. Getting paid for it was not the reason I did all the extra work required to keep an unforgivable helicopter flying. My name stenciled on its side was something to be proud of, but that was in the Marine Corps and crew-chiefs are treated differently in the Corps. The Army has once again screwed the backbone of it's flight operations.

Climbing the steps, I jerk open the door. Fred zips in to see who's awake. Jimbo, Doc, Killer, Scoop, Randy and two new guys,

Nix and a young kid, are moving about.

Jimbo is tossing cans of beer to awakened pilots from the large, freshly stolen and now re-painted, and very noisy, refrigerator. Eyeing me he asks, "You need one?"

With a grunt I catch the cold rusted can hurled at me without waiting for a reply. Once it is in hand, I flop heavily on my bunk.

In the center of the hootch a bewildered newbie, Klien, is examining the mess from last night's gathering. His head's down and shaking in disbelief. "What happened?"

Fred's now on his in-house patrol, nose low looking for food that might be tossed his way or left over from last night. He knows pilots moving about at this hour means it's their day in the air, and a lonely time for those left behind. He's been around long enough to know the game.

In spite of all the booze he drank last night, Jimbo starts to assign flight crews for the day. He's what the Army covets in a flight platoon leader: Tall, good looking — almost the poster type, and college educated. Would have made the Dean's list, providing the subjects had included the supple young virgins at the women's college in Denton. From Mineola, a small East Texas turn-of-the-century railroad town, he must have broken every young lady's heart several times before he left. Big brown eyes, toothy wide grin encased by large full lips and a Clark Gable moustache keep the ladies on his door step. He possesses the natural ability to lead in spite of Captain's bars. Jim "Jimbo" Mitchener and I are old friends, coming from another unit after extending our Vietnam tours for another year to fly with the Griffins.

As 2nd Flight Platoon Leader, Jimbo's job is to get this group of twelve pilots sober enough to fly every day. More important, as one of the Section Leaders, his job, like mine, is to bring these young men back alive.

"I'll take lead with Hunt. Sneaky, you got Klien. Kellerher's with Winston. Doc and Nix will bring up trail. Questions?" The formal assigning of crews for the day is completed.

"Yeah, Captain! Why in the hell do I have to fly with Holiday when I'm senior?" Quizzes a newbie.

"No problem, you'll fly with me Nix. Doc you got Randy," asserts Jimbo with an air of authority he never displays except when pushed by some nitwit.

Small talk begins between the Aircraft Commanders and their co-pilots for the day. Just what I need, idle chatter. Spit-shined boots appear before me. Lifting my head, I face a properly dressed, in a new, non-faded Nomex flight suit, baby faced, Warrant Officer Junior Grade Klien.

"WO-Jug, we'll be flying my plane, Zero-Two-Seven, today. Third revetment on the south side. A servo's been leaking, so make sure the hydraulic level is full. Any questions see Wee Willie. I'll be down there in a few." Seeing a blank stare, I point to the door adding, "*Di đi!*"

"Yes Sir!" A much too anxious young pilot replies, ready to salute, but not sure if it's required.

He hurriedly exits through the back door and I stand, pulling up my well worn, faded to a lima bean color and probably no longer fire resistant, Nomex pants.

"Don't be too rough on him, Sneaky. I flew with him," Doc remarks. "Didn't touch a thing and kept his head out of the cockpit."

"I'm not ready for a nickie new kid flying CCN with me," I snap, looking directly at Jimbo while zipping up my Nomex shirt.

"Work with him. Rick checked him out. Doc and I have flown his FAM rides." Jimbo replied, knowing other pilots are listening to how this newbie was being accepted, and remembering their acceptance when joining the Griffins.

"Since when is a fucking familiarization ride a test of balls? Hell! A test of anything?" I snapped back louder than I want, and the pain of my head is now telling me to shut up and lay down.

"Shut the fuck up!" yells Marty "Chocolate E'Clair" St. Clair, whose day off allows him to recuperate from last night.

"I've got to fly with him, not you! If you want, I'll go back to sleep and you fly," I lash out at the only black helicopter pilot I'll ever know.

After strapping on my personal pistol, I grab a cut down

M-14 rifle with ammo pouches. Pulling it off from the large wall hooks I slip into a stabo rig, then survival vest, and last the chicken plate. Then, grabbing my helmet bag I stomp toward the door, pissed at the scheduling for the day.

"Walk with me to the TOC," Jimbo says, while still getting his gear collected.

Leaning against the front door, I finish the beer. Marty's now sitting up in bed. "E'Clair, keep an eye on Fred today, the old man's on the war path."

"Fuck you. I'll sell him to the hootch maid for a quick piece of ass." He chides, provoking chuckles.

Hearing his name, Fred sits up and looks around at the men who have made him the butt of their joke.

"Let's go." With flight gear still in disarray, Jimbo struts out the front door.

"I'm getting a cup of mud. You want one?" Not waiting for an answer, I duck into the mess hall door.

Coming out of the double doors I see Jimbo's got himself arranged properly. I hand him a cup of steaming hot black coffee. Black because I'm in no mood to chase down the Mess Sergeant to get some sugar.

We start the trek up the knoll to the TOC and Hot Spot. The path is well worn from the many pilots who have made the journey before us. Approaching its crest he breaks the silence. "What do you think of Nix?"

What a question! Hell with it, he wants to know what I think. "An ass. Don't like him. Won't fly with him as a section leader either. And he won't AC in any flight I'm leading." Now it's said.

As if I had said nothing, Jombo continues, "Had a good record on his last tour, just needs some time to get to know how we do things. I flew with him yesterday and had no problems. He's just a bit stuffy."

"Bullshit! He's not with the 1st Cav in the Delta anymore. He's flying in the mountains and it's different. I don't want an asshole who has to think about rules of engagement before he fires."

"Cut him some slack!" Jimbo's tone indicates that he's giving me an order.

We reach the top of the hill as the last 3rd Platoon's two-minute alert aircraft is taking off, repositioning to the revetments. Within ten minutes, 1st Platoon will fly their four Cobras up here from the fuel pit

Walking by the Hot Shack, Warrant Officer Junior Grade Curtis stumbles out. He's loaded down with the gear from the crew going off their twenty-four hour Hot Status. He's trying to hum a Bob Dylan song that is hardly recognizable.

Armorers are in the center of the Hot Spot filling the rocket bins with 2.75 inch FFAR flechette and seventeen pound warhead rockets. Seeing us, one yells, "Morning Mr. White. Flying today?"

I give him a thumbs up. "CCN. Won't be in 'til late. Don't let Wee Willie get drunk," I say, knowing they share the same hootch.

Approaching a sandbag covered mound, we step down into a hole on the end. The Tactical Operations Center, or TOC as it's normally called, is easy to find because of the array of antenna protruding over its sides and top. Dull green in color, it's a reinforced structure built three-quarters below ground for protection against the numerous rocket attacks we receive.

"I'll talk to Rick. If he agrees with you then I'll see the Old Man. 'Til then, lay off him."

"Fair." I grumble.

Entering the dimly lit bunker, the booming voice of the Operations Officer, Captain Roger R. Rogers III, is heard. Regular Army and weighing over two hundred eighty five pounds, he's fat. He's from a highly connected family, which explains the waivers the Army gives him to stay in, and to stay on flight status. We call him Jolly Roger though he's repeatedly instructed us that it isn't a proper way to address a senior officer, especially one of his caliber.

"Good morning Jim." he says, ignoring me, in his self-ingratiating, irritating manner. I'd like to buy him for what he's worth and sell him for what he thinks he's worth. Sure would be plenty of beer money for me.

Jimbo stops in front of the Operations Desk and drops his

flight gear in a clutter at his feet.

In the corner, two radio operators are bent over sets fine tuning them. Muffled sounds of many different frequencies are heard. Chatter from on-going and off-going two minute alert aircraft; avionics shop doing radio checks; battalion frequencies; and the division artillery frequency. All of this adds up to bedlam for the untrained ear. Leaves you wondering how anyone understands anything, 'til you learn the secret of listening to only what you want to hear.

"I'll check weather at Khe Sanh and west," I state while walking over to the small cluttered desk that has weather related items strewn about it. The desk is really a joke, as nothing is current.

Monsoons are over so weather won't be a problem until September. I remember during February '67 it rained so hard every day that the only way we got our flight time was sitting on the flight line in a turned up helicopter and logging the four hours time. We had two typhoons that month and nothing I owned was dry when March rolled around, but this is the dry reason, so weather reports aren't a big deal.

A pock-marked Specialist 4th Class approaches the table. "Morning Mr. White. Can I help?" His southern accent is as thick as the gumbo he was raised on.

"No thanks, Carson. CCN today so weather's not an issue." Less than four hours ago we were drinking together. He was calling me Sneaky, and I was calling him Jimmy Lee.

"Mr. White, mind filling out the Flight Crew Board before you leave?" Rogers asks, now using my formal title. He doesn't like nicknames because he hasn't gotten close to pilots who have earned them, and, with his attitude, never will. Though, he will use mine when he thinks it's being heard by others of his equal rank because he's heard many people call me Sneaky . . . even full Colonels. He picks and chooses those times carefully.

"No problem *Dai Uy*." Walking up to the white plastic board, I grab a grease pencil hanging by a string and fill in the ACs' names next to the aircraft number. Then the co-pilot's name and under "Mission" in big letters I write "CCN." Reaching

Zero-Two-Seven I see nothing entered under the remarks column about the air-conditioner.

"Captain Rogers, you know if Zero-Two-Seven's air-conditioner was fixed last night?"

"No", then as an afterthought, "You don't need it to be combat-ready."

I erupt. "If you'd get out of this fucking air-conditioned hole and fly once in a while, you'd quickly find out what the fuck is needed to be combat-ready."

Charging me in three long strides he wants this confrontation as much as I do, "Mr. White, your job is to fly. Not having an air-conditioner has absolutely no bearing on your mission capabilities. You understand this, Mister?" He's now close enough to smell his aftershave.

Obviously I've hit a sore point. The question, and joke, among us warrants, is how he gets his minimum four hours a month flight time for pay. Rumor is he logs time going to and from headquarters for briefings. Getting flight time while riding as a passenger in the battalion Huey is really the sign of a man who's destined for high command.

Jimbo, trying to get my attention, is shaking his head and rolling his eyes toward the door. I've gone too far but what the hell. "Captain, I've complained to our half-assed maintenance department and they've done absolutely nothing. Now I'm complaining to you."

"I'll have you know Mr. White, our maintenance is the best I've ever been around. If you would learn to exercise some tact, I'm sure whatever little problems you have . . . ah . . . could be promptly resolved."

"You're forgetting I happen to be a school trained maintenance officer and rated test-pilot. Hell, I've forgotten more about maintenance than the slug running things down there knows now or ever will know. What we need are pilots flying combat missions," waving my arms around, "and not hiding in air-conditioned holes in the ground pushing papers around or playing maintenance officer." Spinning around I storm for the exit. As I do, everyone is standing, mouths agape, looking at me. A lot will be said this morning, in both the officer and enlisted mess halls.

Stomping down the hill toward the revetments, Jimbo yells for me. Joining up, he blasts, "What the fuck is wrong? Drink too much?" Disgustedly, he flips me the SOI I forgot to check out during my quick exit. "I don't need this today, you understand?"

I slip the metal SOI chain around my neck and stuff the 6" x 5" flimsy paper notebook with call signs and frequencies of local units behind the URC-10 survival radio in my chicken plate's pooch. Normally we would not carry an SOI on a CCN mission, but Rick has suggested air mission commanders carry one on all flights.

"My air-conditioner has been fucked for the past two weeks and maintenance hasn't even ordered parts. I talked to Sherrily after Wee Willie told me he couldn't get anything done. Fucking Sherrily told me to bear with it. Fucking "Bear with it", the bastard said."

Astonishment appears on his face as I tell him of the exchange between the Maintenance Officer, Captain Jonathan Sherrily, and myself.

Then, as if the subject hasn't been mentioned, he says, "Talked to Rick when he got back last night. Three teams are out and they want to insert another two today. We'll be busy. Let's keep our heads up with these newbies on board."

"Shit! We don't need newbies with us now." Jimbo gives a short grunt in agreement.

Both of us would rather not have any action while flying with newbies, but the nature of CCN missions never allows it. One thing about CCN flights, you're always able to encounter some action while flying in Laos.

Approaching the revetments we can see a green clad crew crawling over the aircraft, pre- and post-flighting our weapons of war. Like a colony of ants swarming over pockets of food, each revetment holding a Cobra is alive with movement. As time approaches to start up, the tempo of activity steadily increases. You feel the beat of excitement growing to a crescendo that finally peaks with the beating of the main rotor blades. As the beat quickens, the awkward looking green machines inch their way to take off positions. When walking the flight line early in the morning, you can't help but be caught up in the sound, like a band playing a John Phillips Sousa march, your legs naturally start to move to the rhythm.

"I'll talk to Sherrily," Jimbo says as he walks toward his aircraft. "And, you'd better lay off the subject of Jolly Roger's flying. He has friends in high places and as Ops Officer he can fuck you over."

"No fucking problem. I'll take him on a weapons test flight and put him in for a DFC like I did Sherrily. Be good for his career. Hell, his father-in-law can come over and present the fuckin' thing to him," knowing my outburst is put aside for now. When one has a father-in-law who is a general, he can expect favortisim.

Walking into the revetment I study my co-pilot now high up on the aircraft inspecting the rotor head.

"Well kid, how does it look? You check the hydraulics?"

I glance at Wee Willie as he finishes cleaning my Snake's back seat plexiglass windows.

Klien responds in some inaudible grunt, which I miss, as I stop to check the tail rotor. Zero-Two-Seven is a newer ship and is equipped with a tractor tail rotor to help with directional downwind hovering control. Normally I wouldn't do this much of a pre-flight, but with a newbie I have to show I'm following some semblance of regulations. Last night I was down here with Wee Willie after ten o'clock, working off some small gripes written up on the Dash Thirteen, or bitch sheet as we call it. Zero-Two-Seven was well pre-flighted last night.

"Willie, what's the word on the air-conditioner?"

"Said they'd try to get the parts on Friday's maintenance run to 5th Trans, but I think I'll steal them out of One-Eight-Eight. It's going into annual inspection this afternoon after Sweet Griffin does some check rides."

"Don't get busted. Sherrily will have your ass, then mine."

"Nah. Got it set with Sergeant Jones to swap units after you get back tonight," he says as he climbs out of the aircraft, holding rags and a bottle of white window cleaner.

Looking up, I question, "Is it ready to go or what?" The angular newbie has no idea what he's about to get into on his excursion west into Laos. "If it's ready, let's get busy. We've got to be there by six-twenty."

Stepping up on the open ammo bay door, I reach into the back seat stowing my M-14 and ammo pouches against the left window. I pull my helmet out of its bag, and throw the empty bag to Wee Willie as he walks toward the large fire extinguisher.

I'm careful with my custom painted flight helmet. Both sides are painted with a white Casper the Friendly Ghost holding an oversized pair of binoculars to his eyes and a mini-gun under one arm. Across the visor cover, written in bright yellow, is "Fuck Communism." It's a carry-over from my Marine days. I was given an Article 15 the same day I won my first DFC because some Marine Master Gunnery Sergeant gave me a direct order to take it off. My Commanding Officer, at the time, dismissed the Article 15 hearing and put me in for the medal. As a reminder, I've always painted it on my helmet. On the back, in smaller yellow letters, is painted "Bring 'em Back Alive."

I get remarks about the helmet. Some good, some down right anti-American. Either you like it or you don't, there's no in-between. My helmet is an extension of my personality. Like my helmet, what you see is what you get, no hidden agenda. Raw, rough, tactless, crude, and loyal. Yeah, loyal to a fault. Committed to my war. It's the only time in my life where I'm my own person. Here in Vietnam, I'm not Robert Bryan White, Junior. I'm no man's son. I don't let people call me, Robert, Bob, or Bobby and I don't use Junior. I'm "Sneaky." There are no fingers pointed, no snickers about my family. Here, it's just me, Sneaky White.

I pull the Velcro strips of the chicken plate around me and secure it tightly to my chest. We only use a front plate as we're encased in an armor seat that leaves only our chests and lower legs unprotected. The plate is uncomfortable because under it, we wear survival vests, and the compartments of mine are full of everything I'll ever need if I go down except for a box of rubbers. Climbing into the Cobra's back seat, I watch Klien scurry around the aircraft and climb into his front seat. Though there is no need for it, I readjust my seat to the position I like, sitting low in the cockpit. I strap myself in, and we hear other 2nd Platoon aircraft start to crank up.

Directing, almost bothered, I order Klien to adjust the mirror so he can see me, knowing that he would have done this anyway. A new warrant fresh out of flight school and landing a Cobra transition meant that he was in the top 10 percent of his class. He knows the procedures.

"When we get to CCN, after your briefing, I'll give you the pushes I want on the radio. Also, what I want on the window, understand?"

"Yes Sir!" Klien promptly replies.

"Name's Sneaky. Everybody calls me Sneaky and that means you, too. You comprehend?" I say to Klien while eyeing Willie's big, toothless grin.

We both know this kid's in for a hard time not just because of my hangover, but because I don't like newbies. They'll get you killed with stupid mistakes. One of the reasons I went into maintenance was the fear that one day I'd have to be an Instructor Pilot, and knowing I'd neither have the patience nor the personality to teach, especially when some snot nose kid is trying to kill me in concert with a helicopter that would rather not be in the air flying.

"Yes uh . . . Sneaky?"

"Wasn't difficult, was it? Let's get this beast in the air and go kill someone!"

Going through the start-up procedure I don't use the printed check list other units would require and Army regulations demand.

"Ready to kick the tire and light the fire, Willie?"

"Clear!" Wee Willie yells as he gives a thumbs up after looking down both sides of the aircraft. He swings the main rotor blade for me to know it's not tied down.

Setting the throttle to just under the Flight-Idle Detent position, I engage the starter button under the collective. The slow whine of the Lycoming turbine starts as it cycles through. The crackling of the ignitors popping to fire raw JP-4 fuel is slowly overcome by a low moan and then a whine as the turbine gains

RPM's. Scrutinizing the Exhaust Gas Temperature (EGT) and the N_1 speed gauges, I ensure a proper start with no problems requiring an emergency shut down. Quickly, we're at flight idle and all gauges are in the green arcs or climbing toward them. Slipping my helmet on, I tell Klien to be quiet. Earphones are crackling with the interplay of the four radios. Radio checks, general bullshit and tower clearances, plus the faint sound of AFVN on the ADF playing some rock-n-roll, might add up to mass confusion for an untrained ear.

"Lets go." I yell over the many sounds my Cobra is singing.

Closing my window, I then check the shoulder harness and inertia system. I reset the barometric altimeter to show the proper reading. Then, gradually roll throttle up to flight RPM. A final beeping up with the RPM button on the end of the collective, until we're at operating RPM. Slowly pulling up the collective, we've become light on our skids. Rotorwash beats down on Wee Willie as he crouches low behind the revetment wall. A Cobra has a different center of balance than a Huey. When a Huey raises to a hover, the nose comes up first, rocking on the back end of its skids. Its hover is three feet above the ground. A Cobra's skid toes are the last to break from the ground. Hovering in a slightly nose-down attitude, usually at a foot or so, gives it a look that adds to its ungainly appearance. Don't let it fool you, maybe we're awkward looking but we'll bring death and destruction on the hardest target quickly and efficiently.

"Nine-Two's up," announces Jimbo on VHF.

"Sneaky's up . . . ah . . . with no air-conditioner," I press knowing this will be monitored by all, including those in the TOC.

"Nine-Two Alpha's up." Squeaked Winston. He is flying with Chief Warrant Officer 2 Tim "The Killer" Kellerher and he's used Killer's call sign.

"Nine-Two Delta is ready but negative Uniform," Chief Warrant Officer 2 "Doc" Holiday advises.

"Nine-Two Alpha, take trail and Delta will move up," Jimbo directs, knowing trail must have an operational UHF radio. "Copy the change, Three?"

"Roger Nine-Two," acknowledges Jolly Roger from deep in

the TOC.

"Somebody ought to switch Sneaky's air-conditioner for the UHF, then we don't have to listen to him." Laughter, chuckles, giggles, and squelch breaks flood three frequencies after this unknown voice mentions my aircraft's problems.

Jolly Roger returns on the air, "Knock off the chatter Griffins!"

"Nine-Two lifting." Jimbo starts backing out of his revetment.

Pulling up the last bit of collective, and while looking out of the left side of the aircraft, I tell my new co-pilot, "Look to the right, we're backing out."

Without waiting for his reply I see Wee Willie waving a thumbs up. Bringing the Cobra to a low hover, I slowly back out of the revetment. As the nose clears, I swing us around and face the take-off pad. Jimbo's in position and we ease up behind him. Continually I scan instruments, double checking operating temperatures, pressures and the positions of a myriad of dials and switches.

"Flight's up," Killer calls from his trail position.

"Evans Tower, Griffin Nine-Two, with a flight of four at the Griffin pit for take-off to the northwest."

"Roger Griffin, your flight is cleared for takeoff. Be advised Phoenix flight lifting at this time. Current altimeter two-nine nine-two. Winds two-four-zero at four. DA four-six-five. You're cleared to cross the active. Negative outbound artillery. Have a good day and good hunting." The harried controller must find this time of day the busiest.

"Nine-Two on the go." The narrow green aircraft slowly starts to move into translational lift.

As he moves, I pull in power and ease the cyclic slightly forward and we slowly move forward from the hover that has left us bouncing for the past few minutes. We dip slightly down, then are mysteriously snatched by an invisible hand that pulls us into a climb. We pass through translational lift and become a flying machine. The wonders of science.

"Griffin Three. Nine-Two Whiskey is off with four at

zero-six-zero-three hours," Jeff "Scoop" Winston radios. Our resident bookworm is also the newest Chief Warrant Officer 2 in the unit, having been promoted while I was on leave. His family sends him a box of paperbacks every few weeks. Doesn't matter what kind, just something to read. Usually they're dog-eared and well read. Sometimes pages, important pages, are missing, and a disgruntled reader will hurl it, and obscenities, at Scoop. If he's not at the controls flying, Scoop's bent over reading.

"Roger Nine-Two Whiskey," thunders Jolly Roger.

"Evans, Griffin flight will be QSY to Quang Tri."

Good day Nine-Two, good..." Is the last thing we hear before I change to Quang Tri Tower frequency.

Chapter 5

"Quang Tri Tower. DMZ Dust Off Seven-Zero-Seven inbound from the northwest along QL-1 to 18th Surg. with two," the deep, baritone voice of the guttiest Dust Off pilot in Northern I Corps calls.

"Roger Seven-Zero-Seven. Cleared direct 18th Surg. Altimeter two-niner niner-three. Winds calm," an Air Force tower operator replies with urgency, then calmly continues. "Phoenix flight cleared to land three-two. Altimeter two-niner niner-three. Winds calm. DA four-five-two."

"Moon Glow, Griffin. Over." Jimbo calls on FM, while Nix calls on UHF radio, "Quang Tri Tower, a flight of four Griffins to the south for landing CCN pad. All weapons systems cold and we have the numbers."

"Roger Griffin, weapons cold, cleared direct CCN."

"Tower, Phoenix will be going to POL," echoed a pilot's voice, punctuated by the popping of his Huey's rotor blades.

"Phoenix cleared off the active to POL."

"Moon Glow, this is Griffin," again on FM.

"Go Griffin."

"Moon Glow, Griffin with a flight of four on final your location."

"Roger. On landing keep turned up and have the ACs come to Operations," murmurs the CCN radio operator. I don't recognize his voice, but it's not Milo or Billy.

"Roger," Jimbo replies, then adds, "Everybody catch that?"

VHF squelch breaks are affirmative replies to the question.

"Find out if we need to refuel," I remind Jimbo, forgetting the hangover that wants to dominate my mind this morning.

"Moon Glow, Griffin. Do we need to refuel right away?" Jimbo asks while beginning his flare to the pad.

"Roger, you'll be going right out."

Touching down, Jimbo's window pops open and he starts to climb out. When you're his size it takes a contortionist to get in and out of these thirty-nine inch wide beasts.

Upon landing, I roll the throttle back to flight-idle, which allows me to feel the rotor wash from Doc's aircraft as he lands behind us. Opening my window and undoing the shoulder harness, I see Jimbo has made it out. "Sit here and listen up on Fox Mike, and write everything down," I yell to my newest charge. Klien gives me a wave like a child waving at one of his parents getting out of the family sedan to get him an ice cream cone.

Climbing out of Zero-Two-Seven, I hope this isn't a Prairie Fire so early in the morning. Jimbo and I arrive at the Operations hut at the same time with Doc and Killer close behind.

"We're busy this morning," Sergeant Major William "Billy" Washburn broadcasts.

He's a moose of a man. His voice alone terrifies you and, when added to his over twenty-five years in the Army, most with Special Operations or Special Forces, you know not to do anything but say, "Yesssssss Sir!" Once past the voice you find two-hundred and twenty-five pounds of body stacked on a five foot six inch neckless frame.   You notice Billy's missing neck right away. Just a large pumpkin shaped head sitting atop a barrel chest with rows upon rows of rippled muscles. Though not an officer, his personality commands respect.

"Here's the problem," Billy bellows, plowing right away into his briefing. He needs no introductions to ACs he's grown to trust, and admire, for their eagerness and commitment to his special missions. "Viper was probed and has been moving the past several hours. Two injured from frags, but they're moving."

He sees concern on our faces when the injured Recon Team members are mentioned. Though we might not know the individual team members, we Griffins are part of the CCN family. Like a family when a cousin gets hurt, you feel concern.

"Sweet Griffin inserted them at dusk yesterday and they

were fine until around zero-one-hundred. We think it's a couple of squads, but Viper hasn't been able to break contact. We'd rather not extract them," Billy says, looking at each AC, then stopping at me with those piercing steel gray eyes.

"We want you to go out there and join up with Covey. He'll give you a mark on their location. Make a few rocket passes and help them break contact. They need to complete this mission. It's important."

All CCN missions are important. Why else would you insert a team of three or four Green Berets and as many Montagnards, seventy-five to one-hundred miles from the nearest friendlies only to leave them alone to hike around for a week or so.

"Jimbo," I ask rolling my eyes toward the door, "what about the newbies?"

"We got two new guys," Jimbo informs Billy. A disheartened expression creeps on Billy's deeply tanned leathery face. He expected a fully experienced crew — not one with cherries flying. "No problem. I've got one and Sneaky the other. We just need the papers signed."

"Okay." Visibly upset, Billy yells toward the darkened rear of the hut, "Stan, go out and have the Griffin FNGs fill out clearance papers, and *di di.*"

From shadows, moving cat-like, appears Sergeant First Class Stan "The Man" Milo. He's the Assistant Operations Sergeant for MAC-V-SOG, Command and Control North, Mission Launch Team 2. As he passes us, he's holding two stabo rigs and forms to sign your life away. Forms are required so the United States of America, United States Army, and any other United States agency, can deny what you're about to do. They promise you that if you tell anyone what you did, the United States can prosecute you to the fullest extent of the law. Yeah I know. What fucking law? All this for telling someone you did something the United States government swears never happened. Nixon's been telling the world, and Congress, that U.S. personnel are not in Laos. Therefore, these operations never happened.

"Unbelievable," thinking to myself, "I've been flying into Laos since 1966. I wonder if the newbies know what they're being asked to sign."

Billy unlocks, then swings open the large double doors of the top secret wall map, then pulls back the curtain covering it. It's of Laos, the five southern provinces of China, North Vietnam, and the area of South Vietnam from Da Nang's Hai Van Pass north to the Ben Hai River. CCN's area of operations.

On the map are neatly laid out grids, each outlined in dark ink. Some have numbers, others have red diagonal stripes. Scattered over the map are small circles that identify recent anti-aircraft gun locations. What would Nix say if he found out CCN didn't plot fifty-one caliber locations, just big stuff like 23mms, 37mms, and larger? I see the markings of four teams in the area of southern Laos. They're east of Tchepone but north of Highway QL-9. These are our babies.

"When did the fourth team go in?" remembering Sweet Griffin had told Jimbo of three.

"Parachuted in this morning from an NKP Blackbird. They're linked up and operational with no problems."

He knows Rick must have briefed us upon his return last night. If the team was inserted by a Special Operations C-130 from NKP it means that it's under CIA control. One of the biggest problems out here is that the Agency usually doesn't tell us when they have teams out. When flying over an area and you see someone, you expect him to be the enemy so you roll in and kill him. How many times have we killed our own? Our teams, like the CIA and other operational teams, go into Laos outfitted in captured NVA uniforms, weapons, and gear. So a casual NVA soldier seeing them will think they're on the same side. It's all part of the deception that often ends up with us not knowing who's who.

"Here's Viper at Xray Delta five-zero-two, five-eight-five." A stubby finger points to a grid well north of the Song Ba River. Officially, it's near the end of our range with a full fuel load. In a year or so this area would become Firebase Ranger-South during Operation Lom Som 719. It'll also be where I end my Army career after dancing with a 37mm, but that's all in the future.

"Indian Country," Killer exclaims, letting out a low whistle.

To the east of Viper's grid is another one outlined with bright red diagonal lines meaning it's seeded with either delayed fused bombs, or bombs that detonate upon any increased magnetic activity. Usually these bombs are thousand pounders. In the past we've been briefed that low flying helicopters will set them off, though I've never heard of it happening. Yet, we try our best not to fly over these grids.

Some grids get personalities of their own and become famous. One, Hotel-Nine, has come to represent an area inaccessible to us. Every time we put a team in, they get blown out or are immediately compromised. Several teams have been totally lost, and have never been heard from again after landing in Hotel-Nine. It doesn't matter if we insert by helicopter or parachute, in daylight or darkness, the results are the same — a shit sandwich. Team members I know would rather not get a Hotel-Nine mission. Whatever's there is very well guarded by the NVA. Maybe Uncle Ho's family jewels?

"Viper's up three-four point seven-five, call sign Whiskey Romeo Papa. Covey's on station and will give you a positive on them. He's on two-four-four point six-five UHF, call sign Long Bow Two-Two. Weather's clear. Covey can get fast movers from Hillsborough if needed, but I'd rather not unless we have to extract them. Da Nang doesn't want a Prairie Fire, they want them to break contact and continue. Your call sign is Night Hawk. Questions?" Billy finishes his quick, but typically professional and thorough briefing. Jimbo and I finish scribbling on our knee pads at the same time.

"What's your load Sneaky?"

"Nails on the outside pods, seventeen pound HEs inside, and both forty millimeters working. But with the newbie, I don't want him firing the turret."

He looks at the Irishman we fondly call Killer who answers before asked, "Got the same, except only a mini-gun working in the turret."

"I'm half and half Jimbo. Both the turret mini and pooper are working good," responds Doc.

"Let's top off and get airborne," Jimbo says as we hear

Hueys landing.

SFC Milo sticks his head in the door. "Want the slicks to stay turned up?"

"No! Have 'em shut down and rig for strings. Get the ACs in here," Billy yells over the noise of the landing aircraft while tugging the map curtain closed. Milo quickly closes the door.

Going out the door, we see Milo standing there, papers in hand, talking to a Phoenix crew-chief.

Climbing into my seat I look over at the slicks, now at flight-idle, cooling their engines before shut down. They see we haven't shut down, so they know something is going on right away.

Putting my helmet on I hear on UHF. "Quang Tri, Griffin Nine-Two with a flight of four at CCN for lift off to the west, then direct to POL. This is an emergency." Jimbo's already light on his skids.

"We're light," the Irishman calls from his tail-end spot.

"Roger Griffin. You're cleared. Be advised C-130 on three mile final for three-two. Altimeter two-niner niner-three. Winds zero-two-zero at six. DA four-five-two." He knows a scramble is in progress.

After lifting, we make a slow wide turn to the south at low level to go under the active approach, then turn north heading directly to the fuel pits.

"Griffin flight on final POL with the numbers, weapons cold," Nix says in his curt manner.

Reaching POL we turn our Cobras to the west facing the pits. Setting down, our co-pilots scramble from their seats to start the topping-off process.

"Listen up. Sneaky and I have newbies so keep an eye on each other. Sneaky, if they need an extract I'll head back early with Doc to re-arm, refuel and escort Phoenix. Any questions?" Jimbo says on the unit VHF frequency.

Affirmative squelch breaks.

Glancing over, I see Jimbo looking intently down at his map. Lucky son-of-a-bitch, his air-conditioner is pouring out condensed air in two thick vapor streams aimed toward his helmet. Reaching up, I feel warm air coming out of my two vents. I glance down to my lap to the plastic covered map I refolded while in the Operations hut, with Recon Team Viper's coordinates circled in black. Checking my fuel gauge it shows we're topped off and I reach out, tap Klien on the helmet, then close my window. Looking up, he sees my cut off sign. Capping the fuel tank closed, he drags the heavy, oily black hose away and climbs back into his seat.

The throbbing has return to my head, and I've got a fucking hot extract. I don't need this today.

"Quang Tri, Griffin Nine-Two with a flight of four at POL for the active. This is a scramble."

"Aaah... Niner-Two you're cleared to the active. Be advised a one-thirty on final roll out."

"Nine-Two lifting."

We overfly the end of the taxi-way on our way to the active.

"Quang Tri, Griffin flight at the active for takeoff. We have the numbers and we'll be QSY to the northwest," Jimbo says, as he starts going through translation lift, without waiting for final clearance.

ARA Cobras are configured with four large rocket pods that enable us to carry a total of seventy-six rockets. We're called "Heavy Hogs." Regular Cobra gunships, or Cav gunships, don't carry this same heavy load. Our Cobras are heavy with fuel and rockets, and as the density altitude, or DA, starts to climb the effectiveness of the rotor system diminishes. At times we use a running takeoff by sliding down the runway, with sparks flying, until our rotor blades develop enough lift to get us airborne.

There's also the challenge of getting enough altitude at the end of the runway to clear the concertina wire curled row upon row. At least once a year some ill-fated pilot doesn't make it and snags the wire. What happens next is funny to look at but deadly serious to the aircraft crew. The skids are jerked down at enough of an angle to cause the main rotor blades to strike the rice paddy. If the crew is lucky, they don't flip over. If they do, they go completely over and the injuries can be fatal. Usually this happens to overloaded, Charlie model, Huey gunships.

Cobras are Army approved to fly at 9,500 pounds max gross

weight. We had one crash after 20 minutes flight time and it weighed 10,200 pounds. Battalion brass wanted to hang the AC. We warrants knew it took phenomenal pilot technique to get it off the ground, then flying for twenty minutes was a test of skills most do not possess, especially those at battalion. Rather than give up rockets for safety, this AC took a full load to deliver to the enemy.

I wonder what battalion brass would say if they were out in the field in need of fire support and some pilot said. "Due to the fact that ARA Battalion brass said I would be overloaded I didn't bring too many rockets and I'm out now. Please try to hang in there, I'll be back in forty minutes or so." Yeah, we all know the brass wouldn't be out there unless it was for a flyover Silver Star for their career advancement.

An Irish brogue on FM reports, "Moon Glow, Night Hawks are airborne in route to Long Bow."

"Roger, Long Bow Two-Two knows you're on the way."

"All right newbie, let's get to work. Write these pushes on your right window... ah... up high so that I can see them."

I give him all the call signs and frequencies, watching in amazement as he slowly and methodically writes them down. I feel like a penmanship teacher in grade school getting ready to grade his work.

"What do they call you?"

"William, but Mom calls me Buff."

"Well William, ah... I'm not your Mother. I'm Sneaky, your guardian for the day. You know Buff means Big Ugly Flying Fucker? It's what the Air Force calls their CH-53 Jolly Green helicopters flying with the 37th Air Rescue Squadron out of Da Nang. You're ugly, but not too big. You'll be 'The Kid' 'til you earn something better." In due time he'll earn a nickname that will stay with him the rest of his Army career.

I change the frequencies on both UHF and FM radios. The VHF is located on the co-pilots panel, and will stay on one twenty-four twenty, the Griffin unit frequency, or push, as we call it, throughout the mission.

"How old are you?"

"Almost nineteen and a half."

Ignoring him for a moment, I report on VHF. "Sneaky's up on pushes." Which is followed by squelch breaks from the others.

"Okay, almost nineteen and a half, here's the ten cent tour. On your right is the Dong Ha fire support base with the little village of Dong Ha to the north of it. You go north past Dong Ha and follow QL-1 crossing the Ben Hai River and you're in North Vietnam, 'bout four miles from here. Some day I'll fly you up there and let you take pictures of the big North Vietnam flag at their outpost, south of Vinh Linh."

He looks up in the mirror at me. Through his clear visor I see a wrinkled forehead questioning me about the flag.

"Usually they don't shoot, just wave. Sort of a mutual admiration society between warriors." He still looks puzzled. He thinks I'm pulling his leg, but in time, he'll get to go up there and take his own pictures.

"Road over the rise to our right will be QL-9. It goes from Dong Ha through Cam Lo on to Khe Sanh then to Tchepone, Laos and ends up in Thailand. We usually follow it into Laos then break off to the area we're working," I say while engaging the rocket systems to <u>HOT</u>, arming the 2.75 FFARs (Folding Fin Aerial Rockets) we carry in our pods, and the front gun turret.

"To our right, the firebase you'll see next is Camp J.J. Carroll, where the 8 inch/175mm howitzers of 2nd Battery of the 94th Artillery Battalion are located. At the base of those mountains over there," pointing south, "is Mai Loc, a 'yard relocation camp. I'll point out some old Marine bases as we pass them. Good reference points that you need to learn quickly. Quicker you do, the safer flying for you during the monsoons."

These old firebases bring back memories of hard combat that gave me my baptism by fire. Flying into fire support bases during the Marine occupation was terrifying at times. Trying to hide behind a M-2 fifty caliber machine gun while trusting a pilot to get you in and out safely without great bodily damage caused me to throw up many a meal.

We're climbing when Jimbo comes up on UHF. "Long Bow Two-Two, Night Hawk Lead." Without waiting for an answer, he continues, "We need more altitude or he's in low working the team."

"Coming up on your right is "The Rockpile." To the south of it, down QL-9, will be Vandegrift, or Vandy. It's named after a Marine General. Before being called Vandegrift it was called LZ Stud. But after Khe Sanh closed in '68, the Marines moved back here and renamed the base. A lot of good Marines gave up their lives for this ground."

I watch his head moving about trying to gather the information as quick as it's thrown at him. Laid out all around him are the fabled mountains of the Northern 'Eye' Corps of Vietnam.

"You flew this area with the Marines." Before I can reply. "That's why you wear that patch."

"Yeah. I was here when we opened most of these bases. Flew with HMM-262, 'Bills Bastards', on their first tour. Then with 'The Flying Tigers', on 262's 2nd tour. It's all home to me. Whenever I come back through Long Binh I ask for 'Eye' Corps. My combat patch is a 1st Marine Division patch, which is rare for us Army types." I'm sure other Griffins already told him why I wear it, as well as Navy-Marine Corps Combat Air Crew Wings above my Army Aviator Badge, and no other rated qualification badges. Question is, what else have they told him about me? I don't like wearing all the junk on my uniforms, part of the Marine tradition I've brought into the Army. I usually fly wearing fatigues, which is frowned upon by brass for safety reasons. Though most pilots wear jungle boots I have two sets of Navy/Marine Corps flight boots, which I rotate daily. So I'm never attired entirely according to Army regulations. This includes the unauthorized personal Ruger Black Hawk .41 magnum pistol I brought back on this tour that stays close to me all of the time.

Regulations say I should wear either the Army XXIV Corps, the Army First Aviation Brigade, the 198th Light Infantry Brigade, Americal, the First Marine Aircraft Wing or the Second Marine Aircraft Wing patch as a combat patch. But not me, I wear the First Marine Division patch, and nobody, at least in the Army, knows the difference. The bright red diamond with a blue number one in its center causes stares. Inside the one, Guadalcanal is spelled out vertically in white letters. Several times I've been asked if I fought on the canal. Hell of a question! Though thirty-two and old by Army line pilot standards, I'm no WWII veteran, which should be evident.

"Were you at Khe Sanh?"

"Yep. Before, then during the seventy-seven day siege, until all the helicopters were pulled out. We won a Presidential Unit Citation. I had a door gunner killed while doing a pre-flight on a rotor head. Hit by a sniper. Never knew what hit him. That's when I knew we'd never come out alive."

Reflecting back to my hardest tour brings back images of lost friends. Though only a few years ago, it seems like ancient history. I try again to push it back into the dark abysses of my mind.

"Will we see it?"

"You'll know when we get there. Can't miss it, even now."

Hoping this talk will end because the memories are painful. Living in holes dug deep in the red ground, fighting bad weather, huge rats, and good NVA marksmen it was my most trying tour. The night Lang Vei was overrun by NVA tanks brought me to the realization that we were only at Khe Sanh with the permission of the NVA, and any time they wanted us to leave they could do it. Years from now it will be argued whether or not it was the great victory, and for who, us or them. It was a victory for me, I got out alive, and I'm sure several thousand others agree. There should be a Khe Sanh Survivors Association, like the WWII Iwo Jima Survivors or Korea's "Chosin Few". It would be a special club.

"Let me explain the radios." He knows the radios from his flight school but I need a subject change. "FM... ah... Fox Mike is used for air to ground communication. Talking to the teams, or grunts, on this one. Sometimes we'll talk to the spotter aircraft with this radio." He waves his hand in acknowledgment.

"UHF is used to talk to other aircraft and towers. When working fast-movers we use it, though sometimes they'll use Victor." Another wave.

"Last but not least is the radio before you. You control the VHF radio. We use this for talking between ourselves. The frequency is the Griffin push, so remember it and check it whenever you get into a front seat. What's our push?"

He looks down then looking back into the mirror. "One-twenty-four twenty."

"Right. Always check this. Avionics guys sometimes change it for radio checks. Here's the game plan. If I tell you to talk, remember which one to use. At times we'll be using all three so you have to keep alert."

"Got it." Waving, I hope, the final time.

Looming ahead is a dark red clay scrape of land extending far out in front of us. Partially overgrown now, there's no mistaking that this was a large fire base. Sections of PSP matting are curled up and now rusting, from long ago impacting NVA artillery, mortar rounds and U.S. bombs. Eight helicopter revetments that I plied my trade from are eroding now. Places that Agents Orange and White missed are now sprouting large columns of bright green foliage of unknown variety. Southeast of the strip, but inside the perimeter, is the old ammo storage dump. The day it took a direct hit I was thrown from my sleeping bag. Peeking outside, I saw thousands of rounds exploding in a 4th of July glory, though it wasn't the 4th, nor was it July. Exploding rounds shooting their lethal charges in all directions. The noise was deafening. What started with one well-placed NVA rocket ended in a rumble that shook the base for thirty-five minutes, and it's shock waves were felt all the way to the bowels of the White House. The insides of every living Khe Sanh resident, two or four legged, for the rest of their lives will remember the day the dump blew. Friendlies had only one Marine killed, NVA viewed a great show, and I can't speak for the four legged rat population. I couldn't hear clearly for days after it. I'm sure the NVA gunner who fired the shot was rewarded with Uncle Ho's Medal of Greatness. Had the NVA gunner been a Marine, he would be a Distinguished Marksman and sent to Camp Perry.

"That's it. My home for eight months."

Feeling stuffy now as the sun starts to heat up our closed cockpit, the tone of this conversation takes a turn I don't expect. A working air-conditioner wouldn't help me now and I know it.

Flying over the base I watch the green helmet bob from side to side trying to take it in. I think back and remember what the base was like when it was crawling with dirty red covered green forms trying to defend it. Not slowing down, it's not a joy ride, we continue west.

I'm happy we've past Khe Sanh. Every time I'm here I remember Jimmy, the smiling round face of the best man at my wedding, who died flying to Khe Sanh in May '67. Our friendship went back to our tour in Vietnam with HMM-262. When I transferred to the Army he was proud that his friend was a helicopter pilot. We had just been on R&R together in Hong Kong, sharing the same hotel room, and yes girls and anything else we could get our hands onto. We got back, and Jimmy had to go to Khe Sanh with his squadron. I had to go back to my unit. He died the next day flying as a gunner on a medevac flight into Hill 861. I'm haunted by Jimmy's face, his smile, and at night I'm shook out of a deep sleep with him leaning over me, talking as if we were still together. Am I alive? Is he dead? Are we together now and if not, will we be together again?

To this day, I keep in contact with my Marine comrades. Whenever I can, I go to Marble Mountain Marine Base, next to China Beach, and spend a night or two with them. We have a good drunken time remembering days past, and them showing off to other Marines a crew-chief that went on to fly, even if only for the Army. I always park in Marine revetments rather than the 282nd Black Cat revetments. Marines would rush over to have their picture taken next to or in the aircraft. I never stop them, what harm can it do? And, if it adds to their otherwise uneventful day, then I've done some good for my Marines. Several times I've given rides to a few close friends. Stick time in an Army helicopter will be something to brag about in years to come.

"Night Hawk Lead, Long Bow Two-Two, over."

"Go Two-Two," Replies Jimbo.

"Hawk Lead we're going to Prairie Fire Whiskey Romeo Papa. They have three soap bubbles injured and compromised. Requested a Prairie Fire and awaiting approval, over," says Two-Two weakly. Another wounded means they're still in contact and a hot extract.

"Roger, we have four Cobras on the way. If we can expend two, and go back to re-arm and refuel, we'll come back out with the package. This way we should be able to provide coverage for Romeo Papa. Will that help?" Jimbo's thinking is the same as mine would be, if I was the Section Leader today.

"Sounds good. What's your ETA?" clearly now.

"About four minutes east of A Loui at twenty-four hundred." Then switching to VHF, "Sneaky, I'll take Doc and expend. You hold back and cover as long as you can. We'll try to get back with the slicks as soon as possible."

"Roger." Then adding. "Killer, you copy?" Which is followed by a double squelch break.

"You get this?"

Looking into the mirror I wonder if he's ready to get his cherry broken. This will be a hot one. There's many fifties out here and given the chance they'll shoot the hell out of you.

"Turn up your UHF and monitor it, I'll be using Fox Mike and Victor. Understand?" Again a gloved hand comes up quickly.

Maybe it's better, I don't have to listen to him. I turn the ADF volume down, no more time for rock-n-roll.

"We going any higher?" Still thinking of flight school tactics.

"We fly by different rules out here. Forget everything you've learned. You fly low and staggered and no formations. Charlie's got the bigger guns. You climb out here... ah... you get blown out of the air. We live low and fast, and with one shot Charlies rather than with the big shit." Wondering if it's impacting on him just what the hell he's gotten into.

"Can't wait to tell the guys from my flight class I'm flying for Special Forces," talking with an enthusiasm that'll be dampened as soon as he gets the shit shot out of him.

"Forget it. Can't do it. Not even to your dear old mother. We don't exist. Didn't you read the fucking papers you signed?" He still doesn't comprehend the nature of our business.

"Night Hawk Lead over A Loui at twenty-four hundred." Nix on UHF.

The slow rolling hills of southern Laos are unfolding before us, as a gentle green wave coming into the beach. Warm lush, thick multigreen carpet that has an appealing, home-like atmosphere, which cleverly hides many NVA traps deep in it's folds and recesses. Under plush layered vegetation are concealed paths, trails and roads used by the enemy. Some roads are all but paved and modern by Vietnamese standards. Two lane, evenly graded fast track roads that allow trucks to drive unimpeded under the blanket of American menacing air power. Co Rock Ridge majestically looming to our southeast looks awesome. It's said to hold a major NVA command center, but I don't think we'll ever know for sure; it is a natural barrier to recon team inserts because of its sheer cliffs. As we continue along QL-9, Doc, with Randy taking pictures, passes to join up with Jimbo.

CWO-2 Randy "Mask" Hunt is our twenty year old resident kid in the platoon though the new replacement may relieve him of this position. We still haven't figured out how he got Cobra transition and ended up in ARA. We call him Mask because his grandfather made him bring a gas mask to Vietnam. His grandfather remembers being gassed in the "Big War" and doesn't want his grandson to go through the same thing. I can't remember him ever missing mail call, sometimes a half-dozen letters. He also gets audio tapes from his family every week. There's times he's the only one from 2d Platoon with mail.

"I'm on your seven, Jimbo."

"I'm holding back 'til you check things out."

Jimbo's and Doc's aircraft pull further ahead leaving a very noticeable separation between me and Killer.

Slowing I look back and see Killer flying a slow left to right wiggling trail pattern a half mile or so behind.

Chapter 6

"Hawk Lead, what's your ETA?" asks Covey.

"We're. . . we're about five out," Jimbo says.

We all scan toward the northwest trying to see the Air Force O-2 Cessna Skymaster flying low over Viper's area.

"Got him! Two o'clock near the top of the second ridge," Mask blurts.

"Hawk Lead, I've got your flight. Proceed west, turn north into the next valley. Proceed half way up the valley and then turn east for your approach. It will be over the low ridge and Papa will be at your twelve o'clock. They're on the west side of a small finger running to the south from this large east-west ridge line I'm over now. Copy?" This Covey FAC is a seasoned pilot with CCN Laotian missions.

"Roger Two-Two. Whiskey up on Fox Mike?" Jimbo asks as he rolls into a wide northwest turn headed for the valley.

"Sneaky, lay back until we expend," says Nix as I look around for Killer's aircraft.

"Whiskey Romeo Papa, Night Hawk Lead, what's your situation?"

A faint panting sound whispers through my headset, as if someone had just finished running ten miles.

"Night Hawk, we're approximately forty mikes from the ridge top. We're in the base of a small clump of trees. Got movement to our Sierra and Whisky, over."

"Roger Papa, hang in there. We'll be there in a minute," Jimbo promises.

"Hawk Lead, we've been given clearance for a Prairie Fire, initials Delta Lima Delta. Copy?" Convey relays to us.

"Roger, Delta Lima Delta," Nix answers.

Flying around in Laos at tree top level must do wonders for his bladder and bowel control. I'll make a point to rib Jimbo about it tonight.

"Put those initials on the window and pay attention!" I yell to the owner of the quickly responding gloved hand, writing hurriedly, but ever so neatly on the plexiglass. "Killer let's orbit clear of the valley while they expend," I order as I start a large, left-hand orbit.

"Rog," acknowledges Scoop, Killer's co-pilot.

Killer is letting Scoop do some radio work today. It's good training because he'll soon be up for Aircraft Commander. He doesn't look like a take charge type and his voice breaks into a high pitch whenever he gets excited, but he'll make a good AC. He just made Chief Warrant Officer 2 and always has his nose stuck in a book. That's how he got the name "Scoop". When we catch him reading we ask him, "What's the scoop?" He's smooth on the controls and a very good instrument pilot. He pays attention to mission details. In Laos, this can mean life or death.

Instruments are my weakness, which is why I learned the valleys so well. I'd rather fly at treetops than on instruments. I'm good at following rivers, roads or railroads to get where I need to, especially during monsoons. Problem is, the only railroad runs north-south next to QL-1 and we don't get any missions in that secured area. I know the valleys and how to get from one location to another by crossing from valley to valley, even during bad weather. But, all this doesn't help when it's dark.

"Hawk Lead, I'll roll in from the north and put a Willie Pete at the western edge of Papa's location. You ready?" the Air Force FAC asks.

Jimbo on UHF, "We gotcha Two-Two." Then switching to VHF, "Doc keep a sharp eye on where it hits, we may not get another fix."

From our location, we can watch the O-2 start its downward plunge toward the bright green finger.

"Night Hawk Lead, Hillsborough over," a crystal clear voice from the high altitude overall Air Mission Controller for Laos booms on UHF. "Will you need fast movers?"

The C-130, flying at forty thousand feet, is equipped with rows of radio booths with controllers to direct air traffic.

"Hillsborough, Night Hawk Gulf. Lead is engaging a target at this time. He'll be with you in a minute," I radio using my official call sign.

Hillsborough would never figure out who Sneaky is. I'm not listed in the SOI as Sneaky White. It would take them forever to figure out we were using unauthorized call signs.

Griffins have a joke where we meet over a imaginary spot and call, "We're at Rastus at 45 angles," mimicking jet pilots talking though masks sucking oxygen. Once a senior, very senior, controller heard us, and for a half hour tied up air traffic trying to figure out where "Rastus" was. Then Jimbo called in at position "Ruby Begonia." The laughter on the air broke the mission's cloud of seriousness.

"Doc, I'll lay a pair just below the Willie Pete. Listen for corrections." Going from VHF to FM, "Papa, Hawk Lead in hot."

"Hawk Lead fire two-five mikes to the two-seven-zero of the Willie Pete," a whispered voice directs.

"Roger, inbound. Keep your heads low," is answered by a squelch break from the ground.

"Breaking right," Nix calls on VHF.

On FM, "Whiskey how was that?"

"Great! Just great! Hawk Lead. . . can you put some three-zero mikes to the one-eight-zero of the last pair," an excited and much louder voice advises.

"Copy and we're inbound," Doc, already in position calls.

"We're hit! We're hit! Taking fire! Eight o'clock!"

The high pitched scream raises the short hairs on my neck.

"Got it spotted! Get the hell out of there!" Covey yells.

"Ah. . . We're hit.. . . ah. . . Lead. . . I'm. . . ah. . . headed east," Doc responds in his normal laid back form, not in the high pitched screams of his co-pilot.

"Sneaky, I'm joining up on Doc. Come over and do your runs from south to north. If you break east it should keep you away from the fifty-one." Jimbo advises.

"Hawk, you took a lot of small arms fire from the top of the ridge as you flew over. Are you hit?" Whiskey asks, unable to hear VHF communications.

"Taking fire! Taking fire! Ridge line to the northeast of Whiskey. Breaking south. Uh. . . We've got. . . ah. . . problems here," Doc radios as calm as ever, though he's just been shot at for the second time in less than thirty seconds.

"I'm closing in at your four. Keep altitude Doc." Jimbo's worry is now evident. There's no place to sit down out here that the NVA haven't already claimed, and we have no Hueys to help with a quick rescue.

On UHF, "Two-Two, this is Sneaky," while still monitoring Doc's condition on VHF, "I'm inbound from the south. We'll make a south to north run with an east break. Copy?"

"Be advised Sneaky, the east-west ridge north of Whiskey has fifty-ones. I'd like to run in some hard tack first."

"Two-Two, Let me first put some nails down and give 'em some breathing room." Without waiting for a reply I switch to FM, "Whiskey, Gulf's inbound with nails. This will be a south to north run with an east break over you."

At the same time, Jimbo's telling Doc, "I'll check you out. Any noticeable control problems?"

"Negative, but we took hits. Gauges went to hell but I think it's only electrical."

"Wow! Got a big hole in the ammo bay door," Nix excitedly points out.

Bet Jimbo loves that. I wonder if Nix has peed on himself by now. "I Peed on Myself While Flying in Laos" would be the title of his autobiography.

"Sneaky, we're RTB. Stay as long as possible. I'll contact base and have them launch another flight. Be careful." Jimbo is escorting his shot-up wingman back to Camp Evans.

The FM comes alive, "Gulf, we have movement to our one-eight-zero. We'll pop smoke for you."

"Negative! Negative! Negative!" interjects Covey, before I can. "Sneaky, I've got you. Follow me in. Whiskey, do not, I say again, do not pop smoke. I'll direct Hawk Gulf."

The O-2 is flying toward us now. He starts his roll-over, turning back toward the north.

"Killer, I'm in with nails. Watch where I take fire, then go after him. I'll break right."

After a single rocket is launched from the small fixed-wing, he breaks into a hard left vertical climb to get out of the way.

Upon impact, I've already lined up my gunsight's glowing red pipper on the growing column of white smoke. With thirty pounds of torque and the aircraft in trim, I massage my thumb across the upper right red button on the cyclic, launching a pair of rockets. I push the button again and lauch another pair. Finally, a third pair is launched on target. Pulling the cyclic back and right quickly as I lift the collective, we sharply break to the east in a steep but slow climb, hopefully far enough from imminent danger.

I announce, "Breaking right."

"Great shot! Great shot! Keep 'em coming," One-Zero's whispered voice cheers us on.

Flying over the team, I see a small, orange panel opening and closing skyward identifying their position.

"Mark! Mark! They're under me."

At this attitude I'm able to look down on them, clustered in a tight circle all facing outward.

"Inbound. Keep your heads down Whiskey."

Killer's now rolling over toward the green finger protruding from the ridge.

"Sneaky, we'll stay up this push. Nine-Three Charlie is launching a flight and will pickup the package," Jimbo advises me. "We're RTB Evans. Doc thinks he can make it. Stay away from the large ridge, the eastern fifty-one is accurate as hell."

"Have Sweet Griffin carry plenty of nails," I reply, hoping that Doc will have a safe flight back, all the while completing a tight one-eighty to prepare to roll in again.

My friend and the best pilot in the unit, First Lieutenant Rick "Sweet Griffin" Frier, is not your normal newly-made real-live officer. He joined the Army after a couple years of college, then went into the Warrant Officer flight program and was class honor graduate. Having a commercial FAA license with instrument and multi-engine ratings prior to entering the Army helped. As honor graduate, he was given a choice of additional schools and he jumped at Cobra transition, doing so well that he became a Cobra Standardization Instructor Pilot. He arrived in Vietnam, via Ft Campbell, and brought the Griffins into SE Asia from Kentucky. After his first year of flying combat and into his second Vietnam extension, the Army felt he would make a good commissioned officer. Personally a lot of us felt he should have stayed a Chief Warrant Officer 2. But Infantry, Artillery, Air Defense Artillery and Armor were all asking him to take a direct commission into their branches. So he became a real-live officer because he felt that it was in his best career interest. Without a college degree, and a major RIF looming in the future, most of the warrants believe he made a bad choice.

If there's a dean of Cobra pilots, especially those flying ARA missions, then it's Rick. If there's a dean of Special Operations helicopter pilots, then Rick is it. His call-sign, lovingly given by us, is "Sweet Griffin." He's a very pragmatic, straight forward, no nonsense young man. For those on the ground, his name means Griffins will arrive no matter what the weather, anti-aircraft fire, or time of day. It means that once on station he will take charge of the mission, though he's sometimes very junior to the stuffed shirts who are flying and think they know what they're doing just because of their rank. He'll direct the mission in the highest standards one could ask for. We love him, maybe not for his personality but surely for the fact he has never lost a Griffin pilot due to enemy fire. Sweet Griffin's bravery is beyond reproach. In the Griffins, where bravery among warrants is nothing but extraordinary, Rick is an example of the pinnacle of courage that we all strive for. His several Silver Stars and numerous Distinguished Flying Crosses attest to this.

As an Instructor Pilot, he's tough and unwilling to accept anything but the best. If you're having trouble with a maneuver, or procedure, he'll take time to repeatedly go over it until it's corrected or learned. These aren't to Army standards, but to his much higher standards. He's not intimidated by rank. In several cases I've known him to refuse to grant the Aircraft Commander or Section Leader status to Captains because they weren't qualified. True, they'd get it via the Operations Officer's say so, but everyone knows without Rick's approval you really didn't make the grade and are suspect until proven otherwise.

Not married, he's a great guy to party with. Doesn't get much mail except from a distant relative. I'm sure he will stay in Nam as long as I do, he's that committed to his job. But after Nam he'll go where the Air Defense Artillery branch sends him, and it may not be a flying billet.

"Long Bow Two-Two, this is Hillsborough. Over." The voice is much too loud.

"Go Hillsborough," while he's doing a tight orbit over the location of the fifty-ones that got Doc. This Covey's got balls.

"Breaking right. Got a positive on Papa." Scoop calls, still doing the radio work for Killer.

"Inbound Whiskey," I advise them.

Killer is breaking southeast and starting his climb back up for another run.

"Taking Fire! Taking Fire! Taking Fire!" Scoop cries in his excited, high pitch squeal.

I kick at the right pedal. The sight's pipper jumps right to the fifty-one's location. It's spewing out rounds that go from white, fade into yellow, and end in a bright green color. A deadly stream arcs towards Killer. Most see the colors blended together producing a greenish glow. For some of us, the three colors appear in almost slow motion. It's eerie. Moments like this warn us that the merchant of death is serving notice.

"Got him!" Lovingly I caress the cyclic's red button like a small supple nipple. The first pair streak toward the gun pit now located in the center of my pipper. If I can just direct the FFARs into the gun pit.

"Too low!" screams the Kid on intercom.

He's too late. I've already made corrections by pulling more collective. Still caressing the button, we watch another pair plunge for the target. "There you go," I talk this pair toward the pit, which is still belching out death. I punch another pair off. And another. And another.

"Breaking," yanking hard on the cyclic and pulling collective. Now it's a race to try and out climb the half-inch diameter fire balls racing toward us.

"Inbound," Killer says.

On FM, Scoop tells the team to lay low 'til we can knock out this fifty-one.

Climbing, we watch as Killer's rockets leave his pods headed for the pit that's still dealing out death and destruction. Each time he fires, a rocket exits from each side of his aircraft, slowly at first then quickly accelerating toward its intended rendezvous with the enemy.

Papa asks Covey how long before the Prairie Fire. He doesn't know it'll be at least thirty-five minutes before the slicks can get on station.

"Breaking," Killer says.

I look down and see he's very low before starting his pull out. Just then, a secondary explosion gushes from the pit and we all know this weapon will no longer be a problem.

"Good," I know he flew the last pair right into the heart of the pit.

"Taking small arms from west of the pit."

"Ah. . . Roger."

My pipper rests on the grayish-white smoke spiraling up. I mash harder on the left pedal as I fire off a pair. Slender bolts shoot out of outer pods, then, as if radar controlled, curve and descend to the area left of the pit.

"How did you do that?" questions the Kid.

He definitely wasn't taught this trick in Cobra transition. It's an old Griffin trick. Use pedals to curve the flight of the rockets. Or pull in more than thirty pounds torque and they'll rise. Drop collective if your first pair is high and the next pair will drop off quickly. After firing as many rockets as we have, you learn how much to use to get the desired results. We are formally taught to fire in trim and with thirty pounds of torque. In the Griffins, we've been schooled on how to bend the rules and the flight paths of our rockets.

A puff of red smoke from the flechettes as they leave the rocket head appears in the air. We all know anyone in the way of these thousands of darts is on borrowed time. With more left pedal, I launch four more pairs from my outside pods.

"Breaking right," as I start the climb out. With added bravado, "Think we got these guys attention?"

Squelch breaks are Killer's answer.

"Covey. Hillsborough with a flight of Spads on station. They're up on your frequency at this time. Call signs, Spad Three-Eight and Three-Eight Alpha."

"Roger, call signs Spad Three-Eight and Three-Eight Alpha."

On FM, Covey tells Whiskey the Spads are on the way. The One-Zero now knows he's got heavy American air power on the way to help with his team's extraction.

"No hits here Killer. How 'bout you?"

"Nah, but real close. If I hadn't broken when I did he'd have chewed my ass."

His calm voice down plays the near deadly misses. Killer's

voice is one of the steadiest in the unit. No matter how hot and heavy the anti-aircraft fire gets, he just talks in the same monotone with an Irish brogue. I surely can't do it.

On FM, "Whiskey, this is Gulf. We're headed back to your side of the ridge."

"Roger Gulf. Got movement to the one-eight-zero," he replies apprehensively.

"Roger Whiskey." Then on VHF, "Killer, think we can run west to east without getting hosed from the other fifty-one or do we take him out first?"

Without hesitation, "Let's get the fucker, then Sweet Griffin can worry about just the extraction."

I can envision the big redhead with a tight-lipped smile thinking of the chance to get another fifty-one this morning. What a great day for the Griffins!

I break squelch twice before going to UHF, "Two-Two we're going to run west to east again," while extending my roll out to the southwest, "then break back for a northerly run once the fucker opens."

"If you wait Sneaky, I've got Spads on the way."

"Negative. Think we can sucker 'em into shooting? If he does, he's a goner."   I start a one hundred and eighty degree turn toward the team and call on VHF, "Lag back on my five. When he opens up, cut in behind me and blast him. I'll break hard to the south and come around behind you. We'll set up a right-hand pattern. Do not . . . do not overfly the big ridge. Break over Papa's location."

"Got it," he's happy, a one-on-one with an NVA fifty-one. Most Griffin AC's like to go one-on-one with a fifty-one.

Weakly, Jimbo's voice emerges through all the other chatter, "Trolling again, Sneaky?"

"You be knowing it!" Scoop quickly responds before I can say anything.

I start my roll out on a heading directly toward Whiskey. "Whiskey we're inbound. We're not firing. This is a dry run. A dry run, understand? Over."

"Roger Hawk Gulf," the One-Zero whispers. His disappointment is evident.

I roll the nose over and the airspeed quickly passes through seventy knots. Abruptly from our left, a bright stream of tracers shoots up toward us, falling off at the final instant.

"Got'em! Break right. I'm inbound. Got the bastard now."

The poor NVA gunner has no idea what he's done to his future, his very short future.

Breaking right, I start my climb knowing Killer's without cover. Adrenalin is pumping in my veins and taking control. The G's become noticeable.

Excitedly, the Kid remarks, "Wow!"

Killer, over my right shoulder, is firing pair after pair toward the fifty. It's a welcome sight to us and one of terror for the NVA. The fifty-one is spewing it's greenish line toward Killer. It's a duel of warriors firing for survival with the loser no doubt being killed. Young men in their finest hour with equally matched weapons now dependent on their own skill and cunning, and a little bit of luck.

"You're taking a lot of fire from the valley floor," Whiskey observes. He's got the best seat in town, watching adversaries, each trying to end the other's life with a well-placed knockout punch.

I hear, "Breaking right."

I'm not completely in position to roll in and provide cover. Starting our roll to cover Killer, I jerk the cyclic back and right throwing the aircraft out of trim.

"Inbound."

I smash the right pedal trying to force the pipper onto the target. The fifty-one is still tracking Killer's climb. Quickly, I fire a pair to get the NVA's heads down or, at least, divert their attention. Trying to adjust, though still off target, I keep pushing the pedal — steering the nose of the aircraft and the red glow of the pipper to the target.

On intercom, the Kid cries out, "Holy Shit!" as greenish

balls now move toward us. The NVA gunners have found a new target — us. They're rounds are headed directly at us. Moments like this seem to take forever, you can't know if it's your last flight or just another war story in the making. As the greenish track moves, the stream looks like young boys having a pissing contest. It looks harmless, but it's deadly.

I continue, now punching the button. I'm no longer massaging it, but being rough as the heat of battle overtakes my emotions. The rockets streak from the inside pods.

"Pull out! Puullll Ooouuut! We're gonna crash!" The Kid screams across the intercom, "We're going to die!"

The Kid has figured it out. We're in big shit.

Killer calmly states, "Inbound."

I haven't called my break but it's obvious I'm ready to. Killer's in position.

All the time I'm watching these big, now bigger — much bigger — fireballs ascending from the ridge, inching closer and closer.

"Shit this slope's good!"

Pulling back on the controls, I hurriedly climb out of harm's way. We can see Killer diving.

"You. . . you got a direct hit, Hawk."

We're still not able to see the target, but we witness Killer send pair after pair.

"Ah. . . We're getting secondaries. I'm breaking off and joining you Sneaky," Killer radios, relaxed as if he just finished a quickie with the hootch maid and had a lazy smoke. Killer is in his environment.

"Good shooting Alpha. That'll keep them quiet for a while."

Covey's verbal recognition to Killer is heard by all.

Looking over my shoulder, I extend our climb. We see smoke engulfing the ridge and, more importantly, the absence of the death stream. "Extend southwest, then we'll turn back into Whiskey."

Squelch breaks.

The duel is terminated. NVA have surely died. More soldiers' families will never know how gallantly they fought their last battle. No parade with medals and honors for these men. Today, Griffins are the victors. What will tomorrow bring, well that is a story that will play out with another set of foes.

"Whiskey, Gulf. We're going to give you a couple of passes then hold back until the package comes. Copy?" We've settled back to the business at hand.

"Roger Gulf. We still have movement at our two-seven-zero and two-four-zero. If you can put a few pairs in there, it will hold us for a while."

Whiskey Papa is calmer now, knowing that the fifties are destroyed and our Hueys are on the way. I bet he can taste the cold beer that will be crossing his lips in an hour or so.

"Roger. We'll be inbound in a minute."

I slow down by pulling the nose higher and higher, a quick way to bleed off airspeed. Doing a tight turn to the east, I roll in on a rocket pass.

"I'll only fire a pair."

We have to conserve on rockets until we either run low on fuel or Sweet Griffin arrives with the package.

"Inbound Whiskey. Heads down!" I call, while lowering the collective 'til thirty pounds reads on the bouncing transmission torque gauge.

The pipper glides to the target area Papa has requested. We plunge toward the target. Ground is rushing up at us, quicker and quicker. Holding back, I fire at the last possible, the most accurate, moment. It also keeps the oppositions' heads down, because the NVA doesn't know your target. There's no proof to back this up. Just a gut feeling that gives me and, I'm sure, others courage to fly in closer.

On FM, "You're taking fire!"

It's too late. Crackling sounds have entered my helmet as dull thuds. I concentrate on the ground rushing toward us. Glimpsing down to the airspeed indicator, it's accelerating through one hundred and seventy knots. I pushing my button. There's no response. Quickly switching to the inside rocket pods, I know we've half expended. Out of flechettes, only HE rockets left and Sweet Griffin's not here yet.

"Breaking right."

With G Forces tugging on us, I pull in more and more pitch. Two wide rotor blades are flexing to their maximum, fighting for clear, undisturbed air. Gladly, I'd trade airspeed for altitude right now.

"Inbound." Killer's rolling in.

Weakly on UHF, there's good news, "Oscar Kilo, this is Sweet Griffin, west of the Rockpile. What's your location?"

Rick's on the way!

"Griffin, Kilo Lead, we're at Khe Sanh, orbiting at three thousand."

I start my roll over.

"Breaking right," I say while pulling out.

We've entered a lazy pattern of rolling in and climbing out of rocket runs, each protecting the other's climb out. Firing a pair or two on each pass, but with a dozen or so left, we may not have that many passes left. Griffins have been known to stay on station, without rockets, and roll in firing nothing. Try to keep the NVA heads down, until relief can make it out. If Rick doesn't get here soon, it'll be one of those missions for us. Bluff the bastards into thinking we're loaded.

"Sweet Griffin, Long Bow Two-Two. Copy your location. We'll get the team ready." Then, "Gulf, I'd like to run in Spads for a few passes before the package gets on station."

"Breaking right Killer stay high and let Covey work the Spads."

I'm halfway through a run and abort, then start a steep climb.

"Sweet Griffin, how long before you can have the package here?" I ask.

"We'll join in ten. Maybe twenty all together. What's the

sit-rep?"

"Waiting for Spads to do their thing. Then, we'll expend and turn it over to you. Hold the package over QL-9 'til I call you. It's crowded over here and there are fifty-ones. Killer's got two and some secondaries. I think they're just waiting for the package."

"Shit Hot! Killer got a couple." Gun pilots get excited knowing there's a chance for a one-on-one with a fifty-one. "Call you at QL-9."

"Spad Three-Eight. Long Bow Two-Two, come up TAC Two."

"Roger Two-Two, going TAC Two," replies the A1-E pilot.

I'd like to monitor the TAC frequency, but another radio would make this cockpit a total goat fuck. It's already too stuffy in here without an air-conditioner. I'm noticing it more and more.

"Hawk Gulf, I'm going to run the Spads. Could you move your orbit south?" Covey asks. Too many aircraft in a small area only increases the chances of a midair. In tight spaces, too much time is spent looking for other aircraft. Any time we're not concentrating on the target isn't good for the ground troops.

"Roger. We'll be over QL-9," I call, turning south.

"Tally Ho. Got 'em in sight," an unfamiliar voice says.

"Sweet Griffin, we have you in sight. We're heading out."

"Roger, Oscar Kilo. You set up for strings?" asks Rick, one of the small group of believers who follow the principle that you should be prepared for anything, at any time, especially on CCN missions.

"Whiskey, I'm going to bring in the Spads on a heading of one-eight-zero. Keep your heads down. We'll be laying napalm to your west. Over."

"Roger Two-Two, we're ready," the One-Zero answers.

Extending our orbit, we try to get a glimpse of the show the Spads are putting on. Air Force A-1E's are our favorite form of close air support. Long endurance time and the ability to fly slow enough to place payloads as close as they can makes them an impressive weapon. Occasionally, after a good mission, they'll join up with us and fly a combined formation. We then expend all our film taking pictures of a combined forces flight.

The Spads carry a wide range of external weapons. The Mark 81 bombs are 250 pounders. The Mark 82's, 500 pounders, are my favorites. They came in two styles, one called Snake-eye, which is what CCN teams request the most. The difference between the two Mark 82's is the amount of drag the bomb has. The Snake-eye is a high drag bomb because of a folding metal slotted umbrella that extends to its rear after the bomb is dropped. The other model is a low drag bomb. Though we don't see them often, except on F4's or A6's, there are also the Mark 83's and 84's, which are 1,000 and 2,000 pound bombs.

The bomb fuse, called a Mark 904, can be preset to go off on contact or with up to a one second delay allowing the bomb to penetrate the triple canopy or, in the case of the larger bombs, to bury themselves deep in the ground or structure before exploding.

The added feature of the Mark series of bombs is the possible addition of a two foot fuse extension to the bomb's nose. This allows the bomb to detonate two feet above the ground. They are called Daisy Cutters because they mow down everything above the level of the daisy growing as ground cover. It's an excellent weapon when the enemy is in the open. The last types of bombs are CBU's, Mark 94's, and napalm bombs. The CBU's disperse two hundred or so small softball-size bomblets from the back of its canister. These come in two types, one being the Type 1 whose two hundred or so bomblets are filled with ball bearing-sized pellets which cover a thirty-eight foot killing radius. The Type 2 goes off with a shower of white phosphorus in a thirty foot or so area, which from the air is a beautiful sight.

The napalm bomb I've seen used the most is a 'Blue 27' or, officially, BLU-27. It's a 750-pound bomb that spews it's deadly jell burning at over 2,000 degrees. Bodies that have been in a napalm attack remind one of the city of Pompeii and it's still frozen forms that were once human beings.

The Mark 94 is used by the Air Force SOS Squadrons when

trying to work a rescue of downed air crew members. There are stories of it being used in some other areas when the enemy is in the open. The 94 is a 500-pound bomb with a gas inside. This form of tear gas causes havoc on the battleground and allows the aircraft to follow up with 'Snake and Nape' or, in the case of a rescue, allows time for the helicopter to get in and out with the downed crew member.

The 20 millimeter cannons on the Spads are different from the ones some of the new Cobras flying for the Cav use. The Air Force's 20mm is an M-39 model firing two types of rounds, sparkles and balls. The balls, as they are called, are the basic ball ammo. The sparkles are HEI's, which produce bright flashes as they hit the target. Some A1-E's are loaded with a sparkle every fifth round to help in locating the impact area. The high explosive incendiary round is really eye catching when fired at dusk or in the dark.

"Sneaky, Griffin Nine-Three Charlie on Victor." Sweet Griffen has called.

"Go Sweet Griffin."

"Sneaky we're at A Loui. What's the situation?"

"Right now the Spads are working. . . just beautiful. Fucking beautiful. Dropping nape. Once they expend, we'll go back in and expend, then mark for you. Be advised they have three WIAs so have the *bac si* on the first slick."

"Sneaky, this is Two-Two, over."

"Go."

"Time to get Papa out of there. You have an ETA on the package?"

"Two-Two, I expect we'll be ready in one-zero. I'm coming over to Papa's location. I'll make a few passes to get any leftovers, then mark Papa for the package. Over."

"Roger Sneaky. You have control of the package at this time." Covey has turned control of the extraction to us.

"Whisky Romeo Papa, this is Night Hawk Gulf." I say while

flying over the southern end of the valley, headed directly for the green finger holding our team.

Barely audible, "Gulf, Papa here. Got movement to our one-eight-zero. Over."

"Roger Papa. We'll be making passes from the west and try to finish up the bad guys. The package should be here in one-zero. We'll bring the package in over the burned out area." There is now a large burned out area from the recently dropped napalm bombs.

"Roger Gulf."

"Sneaky, we monitored that. We've got two slicks and will leave two to the south," Sweet Griffin advises.

"Let's do it Killer! Keep a couple for the trip home. Lay out as many to the south as you can. Try to keep it in a large pattern all the way to tree line."

Double squelch breaks.

"Want me to shoot?" asks the Kid, wanting to fire the turret.

"Negative! Don't fire unless you have a target you know is an NVA. Understand?" All we need now is for an overexcited co-pilot shooting one of ours.

"Yes sir," forgetting my name.

"Papa. You still at the same location?" I ask while trading airspeed for altitude before lining up on the target area.

"Roger Gulf. Victor Charlie are five-zero meters south on a line sweeping the area. They should have crossed the high-speed trail by now. We can hear them. Plenty of AK fire," he replies in a more confident tone knowing the end is near for this mission.

"Heads down Papa."

My airspeed has now bled off so the indicator is bouncing between zero and twenty knots.

"Inbound."

Pushing pedal, I try swinging us around to allow our roll out to stop just to the south of Papa's location. With the pipper on the north side of the high-speed trail, I lower collective. We start a downward plunge toward an enemy that knows we're coming. One pair off! Another pair! Another! We continue to attack the light green ridge. All the time pushing in more and more pedal, allowing each new set of rockets to go further south than the last. Each inches closer and closer to the long tree line and the area from which the Hueys will probably get the most ground fire during the extraction. As I pull in collective and pull back on the cyclic, the ground fire directed at us becomes louder and louder. Before calling my break, rounds hit us.

With a deafening bang, my right leg is violently slammed off the pedal and driven up into the console bottom jamming my knee into the console. Hot searing pain shoots into my right foot and up my leg. Momentarily, I see stars, then adrenalin takes over. I yank both the cyclic and collective. It's survival. With this airspeed, I don't need to worry about loss of rudder control.

"Taking Fire! Taking Fire!"

I'm not sure who's saying it or even if it's on a radio.

"Been hit," I say to no one. During our steep climbing bank I look out and see tan uniformed NVA standing at the edge of the tree line. Hell, they're firing at us!

"Your taking all kinds of small arms from the south, Gulf," the excited One-Zero advises a bit late.

"Get out of there! Sneaky, get out of there!" Killer's calling, "Get altitude and head south."

"We're hit. Ah. . . I'm not sure how bad, but. . . how are you Kid?" The intercom is dead — we've lost radios.

"Kid! How are you?" Still no answer. Looking into the mirror, I see he's moving. He's alive.

"Killer, got hits in the cockpit I might be hit in the leg."

The dead sound continues. I've lost radios. . . no, I haven't. I can hear everyone else. I switch the radio transmitter selector, trying all three. This is scary. I'm not able to talk, just listen.

I check my instruments. I don't need an engine failure or hydraulics problem now. I see everything's green. Surprisingly, the Master Caution Panel is not lit up. Maybe it's not that bad. Taking a rubber tourniquet from my survival vest, I wrap it tightly around my right thigh. Hell, just what I need, to bleed to death before I can get back to the base. My leg's getting numb but we're still flying. I can't feel my right foot, hopefully it's still connected.

"Killer break high. Be careful of the tree line. I saw them standing there shooting at us," I'm still talking into a dead radio.

"I've nailed the whole goddamn hill to the south of the trail. We haven't taken any fire," the ever calm voice says. "How are you Sneaky?"

Hell, I can hear them but they can't hear me.

"Gulf, Nine-Two, how are you?"

"Ah. . . Not sure. Took hits in the cockpit. I'm hit, don't know about my front seater, I can't talk to him," still to a dead radio.

"Sneaky, you okay? I'm fine, but I've got no intercom," the Kid says surprisingly.

Looking up into the mirror, I see him holding up his survival radio. Great thinking, using the outside radio to talk to me.

Tearing my radio out of its pouch, I pull up the antenna to activate it. It's operational.

We're broadcasting on emergency frequency, two-hundred forty-three and double-zero UHF, which means whatever is said the whole world hears.

"We're hit. I can monitor transmissions, I just can't broadcast. I'm hit in the leg. I've tied it off to stop the bleeding, but I've got to get to 18th Surg. Don't know about my co-pilot."

"I'm okay," he says waving his hand.

"Gauges are all green. We need to have someone look us over, especially fuel cells and tail rotor." Then as an afterthought, "Kid, stay off the air. Relax, we'll make it back, no problem."

"Sneaky we'll be on you in a sec," says Rick on FM. "Whiskey Papa, Night Hawk Charlie, get ready for pickup."

"Roger, Hawk Charlie."

"What's the best way in and out, Killer?" Rick says on VHF.

"Need to come in from the southwest and have the slicks start their flare over the burned out area. Papa's at the base of the small clump of trees half way up the ridge. Exit the same way you have'em come in. There's fifty-ones north on both sides of the finger." He adds, "*Beau coup* bad guys south of Papa along the high-speed trail, all the way to the base of the tree line. They got Sneaky. Copy?"

"Roger. If you'll give me a location mark, I'll bring in the package."

"Come on over and bring the *bac si* in the lead slick."

"Roger, Killer. Do you copy that Oscar Kilo Lead?"

"Sweet Griffin, we're behind you. We have *bac si* on board. Kilo Two follow me. Will we need strings?"

"Negative Sweet Griffin, it's a grassy slope. Make sure the *bac si* is in the first aircraft. They have three WIAs," advises Killer, then continues with, "Whiskey, Night Hawk Alpha."

"Go Alpha."

"Whiskey, we have the package. They'll be inbound from two-two-zero. We'll use two ships, call-sign Kilo Lead and Kilo Two. *Bac si's* in lead. They're up this push. Copy?"

The One-Zero now is excited and his voice is louder with new found firmness. The anticipation of getting the hell out of a bad situation is gaining on him. "Roger Alpha, we're ready. You want smoke?"

"Whiskey Papa, Kilo Lead, we'll be picking you up. Negative on smoke. Use your panel." The Phoenix AC must be an oldtimer because he seems to know that smoke only tells the enemy where your team is and where the helicopter is going.

"Sneaky, how's the aircraft?" Rick asks me.

"Okay," I respond, struggling to talk on the survival radio while trying to fly. "Took a hit through the floor. I've been hit in the lower leg and foot. Got it tied off. As soon as you get over here, Killer will mark the RT, then we're headed to 18th Surg. Leg's numb, so I've got a problem."

"Roger. Break off and head back. Spider, escort Sneaky back." Then Sweet Griffin adds, "I'll hook up with Killer and he can mark for us."

"Dancer bring the package in. I'll meet you over the Lima

Zulu." Passing Rick's aircraft over the low rolling hills, I'm headed south to join up with Spider for the long trip back. Sweet Griffin has taken over the mission. Killer's in good hands with Rick.

"Let's do it Killer."

Killer breaks off from my side to lead them to the team.

"Sneaky, keep up this push 'til you get to Quang Tri."

Breaking squelch, I remember I've got to use the survival radio. I repeat it on the small hand held radio.

Killer's now leading the package to the extraction point.

"I'll roll in on the team and give you a mark."

Joining up with Spider, I listen as Phoenix Lead goes in. The few minutes of anticipation is nerve racking. This extraction should have been under my direction, but the hits we took and the unknown condition of my leg has put all that to the side for now. The priority now is Viper and their safe recovery.

"Kilo Two proceed in at this time, the Lima Zulu is cold. Repeat cold." Sweet Griffin's voice allows me to let out a big sigh of relief. A few minutes more and the package will be headed safely home.

"Sweet Griffin. Dancer's at A Loui."

We soon pass over the spot where QL-9 crosses the South Vietnam/Laos boarder. A border with no formal boundaries except those drawn on a map by some cigar smoking men in far off offices. Air-conditioned offices I'm sure. I guess while fixing this battle damage, Sherrily can get the air-conditioner fixed, not a bad deal after all if my leg isn't too bad. Damn, I can't feel it.

"Taking Fire! Taking Fire!" screams a Phoenix. "Got the package on board and we're outbound. Taking fire, three o'clock," says the pilot. Over the background can be heard the sound of his rotor blades popping and the door gunner's machine guns blazing away. "Lead, we have four on board."

"Roger Kilo Two, four on board. How many on Kilo Lead?" asks Covey.

"Got five and are headed direct to the Surg."

"Roger. Extraction complete, you're cleared to return with

the package Sweet Griffin. I'll notify control. You guys did a great job." Now Covey must check on other CCN teams roving in Laos on their appointed missions. Hopefully none are in a comprised position. We need to rearm and refuel. "We're clear of the area. Spad Three-Eight you may go in and expend."

The Spad aircraft will expend their ordnance on the now enemy-infested hill. The Spad pilots can drop their ordnance without a clearance for each pass.

"Moon Glow, Sweet Griffin."

After a moment we hear, "Go Griffin." The voice is Billy's.

"We're homeward bound with the package. We have three going to 18th Surg. Sneaky and his co-pilot will be ahead of us. Please advise Surg, we're inbound and we'll need a security team present."

Rick knows that Sgt. Major Washburn surely has these wheels already in motion. You can bet he'll be at 18th Surg pad waiting for the aircraft to land. We're his men, his teams, and, in a strange way, we're his children, so we'll get the finest care available. Otherwise, some foolish REMF will have to deal with a raging bull with no neck.

Chapter 7

"How you doing, Sneaky?" asks Spider in his deep southern accent. He can lull you to sleep asking for take-off clearance, and if you get him to tell you a story be prepared for a long drawn out one. Spider does nothing quickly in his southern laid-back method.

"Fine. My leg's numb that's all. I... I think it's bad. Hey aren't you too short to be out in Indian country?" I ask the pilot whose days left in country have now melted into hours.

"Nah, Sweet Griffin promised me I'll make it home and get my discharge without any problems."

CWO-2 Warren "Spider" Weaver is a hell of a pilot. When things are tight, you can bet he'll do more than what's required. Besides the normal array of medals they awarded us, he's got several DFCs and a Silver Star.

Spider went on his last thirty-day leave late during his extension, thereby allowing him and me to travel back to the States together. He timed his leave so that he could enroll at the University of Alabama for the next semester. We flew on the same Pan Am flight from Da Nang to the States, landing at McCord Air Force Base in Washington state. From there we, well on our way to being drunk, caught a cab to Seattle-Tacoma International Airport. After buying tickets to Atlanta, Georgia, we entered the first lounge we could find.

We slid up to the bar and prepared to add to our alcoholic content. Military regulations say that while traveling we must be in full Class A uniform, so we were both sitting there decked out in all our ribbons, badges, patches, and doodads. I ordered for both of us and the bartender, an old, heavy-set man with a thick German accent, asked to see Spider's ID card. I asked why. Ignoring me, the thin-haired heavy jowled man, seeing Spider was not quite twenty-one years old, refused to serve him. Now here's a man, Spider, with four rows of ribbons. The top holding the Silver Star and the Distinguished Flying Cross with three Oak Leaf Clusters. It was all I could muster to not punch the bartender in his fat sagging face. A few moments later, the Airport Police arrived to see what was going on, after a bar employee had called for help.

In the yelling match that ensued, I explained that, "... If this fucking country felt that Spider was old enough to go fight a war, fly a fucking helicopter, and lead a flight of warriors into the mouth of the cat, then repeatedly decorate him for his actions above and beyond, then who the fuck was going to tell him, or me, we couldn't drink?"

The Airport Police were understanding and polite. After escorting us to a small hole of an office, they explained that, legally, the guy was doing his job. There had been several bad incidents here of drunken returning Vietnam veterans, and we shouldn't take it personally. A cop then suggested that we grab a cab, go to the nearest liquor store, buy a bottle, and come back here and drink it. He also mentioned that we'd be more than welcome to sit in the four by six foot holding tank and drink until our flight was ready. With that I hailed a cab and after a mad drive to the nearest store, rushed in for a couple of bottles of booze. Getting back in the waiting cab, I made sure the fare included a large tip. What the hell, it was only money and I wanted to get drunk.

Sitting in the holding tank, the cop was able to round up several glasses for us to drink from, though he apologized for not having ice. He was going to get some when we told him to sit down and not worry about it, after all, in Nam we never had any. He asked questions about where we were stationed, what we did, and how the war was really going, not what he read in the newspapers. Are we winning or not, was a question he asked several times. Then if we thought we would win the war. He told us how he "missed the war" because he was married, then had children and, of course, he was a law enforcement officer. In my years of going to and from Nam I'd never had a long talk with a non-veteran. It was a shame that I was too high to remember the rest of this talk. I'm sure it must have been interesting.

When the flight was ready, he escorted us to the gate and made sure we got on the plane for Atlanta. His last act was official and he took the near empty bottle of Scotch from me, citing some obscure FAA regulation.

While strapping in the 707s seat, Spider remarked that he was a nice guy but still took our bottle. I opened my briefcase, and showed him the second bottle that would provide us with a big hangover the next morning.

Spider extended for the "early out" immediately given upon his return to the States. It's the Army's way of keeping pilots in Nam, especially experienced warrants. Promise them an early discharge rather than a full four-year obligation if they spend at least six extra months in Nam. Spider's completing his second tour. Great deal for the Army, but I'm not sure about the warrants. With an average life expectancy of 170 days, who needs an extra 180 days added to your basic 365 before DEROS? We get killed quickly enough without extending the window of opportunity.

"Knock it off!"

I don't know the voice, but it's Captain Crane's style. He must be with Rick, and if so, I know Rick's not enjoying himself. Crane, by virtue of being the Third Platoon Leader, made himself an AC. Didn't hurt to have the gracious help of a fellow ass, Captain Rogers. He doesn't have 400 hours total time, including flight school.

With Sweet Griffin as senior pilot, at least the other guys in the flight will be safe from any dumb command decisions. I'm sure

Crane logs AC time while Rick logs IP, so they are both happy. The only real issue arises when this prima donna tries to make a decision. Then a lot of warrants get pissed. So far it hasn't happened in any life-threatening flight, but it's just a matter of time before it will. Then the warrants will rise up and express their concerns and fears.

The Kid writes on the window, "You okay? Can you land?"

I give him a thumbs up. He's got a story to write home to his mother about. Hell, he couldn't believe that I would let him land this wounded beast. Flying a Cobra from the front seat is awkward at best, but to land after being shot up would take a very good pilot. I wasn't shot in the fucking head, was I?

"Quang Tri Tower. Griffin Nine-Three X-Ray."

"Go Nine-Three X-Ray."

"X-Ray at The Rockpile inbound. We're declaring an emergency. Ah . . . my wingman has been shot up ah . . . we don't know the damage."

Damn! Spider has really blown this out of proportion. Hell, everyone will know that I've been hit.

"Roger Nine-Three X-Ray. What's your wingman's call-sign and the extent of damage? Ah . . . will you need fire trucks?"

Another controller breaks in. "Nine-Three X-Ray, be advised we've notified the Surg of your status."

"Quang Tri. Call-sign is Sneaky White. He's flying a Cobra and will make a running landing on the active. I think his weapon systems are cold, but I don't know for sure. He can monitor you but can't transmit."

This has gone too far. Grabbing the radio off of my lap I announce. "Quang Tri Tower, this is Sneaky White. I have the numbers and would like to try a running landing to runway three-two." The noise level from talking on the hand-held radio must make it difficult for the controllers to understand me.

"Roger Sneaky White. We have medical and fire on the way. You're cleared direct to two . . . barometer is two-niner niner-four. Winds are calm." Then as an advisory to all listening, "All aircraft in the vicinity of Quang Tri Field, be advised we have an emergency in progress. A Cobra from the west will be landing. The field is closed 'til further notice."

"Quang Tri, Sneaky White. I think my tail rotor is working. My engine instruments are in the green. This will be a precautionary landing. Weapons system is cold."

"Roger, weapons cold. Please state your location."

"Quang Tri, this is Nine-Three X-Ray. We're over Mai Loc, starting a very long extended downwind leg. Sneaky, I'll do the radios. You'll be busy."

He's perfectly correct, flying and talking on a hand held radio is awkward.

"Be advised, all aircraft in the Quang Tri field area, the airfield is closed at this time we have an emergency in progress." The controller will probably repeat this several times.

"Come on Sneaky. This is Seven-Zero-Seven. You can make it." The Dust Off crews must be monitoring from their radio room adjacent to 18th Surg pad.

"Keep your airspeed up until you're on the runway," reminds our unit IP, Sweet Griffin. He must be past the Khe Sanh Valley escorting the package back to CCN.

I test my right leg, it's totally numb. A bad sign. Using my left foot, I can feel the floor panel skin has been peeled back by the bullet, which now is lodged somewhere in my leg. The floor skin feels like a rose that has sprung to life, probably beautiful except for the problem of how it got this way. Shit, if it's in my leg, I'm in trouble.

Putting my right foot up on the pedal I try to see if I'm able to use it to counter my good leg. It works as I put pressure on the left pedal, the right moves back. Still no feeling. If I can only keep flying, and hopefully not lose my tail rotor on final, we'll make it. I start the gradual left-hand turn.

"Quang Tri, Nine-Three X-Ray we're turning a very wide base. We have the numbers." Then Spider reassures me with, "This will be a one-shot Sneaky. Get it down and then ride it out."

I want to respond, but I'm too busy checking everything for the last time. Spider's close up on my wing. I give him a thumbs up then get back to the task at hand, landing without rolling us into a ball. Shit, I hope this turns out okay. Starting the roll out, I line up on the runway's striped white line painted down the center of the sixty-foot wide PSP strip. Once this is accomplished, I let the nose come up slightly to bleed off airspeed.

"You're clear to land Sneaky White! Ah . . . Good luck." Reassurance from the tower, though at this point I don't think I could do a-go-around, at least mentally I couldn't handle it.

"Easy . . . Easy . . . does . . . it!"

The runway goes under us. To the left and right, helicopters are on the ground turned up with crews intently watching us. Hanger areas are lined with spectators. Guess they've made their bets and are now awaiting the outcome. Will he make it or not? They're here to see if I end up in a tight little ball, or just skid to an uneventful, safe stop. For some, it will be a payday. Others with cameras, it might be a picture to send home and tell about the dumb son-of-a-bitch who bought it, RIGHT BEFORE MY EYES! God, I hope it's a payday for the good guys.

Our skids touch the PSP matting and the airspeed drops off quickly. I immediately close the throttle and turn the battery switch to the OFF position. My body is jammed into the shoulder harness. The inertial system works as advertised.

"I hope this works out," I mutter as we continue our skid.

Coming to a stop the nose swings to the left in a herky-jerky motion, as if someone gave us a tug with a rope. It's deadly quiet. Looking to my right, at a fifteen-foot hover, is Spider who now dips his nose and hovers to the next taxi-way.

No sooner do I get the window open, and there appears the Kid. "We made it . . . WE MADE IT! You saved my life! I can't believe it!" He's screaming uncontrollably. I'm surprised how quickly he got out and climbed up to my side of the aircraft, I never noticed him leaving his front seat.

Brakes squealing, a jeep abruptly stops near our Cobra.

Bounding out is a tall slender officer in a sweat stained non-nomex flight suit and what appears to be a doctor, bag in hand, running behind him. It's Seven-Zero-Seven. Unstrapping, I now decide to face the music. Either I'll lose my foot or be a cripple for the rest of my life. My flying days are over.

"Don't move 'til the Doc gets up here," Seven-Zero-Seven yells at me.

He's much older than his boyish looks and it's very deceiving for some of the men he's rescued. If you're shot down you want Seven-Zero-Seven to come and get you, he's a natural life-saver. DMZ Dust Off Seven-Zero-Seven "The Freedom Bird" home, as he's affectionately known. For a man who looks to be only sixteen years old, he has an amazing amount of experience and savvy. I wonder if he ever had a chance to be a kid. War snatches away youth, both physically and emotionally. Boys are old men before their time. In Nam, as their tours get shorter, the aging process progressively speeds up. Nobody goes home young. Either you're dead or old on the outside, and if you're old you're dying inside. Where does our country get these young men who rush to become old men? Why not let the older men, who make the decisions to send us, go instead? Their aging process would be insignificant and a generation would be spared from the loss of enjoying its youth.

"How you doing?" the Doctor asks as he peers into my cockpit.

Hell, does it look like I'm okay? "I'm hit in the leg. Don't know how bad, but I can't feel it. Tied it off with this tourniquet so I wouldn't bleed to death." At least twenty vehicles now encircle the aircraft. Some idiots are still clicking away with their fucking cameras.

"What we'll do, ah . . . is pull you out. Ah . . . get you on a stretcher then over to the Surg. It's going to hurt, but hang in there."

Nice for him to tell me it's going to hurt, I can't feel a thing now. Now they tell me it's going to hurt.

"Sneaky, that was some great flying," Seven-Zero-Seven is always positive. I guess it's why he's such a good medevac pilot. Right now he'll say anything to get my mind off of my foot, or lack of one.

The burning is long over, and numbness has set in. Earlier, it felt like a hot poker had been punched into the bottom of my foot, but now there's no feeling. I know I might pass out if I see my foot is gone, so I close my eyes as they pull me out. Can't pass out in front of these guys, especially with all the cameras. As they lay me in the stretcher, I hear the Kid.

"Look, look! Look at them holes! Six of 'em! Lined up from the back seat to the hell hole!"

Can't he shut up? I lean up on the stretcher as they shove me across the back of a jeep. Looking down I think I see, then don't see, blood. There's no blood! The tingling sensation tells me there's something wrong. I try to think back to anatomy classes at Texas A&M, where I studied Pre-Veterinary Medicine. Right now all I can remember is screwing the big breasted girl under the Owen field bleachers while at a football game up at Norman, Oklahoma. If all I can remember are the girls who I screwed while in college, no wonder I quit school after two years.

Bouncing to a stop. "Do you fly this bad?" I ask Seven-Zero-Seven, who's made it his personal responsibility to drive me to the Surg.

Gears grind as he hunts for reverse. After finding it, we bounce backwards until stopping in front of the triage double doors. My adrenalin is rushing. Light headed and clammy I drift off.

"Can you believe this?"
"He's got the wound of a life time."
"Knowing him, he'll never live it down."
"Damn lucky. That's what he is."
"Talk about luck."
"Hell, I've never seen one like it."
"Let me see. Come on . . . let me see."

Am I dreaming or are they all talking about me? Squinting into a blinding light I find myself nude and cold, and a crowd of people gathered around my legs.

A beautiful nurse, yeah I'm sure she's beautiful, sees I'm awake. She gives me a motherly pat on the shoulder. "You'll fly again. You're just fine."

Bullshit! I remember telling this to David Koons when he lost his leg at the knee from a fifty-one. He knew, I knew, we all knew he'd never fly again. The fifty-one took it cleanly off. Last we saw of him was the morning they carried him to a C-130 for the ride to Da Nang, and onto the States for a medical discharge.

"Mr. White. I'm Major Doyle. We've checked you all over. You're lucky. The bullet pierced the bottom of your aircraft, came through your boot and lodged in the bottom of your right foot. You have no broken bones. You have some damage, though not much, and no muscle damage. Very little co-lateral damage, I'd say. It'll be sore for a while. You have, or should I say ah you will have, a very serious bruise. I put in six stitches and you'll have a small scar after it heals. You'll be just fine though. Probably back flying within the week if your Flight Surgeon clears you and no infection develops. You're lucky, very lucky."

His face is triangular, and has an excessive amount of black hair protruding from his ears and very thick, bushy eyebrows. He peers over his glasses, half moon, and turns to walk away saying, "We'll keep you here overnight. You can go back to your unit tomorrow. I don't expect any complications and probably a lot of war stories," grinning like the cat who ate the canary. "Relax. You're fine." So much for his bedside manner.

This doesn't make sense. I must be dreaming "Doc, you sure? I can't feel a thing." Convinced that he's just being nice to me before they take me into surgery and cut off my foot.

"No, you're fine. What you did was tie the tourniquet too tightly. It cut off the circulation. That is why your leg was numb."

"Thank you Doc. Thank you." I try to wiggle my toes and suddenly realize I'm nude and laying on a concrete slab with a dozen or so people peering down at me. "Shit! Can I get some clothes on!"

"Make way here. Make way!"

Thank God it's Sergeant Major Washburn. He has a big grin on his face. Seeing me nude, he laughs. Just what I need, a Green Beret laughing while I lie here, butt-naked and defenseless.

"Milo has a wheelchair for you, Sir! I've got to go down to surgery. Two of the 'yards are there. After you get out of X-Ray I'll come by." Then with full military bearing he spins toward the set of open doors and vanishes.

Left standing there is Milo, grinning from ear to ear. Tossed over the wheel chair back is a towel. "Will this help, Sir Sneaky?"

"Fuck you Milo! You understand. Fuck you Milo!"

"That's Sergeant First Class Milo. Milo with a towel, Mr. White! Does this sound about right?"

"Okay! Okay! Enough! Let's get the hell out of here."

"Sergeant, would you be so kind as to wheel this injured pilot down to X-Ray so we can find out if there's any metal left in his foot," the beautiful nurse, who on closer inspection really isn't, orders. But she sure was a pleasant sight to wake up to.

"Yes Ma'am. With great pleasure. I'll gladly take this most ungrateful officer off of your hands."

"When he's through, they'll tell you the ward he'll be spending the night in," she replies, still talking to Milo, but looking at me.

"Let's go Milo. I'm cold."

I slide off the concrete slab and into the wheel chair while grabbing the towel and covering my lap. The nurse gives me a warm smile, and the small gathering breaks away from the slab and the chair. I look back up into Milo's face, a big grin with pearly white teeth lined up like bowling pins. "Let's go!"

"Yes Sir!" Shoving me toward the double doors. "Thank you ladies. I'll teach this officer some manners later."

Chapter 8

The DMZ Dust Off Huey is now on short final to the Hot Spot. Looking over the AC's shoulder I see a half dozen guys milling around the Hot Spot waiting to greet me. I don't feel like a lot of harassment this morning. My sober night at the hospital was uneventfully and boring, and it put me in a bad mood.

After x-rays and being reassured that there were no metal fragments in my foot, I was given a clean bill of health. From there, Milo pushed me to a ward, and I gingerly climbed into bed and tried to sleep. Billy and Milo stayed with me until I dozed off.

I woke up in the dark and the ward was cold and quiet. With thirty other beds, some filled, it appeared to be a non-serious injury ward. I surely didn't need to be held over night. A heavyset First Lieutenant came by after I sat up and asked if I wanted anything to drink. Returning with a can of soda, she told me of my many visitors during the early part of her shift, but she shooed them away so I could sleep.

She then proceeded to tell me, in medical terms, all about my wound. It didn't seem serious. She did say that she was given strict orders not to allow me to go to the Officers Club and that I was to remain in the ward for the night.

No matter how nice I was, she wouldn't allow me to leave or make a phone call to have a couple of beers delivered. With this at a dead end, I asked for something to put me to sleep, and went to sleep earlier than I ever had while in Vietnam.

Morning rounds were conducted by a strange looking Captain and a gruff Major. Immediately, I set them straight on the fact that I didn't belong here. The Major agreed and by 10:00 am I was headed out. I caught the 11:00 am logistics flight on its trip to Da Nang, but was not allowed in the club while awaiting the flight. They were determined to keep me sober. The DMZ Dust Off crew was more than willing to drop me off at Camp Evans.

Upon landing, several guys come out of the TOC to be witnesses of my return. I hobbled out of the Huey on a single crutch carrying a small light blue bag containing my cut open boot, some crumpled up medical files, and two sets of x-rays. One for my medical records files, and one for a souvenir. They also said I could keep the bullet ridden boot if I wanted. As soon as I can, the boot is going into the trash.

As the Huey lifts off, I wave thanks. Cat calls, laughing, and jokes start as the noise of the departing Huey's beating blades die off. Surely I'll be the butt of their insidious humor until another pilot does something to relieve me of the harassment.

While I stand around with the aid of the crutch, an armorer saunters up.

"Sneaky. They're coming to get you," he says, pointing to the activity outside the Administration hut.

Others walk toward me, starting their kidding. Sounds of a jeep revving up the hill, hopefully to pick me up, are one of relief.

I hobble around to see the Old Man, Major Stafford, driving onto the Hot Spot. He's got an entourage with him. As he skids to a stop, I'm greeted by smiles and several cat calls. The calm before the storm, and I can feel it. Hopping the last couple of feet to the unoccupied passenger seat, I flop down. I let my bandaged right foot hang out, it's too painful to put down on the floorboard.

"Our wounded warrior has returned. How're you feeling?" Asks the short thin man, our CO.

He's on the tailgate assignment of his career. His face is leathery and deeply streaked with lines of age as well as too much sun, and probably one or two too many drinks along the way. As an enlisted man during the later stages of WWII, he didn't get overseas, but he decided to stay in the Army anyway.

He fought in the Korean War, with his first three or four months as a Sergeant. Then, after being wounded, he went to Officer Candidate School before returning to Korea for a tour as an Artillery Lieutenant. After Korea, he went to flight school at Fort Sill, Oklahoma, and flew spotter aircraft for Army Artillery.

He's been passed over for Lieutenant Colonel three times so this is the last assignment he'll have before forced retirement. Because of it, he doesn't take the power of command too seriously. He remembers his enlisted days, and knows things are tough enough in combat without some crazy CO trying to win the war at the sacrifice of his men.

Before I can answer him, Jolly Roger comes out of the TOC and with long strides approaches the jeep. "Mr. White, it's good to have you back. Any word on how long before you'll be back on flight status?"

This guy can't wait, can he? "Well *Dai Uy*, I've got to see the Battalion Flight Surgeon tomorrow. It's up to him. As soon as I can wear a boot I'll be ready if," I point down at my foot, "there's no infection." Now I get a dig in. "Captain Rogers," saying formally and sarcastically, "maybe I should fly without a boot, just a sandal, if we are that short of pilots to fly combat missions."

I glance over to the Old Man and he starts laughing. Others join in, but only after the Old Man has started laughing. Though I said it with rancor, everyone else takes it as a joke. Rogers eyes indicated that he understood my meaning.

"You're off 'til the Doc clears you. You can help Captain Sherrily in Maintenance until then."

Shit. Talk about the kiss of death. The last guy in the world I want to be around is our Maintenance Officer.

"Good idea, Sir." Jolly Roger sees humor in this especially after our last confrontation about maintenance, or the lack of it. "Maybe Mr. White can see to it that his aircraft's air-conditioner is repaired to his personal satisfaction."

He knows he's got me and the frown has turned in a slight smile as he rubs it in. As Jimbo has repeatedly impressed upon me, Captain Rodgers does get even. Though this does not appear to have been his idea, I'm sure that he put the bug in the Old Man's ear about how they could put me to good use while I'm limping around.

Everybody within earshot starts to laugh. Everyone except me. From a distance it would appear to be good natured joking, but listening closely, one could hear the venom and know that all is not as it appears.

"Let's get you down to the hootch. I'll call Sherrily and see if he can put you to some good use." Without fanfare, Major Stafford slams the gear shift and pops the clutch, letting tires spin as we accelerate off the Hot Spot.

The Army, like the other U.S. services, frowns on it's officers driving vehicles. It goes back to the era of horses and horse drawn carts, wagons and carriages. Back then, officers rode their own, usually privately owned steeds. Enlisted, who were not in calvary, would sometimes be relegated to ride on the carts, wagons, carriages, and even cassons. So, when it was required for officers to ride on horse drawn vehicles, it was only natural to have the regular drivers handle the horse teams.

Major Stafford, since his arrival at the Griffins, has refused the services of our enlisted drivers. Even when with other officers, he does the driving. The first time the batallion CO showed up, the word was that he was stunned to see that Stafford picked him up and drove him around the compound. If anything was said, I'm sure that Major Stafford reminded him of the shortage of men in the unit, and that he only had less than a year left in the Army. At first, we thought that his driving was a silent protest to the Army for forcing him out. But, when quized at the club one night, he gave a convincing argument about how he was driven around for almost twenty years, and he was tired of being chauffered. In addition, in a year he would have to drive himself everywhere, so why not start now.

For the sake of the United States population, we're all glad he's having the six months to practice these lost skills. Whether grinding the gears, popping the clutch, turning too sharply, cutting off those he had just passed, refusing to use hand or mechanical turn signals, or trying to stop on a dime at the very last moment, Major Stafford's driving had become a symbol of his command. Not conventional, but it works.

My ride to my hootch ends in one of his typical abrupt stops. As I swing my legs out, Major Stafford asks me to stop by his office later when I'm feeling better. Before I'm able to ease out of the seat and onto the crutch, the front door swings open and E'Clair, Doc, and Scoop step out with a chair and an open beer.

"Here's a beer," E'Clair says, as he shoves the foam covered can at me. After I accept, he shakes the foam from his hand.

"Sit!" Doc says, pointing to the chair as if they are going to carry me into the hootch. Looking past me to the Old Man, he says antimatedly, "We'll carry the wounded veteran in, Sir"

By now, everybody is busting a gut. Fred is at the door, tail wagging, and looking up at the gathering. At least I'll get some solace. He sure won't be on my case about the wound. Disgustedly, I hop past the laughing pilots and yell back to the CO that I'll be up at his office in an hour or so.

Inside the hootch, I see the pranks have begun. Over my cubicle a large cardboard sign is hanging. Crudely drawn on it is a purple heart. Written above, and in very neat form, is my name in thick blocked black letters.

"Kid, if you're involved in that drawing, you're in big fucking trouble," I warn as I hobble by Klien who's sitting at the low table, made of discarded rocket boxes we use as the platoon bar. I bet he's writing his Mother.

"Good to see you ah...Sneaky" He used my name almost timidly, but at least, he used it. "You did a great job flying us back. You seen the plane? It's in the hanger. They're going all over it. Had holes everywhere." He opens his arms to further explain the damage. "I took a couple rolls of film and I'll let you have some of the flicks when I get them back."

Ignoring him, even though he has followed me to my

cubicle, I hobble up to the sign and yank it down. Hopping around, I sail it toward E'Clair who's laughing so loud that Fred has scampered over to him and looks up at the big black man. His laughs have overrun all the other noise and laughter in the hootch.

I stand as formally as possible and give E'Clair a salute.

"Don't throw your award away. You're supposed to be honored to receive such an award from your most grateful country."

Everybody's laughing at the point of near hysteria. It even gets to me, though I try not to laugh as loud. Hell with it, if you can't beat 'em, join 'em.

"Fuck you E'Clair."

"By the way the Old Man is going to talk to you about Fred. He got caught pissing on the 1st Platoon hootch. They're hot! Seems Fred missed you last night and spent the night looking in gutters, bunkers, or laying along the road in hopes he'd find you."

"Listen E'Clair I left you in charge of him." My anger is rising. "If he's in trouble it's your fault." I turn and throw my crutch down and lay on my bed.

"Want a beer?" The Kid has followed me into my cubicle.

"Yeah, give me one Kid. By the way, lowering my voice, "That was smart of you using the survival radio."

Fred jumps up on the bed, wanting attention. Licking my face, he reacts to the attention I'm now giving him. It's hard to say if he got any while I was gone, he's always excited like this when someone pays attention to him. But he knows that I'm the one who keeps him here. Maybe E'Clair was right and he spent last night looking for me.

"I learned that from one of my IPs," the Kid replies as he brings me a cold beer. I notice that he hasn't taken one for himself.

Jimbo opens the back door, arms full. "Need some help out here. Did a booze run." Seeing me he stops, shakes his head, then continues to the front of the hootch, saying, "Well look at what the dog brought home. Nurses throw you out?"

"No! Wouldn't let me in their club either. Said Griffins have a foul, can you believe that word, FOUL reputation."

As the pilots go out the door they're laughing. "I heard the Old Man tell Sherrily you'd be helping him 'til you get medically cleared. You know that?" Jimbo knows my feelings all too well.

"Yeah. He told me to come by and talk. I don't want to work down there. I'll be able to fly as soon as I can put a boot on," remembering that the 18th Surg medics had ruined my Navy/Marine Corps flight boot while cutting it off my foot.

"Sneaky, don't go shooting your mouth off and end up telling the Old Man something you'll regret later. By the way, I talked to Rick about what we discussed." Then he disappears out the door for another handful of packages.

"Jimbo!" I yell, wondering how the talk about Nix went. My answer is the back door slamming against its stop.

"Damnit!" I swing out of bed, missing Fred who's curled up at the foot. "Might as well go up and see the Old Man."

I gulp the last of the beer in one long and near choking swallow and reach under the bed for a shower shoe. After trying to put it on, I realize that it's far too painful to wear it. Nothing seems to be going my way today.

The pilots return carrying more packages, while Jimbo holds the door open for them. After everyone has entered the hootch, Jimbo steps into my cubicle, bends down and in almost a whisper says, "We'll talk later, but you may have a point."

"Damn right, I do!"

Jimbo stands and shakes his head. He heads for the front of the hootch, where he'll direct what goes where. I try to keep up with him, but the hobbling prevents it. As I start to push the front door open, the Kid steps in front and opens it all the way.

"Fred stay here, I'm going to see the Old Man. You got me in all this trouble, so land." The dog cocks his heads then sits down. It's the only command we've been able to teach him, he's not too smart. My goal, when he was a pup and long before I realized he was dumb, was to teach him all aviation commands, but haven't got around to it, because it took months to teach him this one command.

Entering the Battery Administrative office I see Sergeant First Class McPherson, who's filling in as the unit First Sergeant. The two battery clerks are hunched over typewriters pecking away at some non-important memo, form, or maybe just a letter home.

"Hi ya Top?"

"Well, how are you doing Mr. White? See you're up and at 'em."

With twenty years in the Army he really doesn't like being the Acting First Sergeant. But our battalion is under-strength so rather than working on the flight line that he loves, he's been assigned this position for the past five months.

"Heard you were lucky. Looking at the plane, I'd say damn lucky."

"Yeah, you know Top, some days you eat the bear, and some days the bear eats you." I wait til he's through chuckling. "The Old Man in? He wants to see me. I'm probably in some kind of shit."

"He's on the other side. I'll get him. It's the dog, Mr. White. Dog's trouble around here. Also, they want you to work in Maintenance for a while. They're way behind in their work."

"I was afraid of that," though I'd already been told of this.

"Dozer! Tell the Major, Mr. White's here."

Specialist 4th Class Dozer stops typing and expels a chest full of air. He's always unkept and looking bewildered, but there's no doubt that he's the only administrative person in the unit, maybe the battalion, who knows what he's doing. The unofficial word is that he has a Masters Degree, in Chemistry of all things, from California-Berkeley.

Though Berkeley is a lightening rod for radical thinking, they must have an active draft office, as we have three who have graduated from there. If Dozer is like the other students from

Berkeley, then the 4th Estate has painted a lousy picture of the student body. Since the 4th Estate's picture of Americans fighting in Vietnam is a bad one, I guess Berkeley students get some of the same slanted press. All of our three, though I have no idea of their political leanings, have been good, if not outstanding, soldiers.

Each, PFCs Fredrick and McCluskey along with Specialist Dozer, have tackled their respective assignments with a zeal that has surprised everyone, especially after learning their education and Alma Mater. Each has taken to wearing peace symbols and FTA emblems, but here in Vietnam that is done by about a third of the troops. The continual need for haircuts and general sloppiness of uniform does make them standout, but their work habits are on the other end of the scale. Each, though they never met before their arrival here, has the same, almost carefree attitude, that misleads you.

Dozer's attitude, because of his high profile job as a clerk, is really noticed. Bypass the appearance and the don't give a damn attitude, and you find someone who does his job, and everyone elses in the office, quickly, efficiently, and without errors. For a slob, he does the neatest paperwork I've ever seen.

Fredrick is an armorer, known for taking on repair jobs no one else wants, or can do. Many times he's fixed weapons systems that would normally require being sent to out upper echelon maintenance unit. Rather than lose the aircraft for at least three days, Fredrick will take on the repair, working alone surrounded by the Field Manuals. He also works a job straight through until it is finished. Once, he went from afternoon one day until noon the next day to fix a problem. Even the Old Man couldn't talk him into taking a break for chow. He kept telling Stafford that he'd be up there in a while. Even after the Old Man ordered food brought to him, he never touched a bite. He was in his own world. He usually dresses in cut-off fatigues, a tee-shirt which is three sizes too big, and US Keds high-top sneakers, with the toes cut out. I can't remember seeing him in any other attire. But, he weaves his magic and fixes the problems, adding to anyone who is listening that the Army is screwed up for buying such a cheap piece of equipment. I often think of his statement when I strap in. Just how cheap is this Cobra I'm flying?

PFC McCluskey works in Supply. How he got there with a degree in Electrical Engineering, nobody knows. Surely someone would have wanted him in Communications. But within his first thirty days with us he proved his worth. Now he is only in the supply room for a half an hour or so after breakfast and again after lunch. Our Supply Sergeant says he gets everything done, ordered, and cleaned up during these two visits, and doesn't hang around after that. To back this up, the Supply Sergeant let one of his other clerks be assigned to the perimeter guard because he didn't need the help. Here in Vietnam, everyone needs help. McCluskey is really good. With his efficiency, it allows the Sergeant to open his card room earlier.

The card room, though illegal, has been running in the unit for as long as anyone can remember. It not only attracts the few NCO gamblers here at the Griffins, but also from all the other units located here at Camp Evans. It used to start after lunch and go until the money ran out. Now with McCluskey, the Sergeant is allowed to start his poker game as early as nine am.

One night the Supply Sergeant, after releaving me of sixty or seventy dollars, told me he wished that he'd found McCluskey a few years earlier. I assumed it was because of the money he was raking in with the games of chance that always seemed to favor him. But no, it was the Sergeant was sure he would have been a SFC by now, because McCluskey was the best supply man he'd ever come across.

McCluskey weighs over two-hundred pounds and always looks like someone threw a bucket of water on him, no matter what time it is. He sweats continually, but strangly enough never loses weight. His hair looks like it hasn't had a comb in it since boot camp. It's a tangled web. Discounting size, you can still tell who it is, from a distance, by the black bushy mop.

Specialist Dozer swings his chair around and knocks on the

office back wall. The Major and the XO live in the back half of the building. Although there's no door between the two large bays, one can yell back and forth through the walls or, if needed, walk around to the front to enter.

"Major Stafford. Mr. White's here. You want him here or would you rather he come around to your room?" Dozer yells nonchalantly.

"Send him," someone, other than the CO, answers.

"See you Top," I say as I hop out the front door.

I slowly make my way around by using the crutch and one hand against the side of the building. The building is identical in style to those used for the unit's living quarters, and most others at Camp Evans. This one has the back half partitioned off to form a small living area big enough for two bunks, a small desk, and some personal items for the Old Man and the XO. As I reach the screen door, it's shoved open. I squint to see who's inside, but the sunlight outside, and the darkness in the hootch, prevent me from seeing it's occupants.

"Come in Sneaky!"

With an exaggerated motion, I hobble in. The Old Man is sitting on his bunk. The XO, Captain David Westrock, is stretched out on his bunk clad only in faded green boxer shorts and drinking a root beer. Lounging in chairs are Captains Sherrily and Rogers. Now this is going to be interesting.

"How are you doing? I was going to fly up and see you, but when I heard you'd be back today I thought I'd wait," Sherrily says, while shifting uncomfortably in his chair. This statement is more for the others benefit than for me. He would never go out of his way to see anyone and especially not to a hospital. It would be a painful reminder of his vulnerability.

Captain Jonathan Sherrily is our Maintenance Officer. He's a scrawny, almost sickly looking man, in his late twenty's with thin hair that will ensure his baldness by the time he hits forty. His facial features are on the edge of being delicate and feminine. Thin lips, light eyebrows that appear plucked aid this look. His small nose could be accused of being pointed, but it isn't long enough. I've never heard him raise his voice, except the day he was flying with me in A Shau Valley. That day was a rite of passage for him, and though he was subsequently awarded a DFC, he knew from that day on that his calling was in the Maintenance Department. He knows, just as we all know, he's no warrior.

Being around warriors strains him. To see them go off in the morning and watch their return, with occasional aircraft shot up, reminds him that he's an outsider. The tests they have passed while in the air affect the warriors when they return. It can be seen in the mess hall, the Club, and even in the shower. Warriors walk, talk, and act differently. It's all through their mannerisms and especially in the eyes. Someone said years ago, that the eyes are the windows to the soul. If true, then warriors must scare the hell out of normal people. I've noticed it with the grunts, its the look. Sherrily, like a few other Griffins, walks with a different step. As we go along in a hunter's lope, the non-warriors walk with an uneasy motion reflecting the insecurity within themselvs.

When around pilots, Sherrily seems to tense up, his features become more finely drawn, and he begins to fidget. The place that gives him comfort is the maintenance hanger. It's his domain. There, he is not only familiar with the going on, but he is in charge. Some may call it an escape, others see that he is giving his best to the war effort. He has done an admirable job with our maintenance. And if my air-conditioner worked, I would have no complaints.

To defend against some of my own short comings, I have developed the style of picking on others. It's not that I'm a bully, but it is easier to complain about someone else rather that let them complain about me. As a school trained maintenance officer I could be sent or 'requested" to go work down there full time. It would mean no more daily flying and this is what I'm afraid of. So the way I have chosen to avoid this is to build a wall between us. This way Sherrily will never go to the Old Man and ask to have me permantly assigned to him. Sherrily is paying for my reluctance to work in maintenance.

Captain Sherrily is a Maintenance Officer by virtue of graduating from the Aviation Maintenance Officer's Course, or AMOC, at Ft. Eustes, Virginia, just north of Norfolk. He got this assignment because he was a Transportation Corps aviator. For some reason he didn't go through the Test Pilot School which initally made me think he wasn't good enough. But in my AMOC class, the four of us that got it were the top four in the class, and I know there were a couple of other good candidates for the class. Maybe he was in a class like this, but I'll never let him know that I think this.

I went through both schools some time ago. Going through them as a lowly WO1 was a privilege the Army extended me, which caused many looks from the other classmates and instructors. I've only worked formally as a Maintenance Officer in three units. I have a 671CP MOS which means, among other things, that I'm an aircraft maintenance, rotary-wing, parachute qualified warrant officer. That and a dime will get you a cup of coffee.

"Sit down. How about something to drink?" The Old Man is going to make this as easy on me as he can. He is being gracious, in a casual unassuming way.

I gingerly slide into the only easy chair in the room, which, thoughtfully, has been left vacant for me. By sitting at an angle, it allows me to rest my wounded foot on a hi-fi speaker. I let my calf rest on the wood veneer speaker and the bandaged foot hangs over for all to inspect. It looks worse than it is, with the wrapping oozing of yellow-orange antiseptic that was swabbed all over the foot.

"Yes Sir, something cold would be fine," I reply. Getting these pleasantries over will be a relief.

Westrock leans up and opens the refrigerator between the two beds and quickly reads off the list of its contents.

I want a beer though I'm not sure what the Old Man will say. After deciding I don't give a damn about the others, I continue, "How about a beer? I'm not flying today," smiling. Might as well get all I can. Sort of the kiss before the fuck.

The Executive Officer reluctantly takes out a beer and, after looking at Stafford for a sign of disapproval, opens it letting the foam bubble over its lip and onto the floor. He passes the cold non-rusted can of Budweiser to me, then lays back on his bed. He's got two oscillating fans hanging upside down by wire at the foot of the bed. Both are turned up to high speed and aimed directly at him, yet he still sweats profusely.

"Your health. Good to have you back," Stafford says in a genuine tone of compassion. The Army is going to lose a good man when they let him retire. He cares about his men. The years he spent in the lower ranks lets him understand there are times when compassion is more important than protocol.

Heads nod as they hold their cans, waiting to see if the Old Man takes a drink before they do. Army protocol is ridiculous at times.

"I asked you over here for several reasons. First, to let you know you did one hell of a job bringing the plane in. It's got more damage than you thought. When you get down to the hanger you'll see, but I want to reiterate that you did one hell of a job not rolling it into a ball."

The others are sitting hunched over, not wanting to make eye to eye contact with me. Westrock sits up to adjust a fan for the second time. With the pillows propped up, he appears to be a Roman Emperor waiting to be served.

"There was no place to put it down out there. I didn't want to have an extraction team go out there and try to retrieve it," I reply, knowing who would have led the recovery crew. Sherrily leading would mean others would have been at risk trying to sling the Cobra out. Destroying it in place would mean we'd be without a replacement for at least two weeks. It would have put a strain on all the other planes and crews. We need so many flight hours a day to complete our missions. The more planes you have, the more time you have for inspections and general maintenance. It translates that the Cobras will be in better mechanical shape which means pilots have a better chance of survival. That's all we care about — survival.

"I'm not sure how long you'll be grounded. But the problem in Maintenance is, they are lagging behind and they need some help. I thought you wouldn't mind going down there and helping Jonathan with whatever he needs." He looks first at me then over to Sherrily, then back at me. "I know there's been some differences of opinion. Maybe this will be a time to iron them out." Major George D. Stafford is wise enough to know that to order us to get along won't work. As the days go by with this old retread, I find a genuine liking for him. One that could easily extend outside the Army. "This talk is not only meant for you Mr. White. I have already talked to Captain Sherrily, and I think we have come to a common ground on this."

Looking at Sherrily I see in his face the look of a man who's been raked over the coals, and he's starting to fidget.

"If you gentlemen have anything to say, this is the time. When you leave here I expect you to work together." Looking over to me. "Sneaky, you have a lot of experience you can share. I know that you'll help us out during this time."

Might as well say it now. One thing I have learned in the military, if given the chance to freely speak your peace and you don't, then you live with it. "Sir, the problems I see with maintenance may or may not be with the Captain. I don't go down there and tell him how to run his shops. But when I do say something, I expect the common courtesy of being listened to and not ignored. Not being told and I quote, 'To bear with it.' Fucking bear with it was what I was told. I know maintenance is behind. I've never been in a unit where it wasn't. I also know what things are needed to make our aircraft combat ready." Now looking over to Jolly Roger. "In my case, an air-conditioner is needed. Flying for four to seven hours in a closed cockpit is not easy or comfortable. Especially when the sun is blistering your ass and the dinks are shooting at you." Now looking back to Sherrily. "I know the Captain doesn't fly that many combat missions. I also know that every pilot wants his Snake to be in the best shape. But

I also know damn well that I'm the only pilot in this unit that has ever changed a transmission or an engine. And I don't mean watching mechanics do it. I am talking about doing it myself. You know Captain, that any major work done on Zero-Two-Seven is done while I'm there. I get dirty! I help! Whatever it takes to get it mission ready."

Shifting in the chair to face the Major. "Sir, I don't like getting told to bear with it when my plane needs parts. In fact, I don't think the parts have been ordered yet." I see Sherrily's head is down, staring at the floor. "This is all I have to say. I'll do whatever you say Sir, but I want you to know that a lot of things happen that fail to get reported to you," I say, shooting a look over at Jolly Roger, "Just complaints about me and my tact seem to be all that arrive here."

Well it's all said now. We'll see what happens. Maybe Sherrily won't want me down there.

"I've got a lot of problems. Hell, I'm buried! Besides being short of line people, I've no night crew to speak of. Experienced mechanics are at a premium in the battalion. I've been more worried about getting the planes in flyable condition rather than the small things. We have planes flying with only two radios, leaky hydraulics, only one gun working in the turret. There are a lot of problems down there. Parts are hard to get. People are harder to get. This war is getting to be a paper war, and headquarters is more interested in the requisition forms being filled out correctly than our needs." Sherrily's excuses are true.

"This is why you're getting Mr. White. Now, is this settled?" No answers, heads just looking downward. "I'd like a few minutes with Sneaky alone if you gentlemen don't mind."

With that they stand up and as they go out the door each pats me on the shoulder. Hell, they must think I'm a dog. Just out of the door, Sherrily opens it back up and offers. "When you're ready, call down, and I'll have a jeep come get you." He says this genuinely happy to hear that he will have me helping him.

"Thanks Captain."

Tipping the beer up I find it's empty. I don't remember drinking it during the past few minutes. I try to put it quietly into the rust covered trash can by the desk.

Putting his Fresca down, the Old Man leans over to the refrigerator. Taking out two beers, he pulls one of the now empty chairs up in front of me. Sitting down, he opens the cans and hands me one. This time it doesn't foam over.

"We don't get Budweiser often. Battalion S-4 sent up a couple of cases for me." He takes a long drink. Then, looking at me, he starts, "What's the problem with Nix?"

Nix? How the hell did he find out about that? Jimbo or Rick must have talked to him. I'll be damned.

"Well Sir . . . " Got to be careful. Stafford hasn't flown that much and he's never flown a CCN mission, or at night. Word is, he's been ordered not to. But I would have thought he would get out at least once to see what's being asked of his men. When I was a Marine crew-chief, I flew with CO's that lead missions. Being a Sparrow Hawk mission, which Prairie Fire missions were called back then, didn't prevent a Lieutenant Colonel from leading them.

The Major I had in the 282nd didn't fly that much, but he was a new aviator going though flight school just to lead an assault helicopter company in combat. In CAV units, the CO's fly, so I've wondered why Stafford didn't fly that much. Is it that he's tired of war, having been in Korea, and now on his second tour for this one?

Repeating, "Well Sir . . ." Nix has friends I'm sure, and we'll cross paths again in our careers. "To be honest, I think he's scared. I know he had a good first tour. He's was a good IP, but he's not used to our style. Also, I think he's a bit put out because he's not in charge. He's the senior warrant in the platoon, but he's not an AC or Section Leader. That might be an affront to him."

Looking at me intensely, he takes a slow sip of beer. He's thinking. Letting out a sigh, he leans back rubbing his forehead.

"Sneaky, you're learning, though slowly, about using tact," smiling, "you don't want to say he's yellow, but this is what you think, right?"

Looking down at the floor, I nod my head. I'm uncomfortable with this. I've said it to others but they were all front line pilots, and not the CO. There's no doubt that Nix had a good first tour. Many hours, a couple of DFCs, but that was then and this is now. There's an old saying that you're only as good as your last mission. I'm sure one day someone will be saying the same thing about me, if I live long enough.

"Let me tell you something, and it's not to leave this room," the Old Man continues as he takes another slow sip. I too gulp down some of the cold liquid as my throat is now bone dry. "I don't expect him to be around too much longer. He's been talking to slick units, looking for a home. Without him knowing it, I talked to a friend at 2nd Brigade seeing if they could use him, possibly as the Colonel's pilot. When Rick gave him the FAM ride he came to me and told me of his concerns. You know Mitchener's been in here twice about him. But I'm not going to throw him out. I won't ruin his career because he's having a hard time with CCN."

I'll be damned, everybody's been to him about Nix.

"I'll not ruin him because I understand there's times in one's career that you take a different approach to things. I don't fly CCN. When I was younger, you would have had to fight me to keep me from flying hot missions. But we all change. You will too. As you get up toward the end of your career you'll look at things differently. At least you'd better."

He takes another drink of beer, and I do too. "The war's winding down, and you won't survive in a peace time Army unless you change. I've been though it twice. You're a damn good man and, when you work maintenance, you're an excellent Maintenance Officer. I have the utmost faith and confidence in your flying abilities. But after this war, and it's going to end, you may have a hard time in this man's Army. I've met guys, Korea and here, that should stay and not come home to Army garrison life. You're not the spit-shined, shaved-tail-haircut, cocktail-parties-at-the-Colonel's-house type. Hell, the way you drink you should only be allowed in stag bars." He's smiling. "In war, the Army can't survive without you firebrands. But in peace time, you can't survive the paper pushers. Sneaky, you need to think it over. If you're going to stay in, you've got to change and I mean it. To me, you'll never be happy back in the States." Pausing, he takes another sip. "I think Vietnam is your home. You understand what I mean?"

I do, though I've never thought of it like this, and no one has ever said it to me. I feel like it's my home. I'm happy here. I gulp the rest of the beer down.

Abruptly, he changes the subject. The change leaves me cold. I have to think about what he has said. If the war ends, what will I do? Try to finish my last ten years out, trying to conform and hoping for another war. Hell, no one hopes for war! Or do I get out, and try to stay over here and fly. Maybe Air America, it's quasi-military and they'll always be over here. I wonder? Who can I talk to about this? Shit!

"Nix will be leaving. I don't know when, but he'll be leaving. He's not happy here, and he doesn't like flying Cobras. He's a slick IP so there's a home for him somewhere, we just have to help him find a good one. I'll talk to him when the time is right. But for now, I don't need you causing problems. We clear on this?"

"Yes, Sir!"

"If there's anything you need, let me know. Don't let that" pointing to my foot, "get infected. I need you here."

"Yes, Sir!" I know our conversation is over as he stands up.

"One last thing, Sneaky. I'd advise you to temper your tongue with Captain Rogers. If you want a long Army career, you know you'll be running into him again. If you piss him off now, you might have to pay for it later. Do we see what this could do to your career?"

He opens the door for me. Standing there, in his boxers, is Westrock talking to Captains Sherrily and Rogers.

I climb out of the chair and pickup the crutch.

"Yes, Sir. Thank you. I'll do what it takes to smooth things over."

Hopping out the door, I start the forty-yard hobble to my hootch.

Halfway there, he yells. "What about the dog?"

Turning around, I see him smiling, then he waves at me to keep going. Fred has survived banishment for another few days.

Chapter 9

"You've been off for two weeks. You're cleared to fly. So, this is your day."

"Son of a bitch! Why didn't you tell me this last night? I wouldn't have gotten drunk if I thought I might be flying today." Well that's a lie, I would have got drunk anyway.

I sit up and kick at Fred. He's continually bumped my bad foot when I've been in bed. My time off has been enjoyable but short.

"I've told you for three days to get ready. You laughed. You're lead today, I'm going to Da Nang. Set your crews." Jimbo leaves my cubicle.

"Shit, you could have said you meant it this time."

I plod barefoot over to the platoon flight status board. Looking it over, I check who the low-time pilots are. I call out Lieutenant Poole, and CWO's McIntyre and St. Clair. Then, assigning the co-pilots, I find that I'm left with the choice of who will fly with me.

"Captain Lardo, you'll be with me today," I say to the newest member of the platoon.

He arrived the morning after Tex left. He's sitting on his bunk drinking what appears to be coffee. A newly minted ADA Captain, he spent a tour in Germany prior to coming to Nam. On his way here he went through flight school.

Pilots are moving about knowing it'll be a busy day. Last night on Rick's return from CCN he told us of plans to insert several teams into the Anvil area.

The Anvil is a very small area south-southeast of the abandoned Lang Vei village. It's a part of Laos that pokes into Vietnam and is shaped like an anvil, whence its name. Enemy activity has been building up in the area so CCN has been asked to check it out.

The problem with the area is threefold. First, it's always been a hot area because of the direct and very accurate gunfire received from the northwest. The northern side of the Anvil is overlooked by a looming escarpment called Co Roc Ridge. There are very few places in Southeast Asia where you can fly and get shot at from above. The Anvil area is one. Another is the Mugia Pass on the border between North Vietnam and Laos. The pass is surrounded by fifty-three hundred foot ridges. (I'll get my chance to fly through Mugia in a few years when flying for Air America.)

The second problem is the Xpone river which twists and turns throughout the area. This allows plenty of hiding places along its banks and has become a favorite NVA hiding place.

The last problem is that it is level. There are no ridges or hills to duck behind. Scrub vegetation, not more than four feet high, allows the NVA to see your movements easily. They see you coming, going, and what you're doing while there. Too many aircraft and crews have been lost in this area.

"E'Clair, walk with me," I say as I finish getting my equipment together.

I'm carrying my survival vest and stabo rig in my hand. I usually opt to put them on once I get to my plane. My plane, Zero-Two-Seven, was up and flying within a week after the Viper extraction incident. Sherrily fixed the air-conditioner with parts taken from one of our hanger queens.

This war will not be won without the valuable assistance of the hanger queens. Aircraft stripped of every conceivable part to be put into other aircraft. We probably have an extra complete set of parts on hand. Just hope that your unit doesn't have to move, otherwise you've got a major problem trying to get the queen up and flying. Usually it's slung loaded to the next camp. I've known of a few airframes stripped naked for over a year, hoping it would take a direct hit from a mortar round during an attack. Many a Maintenance Officer has written off an entire aircraft that was already stripped to its bones for parts after it was hit by an NVA mortar or 122mm rocket.

"I'm ready," Marty says with gear on. He's standing by the door.

We walk up the path to the TOC. Flying with Marty St. Clair is relaxing. He uses the radio only when necessary and seems almost telepathic. He always seems to know what you're going to do next. Not a man of many words, he is one of action. He never shows the probable strain of being the only black pilot in the unit. His goal is to get out of the Army and fly for an airline. He'll make it if they give him half a chance.

Marty, who brought with him when he arrived at the Griffins, the nickname Chocolate E'Claire, is a good natured sort. From the East, Philadelphia area, he was raised in an upper-middle class family. When listening to him speak, if you are not able to see him, you would think you were talking to a WASP. I went to private school and had been around several blacks who's diction was a whole lot better than mine. Marty would fit right in with this group. Every so often he uses a word and everyone does a double take, not only because of the way it's pronounced but the word is very upscale for us.

Marty, though large, doesn't convey the overpowering image one would think when told of his size. He's not at all timid, but brings an unspoken commanding presence into a room. When he does speak, he keeps his verbiage at a minimum and is very polite. But he does convey his thoughts and ideas quickly. He has a knack, which I've seen him use many times, of letting others think that Marty's idea was theirs. In an unassuming way, he usually influences what is going on around him, but never, at least visually, revels in his accomplishment. But I think that being so polite is what really throws everyone off.

His free time is spent reading through, several times that I know of, a stack of books on his refrigerator. These are about flying, and especially instrument flying. He plans on taking FAA exams when he returns to the States. When asked if he was going to extend for the early out, he promptly said no, as he wanted to get a year or so of flying in the States before he applied to become an airline pilot. Other than the one or two beers he might have after a day of flying, he does not make it a point of getting knee-walking drunk with the rest of the platoon. Our nightly excursions to the Club, more than likely, will not have Marty tagging along.

He does get mail, in fact it's as regular as clockwork. Every other week he'll get five letters, all delivered on the same night. One is from his Mother and Father, though it's written by his Mother in a diary form. One is from his Grandmother or Aunt, or maybe a distant relative, who sends a short note inside an ornate religious card. One night while kidding him about his Southern Baptist background, he told me I better never let Miss Buella hear me say that. I can only gather that Miss Buella and the lady sending the religious cards are one in the same. Marty also receives three cards, usually in some pale colored envelopes, from his three younger sisters. He has several of these tacked to the wall next to his bunk, and he rotates them with military regularity. One time when the hootch was empty, I walked into his cubicle and looked closely at the cards. It was easy to see who had sent each, as the handwriting improved drastically when compared to each other. I quickly left and felt for quite some time that I had invaded his privacy. It wasn't something that I would normally do, but the half dozen cards drew me to the cubicle.

Marty, along with Jimbo and the just departed Tex, brings a sense of honor to the platoon. I try to live my life within this code of behavior. It's not the type of behavior most think about, for if it was, they would think we were all a bunch of drunks and misfits. No, it's a code that becomes a debt to your fellow warriors.

It's a debt that was felt, and carried by, Samurai warriors, by Knights of the Round Table, and men who are practicing warriors. You will not let your fellow warriors down, therefore you don't let yourself down. It's not as much about being the best, but it is the fear of not being able to follow through on your commitment that drives you to this level. Neither is it a spoken debt or code. If anything, it's a silent code. Some might think of it as mystical, but it isn't. It's just there, around those that are blessed with it. I know who has it, therefore, I know who I can count on. It's not just counting on someone, but being allowed to do so without disclaimers. I know that whatever asked, implied, or seen being needed, will be acted upon without reservations or questions. Even after the fact, this code is above questions and answers. It is not one talked about over a cold beer in hushed tones. If you are embodied with this, then you live by it, so therefore when you see others with it, you know you can count on them. This code of honor is not only a debt owed to others, who never ask for it, and in almost all cases it's not even known that it's owed. But having it lets you share in a bond, a bond that transgresses all other bonds that mortals speak so freely about. It's a bond with others, who, like myself, Jimbo, Tex, and Marty share.

Warriors have a sense of debt. We do not go running along into a bad situation to get a medal or some fleeting recognition. We do not spend time gloating over some measure of the honor code, nor do we plan our actions. Those who owe the debt, gracefully and without fanfare, stand up when needed. It's just that simple. When a need arises, we stand and cross the line. Texas folklore tells of the line drawn in the dirt at the mission in Alamo, and how to a man, they stayed on to fight, without much time, they made their minds up to stay, even though they each knew the chances of surviving. The number, in the thousands, of Mexican soldiers marching to the Alamo was surely a death warrant, just waiting for execution. But the code was with these few men. As officers, our line in the dirt was drawn the day we signed up. It was not an issue of if, or when, I'll be sent to Vietnam. Hell no! If you signed your name on the line, and graduated everything the Army put you through, then you were going to Vietnam. After all, this is the

Army's part. They had no idea who had the code within them. Sure, maybe a half dozen in each flight class had prior service, had seen combat and maybe even been decorated. But the number was small, very small. The Army needed large numbers of helicopter pilots each week, and prior service types are not running around to sign up to go to flight school then be whisked back to Vietnam and get killed.

If, after a few months flying here, those that possess the code surface, then they will meet with others, and each will know. For the first timers, they never know until they have been under fire. Then, even though you were rattled and shook-up, though your body was injected with flushes of adrenalin, and your mouth was dry as a bone and your tongue feeling like it was three sizes too large for your mouth, you'd say to yourself, hell, I can handle this. Usually right after this, if the incident was bad enough, you threw-up or had the dry heaves. No you don't know for sure at the moment, but you feel different. After a few more times under fire you begin to know you are different. This leads to looking around you. Studying those men that work with you. You want to see if, and more important, who has this same aura. In 2nd platoon, Marty has it. Jimbo has it. Tex, who left ten days ago, had it. And yes, I have it. We walk a bit different, not cock-sure, just with the knowledge that we will pay our debt when asked.

As Marty and I walk up to the TOC no words are spoken. But I feel good, even safe, as I'm around the code of honor. And in my heart I know that Marty feels the same way.

After going into the TOC, I read artillery advisories and some bulletins regarding recent AA fire. I check out my SOI and walk over to the Flight Crew Assignment Board, and without being told, I fill it out.

It's the first time I've been in the TOC since my outburst. Glances are stolen toward me then over to Jolly Roger, but words are not said.

We're starting to leave when St. Clair says, "I'm glad they

fixed your air-conditioner Sneaky."

For a moment it's quiet and then uncontrollable laughter erupts from everybody. Turning around, I see the one laughing the hardest is Jolly Roger. Our incident is over and the ice has thawed. I'm sure working with Sherrily helped. Peace for now, though tentative, has been made between us.

"Fuck all of you!" I chide, giving everybody the finger. Then I laugh too as I think of just how funny the whole thing is. "Let's go, Marty, before someone sees how ridiculous this is."

Walking down the hill, Marty tells me Jimbo had asked him to say it. He didn't even know I was going to have Marty walk with me to the TOC. Marty tells me he would have walked up there anyway to get his SOI and he really though it would be a good idea. Probably because Marty is a warrior, he can do this without worrying about my temper.

At the revetments, I go through a preflight with our new Captain watching. I explain what I want checked, and why. Though the Army has a prescribed check list, there are things I want checked beyond it. I know her quirks as she's been my aircraft for over eleven months. I explain that the sooner he learns each of the platoon's aircraft personalities the better off he'll be.

Captain Daniel Lardo is a heavy set Mexican-American. Since the day when I first heard that he went to college in Oklahoma, I've been on him. Being a Texas A&M Aggie, I feel this is not only my right and privilege, but surely a responsibility to my fellow Corps of Cadets.

Lardo hasn't appreciated it. First he tried to counter with rank, but that got everyone on his ass. Then he retaliated by bringing up my Marine Corps background. After that proved fruitless he used the old Texas - Oklahoma rivalry. Honestly, this is the way I started it in the first place, after all he went to Oklahoma, not I. One night at the club I ask how he got across the Rio Grande and made it all the way up to Oklahoma. That brought out the most scathing remarks yet. Later that night, fellow Texan Jimbo, told me to lay off the Mexican jokes, but once I found out he was sensitive, he became fair game. Now it's to the point things are being said out of spite rather than good natured joking.

Climbing into the back seat, I notice Wee Willie has stenciled another small gun on the Cobra's side denoting a fifty-one. Looking over at him holding the main rotor blade tip, I yell, "Willie, why not paint a foot on the side."

Laughing, he replied, "I was going to, but some of the guys said you'd get pissed."

"I sure would have." Lying, as Willie knows it's not true. I harass any and everybody, no one is immune to my attempts at humor or cutting remarks. But this is my defense, because I take a whole lot because of my Marine Corps service — being a New York Jew hasn't helped either.

"I had to repaint your name underneath. Fucking tin benders screwed up the belly trying to fix it." Referring to the large white letters spelling "SNEAKY" that are painted along the belly of my aircraft.

The paint job has got me into trouble several times when flying over brass from other units who don't like, especially in the 101st, the painting of personal names on Army-owned aircraft, at least by warrants in the 101st. It's been painted out several times just to have it mysteriously reappear a few days later. Once it was painted out at six or seven one night, and by midnight had been replace, though it was light green in color.

"Clear!" I yell while Wee Willie swings the blade free.

Engaging the starter, I start the ritual that brings us to flight conditions within two minutes. ARA ACs have to be able to get inside a Cobra, strap in, start it, and be ready for take-off within two minutes. It's a standing unit requirement that we have to perform while on two-minute hot status, which can happen several times during our twenty-four-hour alert shift. When the siren goes off, we have to be airborne in less than two minutes. It's an ARA trademark. And the Griffins are the best of the ARA.

"*Dai Uy* turn up the Victor." Talking into the small microphone pressed firmly against my lips I use a tone that will ensure he knows I'm the Section Leader and AC for the day.

"Sneaky's up," I say to other members of the flight.

After getting all the ACs replies and receiving clearance, the flight is airborne and flying low level along QL-1 headed for CCN.

"*Dai Uy* we'll be working the Anvil, doing inserts. You need to keep all the teams listed on the window. I figure we'll be lucky if we can get them all in. If something happens we'll be busy and we don't need to waste time getting pushes and call-signs again."

"I understand." His reply is short, and judging from the tone he's not happy being in my front seat.

It's his second CCN flight so he should know what to expect. His first flight was with Jimbo as lead, and the relationship was much different. They are fellow Captains, with one hopefully taking over the platoon from the other at some point in time. Now he's got an arrogant warrant officer telling him, a captain in the United States Army, what to do and when to do it, and to top everything off he's flying as a mere co-pilot. He's not a happy camper. He's signed the papers and knows where we're going, but this is the first time we've flown together. Being the Section Leader, I'll be busy with other things. Maybe I should have taken one of the senior warrants instead, but out of respect to his rank, I didn't. If he's going to take over when Jimbo leaves, he's got to have experience in the lead aircraft.

After landing at the PSP pad and starting my shut down, it becomes evident how busy we'll be. Several recon teams are milling about, and it looks like a large Hatchet Force is gathered at the northern end of the compound.

"Good to see you Sneaky!" Milo's busy, but not too busy to walk over to my aircraft and welcome me back. "How's the foot? Bruised as the ego?" His smile is infectious, and I know that he's kidding me but also letting me know there was concern.

"Nah, ego took it hard. But it wasn't that bad and I did get down to Da Nang and visit the safe house. Also got thrown out of the Da Nang Hotel, but for a while they thought they had a real live colonel with them."

MAC-V-SOG operates safe houses throughout Vietnam. In the Da Nang area there's one operated just for CCN's guests. It's an old French style villa. When you first drive into the compound, you expect Humphrey Bogart or Peter Lorrie to walk off the long porch, wearing a white suit and Panama hat with some kind of tall exotic drink in his hand.

Though there are no women, except one, living at the villa, why I go is the camaraderie, booze and food. It's totally escapism when here. And without much thought you can really believe you're living in the 30's in some far off distant land. Within the compound you can get, have, or do anything, except commit murder, without fear of it, or tales of your actions, leaving the compound. It also helps that CCN provides its own security force at the compound, so your guard is down without the worry of the war intruding into your realm of bliss. Usually these excursions only last three or four days. But you can really get your batteries charged in that short time. You come out of it a new man, which is really why MAC-V-SOG has gone to all the effort and expense to provide this retreat for the few warriors that it covets so dearly. A few, very few, helicopter pilots are able to get into these houses. I'm one, and I do so whenever I get time off and I'm not with Twit.

The house in Da Nang is called 'House 22,' because it is located on 22 Le Loi. Le Loi runs north/south adjacent to Duy Tan, from Da Nang Harbor into the heart of Da Nang City. At the northern end of Le Loi, nearest the harbor, you can turn right, or east, go a few blocks and be at the Da Nang Hotel.

Across the street, from 22 Le Loi, to the north, was a French style cafe restaurant with a few outdies, or as the French say, Bistro tables, and the half dozen small tables located inside, which I never use unless its raining. The owners were French-Algerian, which added to the wide range of the menu. Because House 22 had no kitchen, or cooking area, all our food while staying there had to be purchased on the economy. But after a day or two, you quickly tire of the French bread and meat which gave you the running trots within two hours. I only duck in for the Ba Mui Ma '33' beer, at least that is served cold, but the price, was as one would expect of something French, expensive!

The quickest, and to me the best place to eat, was the Chinese Soup Kitchen, just across Le Loi to the east. So close, that you could yell out your order from the second floor balcony. The food, well the only meal they served in all the years I've been going there, or having it delivered, is a thin, runny, murky broth, called soup, which has some vegetables including the ever present stable to an oriental diet, rice. It appears to me, that after the soup is ladled into a bowl, they add a small piece of substance - which floats on the top. I've heard many swear it was chicken, but then on the other hand I have heard about the same number swear it is rat. I do know this, its white meat and tender, and I've never been sick from a bowl topped off with it. So for me, it must be a very small chicken's breast, at least I hope so.

For those that go to 22 Le Loi, and strike out for the night at the local bars, there is a very sad looking worker, I guess you could call her a domestic, as she tries to keep the upstairs rooms clean, called 'Miss Sweet Lips.' Miss Sweet Lips seems to enjoy her status at the house, though I am sure a New York City hooker wouldn't envy her job, but when everything else has failed, Miss Sweet Lips will give one a few minutes of pleasure, as long as the lights are off and your imagination was running wide with thoughts of some blonde back in the States.

The word is, MAC-V-SOG, Phoenix, and the Agency, all have villas like this scattered throughout the city. Usually, and the rumor I heard is at least once a week, someone from one of the houses tries to invade the Da Nang Hotel. The Da Nang Hotel is the most formal hotel, if you can abuse the word formal this badly, in Da Nang. There is no doubt that in years past, prior to World War II, it would have been considered a posh place to rest during a weary traveler's trek. But that was then and this is now. The lack of upkeep, the constant war, the general lack of guests paying on the high end, have left the place in not only disarray, but scruffy as well. Even the staff has become aged and threadbare.

With the arrival of the United States advisors, and later US troops, the hotel didn't spruce itself up, even though there was the infusion of money from the cash rich Americans. Americans, not like French troops, will over pay for just about any service provided for them. Quickly senior Air Force and Marine officers took over. As the build up in the Da Nang area continued, it meant that higher ranking officers became more plentiful. So what once was a hangout for American advisors, became a hangout for American officers, which in turn became a hangout for American Field Grade officers, till its present status of being unofficially only for full Colonels and above, as well as becoming the official residence of all MAC-V personnel assigned to Da Nang.

When in Da Nang, I wear civilian clothes, carry a semi-concealed weapon, and instead of a military ID, I carry a MAC-V 'fuck you' card, or as Sweet Griffin calls it, a 'get out of jail free' card. This little four by two and three quarter inch card is worth its weight in gold. Few have heard about it, and fewer yet have ever seen one. It has on one side, a photo of the bearer, but no rank or military affiliation. But on it's back side is all in Vietnamese that no one may ask questions or detain this man. MP's don't like the card as it takes away their assumed right to harass combat troops, and even the South Vietnamese White Hats, their cross between police, MP, and Shore Patrol, leave you alone.

Going to the Da Nang Hotel, in civilian clothes, making an ass out of myself, and getting politely asked to leave has become a pleasure that I look forward to when I go to Da Nang. I always take two or three Vietnamese ladies and when stopped at the front lobby by an elderly Vietnamese, I quickly flash my 'get out of jail free' card and then make as grand an entrance to the dining area as possible. This always produces looks, which quickly turn to stares because of the clearly non-MAC-V colonel that has entered their inner sanctum. After the stares grow old, the men throughout the room then try to ignore me.

This would work except I didn't just sit down with my lady

friends and order a meal and eat it quickly. No, I made it a point to order for each of the girls, and kept several waiters coming and going. The men, in their freshly starched fatigues and shiny boots, each know that I am not a high ranking military officer, nor am I a high ranking US civilian doing some much needed service for the US interests. But they are correct in their thoughts when they think that the only way someone like this could get in their secluded bastion was if he, or in this case me, held a 'get out of jail free' card. So with this thought it means that I'm some lowly peon who has in someway become involved in doing some dirty work for the cause.

In the past I've had one of the men come over to the table and ask to speak with me privately. My reply was taking out my wallet and flashing the card. It was the mere sight of the card that quickly backed away the intruder. I'm sure, though it took all the self-control he could muster, that his return to his table was done with nods of disgust to the other officers.

The staff of the hotel treats me well, except they know that I am going to impose hardship on their business for the night. The balding men not only eat quickly, but then rather than sit around and take in the respite from their hectic assignments, they leave. What would have been a three or four hour escape now ends up an hour or so dinner and a swift departure. Me, well I take the girls to the dance floor, one at a time, except when the rock tunes are played. Then I bring out all the girls and shimmy, shake, and make a general ass out of myself. Booze does wonders to one's decorum. The staff allows us an hour or so of drinking and dancing, then the services get slow and sloppy. This is their polite, but effective, way to tell me that we have worn out our welcome.

For an outsider to look upon my visits it would be a contradiction. The hotel in its classic French colonial architecture is fine and delicate, but now faded interior furnishings, and its dimly lit high ceiling rooms overcome its once beauty with a pallor. The staff, in their old faded, formal clothes, scurry around to wait on guests, who themselves are older, more distinguished men all looking like they are pressed for time, but are forcing themselves a few hours relief. Then in the center of the dining room, as I would never accept a table near a wall, was a noisy young man with a table full of beautiful ladies having an apparently great time. And if, and this usually took a ten dollar American bill, I could get the band to play 'Louie, Louie', or 'I Can't Get No Satisfaction', the table's participants move to the dance floor and begin mass dancing in frenzied gyrations. Then, and only then, has the serenity of the old hotel been broken. But it ends, once I realize that the management, through its staff, is sending me this message. I tell the girls it's time to head for better music and wilder times. It ends, for the brass, a ruined evening! But then they don't have to risk death the next day, do they?

As I walk toward Milo he laughs harder. Quickly he joins in step with me as I head directly to the Operations hootch. Upon entering I see the map case on the far wall is wide open and Billy is talking to two Air Force Covey pilots.

Turning around to see who has entered, Billy quickly smiles. "Good to see you up and alive. You know Captain McDermott, he was the Covey when you received that near fatal wound to the little pinky." Then nodding his head toward the other man standing in the grey flight suit, "And this is Major Henter. We've got two Coveys today because of the work we'll be doing in the Anvil. Like it or not, you're first day back will be a busy one."

Returning to his map, Billy continues, "Here's what it looks like. We're putting four teams into the Anvil, about... ah... here. They'll be inserted one klick apart, in a box pattern. Then we'll wait and see what we flush out." His eyes sparkle when he speaks of getting the enemy to start any action with his teams. Within Special Operations, Billy is known for his daring and unorthodox schemes.

"If things go the way we think, one of them will get in contact within an hour of insertion. The other three teams will then move toward the contact and not only provide fire support but if needed, a blocking force for any NVA re-enforcements. If necessary, we'll launch the Hatch Force. They're assembled and ready to go." He casts an eye around to all three of us standing before him. "Our mission is to see who's out there and what they are up to. It's not a walk in the park, but a recon by force so to speak. I do not expect them to be out there for more than twenty-four hours."

He then concludes his briefing to the Coveys, during which the helicopter pilots start entering the hootch. The door slams several times as the Ghost Rider ACs straggle in. Billy will repeat this basic briefing again, but will add the call-signs and other information that I missed, but the Coveys noted prior to my arrival. Once everyone is seated, Billy calls to Milo to drive the Covey pilots over to Quang Tri Airfield so that they can get airborne. They'll need to check with all the teams we have out in Southern Laos before they cruise down to the Anvil to check on weather and the prospective LZs.

After the two leave, Billy brings our group to silence with a simple cough. Though Sergeant Major Washburn is a lower rank than a Warrant Office One Junior Grade, and at least twice the age of most of the pilots sitting in the room, his simple clearing of the throat has caused all of the men to not only sit up straight but give him their undivided attention. We find out that the Riders have brought up six aircraft. Billy tells them that one, who will fly trail on all flights today, will carry two *bac si* on board. The other extra slick will be used on all flights as an extra aircraft, but really will be needed if we have to insert the Hatch Force. Then, as if just thinking about it, Billy says we can use the fifth Huey to carry out team members for the first four insertions as well. Without directly implying it, the message is clear through the briefing; we'll be in for some heavy combat all day. After all, we are going there spoiling for a fight, and in the Anvil you can get one without looking too hard. We'll get plenty of flight hours today, and we'll each get to use our weapons systems frequently.

After an in-depth briefing and far too many questions from a

Ghost Rider Captain, we break up and go to our aircraft. We won't take off for thirty to forty minutes while the Coveys check out the area and radio back that they are ready for us. Then things will be busy. Now, milling around several of the aircraft are small groups of men; joking, smoking, some rechecking the machine guns one final time, and the Griffins sitting on the sides of their aircraft's ammo bay doors.

Billy takes this opportunity to get some good-natured ribbing in, stopping by each aircraft to explain to the crews that if shot in the foot inspect it first. Someday, I don't know how, I'm going to get even, but today is all his.

Milo, running out of the Operations Hut, is waving his hand in a circular motion. This is it, I climb into the back seat and strap the four belts into position. I'm now a part of the aircraft. Cinching the belts tightly is like pulling a second skin around you. You and the Cobra become one. Quickly my mindset goes into its combat mode. Play time is over.

With your right thumb massaging the red cyclic button it becomes an extension of the electrical connection touching the end of each rocket. You push the button, it throws the switch and a charge goes though, igniting the rocket and sending it on its fiery way. Think about banking right and the Cobra banks right. No need for erratic cyclic movements, you think movements and they happen. Just as you breathe without thinking about it, your subtle movements are done without thought. You and the Cobra have become one.

Looking up on the right front canopy window, I realize I can barely read Lardo's scribbled call-signs. After getting turned up, I jot the needed call-signs down next to me so I don't have to try to figure his scribbling out or look down to my knee pad. His writing is as bad as mine, but smaller.

Sitting with my helmet on, I watch RT Mamba load into the slicks. Upon refueling we'll head out to the AO together. "Double D" McIntyre tells me the Griffins are ready.

"Quang Tri Tower. Sneaky White with a flight of four

Griffins at CCN for POL, we have the numbers." I close my window since we'll get the clearance right away.

"Sneaky White you're cleared direct to POL. You have the numbers."

"Roger, we have the numbers. Sneaky White and flight lifting."

We reposition to the fuel pits. Upon landing, the co-pilots get out to top us off.

On our unit VHF push, I remind the AC's. "Keep a close eye on everybody. We'll have a lot of aircraft out there. This can turn into a goat fuck real quick."

VHF squelch breaks are confirmation that everybody is up and listening. We watch as the Ghost Riders, from A Company of the 158th Assault Helicopter Battalion of the 101st ABN, land to refuel. RT members climb out, loaded down with belts of extra ammo and extra hand grenades hanging from every conceivable spot. This is not going to be a multi-day patrol. Most have green scarves tied tightly around their heads, though a few have boonie hats crumpled in a manner to break the straight line that's obvious when hiding in the foliage. They're using US issued web gear and weapons, not the normal captured NVA gear used in regular cross-border operations. Almost all have either a .45 caliber or 9mm automatic pistol strapped to their waist, and several have M-79s slung across their backs. Two of them are carrying shotguns. It's obvious they're going in for a fight and all they need is ammo, not food. The mission is simple, get in and shake things up. Once the shooting starts, we'll try to overpower the enemy with extra teams and air power. If we're lucky and some unlucky NVA, hopefully an officer, meets up with us, we'll capture somebody. At least Billy had mentioned that a POW snatch would be something to try for.

The Ghost Rider Lead, the inquisitive captain, gives me a thumbs up after the crew-chief and door gunners help the heavily laden green forms back onto the bare Huey floors.

"Quang Tri, Sneaky White with a flight of four snakes and six slicks at POL for take off."

"Sneaky White your flight is cleared. Altimeter twenty-niner forty-four. Winds are calm. DA seven-eight-zero. Have a good flight Sneaky." It's apparent to the controller, an untrained non-combat eye, that the bodies sitting on these Huey floors are going to look for some trouble and one shouldn't delay them in their search.

I know the duty Air Force controller from my days with the Sneaky Whites at Dong Ha. Not many pilots in Nam have units named after them. The only other Army ARA unit, the Blue Max, was named after one of their senior warrants, a guy named Maxwell. The 108th Arty Group is now named the Sneaky Whites. What started out to be the Black Maria's was changed because of a night I spent leaving a whorehouse.

The slicks, now at a hover, start their dance to the active. It's not like the normal one. No, these Hueys are loaded down and seem to be straining to reach the recommended three-foot hover. We let their rotor wash blow away before we start to the active. They're ahead of us in a lazy straggling formation, straining for all the power they can get. We're in no better shape. Overloaded with rockets, turret ammo and fuel, we're barely able to pass through translational lift and get airborne.

"Quang Tri, Sneaky White's flight is QSY to the west."

Changing the radios to the Covey push, I hear the FACs talking to Billy. The primary LZ will not be used. We'll be inserting into the secondary, though I didn't catch the reason why.

We pass Camp Carroll before we've closed around the slicks. It's an uneventful flight to Khe Sanh. I would normally give my co-pilot a running commentary of the area and the many battles fought here, especially if it's the first time he's flown with me. But with Lardo, I pass it up. As we pass over Khe Sanh, the lead Ghost Rider directs the extra Huey to orbit over the old Marine airstrip at a thousand feet rather than follow the package to the Anvil. It's not normal to leave an aircraft alone this far out in Indian country, but their lead is a captain and he's in charge of his flight. Our safety is in numbers, but a high orbit over Khe Sanh is as safe as one can get out here.

"Black Market, this is Huckleberry Finn Three-Four. Bring the package over. We'll be inserting into the secondary Lima Zulu. I've over flown the primary and there was activity."

Hell, activity means NVA are in the area and you can bet the other LZs will be hot.

"Roger Three-Four, we're on the way."

We maintain our altitude, though it will cause the slicks going into the LZ a lot of exposure time. When flying in Khe Sanh valley, altitude is a good thing.

"Fox Bravo, advise you approach from the November Echo. Depart by taking a sharp right one eighty and exit the same way you came in. Try not to overfly the road to the Sierra," the lead Covey, Huckleberry Finn Three-Four, Cpt. McDermott advises.

We're approaching the Coveys' tight orbit. One is Major Henter who is four or five hundred feet above and flying to the one-eighty from his wingman, Captain McDermott, but always keeping him in sight. If we take gunfire, it will be from the high speed trail, really almost a two-lane road running east-west. After the insertion of the second recon team, we'll have to deal with the large anti-aircraft guns from Co Roc. I expect this will be a busy day with a lot of gunfire delivered by both sides.

"Three-Four, ah . . . we'll start our descent if you will give us a positive on the Lima Zulu. E'Clair and Double D hold back and escort the package. Cool and I will prep the Lima Zulu."

We're less than five hundred feet above the ground as I start searching for the secondary LZ. Covey Lead, Finn Three-Four, is diving down before us to an area of scrub vegetation, when he fires a single Willie Pete. I wasn't prepared for it, but it's the quickest and best way to get a positive on the LZ. Looking over my shoulder I see First Lieutenant James "Cool" Poole has closed up on my wing.

Cool has the Kid as a co-pilot. Since the day we got shot up, the Kid has been in the air on every Second Platoon flight. Flying with Cool will be new to him. Cool earned the nickname from having a head full of blond hair, blue eyes, and being a native Californian who goes around being "cool". At least, he thinks so. He's from a place called San Fernando Valley. I'm not sure if it's a town or just a rural valley. Californians are not only different, but the people from this "valley" area are even more so. A subculture of California, which is a subculture of the United States. Though twenty-three, he acts sixteen and is in constant search of a party. Other than a beer once in a great while, he spends most of his time with the enlisted troops listening to music and smoking grass. Though a good AC, he'll never make Section Leader because of the grass smoking.

In the Griffins only a couple of pilots smoke marijuana. The lower junior enlisted men seem to enjoy it more than booze, probably it's cheaper and more accessible. Those not smoking it turn their backs to those that do. Me, I don't, nor do I party with those that do.

Vietnam's American military visitors can be broken into two groups when classifying their form of relaxation. The boozers, who are further divided into two groups called alkies who drink only beer, and the lushes who drink anything. Usually, only the lowest three enlisted ranks are the alkies. The lushes are mostly NCOs and Officers who are able to purchase beer, wine or hard liquor either on ration cards or in their respective clubs.

The others are the pot-heads and dopers. The dopers are usually the younger men from the urban areas of the States and have turned to drugs because our military, under the leadership of USARV military commanders, have restricted them from buying hard liquor. So the local population, exercising the free market economy we're trying to teach them, sells drugs of all sorts by the roadside, through hootch maids, barbers, and prostitutes. If it's a Vietnamese national you're talking to, by and large they either have dope for sale or can speedily direct you to a site where it's cheaply available, though they do not use it, they see the need to supply the young Americans with it.

While I was with the 484th TC Detachment (KD) unit

attached to the 282nd Assault Helicopter Company at Marble Mountain Air Station south of China Beach, we received some incoming 122mm rockets overnight. As soon as the first one hit the compound I was up and sober as a judge and headed for the shelter even though I had been passed out drunk, hours before. Two pilots, known potheads, at the other end of our hootch were too far gone and laid in their bunks throughout the barrage. The hootch took a direct hit killing one of them and causing the other to lose both his legs. That night, amongst the blood and gore, I gave up any thoughts about marijuana.

"I'll fire a couple pair then break around and meet up with the package."

Cool immediately answers, "I'll stick on you."

Every rocket must count out here. Seeing the wisps of grey-white smoke spiral into the air, I know where to shoot. I start a gradual glide toward the target. This shallow gun run is risky, especially in the Anvil area.

When firing nails, you control the spread of the flechettes by two factors: distance from the target and firing angle. The closer you are to the target, the smaller the impact area will be. The angle allows you to have a pattern that can vary from an oval, steep angle, to a ray pattern when you're firing from a shallow angle. When training new pilots, we take them over the South China Sea so they can watch where the flechettes hit the water. Then, after many passes, they learn what altitude and attitude they need to be in to get the pattern they are looking for.

Flechettes, or nails, are the best ordnance we fire. Inside each flesh colored domed warhead are 2,200 inch-and-a-quarter darts. Once leaving the warhead, they're effective, very effective! Not good against buildings or reinforced bunkers, but in the bush or sparse vegetation, they'll kill everything on the ground. It's said that if you fire a pair from the standard gun run approach starting at fifteen hundred feet above ground level, you could put a dart in every square foot of a football field and it would produce 97% casualties. So far, I've never been able to fire at any NVA milling about on a football field, but I'm keeping my eyes open for the chance.

Several months ago, while flying a CCN mission, Sweet Griffin caught some NVA on a gentle slopping hill. They tried to hide behind the trees. When Sweet Griffin rolled in from behind, he literally nailed them to the trees. For a reward, the Recon Team brought Sweet Griffin back several shirts with little blood stained holes. The darts didn't stop with the shirts or flesh, but imbedded into the trees. So the team had to literally peal the shirts, with body, away from the tree.

When firing for the purpose of clearing an LZ with no friendlies around, I try to make the impact area as large as possible. For this mission, I want some altitude, but this run I've got little. So it'll have to be a run where the darts go all over the place.

"Inbound."

The pipper's at the base of the smoke and I stroke the red button once, then twice. Rockets plunge for the target. Prior to pushing the button the second and third time, I've pushed the rudder pedals, to spread the rockets around.

"Breaking left." I start my climb out.

"Taking Fire! Holy Shit! Taking Fire!" my front seater yells before I have a chance to call, or for that matter react.

Slamming the cyclic back to the right jerks us out of trim and into a slip. A fifty-one is firing at us from the dirt track that might pass as a road.

I get the pipper onto the source of the stream of tracers. It's more than one. A quad fifty. Rare inside South Vietnam. Deadly for those within it's range. Our rocket's range is about the same as a fifty-one. Cobra pilots find it challenging to go against them. It comes down to who is the better. In order to kill him, I have to be in his range. In order to kill me, he'll be in mine.

"We're on the fifty-one!" I scream.

"Break away! Break away!" someone is yelling.

No fucking way. I've got 'em right where I want. I'm low and fast. The red glow of the pipper is now dancing on the offending clump of brush. I have a perfect bead on the gun emplacement. I keep flying toward him, massaging the red button of death as we close in. I'm "into the mouth".

"We're hit! We're going down!"

The NVA gunner has found his mark. Flying toward him firing rockets I've let his stream of rounds hit the right side of our aircraft. I keep firing. White-greenish balls keep coming at us. Looking like basketballs now, they're not falling away. We're in each other's range and both of us are scoring hits. Like a pinball machine with it's buzzers and lights flashing all around trying to distract you from the mission at hand, the flashes of gunfire erupt from the ground.

"Get out of there! It's a ZPU! Get Out!" Poole's yelling.

ZPU! Shit, I'm in trouble. A fifty-one-caliber gun, classified as a 12.7mm by the NVA, shoots a round approximately a half inch in diameter. A ZPU shoots a 23mm round which is almost a full inch in diameter. Usually mounted in a quad emplacement and on the back of a truck, officially called a ZPU-4. A couple of times I've seem them mounted on a small two wheeled trailer, but when mounted this way it usually has only two barrels. Its range is twice that of a fifty-one.

Can't break away. I keep flying unthinkingly to the target. If I change direction, he'll have an unmolested shot at me. Cobras have no door gunners, nor any defense from a broadside shot. The turret can be used with limited success, but not today and not by Lardo. My only option is to give him the narrowest target possible. Like a prize fighter defending himself in the corner while being plummeted, I instinctively stand and exchange blows rather than try to slide away. It's survival.

A Cobra is only thirty-nine inches wide, except for the stub wings mounted on the sides. The wings have four hard points for mounting armament. Mine are holding the four nineteen-tube rocket pods which I'm trying to empty as fast as I can. It will take a good shot to hit me in a frontal view.

An explosion rocks us to the left, then we're jerked around to the right. We're taking more hits!

"We're hit! Ah, going down!" Lardo is still yelling. At least he's started shooting his turret.

Zero-Two-Seven has twin 40mm cannons. They can't be fired simultaneously; but for the type of area we're in, it's the best turret weapon to have. Under us, the ammo bay compartment is holding the two shiny stainless steel drums, each with four-hundred rounds of 40mm ammo. There are no friendlies on the ground; so wherever the rounds go off, they're only going to kill enemy. In scrub vegetation, the round will cause a lot of damage. A variation of the 40mm M-79 round used by our infantry, it has a good fifteen meters killing range. The round flies through the air so slowly that if the sunlight is just right you can watch it travel. I bet Lardo isn't watching the rounds glide through the air. He's just firing.

"Hit the road!" Screaming as impacting rounds rattle me. I don't like getting shot at.

"Break away Sneaky!" Poole's still yelling from his trail position.

"Do not! Do not bring the package over! Break away and go to Khe Sanh!" Covey is aborting the insert until we can get things straightened out.

I'm a few hundred yards from the gun and I see it's sitting on the bed of a truck. Looks like an old WW-II Japanese model probably left over from their occupation in the late thirties and early forties. Now it's all covered with a makeshift camouflage of brush. Brown-suited soldiers are running about but not for long.

Why scan instruments? At this point, it isn't going to help. We're in Indian country where the big guns are. All I can do is lay out as much fire as I can and hope we can limp back to the Khe Sanh airstrip. Right now those fifteen-sixteen klicks to due north seem a long way away. I sure don't want to walk out and any slick trying to land to pick us up is in for a rough ride. I've got to keep us flying.

The truck takes four rockets directly onto its bed. Almost ten thousand darts are concentrated into this small area. Instantly, all fire from the gun stops. With only nails, I'm not able to destroy the gun, just kill the gunners. They'll replace the gunners as fast as we can turn around. Flying directly over it at less than fifty feet, and going two hundred knots, it would take a good rifleman to hit us. But it seems they have a lot of riflemen out here today.

"We're staying low and are headed back to Khe Sanh," I scream into the radio and, for the first time scan the instruments. The Master Caution Panel has not come on and things seem to all be in the green. "Took a hit and will have to RTB."

Looking out the right canopy window, I see damage. Flapping in the wind, sheet metal is bent out of shape from a 23mm round. This is major damage, judging by the size. But it's only on the stub wing, and this contains no flight control equipment, so it should be an uneventful flight back. But the noise and the yawing sure felt like a lot more.

"You're crazy! Get altitude asshole!" Lardo is carrying on, while blazing away with the pooper.

"Hold your fire unless you've got a target." Saying on UHF instead of intercom. "Covey, Market Lead, we've got damage but we're still in the green. I'll head for Khe Sanh, then if I can, I'll return to Evans. If you want to go ahead with the insert, Market Nine-Two Kilo can do it. I'll have the slick at Khe Sanh escort me back."

"Negative Black Market Lead. All aircraft abort and return to Quang Tri." Covey must have relayed what happened to Billy. "We're going to run in some fast movers, then wait for clearance to go back in."

At least someone is thinking. Now to nurse this wounded and maimed beast home. The second time I've got it shot up since coming back from leave.

"E'Clair, you escort the package, I'll follow with the extra Ghost Rider. I'll cut him loose at Quang Tri, then single ship to

Evans." Before getting a reply I switch to VHF. "Griffin Three." A lot of static. "Griffin Three. Sneaky, over." Static. We're too far out.

"*Dai Uy* turn the Victor all the way up." Without altitude they're not able to hear us.

I try again, but still not enough altitude.

"Covey Lead, would you tell Rabbit Hutch to relay to Griffin Three I'm headed back. Also, have them get another aircraft ready." One of the Covey's aircraft darts into a steep climb getting a line of sight transmission to Quang Tri.

"You're fucking crazy! You know that? Fucking crazy! Those rounds were coming right at us."

He still hasn't quit. Fuck him. "Listen asshole. I'm driving. Not you! Sit there and shut the fuck up, until I tell you to talk!"

This is not the tact Major Stafford has wanted me to exercise, but I'm not in a good or tactful mood at the moment.

"Roger Sneaky, we'll forward it." Covey breaks.

Chapter 10

It's an uneventful trip back except for the normal chatter that comes after a mission, even an aborted one. After passing over Camp J. J. Carroll, I release the escort Ghost Rider Huey to return to CCN and proceed southeast toward Evans.

"Griffin Three, Sneaky White inbound to maintenance with severe battle damage. I'd like to have another aircraft ready." Telling them there's damage will expedite the normally lazy pace that Operations and Maintenance Officers seem to instill into those working around them. They're not out here flying, where time can mean lives.

"Griffin Nine-Two Gulf, go directly to the Pit." Must be Jolly Roger, he never replies to me with my Sneaky White call-sign. "You'll be met by maintenance, and they'll assess whether another aircraft is needed, over."

"Three, I know you still don't think I know too much about maintenance, but on landing I'm sure that Four-Six will advise you I have damage." Jolly Roger can't believe I can tell if a plane is mission ready when I've got it strapped to my ass.

"Nine-Two Gulf, I have notified Four-Six you're inbound. Over." It's a crisp over, meaning it isn't.

"Evans Tower. Sneaky White with one snake inbound to the Griffin Pit. We're northwest and we have the numbers, over."

"Roger Sneaky White. Call when you're at the boundaries."

"Griffin Nine-Two Gulf, this is Griffin Four-Six. Could you describe your damage? Over."

Captain Sherrily is now on the radio for an in-flight

evaluation of the battle damage. Jolly Roger probably told him it may not be that bad.

Might as well stir things up further. Our VHF is monitored by the Griffin TOC, Griffin Maintenance, a radio in the Old Man's office with speakers in his living quarters, and in the Battalion TOC.

"Be advised Four-Six, we have taken several 23 mike-mike hits. Do you copy, Two . . . Three . . . Mike . . . Mike . . . Hits! No injuries but . . . Ah . . . We have some new air-conditioning. How do you copy? Over." Surely this will get everybody to sit up in their seats.

"Ah . . . Roger . . . Ah . . . You what?"

"Break . . . Break! This is Three, did you say two-three mike-mike hits?"

"Be advised, please repeat as the last was garbled." Now I have them listening.

On UHF. "Evans, Sneaky White on final with a direct approach from the northwest to the Griffin Pit. Weapons cold. I have the numbers."

"You're cleared, Sneaky. Cleared across the active direct to the Pit. Winds are calm. Altimeter two-niner four-one."

"Roger, cleared direct, winds calm, altimeter two-niner four-one."

Switching back to VHF, "Sneaky's on long final."

"Roger Sneaky."

A new voice from the TOC which means Jolly Roger has left and is headed to the pits. It's the deep, slow, southern accent of the Spec Four who lives with Wee Willie.

As I flare to the PSP pad, I observe several jeeps parked in front of the hanger. It's the greeting party of non-flying flight officers, now gathered and looking intently in our direction. Hovering to the front of the hanger, I turn, letting the right stub wing with its peeled-back metal face the group. The exit hole is at least a foot and a half in diameter and with metal flapping in the wind it appears much larger.

Heads are shaking. I'm not sure if in disgust or amusement. Either way it means work for the metalsmiths. I'll be sure to buy several cases of beer for these guys, especially if they can fix it quickly.

I start my shutdown procedure as Captain Lardo climbs out. He takes his helmet off and throws it to the ground. Apparently he feels it's his place to put on a display like this. He comes around to my side and, and opens my window while I'm taking my helmet off, and starts yelling.

"You fucking bastard! You goddamned son-of-a-bitch! Were you trying to get us killed? Look at it!" Then he turns pointing to the stub wing I've looked at for the last twenty-five minutes.

"Calm down. It's nothing. I got us home, didn't I." I look past him at the dozen or so inspecting the stub wing. The grin on my face is all part of the Sneaky image. It's appropriate to display this bravado every time I get my ass shot up.

"Fuck you! I'm talking about on the other side!"

I look out the left canopy window and see nothing out of the ordinary. This guy's not going to make it if he feels this bad over one hit. Undoing my harness I see the crowd of men moving to the Cobra's left and pointing at that side of the aircraft. What's wrong? I climb out and shove past Lardo, who's still putting on a big scene.

"Sherrily, you got another aircraft? We'll need all we can get up there today." Still ignoring Lardo, I walk around to the other side.

Pushing through the throng, I see what's got the wrath of my co-pilot. On the left side, going down the side at about waist level from the copilot and knee level for the Aircraft Commander, me, the metal has been peeled back. It starts within two feet of the nose, which is a fiberglass cosmetic cover now that they've moved the landing light to the belly of the aircraft. It ends at the base of the engine, beyond the hell hole, where the aircraft fuselage narrows.

I have taken a twenty-three hit on the left side as well as the right stub wing. The damage is bad but we had luck, it could have hit our tail rotor and we'd have been in big trouble, maybe even gone down. This round traveled down a reinforced metal plate on the aircraft's side.

Lardo, now next to me seething, "See, goddamn it! You tried to kill me. Shit, you went right at it."

"Right. It's why I have a fat fucking captain in the front seat."

Everybody's looking, as we stand face to face. Are blows going to be exchanged? It's happened in my past, with a West Point major who was the 108th S-1 and had peed on himself during a hairy scout mission.

"Always wanted a fat bastard in the front seat to stop any stray rounds that might be headed my way."

My contempt for the new captain has boiled over and is showing to everyone. They know what kind of pilot I am, so their thoughts must be that the captain screwed up somewhere during the flight. He may have, if the feedback I felt in the controls can't be traced back to battle damage, then he tried to override me. But for me, this is two battle damaged aircraft in the past two flights. Am I getting old, out of touch??? It might be me.

"That's enough Mr. White." Major Stafford interjects. I didn't see him arrive. "Do you need to get back up to CCN?"

"Yes Sir, they'll need us all day. In fact, if we can spare another two crews, it would help. They have some heavy operations planned today. This was the first and we didn't even get the team inserted. We should have two Section Leaders. It'll be that busy. They've got a Hatch Force sitting on the pad, so they know it's going to be a shit sandwich."

"Roger," Stafford looking at Jolly Roger. "Can you get it cleared with Battalion?"

"I'll get right on it Sir," Still looking at me. "What aircraft will you be taking back up Sneaky?"

Glancing over to Captain Sherrily for an aircraft assignment, he points to the last revetment. "Take One-One-Five, but the turret doesn't work."

"Got it." I walk through the ever-increasing gathering to get my flight equipment. Already Wee Willie has climbed up and hands the gear down to me.

"Do you need all these freqs?"

"No, got it all on my knee pad. I'm sorry. I didn't want to get it blasted like this."

Wee Willie worked so hard to get it flying right away. The life of a crew-chief in Nam is one of never-ending work. Though he knows I didn't do it intentionally, he still has to pay for my actions.

"No problem. Big shit today." He smiles.

Though our crew-chiefs don't fly with us, they're very much a part of each mission. I try to include Willie in all of the things that are going on when I get back in at night. If I were flying Charlie model gunships, or LOHs flying scouts, he'd be my crew-chief. His sense of humor is great and he wouldn't let fear take control. Flying combat missions always generates fear. The issue is whether you let it take control of you, or you take control of it. It is a delicate balance.

In the Marines, I learned that size doesn't tell you who's brave. Once I was flying with the largest door gunner in HMM-262, a newly re-enlisted staff sergeant. We got into trouble and he fell apart, just laid on the floor. Several months later while going out on a night medivac, I had a gunner assigned to me that was so puny that no one could understand how he made it through boot camp. We took a lot of fire that mission and all through the mission this one hundred and forty pound, skinny, Marine hung out the door exposing himself while I worked the winch to bring up the wounded. The kid had balls. Lesson learned. Size don't mean shit.

Nix joins me as I walk to the revetment. "What was it? Too big for a fifty-one."

"I thought it was a quad fifty but it turned out to be a ZPU-4. Scared the hell out of me." I'm not used to talking to anyone about my fears. It's uncomfortable, especially at a time like this. "Guess we came close to buying it. The Captain didn't do too good." Being able to tell someone that I was scared takes a load off me, even if it is Nix.

Jimbo has been loaning him to Sherrily to help with maintenance. He and I worked together while I was recuperating these past weeks. We've come to a mutual understanding and have gained a respect for one another. One afternoon, I was going to take an aircraft out on a test flight. It had just come out of an annual inspection and would have had many gripes written up once the flight was finished. Nix asked to come along. After a long and very detailed preflight, I, at the last moment, told him to take the back seat. For an hour and a half, I took him though the test flight syllabus, then I passed the test flight manual back to him. He, for the first time in his career, took an aircraft through the syllabus. When we finished refueling, I suggested we do it again, and, for the second time and a lot more relaxed, he went through the syllabus. That night, in the club, he bought me a beer and thanked me for the time I'd spent with him. Major Stafford would have been proud of my tact, if he'd only known.

Rumor is Nix will be going in the next few days to 2nd Brigade, called Brandy Flight, to fly the Brigade Commander. This talk lets him know that I do realize just how bad things were this morning and I'm not a carefree pilot. Maybe his departure will end on an up note with me.

One-One-Five's crew-chief is getting the plane ready as we get to it. He's an older Spec 4 on his third tour. He's been busted several times. According to rumors, he was escorted out of Germany after getting caught with some high ranking German officer's daughter in the back seat of a Volkswagen. How he did whatever it was to the Fraulein in the back seat, I'll never know, but it makes for a good story. He's a good crew-chief but short on words around pilots. We get along only because as Wee Willie says, "He knows you were a crew-chief."

I start a quick preflight. During my walk around, Lardo comes up and throws his equipment into the front seat. "White!

When we get back tonight, you and I are going to have a long fucking talk. You understand me mister?"

"No problem, I'll be at the club," I smile because his outburst after our landing will be considered as a response to fear. With everyone watching, he'll have to try to straighten this out or carry a yellow streak down his back that will follow him throughout his career.

Fear is permissible, but not allowed to be expressed in the Griffins. You just repress it in the pit of your stomach and the back of your mind. In the Griffins we have three levels of pilots. Those who'll fly anywhere anytime, and any weather. There's the group who avoids CCN missions or just flat out refuses to fly them. Officially, they don't have to fly the volunteer missions. Hell, you can get killed going from Camp Evans to Fire Base Nancy; so what's the difference. Dying in Laos, South, or North Vietnam wouldn't make a hill of beans to anyone. If you're dead, you're dead! Then there are the non-flying flight officers. These are the men whose silver wings mean a couple hundred extra dollars a month and the prestige of being an Army Aviator. They're not good enough and they know it. Whether it's fear or just being a lousy pilot, in their own way they're probably saving the line pilot's lives by not adding their uncontrolled or unchecked fear to a dangerous mission. When you mix it up with the bad guys, you'd better come prepared, and this means all crew members.

I climb in and quickly strap in. I start the engine and, while waiting for the temperatures to climb to normal, I write the pushes onto the left canopy. After getting clearance, we back out and hover to the pad. A jeep with Sweet Griffin and three pilots drives by. They will be the extra crews coming up to CCN. This will help with the amount of work and the area. Especially having Sweet Griffin up there.

We fly back to CCN in silence. Lardo's stewing over the hits we took. On landing, it's time to break the ice. If we have another hot mission today, I want him alert.

"*Dai Uy*, I would say we flew right down the mouth of that

bastard, wouldn't you?"

He looks into the mirror and shakes his head.

"Yeah, taking hits on both sides was weird. You know, I wasn't trying to get us killed." Before he has a chance to comment, I pull off my helmet and hang it on the small hook hanging down from the upper canopy. I finish the shutdown in silence and without looking at the mirror.

Several of the pilots walk up. E'Clair looks up at me and shaking his head says, "Asshole! Didn't you know what it was?"

"Hell no. If I had, I sure would have let the fixed-wings fuck with it." I say, but not too convincingly.

"I've heard that one before. Before we go in there for the briefing you had better watch Rider Lead. He doesn't want to fly any more today. Says the area is too hot and he doesn't want to lose any of his aircraft or crew."

"What's Billy say?" His will be the final decision.

"He's in there having a talk with Captain America. There is no doubt we're going back out. I expect we'll insert the Hatch Force and have a real donnybrook. Then . . . a quick extract with fast movers cleaning up any leftovers." As an afterthought, E'Clair points to the end of the pad and where the Hatch Force members are all suited up and pacing. Their adrenalin is starting to flow.

"Okay. Lets see what the deal is."

Climbing out I walk to the Operations Hut. Opening the door, I see the pilots sitting on the wooden benches looking at an animated discussion between Billy and Captain America.

Captain Steve Stanton, also known as Captain America, is the Detachment Commander of MLT 2. He's on his fourth Vietnam tour. His first was with a Special Forces A Team, then two tours running recon with one of the CCN teams. This newest assignment will help him in future career assignments as this is considered an administrative or staff assignment. He hates it, and he'd rather be out in the field but he knows the rules for career advancement. Young, blond, well built but not overly muscular, and highly articulate. He's from Colorado and loves to snow ski, so every leave is scheduled in the winter and to the slopes he goes. Years ago someone gave him the nickname Captain America and it's stuck.

"Nice of you to make it back. You get another aircraft, or is yours still flyable?"

Billy and I are good friends and as the years go by I find he's the closest I'll ever have to a father figure, and over the years has become my surrogate father. His wife works at the Smoke Bomb Hill mini post exchange, and acts as a grandmother to my, and many Green Beret's, children. They call her Auntie Stella, and when visiting her, kids can do no wrong.

"Got a bit hot out there for ya?"

"Yeah, got another plane and had my fat captain clean his shorts."

Warrants sitting around chuckle. Most know there's probably some truth to it. Going against a ZPU can be deadly. Plus Lardo isn't here, I left him sitting on the open ammo bay door, pouting.

"Supposed to be another two coming up."

"Yeah, saw Sweet Griffin with another crew headed to the pits when we took off. He should be in here soon."

"We'll wait for them then have a briefing. If you want to eat, the 'yards are cooking in the back."

Captain America knows I love to eat native food, rather than the coveted LURPS that most of the flight crews try to get. Whenever possible I go to the 'yard's hootch and see what's in the pot. Well, pots; 'yards cook many course meals.

While going out the back door I pass Master Sergeant Earksen sitting at the radios, and hear Sweet Griffin announce he's on final. This won't give me much time to eat. Eating with 'yards, or Vietnamese for that matter, can be quite a long, drawn out experience. It's more a social event than what Westerners make of it.

Entering the 'yard hootch I see that I'm just in time.

I walk to the right to the end of the hootch. At the end is a small, by 'yard standards, make-shift kitchen. Quickly the old 'yard fills several small mismatched plates of steaming food.

I sit on the bamboo rug and immediately start to eat. What normally would take an hour, I complete in less than fifteen minutes. As I'm cleaning up the last from the plate, the Kid yells for me to come to the briefing. I thank the old 'yard, get up and walk out feeling full and content. I really would like a nap but business calls.

Billy and Captain America are taking us through their plan for the insertion. Pilots and some recon team members are seated in the Operations hut. In the background, Hatch Force Team members are leaning against the wall. Though only Americans are allowed in the briefing, the 'yards going on this mission know what is expected of them. I'm finishing a luke-warm soda after a quick but filling meal of rice and fish the old 'yard shared with me.

Billy has given all the frequencies and call-signs. He's surprised us with the disclosure that he, Blister and Valentino will be going in as strap-hangers with the Hatch Force. Captain Stanton will be directing the operation from overhead in one of the Coveys.

It's a straight forward plan. We'll insert the Hatch Force Team and two of the recon teams onto the ZPU's location. We'll use the other two recon teams as a backup in case things get out of hand. Billy wants to go quickly and move to an intersection east of the ZPU's location, while grabbing a prisoner on the way. We're fairly sure it is well defended because of the heavy guns deployed in the area. We'll extract immediately after a prisoner is captured. He stresses that this will not be an overnight mission but one of getting in, then getting the hell out.

Captain America points out we'll be using the old Khe Sanh strip as a mini-staging area. While the pilots understand his concerns, we're not all in favor of this. His plan is to have the two backup recon teams at Khe Sanh, so they'll only be ten minutes away if needed. This is better than having to wait the hour and twenty minutes for the round trip to bring them from the MLT.

Using the radio relay site, Hickory, is out of the question. From an observation point it would be helpful, but it's too far out of the way. Also its altitude would require carrying only three team members per ship up, and off, the mountain peak. Hopefully the Ghost Riders can carry six team members per ship.

It's decided to first carry the four recon teams out to Khe Sanh. We'll return, refuel, pickup the Hatch Force at 90 to Khe Sanh. We'll land and pick up two of the recon teams, then insert the whole package. This will leave a reserve of two teams sitting on Khe Sanh airstrip. We'll escort the package with two Cobras each way, then use four Cobras on the insert while the other two are refueling.

Sweet Griffin and I have decided that Poole and I will fly the two ship team. Sweet Griffin will control the four ship flight. It's a highly experienced group with Sweet Griffin. He's brought CWO 2 "Doodle" Woodruff, who's also a section leader and the unit artist. (The Battalion staff found out about his handy work and he's had to go to Camp Eagle to do work for them as well as the many requests he gets within the Griffins.) Though I should lead the four ship operation, I worry about how much cooperation I'm going to get from Lardo. With Sweet Griffin up there, things are in good hands. In an operation this size, section leaders are busy with many things and don't have time to baby-sit. In my case, there's also the worry about an arrogant and scared Captain who might try to override the flight controls, plus I have no operative nose turret.

After all questions have been asked and duties gone over, Billy excuses most of us to go to our ships and get ready. He asks for Ghost Rider Lead, Sweet Griffin, and me to stay back during his briefing with the team members. Captain America tells Milo to drive him over to the Quang Tri airstrip to meet with the inbound Covey.

Billy's second briefing is short. They're to be inserted and move to the east along the road. They'll be just south of the track with the intention of capturing a prisoner and gathering any other intelligence materials laying about. He then assigns the positions of the recon teams in respect to the Hatch Force. It's to last no longer than a couple of hours. There are no questions—these men know their business and have trained many, many days for a mission like this. Billy steps back and lets the teams pore over the map. The One-Zeros cross-check their pocket maps against data on the large one. They all want to be sure they know where they'll be and what the others will be doing.

Sweet Griffin and I leave the hut, with the Captain muttering how bad it is going to be. We each go to our respective aircraft, waiting for the word to turn up and take off—the typical Army 'hurry up and wait' mode has set in.

Milo returns and signals us to load up and head to Khe Sanh. I'll escort the first flight of slicks out, then stay overhead while the slicks go back and get the Hatch Force. Sweet Griffin will escort their return. When they reach the old Vandegrift Marine base they'll call, then Cool and I will depart Khe Sanh and go refuel. This way we'll maintain gunship cover over the teams sitting on Khe Sanh strip for most of the time.

Sweet Griffin's flight will overfly the pickup of the extra teams, then lead the insert. As soon as possible, I'll return to overfly the Hatch Force's movement to their objective. Sweet Griffin will have two Cobras go re-arm and refuel as soon as I get on station. Our goal is to have Cobra coverage at all times, hopefully four of us.

Covey has laid on a flight of four Spads and several flights of fast movers. Need all the fixed-wing support we can muster. From this morning's experience, I think we will need it. It's normally a hot area and, if the encounter with a ZPU-4 is any indication of what's out there waiting for us, we'll be busy from the moment we arrive.

"Ghost Rider Lead is up."

"Roger." I switch over to VHF. "You up?" I ask Cool as I look over and see him giving a thumbs up.

"Quang Tri Tower, Sneaky White with a flight of two Cobras and six slicks at CCN pad for departure to the west."

"Roger Sneaky." It's the familiar Air Force controller working his long twelve hour shift. "You're cleared for take-off. Current altimeter twenty-niner forty-six. Winds three-two at one-five. DA niner-four-zero. Have a good flight."

"Roger we're lifting."

I lift to a hover while turning sideways into the wind, to get a better view of the Hueys. With my left hand I wave for the lead to go. Hueys need to get off first. We Cobras will need all the extra room possible to get over the concertina wire.

"Rider Lead's up,"

He starts to enter translational lift and moves into flight. Behind him the other five green machines are now moving. Each takes its turn to get airborne.

Turning after they pass, I start my lift off. To our right the Hatch Force is all lined up, awaiting the return of the Hueys to take them into battle.

"Sneaky White's flight is clear of the field," the Kid, WO Klien, calls to the tower. Cool must be letting him do more than sit in the front seat.

Since I got shot up, his mother has sent me several get well cards and a very nice personal letter thanking me for saving her son's life. I guess he sent her photos and told her everything, because she said she knows how to keep a secret. Getting mail was a big surprise for me, at first I thought it might be divorce papers. In all my tours in Vietnam I've only received a few letters, but then I don't think I've written but a few either. In her last letter, she told me she was sending me a surprise, which I'm sure will be a tin of her homemade oatmeal cookies. Her postscript was the reminder that she prays for us all. I didn't know how to respond to her first letter. What do you say, "Listen lady, I wasn't saving your snot nose kid's life, I was trying to save mine!"

I change the UHF push from Quang Tri tower to the Covey's.

Once up, I listen as Milo advises that the first package is in route.

It's only 12:20 and it's been a busy day. A major change in plans shows just how ever changing the ebb and flow of battle is. We at CCN are only involved in intelligence gathering. I hate to think what conventional unit's slick and gunship's pilots must endure flying ever changing missions. I know pilots that have flown day after day for more than fourteen flight hours at a stretch. You get so tired that when sitting on the ground awaiting a mission change or to be loaded, you cat nap. It's really not a nap. It's just pure exhaustion overwhelming you. You become a zombie as you fly hour after hour. You leave the revetments in the early morning darkness and arrive back in the evening darkness. In the 282nd we used to take turns napping as we'd fly out to and return from missions. Once I had a crew-chief yell, asking who the hell was flying the aircraft. Both the co-pilot and I looked at each other, thinking the other had the controls. After flying nineteen hours the day before and into our tenth hour that day we had simply lost it. It's one of the few times I've ever aborted a mission. I called back to Marble Mountain and told them we had a feedback in the flight controls. The crew knew it was imaginary, but no one said a word as we returned. Better to go home, than kiss a mountain while asleep.

Chapter 11

It's a typical quiet flight out to Khe Sanh Valley. Before the slicks land on the old PSP strip, Cool and I fire a dozen or so flechettes to kill any NVA in the area and to set off any traps that may be set up.

The men immediately get off the Hueys and set up a defensive position. Within a minute, we hear the double squelch break on FM, signifying they're okay. The slicks are already on their trip back to pick up the Hatch Force.

Climbing to five hundred feet above the battle-scarred red dirt, we extend our covering pattern out about a half a mile from their position. We're in a staggered trail formation not going anywhere in particular, just looking. Looking up, I see Lardo's head bobbing. He's lost without an operative turret. Flying out here like this, he should have one, but with my luck he'd shoot up our guys and we'd have a friendly fire incident. I understand his frustration because I've been there before. I know he's feeling naked in the front seat and the thought of flying with me back into the same area must be tough on him. The front seater of a Cobra, the co-pilot, sits lower than the Aircraft Commander in the back seat. The canopy is lower than the AC's back seat. You feel as if you're perched out in front of the aircraft — a target for the enemy with their destructive fire. Normally, with a new co-pilot, I would give them the twenty-five cent tour of the Khe Sanh Firebase. But it's obvious that neither the captain or I would make good conversation right now. This morning's flight is still thick in the air. So I'll just fly around and leave him perched out in front naked and alone in his thoughts.

"Black Market. Huckleberry Finn Three-Four."

"Go."

"Package is on the way. You're free to refuel. Over."

"Roger. Ah . . . We'll wait 'til they're at Vandy, then head back."

He's answered by squelch breaks.

"See anything that might give them trouble, Cool."

"Negative. Heard Sweet Griffin on Victor, he's at Vandy."

"Roger." Switching to FM. "November Delta Foxtrot. Black Market Nine-Two Gulf, will head back now. Your package is about one-five out. You'll be okay. If you have problems Finn Three-Four is overhead, give him a call."

"Roger Nine-Two Gulf. It's quiet down here."

We make a pass over their location and continue down the strip, at less than twenty feet and at one hundred and eighty knots. East of the airstrip is where the stream and small waterfall are. Upon seeing it, you're lulled into thinking how peaceful and serene the area is. So far from the truth. This valley is one of the two major infiltration routes into the I Corps area of South Vietnam from Laos.

Following QL-9 east through the mountains, we pass Sweet Griffin and the package. There's no radio communication. Everything's been said. This is business time. My job is to get refueled, re-armed, and return as soon as possible. Passing the Rockpile, we lose communications with the flight and have to rely on Milo to relay any news.

Re-arming goes quickly as we only need four rockets per side. The armorers load nails into the empty receptacles in the outside pods. The inside pods, not expended, have their full load of nineteen HEs. We'll have use for nails in the next hour. As long as we have friendlies on the ground, we'll need to be careful though. HEs allow us to put shots within twenty-five meters of our guys. Though close, our teams can survive, and out here, survival is what it's all about.

While refueling, I remind Cool to load all he can. We'll need to stay on station as long as possible. I'm not familiar with this Cobra's power. I fill up against the hope that we can get airborne.

Once topped off and trying to come up to a hover, I find that we're too heavy. This engine doesn't have the power that Zero-Two-Seven's does. I pull all the collective I have. As the rotor RPM starts to bleed off, I swing the aircraft to the right, into the wind. Though not at a hover, we're light on the skids and scraping the ground. I work us to the active, lightly sliding most of the way, and start our take-off.

Cool, with more power, holds back while I use every known trick to get off the ground. We all know and can clearly see the rolls of concertina wire waiting at the end of the 1800 foot runway. It just waits to snag some unsuspecting or careless pilot. It's not my day to be that pilot, I'm needed at the Anvil.

Clearing the wire, at only sixty knots, we're flying. Cool gives us a very graphic description of the amount of clearance, using his California vernacular.

Milo advises us that the insertion has started and it's hot. Several slicks have been hit but no injuries, and nothing major damaged. I tell him to relay we're on the way.

Our trip out to the Anvil is full of anticipation. Already my mouth is getting dry. My tongue enlarging. I several times pull on the straps to tighten my harness. We know they're on the ground. The wheels are in motion and we don't know if all the cogs will fit smoothly into place. For the next hour, Cool and I will be their close air support. The radio is already buzzing with Covey directing a flight of Spads to several anti-aircraft gun emplacements west of the team.

We meet the Huey's, flying formation, on their return for fuel and then wait. They'll wait for the word to go back out into harm's way and do the extraction.

"Sweet Griffin, Sneaky's at Khe Sanh," I call as we enter the valley. We're less than five minutes from the action.

We see, looking south, Cobras circling like bees around the

hive. There are plenty of targets. Hopefully, we can get this done without losing anybody. Missions like this sometimes get out of hand. Even one crew shot down here would be hard to extract. Once one goes down, others seem to follow, in an attempt to rescue the first.

I used to hunt crows. It's very difficult to call them in to get a good shot. But once you've got one down, the others flock to his aid creating mass hysteria. For us, loading our long barrel shotguns as fast as we could, it was easy hunting. The key was getting the first one down.

"Come on over and get in a high orbit to our north. I want to expend before I go back and refuel. Dinks all over the fucking place. Breaking left!"

I see Sweet Griffin's Cobra as he starts climbing out of a gun run.

"Taking fire! Taking Fire! Fifty at two o'clock," Woodruff says.

"Got him, break now! I'm inbound!"

Confusion sets in as the number of targets increases and the sense of urgency sweeps all the pilots. When you have this many targets, it ends up that the left doesn't know who the right is shooting at and vise-versa. Hopefully, we can prevent a cluster fuck by staying coordinated. We're only one step from a goat fuck right now.

"Sneaky I'll break off and head back. E'Clair, try to stay until you get a twenty minute fuel light. Mark the targets and Foxtrot's location." We see a pair of Cobras climb out to the northeast.

"Roger. Come on down Sneaky. We're using nails to the north of the brown. Foxtrot's on the south side of the brown just west of the split. You can see the panels on their packs."

"Coming down. We'll join in your pattern." Then to Lardo, "Get a positive on the team, I don't want to hit any of them."

Getting low, we see people running around as if there's mass panic. It's hard to figure who's who. This is even with our guys using orange panels on the top of their ruck sacks to mark their location.

"Inbound!" I call as I watch the Cobra in front of us fire off a pair, then break into a climbing left. The small arms fire is noisy even inside a closed cockpit.

"Find the team! *Dai Uy* you hear me? If I get too close, let me know."

"Black Market we're getting a lot of fire from one-zero-zero. About two-five mikes. Can you help us out?"

"Roger," I answer while rolling in. "Keep your heads down. Cool put a pair just east of the team." I'm in a bad position to be firing. If a rocket goes low I'll hit friendlies.

"Got it! Get out of there Sneaky. We're inbound!"

"Breaking left!"

We go into a steep climb getting out of the fray. AK-47 rounds are hurdling up at us and everyone else, in a fusillade we're not accustomed to. It's only a matter of time before we take hits. The Cobra strains under the added weight and G's I'm subjecting it to.

"That's it! Keep 'em coming! We hear 'em." The Hatch Force One Zero is now directing Poole's rocket pass.

"Breaking!"

"Inbound! Ah . . . This will be my last pass we got a light."

E'Clair is at the twenty minute fuel warning stage of his flight. He and McIntyre must leave immediately in order to make it back to Quang Tri. Though the light says you have twenty minutes of fuel, it depends on the calibration of the gauge. Sometimes you have more, sometimes you have less. When flying your own aircraft, you have a good sense of the guage's accuracy. When flying some other AC's aircraft, you have absolutely no idea. Running out of fuel is not healthy out here.

"Roger we've got it. Hurry back. This could really get bad."

In a few minutes the NVA will know the only Cobras left will be Poole and me. I expect things to heat up.

"Black Market this is Finn Three-Four. I'd like to run Spads in on the area north of the brown. Can you move your pattern south?"

"Roger."

This will put us over an area with more anti-aircraft gun emplacements. But, the few passes the Spads will make make the risk well worth it.

"Cool, be careful over here, I expect to have big guns shooting. Inbound!"

He answers with squelch breaks. Talking takes up too much energy in the confusion.

Rolling in on a small clearing, I see brown-suited NVA running toward our team's location. Firing several pair of HE's in between groups of combatants, I hope to break our team's contact.

"Got 'em in the open!"

"They're ours! Don't shoot!" yells Lardo.

"Black Market, those were close."

"Roger. I'm breaking!"

"Inbound!"

Cool fires at the shooting holes dug in next to the intersection. We clearly see the holes running along the road and in the clearing. Bright flashes from the gunfire stab up at him from the slits dug along the side of dirt packed track.

"Breaking right."

We use a right-hand pattern while the Spads are making their runs. Overflying the path of fixed-wing aircraft dropping bombs and firing 20mm cannons is not good for one's longevity.

"Huckleberry Finn Three-Four we've have WIAs. One soap bubble hit."

Damn, I hope it isn't bad.

"Inbound! I'll only shoot a pair. We need to wait for Sweet Griffin." We pick up the answering squelch breaks, as not only Poole but the two Coveys are all on the UHF.

We must conserve as many rockets as we can but still provide good close support. Without a turret, I'm handicapped on this mission. I know Lardo is feeling the loss greater than I. In other Cobra units, not having an operative turret is a non-mission ready status. But not in ARA, our primary mission is as a rocket platform and the turret is only a limited defensive weapon. We rarely use it because of the turnaround time needed to reload the drums. With a co-pilot and a couple of armorers we can reload our rocket pods in three minutes or so. It would take twenty minutes to load the turret even if you had an experienced armorer loading the drums and pulling the ammunition through the belts to the guns. Time is too valuable for us to waste. We shoot rockets and carry many more because of it.

"Huckleberry Finn we got a snatch! A double snatch." There's jubilation in the voice as the mission is now ready to close. "Let's get the hell out of here."

"Roger Delta Foxtrot, you have a double snatch?"

"Roger! Get the package!"

Lead Covey is now calling MLT to have the slicks launched and extract the team. Only one injured so far and they've captured a couple of NVA, this may be a good mission after all. We continue to roll in, firing a single pair at a pass, letting the team get ready for the extraction. The slicks will take twenty-five long minutes to get here.

"Sneaky, Sweet Griffin entering the valley."

"Roger. The slicks are called, we're going to Prairie Fire."

"Roger Sneaky. How is it going?"

"We're making dry passes, keeping heads down. There's too much gunfire down here. A guy could buy it out here. We got a double snatch."

"Market aircraft. Ah . . . Finn Three-Four. We're going to run a set of fast movers from the west to east, north of the brown. You'll need to get out of there."

"Roger Four, we'll move south and let Sweet Griffin's flight join up with us." We're now flying over the intersection and climbing out in an extended right-hand pattern.

"I'll drive straight out and climb to the right, Cool."

"Gotcha!"

"You had better go further east Sweet Griffin. Fast movers are set to roll in."

"I heard. Got you in sight, we'll be there in a minute."

"Climbing!" Cool calls.

"Taking fire! Eight o'clock, fire! That fifty's close," Doodle calls, flying on Sweet Griffin's wing.

They've flown over a gun emplacement to the northeast of the area we're working. Anti-aircraft emplacements firing at our aircraft that far away from the LZ we're working is a sign the NVA are well dug in and with plenty of resources.

Joining up, we fly a pattern allowing us to watch the F-4s roll in and drop their bombs. First are the napalm's two-hundred and fifty pound canisters spreading the jelly indiscriminately. Explosions and heat rock the team. No complaints, just cheers and colorful descriptions to pilots of their accurate delivery. The F-4s will drop CBUs to kill any leftover NVA when we've completed the extraction. The CBUs are difficult to use this close to friendlies.

"Fox Bravo's in the valley."

Good news, slicks are inbound. We don't have much fuel left and Sweet Griffin would rather run an extraction with four Cobras instead of two.

"Sweet Griffin, I've only got a few minutes left on station. Want to extract them now, or wait for E'Clair?"

"Finn Three-Four. Sweet Griffin, over."

"Go."

"Four, can you raise Market Nine-Two Kilo to get an ETA?"

"Black Market Nine-Two Kilo this is Huckleberry Finn Three-Four. Over."

"Kilo what's your ETA?"

"Roger we'll be in the valley in two to three minutes."

"Finn Three-Four could you have them come straight to the package."

"Kilo, Griffin advises go directly, ah... directly to the Lima Zulu. We're ready for extraction."

I'm able to hear Marty's reply meaning he's entering the valley and only minutes out.

"What's your fuel, Cool?"

"Ah . . . lets see, ah . . . got another five I think."

"Roger. Sweet Griffin we'll stick around and help you with the first couple of slicks."

"Roger."

"Fox Bravo Lead this is Griffin Lead ah . . . We're ready for extraction. We need the *bac si* in Chalk One. He'll have five going out. One is injured. Chalk Two will take out five including the two POW's. Chalk Three through Six will each have six on board. Make sure you call your load before you lift off."

"*Dai Uy*, as they call off add 'em up. Don't want to forget anyone out here. When Chalk Five comes out tell how many are supposed to be left for Six. Understand?"

"Got it!"

Sweet Griffin, both Coveys, and Ghost Rider Lead are doing the same thing. Getting their counts ready.

"Fox Bravo Lead will be going in last. We'll try twenty second separation." On FM to the team, "Delta Foxtrot this is Fox Bravo we're inbound for pick up. *Bac si* on Chalk One."

This is going to be tight. With a twenty second separation, we'll have to fly a tight gun pattern to protect the slicks. Three to a side, each Cobra will pick up a side of a slick and protect it as it goes in. Hopefully the whole process will only take five minutes or so. For all of us, those five minutes will feel like eternity.

"Lead, we'll mark the team for you. Head in at two-two-zero and come out at zero-four-zero then direct to Khe Sanh. Do not climb out 'til you've passed the old Khe Sanh village. Do a high orbit over the strip."

Sweet Griffin directs the slick's approach and departure over the freshly napalmed area. It should be the path of least small arms fire. If one goes down, it will be in an area we can all see. Flying low level will keep the larger anti-aircraft guns from getting a good shot at them. Once past the destroyed village, they'll be on they're own until they get over to the abandoned strip.

"Griffins, Doodle and I have Chalk One, Sneaky and Cool Chalk Two, E'Clair and Double D Chalk Three. Use the same rotation for Four, Five and Six. Lets get 'em in and out." The call is followed by numerous squelch breaks.

We all have our assignments and know what needs to be done. If we have to, we'll slow up and get between the anti-aircraft fire and the slicks. We've done it in the past and not one Cobra AC out here today will hesitate doing it again. Though small arms fire isn't of much importance to us, we need to protect the vulnerable slicks from the fifty ones and larger guns.

"Ah . . . Griffins. Everybody's ready and we're inbound. Let's see a good twenty second separation, Riders."

The Ghost Rider Lead has his flight in formation and in intervals.

"November Delta Foxtrot, this is Finn Three-Four, pop smoke. I say again, pop smoke!"

In the low scrub a wisp of smoke appears right away—in not only one location, but in three.

"I have goofy grape," Sweet Griffin says as he leads the first slick in.

The other two columns of rising smoke are yellow. They are over one hundred yards from our team's location. The NVA obviously know what we're about to do. The problem is, the NVA don't know the color of smoke we're using.

An old NVA trick is to try to get a Huey to land at a site with the wrong color of smoke. They wait until the Huey hovers, then spring a trap on the unsuspecting crew. When successful, this trick cam cost at least an aircraft and sometimes the lives of the crew.

Sweet Griffin fires several pairs of nails into the enemy's yellow smoke. Whoever ignited these grenades are no longer our problem. They will find the task of escaping flechettes in low scrub to be impossible.

"Fox Bravo Six on final."

Far ahead of me I watch a Huey sinking into the scrub to pick up its load. All I see is it's main rotor turning, with one blade painted white, which gives the illusion of turning slower than its actual RPM.

"Bravo Six lifting with five."

"Roger with five."

Covey will be doing the official head count, though each of us has that responsibility. With Captain America flying in Covey Lead, he'll have the final word.

"Bravo Two, in!

Our slick goes into the sea of undulating green brush. We orbit around it and watch as two forms are thrown into the Huey. These are our rewards for being out here.

"Two's out with three and two."

"Roger three and two."

"Three's taking fire at ten o'clock. We're in!"

"Six on board and lifting. Gunner's hit, we're taking fire! Shit!"

On one side, the red tracers stop pouring out of the Huey's well as the gunner is no longer able to respond with his M-60. The other side is still sending its steady red stream, snaking out from the aircraft toward unseen targets.

"Sneaky, that's sixteen out so far. Eighteen more to go."

Lardo is doing his job. Even writing high on the window with the black grease pencil so that I can see. With no operative turret, he needs to have his hands doing something.

"Chalk Four's in. Took AK fire along the brown to the south. Ah . . . we got several hits, but we're flyable."

This is turning into a bad scene for the last two Hueys.

"Five inbound. Get out of there Four!" The Huey we're escorting starts his flare early as the LZ is filled with Chalk Four.

"Four lifting with six."

"Five on the ground. Taking fire in the LZ!" We all hear the rounds over the radio as the pilot transmits. "Out with six. Fire from eight o'clock. Get in there Lead!" Without a turret, we've not been able to fully support Chalk Five.

"Lead's in."

The last Huey descends into the swirling vegetation and seems to hang there for a long time.

"Taking Fire! Taking Fire! Got six!" The background noise over his radio sounds like sheer hysteria.

He's now lifting, slowly, almost waddling, and moving to the west. He's extending his exit too far to the west.

"Break Right! Break Right!" Sweet Griffin is yelling.

Next to him, E'Clair is firing rockets in front of the Huey.

"Ah . . . we've got problems with the hydraulics. Ah, there goes primary. Come on . . . baby. We'll be nursing this back." Still hearing rounds across the radio, we don't know if it's 60 or AK fire.

"I got him, break around and get behind me!" yells Sweet Griffin as he closes in on the limping aircraft, wobbling and fishtailing in a slow turn to the north.

"We're with you!"

"I'm on him!"

All the Griffins are yelling their intention to cover the wounded Huey's escape.

"Shit! Got a fuel light!" I yell. This is not what we need right now. We need to help this sick and lame bird back to Khe Sanh.

"Me too." Cool probably has had his blinking in front of him for a few minutes and said nothing until we got this last slick out.

"Sneaky, you and Cool go ahead and return. Escort Three, Four and Six back. We'll follow with the rest of the package. We need to get the injured to 18th Surg fast."

"Roger we're breaking off," I reply and turn north.

"Fox Bravo Three, Four and Six, you monitor?"

"Roger Sneaky. We're orbiting at one-thousand and will meet you at the falls."

"Roger Four and Six. Bravo Three how are you doing?" I ask the Huey flying in front of me.

"Got it under control."

The Ghost Rider Three has turned northeast. He's no longer trying for Khe Sanh, but flying to the mouth of the pass leading back to Quang Tri. I don't blame him. Any extra flying with a wounded door gunner would be too much for any pilot.

"Roger. We'll be with you all the way back. Sneaky stay with him. I'll get the rest of the package. Covey we have everybody and we're headed back to Khe Sanh." Sweet Griffin is now rounding up the rest of the package.

"Roger Griffin. Good job."

"Who was hit?"

"Ah, a strap hanger took shrapnel, nothing serious."

Holy Shit! Billy was one of the strap hangers, the extra men on a team, and he may be hit. I didn't even think of it. I hope it isn't bad.

"Bravo Six, we've got you," I say, as I see a pair of Hueys ahead of us turning to start the trip through the pass.

"Bravo Two, think you and your flight can pick up the other teams at Khe Sanh?"

Good idea, it'll save us from having to fly back out here to get the twelve team members left on the ground. With the slicks low on fuel, we might be able to do it. At least, get them to Camp J. J. Carroll.

"Fox Bravo Five, you think you can each carry another six."

"Fuck it, let's try. Better than coming back out here," an unknown Ghost Rider pilot states.

"Ah . . . Griffin, we'll give it a try." Being light because of low fuel load and having a long runway to take-off from should make it easier.

"Sweet Griffin. Sneaky and three Riders at the Rockpile, QSY to Quang Tri."

"Roger."

Changing pushes, I hear Four on the air, "Quang Tri tower Ghost Rider Three-Seven."

"Go ahead Ghost Rider Three-Seven."

"Three-Nine and Three-Five at the Rockpile, inbound for

18th Surg. Three-Seven will co-direct to CCN. We have two Griffins with us."

"Roger Three-Seven we'll notify Surg. Call at the boundaries."

"Rabbit Hutch this is Sneaky, Ah . . . We're about five out of the Surg with two."

Milo is already on top of things. "Security's on the way Sneaky. Will meet your flight there."

"Roger."

Milo lives up to the standards Sergeant Major Billy Washburn requires for all those around him. Keeping on top of things is a common trait for Special Forces, but Billy's operations are always a cut above the rest.

"Quang Tri Tower, Sneaky White with three Ghost Riders to the west. Weapons cold. Two Ghost Riders will need a direct to the Surg. Ghost Rider Three-Seven will co-direct CCN. Cobras need a direct to POL, we are low on fuel."

Not hard at all to say when you're looking at a light that has been blinking for far too long. You can reset the Master Caution Panel, but the light still blinks.

"Roger Sneaky White. Weapons cold. Riders are cleared direct to Surg. Cobras cleared direct POL. Rider Three-Two call at extended base. Altimeter twenty-nine forty-seven. Winds are zero-three-zero at one-two. You're cleared."

"Roger cleared POL. You're cleared to Surg Riders."

"Rider Three-Nine and Three-Five, final Surg."

"Quang Tri, Ghost Rider Three-Two on extended base to CCN."

After landing next to the POL area and Lardo has started our refueling, I call over to Cool, "On fumes, how about you?"

Though he's not answering, I watch him wipe his brow. I know that we both stretched this flight.

After we've repositioned to the CCN pad and started our shutdown, several quarter-ton trucks speed out of the compound. They're headed for the Quang Tri field POL to pick up the returning team members on Ghost Rider Lead who just made an emergency landing. It's the end of a hard day, not only for team members, but flight crews as well. Though several teams are still in Laos, as long as they're not compromised and no Prairie Fire is called, we'll call it a day.

I'm in the Operations hut and downing a cold beer as Ghost Rider slicks start their landings. All but the Ghost Rider Lead. His slick will have to be repaired before he can fly that plane again. He'll catch a ride on one of the returning trucks, and leave his crew to start the repairs.

Our Cobras are landing. Things are unwinding. Four of the slicks have taken hits including the Lead's. The Griffins received none, but there were several close calls. The elation of completing the mission is setting in around the compound. Each crew member gets out of his aircraft throwing off his chicken plate and survival gear. Their expressions change from worry and anxiety to smiles and relief. They converge at each bullet hole, hands gliding through the air describing attitudes and altitudes as bravado now expands the crew-chief's and gunner's versions of the afternoon's events. The word that their fellow Ghost Rider door gunner was only slightly wounded relieves them. They inspect his well where the blood will be quickly hosed off. A new gunner will fill his seat tomorrow.

Sweet Griffin comes in and grabs a beer. A jeep screeches to a stop. Milo and the blond Captain America hurry to the back of the Operations hut, headed directly toward the secure radios. Captain America will debrief and get his reports out immediately. Headquarters has surely requested an update on the mission by now.

Rather than disturb him, I get Milo's attention and tell him Sweet Griffin and I will be going to the hospital to see Billy. The two NVA POWs are also being patched up. They will be interrogated by the Assistant Intelligence NCO before being shipped to CCN Headquarters at Da Nang. They'll talk . . . once they're given proper medical care, some food, and find out the large round-eye Westerners aren't going to beat the information out of them.

Putting the jeep in gear, I holler to Lardo, "If there's a mission, fly over to POL. I'll meet you there."

Sweet Griffin's told WO-1 Leonard "The Lizard" Mock the same thing.

As we drive up to the fence, a Montagnard sentry pulls it back and waves us through. Though already inside a military base controlled and guarded by the 1st of the 5th Mechanized Division, the MLT compound is enclosed by rows of concertina wire and has an internal armed guard. The 'yards walking guard have a reputation of shooting first, and asking for a translation of the request later. 5th Mech soldiers know that whatever you do, don't try to break into the Special Forces compound or you're dead meat.

I realize I'm driving a new jeep. It's an even bet it's freshly stolen. MAC-V-SOG, and Special Forces in general, have a wonderful method to keeping their vehicles running. When one breaks down, they steal a new one. MPs looking for a stolen vehicle will have its serial number.

One way to avoid detection is to peel the serial number plate off. If it's inspected though, the lack of the plate will alert the MPs that it's stolen.

The other way, and one used exclusively by Special Forces, works because of the large number of organic aircraft. When a new vehicle from 5th Mech is stolen, it's sent on the next C-130 Black Bird going south to Nah Trang. Then, the Green Berets in Nah Trang steal a vehicle from a local unit and send it back up to us.

If we get pulled over or have the numbers checked by MPs, they have no record of the vehicle stolen down in Nah Trang, nor do the MPs in Nah Trang know about the 5th Mech theft. It works out well for us all. Our Mission Launch Teams don't have enough personnel to do the general maintenance, so it's far easier to trade one in when it doesn't work anymore. Anyway, if we're all in the same military . . . fighting the same enemy in the same war . . . is it really stolen? Or, is it just being appropriated by another unit with a higher priority need? We don't sell them, or strip them for parts. If it's old, out of tune, or dirty, we just trade it in for a new model at the local PX parking lot. If the finder will repaint it from black back to OD green and paint out the bumper markings of MAC-V-SOG CCN, then they shouldn't have problems either. Very effective use of limited, and sometimes down right scarce, vehicles. After all if a colonel or general loses his jeep, he'll have a replacement within the day to go to all those important meetings, briefings, and get togethers where they award each other medals for superior paper shuffling. We too have a need and a good way of filling it.

Arriving at the Surg, Sweet Griffin and I go straight to triage to find Billy. I see the nurse from my stay a few weeks ago. I ask her about the Green Beret that just came in.

"You mean the arrogant, loud mouthed Sergeant Major!"

Billy's already worn out his welcome.

"Yes Ma'am, that'll be the one."

She points to the doors going to the other medical departments. "He's in x-ray. Hopefully they've quieted him down. Don't you men know anything other than profanity?"

"Thank you Ma'am." I cut off the conversation. There would be no way to explain why we talk this way, there's really no excuse.

I quickly catch Sweet Griffin as he pushs his way through the double doors.

We walk down the covered pathway to the hut with a small canted red and white sign printed in large block letters, "X-RAY". We're greeted by the sight of a large, white ass protruding into the air. It's Billy's.

"Well, if it isn't the big bad Green Beret."

"Fuck you Sweet Griffin!" Billy is facing the other way and can't see us. "Fucking Sneaky got me. I'll strangle the motherfucker when I see him."

"Stay still! I need to get these pictures to see if you have any other shrapnel in your posterior," cuts in a lanky, long haired medic with sunglasses on. He's operating the machine and having a hard time with Billy.

Walking up to him, we see his ass is peppered with small red pin holes. The pinholes cover him from the base of his back all the way down the top half of his thighs. There's amber antiseptic washed over the area. You can see where some of the holes have been probed.

I start laughing giving away my presence.

"That you, asshole? You son of a bitch, I'm going to kick your ass. Is that you Sneaky?"

"Billy, what the fuck happened? Get too close to a frag?"

"Fuck you! You tried to kill me. I know damn well it was you."

"Bullshit! You probably got in the way of some NVA. You're too old to be out there. This isn't World War II or Korea. You're fucking too old to be out there. You understand that, old man!" There is no doubt, but if he's alive in the year 2000, he'll be involved somehow in a military operation somewhere in the world.

"I saw you. Yes you, you son of a bitch." Billy swings his tightly balled fist in my direction. "Saw you when you flew over. Your fucking helmet is the only one like it. When I get up from here, you had better *didi.* AH! That fucking hurts . . . Damn it! Otherwise you'll be spending the night here with me, in the bed next to mine."

Chapter 12

I ease up to the revetment after landing. Willie and Jimmy Lee Carson are sitting on ammo cans, with open beers in their hands. With all the problems I've caused for the maintenance people today, I'll be buying the beer tonight. The added work from the battle damage to Zero-Two-Seven will cause Wee Willie and others a long hard night if, and I doubt it, they can get it fixed in just one night.

Setting the Cobra down and rolling the throttle back to flight-idle, I let the temperatures prior to going through a normal shut-down procedure.

Before I'm unstrapped and the blades finish free wheeling, Captain Lardo has already climbed out and, with his survival equipment slung over his shoulder, is storming toward the hill and our hootches. He and I will have a meeting of the minds tonight or our flying together will cease. If he becomes the platoon leader when Jimbo leaves, he'll have to fly CCN if he wants any respect in the Second Platoon.

After our return to CCN with the replacement aircraft, Lardo sat alone, between the Admin and Operations huts, ignoring conversations with the other pilots. No telling what is going through his mind, but the time away from me gave me a bit of solace as well. Other than the instructions I gave him when going over to see Billy, we have not interacted very little since the incident. Usually I let the front seat fly the aircraft back from CCN, but not today. On the trip back I flew east, over the South China Sea, and called for Evans GCA for an approach that ended with a high speed fly-by of the active. It's obvious that we're headed for a blow-out. Normally I would relish such a chance, but I am not so sure on this one. It's not so much of Major Stafford's council with me about tact, though I ought to listen to him on this one. But there is something more with the Captain, and I can't seem to put my finger on it. If I knew more about his background I'm sure this would help. Hell, he's a Captain, so he's had to do the right thing up to now. Though a newly made Captain, and an even newer pilot, he still had to pass muster along the way. If he's that sensitive about being Mexican-American, then he ought to look around as the Army is loaded with Mexican-Americans and especially in the elite units. When looking at Special Forces, you'll find at least 25% and there is no doubt that if you don't carry your weight there, you're sent packing and quickly. So I need to think this one out. But I'll do that tomorrow for tonight I plan to get totally wasted. Tomorrow I'll try to reason out a way that we can get along, even if I have to sit down with someone and talk it through.

I climb down the side of the Cobra and start my post-flight inspection. I do it without the usual banter with Wee Willie. Not only am I inspecting the aircraft, but I feel Carson's eyes on me, inspecting me as well. The whole time Carson has not said a word, but his eyes have betrayed him. I know that if I rushed through the post-flight and missed anything, no matter how small, he would take note. I'm sure he would not correct me, but would log it in the back of his mind. The next time a group of the crew-chiefs were sitting around and pilot's names came up, he'd wait until mine was spoken. Then he would bring up his assessment of my post-flight and how I missed whatever. If I pass, and I'll probably never know, Carson would just keep his mouth shut at the gathering with the other crew-chiefs.

Once I finish, I carefully go over the Aircraft Log Book, double-checking the 2408 as I close it out. Carson surely will inspect this as well. Once done, I gather up my stuff and tell Willie I'll buy the beer, to see me at the Club tonight. Then I give a more formal goodbye to Carson, which he responds with a slight nod.

I walk up the hill past our hanger. Zero-Two-Seven is resting in one of the bays. Sheet metal mechanics are swarming over the wounded bird as I pass. Panels are stripped from its side, extra flood lights aimed at the gaping open wounds, and two men are laying on their backs under her belly. One other man is sitting with half his torso stuck up into the hell hole, which is just what it sounds like. The cramped open hole below the transmission area is not only small but because of its location is, at best, difficult to get into. This spot has become the home for the smallest of the men within the maintenance platoons. It's also dark, so a flashlight is required. If you are safety wiring something, you then see that you need a third hand to hold the flashlight. Up to now, we've not found a three armed little man to fill our needs in this department. Looking back, I see the crew is working with an air of urgency but in a methodical method as they try to bring Zero-Two-Seven back to life. I'll have to get a couple cases for these sheetmetal men as well. It's going to be a long night of stripping, inspecting, fabricating, and reinstalling metal. At four-eighty a case, this will be a twenty dollar night, but it's the least I can do after I brought her home tore up like this.

A jeep loaded down with returning pilots approaches and, not waiting for it to stop, I wave it on. I'm not in the mood for idle conversation, I need time to think today's incident through.

Someone's going to say something about us getting shot up. Not the fact that we got it, but about me going after a ZPU-4. It isn't the smartest choice a helicopter pilot could make. Honestly, though I'll not admit it to others, I didn't know it was a ZPU until I was already locked in. If we had Cobras with 20mm cannons like the 2nd/17th CAV, it might not have been so bad. But an overweight heavy hog is the aircraft we use, not the CAV's 20mm aircraft. I know that the most stinging comments will come from the commissioned officers. The warrants, who know that it wasn't a smart move on my part, will hold their comments to themselves. I'm sure it will come down to the warrants circling the wagons around me, and closing the ranks to protect one of their own, even though they're not pleased with his actions. But those that have flown into Laos know that things happen quickly, and reactions to incidents are made without a long thought process. For me, I'll defend my actions on this one, but it's just another instance where Sneaky has gone and done something that wasn't the norm. If Rick had done this today, there would have been things said, but nothing like what I'm going to have to defend. If Rick comes to me and tells me I screwed up, which he will not do till he heard my side of the incident, then I'll agree. But right now I don't think this is going to happen. Time will tell as far as Rick is concerned.

I cut through the enlisted hootches, and catching a glimpse of our hootch, I see Jimbo in ragged cut off fatigues bending over a smoking grill. At least we'll have a good meal for a change. One gets tired of Army chow within a week of arriving in Vietnam. This is one reason why clubs, for all the ranks, have flourished so well. The mess hall fare is usually meat and potatoes and it's the same bland-tasting meal, no matter how it's served. The dessert, Jello, is served slightly cold and wiggly but runny, or if served warm it's in the Kool-aid container. For us here, it's Red Death, whether cold or warm. Also the premise about weight loss suffered here in Vietnam is that it's caused by the heat which forces your body to sweat out all your body fat. Some doctor came up with this theory, but I'm sure he did this while he himself was eating in some General's mess, with table linen, silverware, glassware and stewards to fetch whatever he wanted. It sure wouldn't have been here in this 101st Airborne Artillery mess hall situated on the front lines. No way. The meals, if you believe the published menu, sound good. But after going though the line it's very apparent that the truth is left outside the mess hall doors. But one cannot fault the mess sergeants. They are given what they must work with, and personally, I think given their circumstance, they do a good job. It's just I'd rather have a steak, and it looks like Jimbo is going to fulfill my desire tonight.

"Looks like the trip to Da Nang was worth it," I say, as I

near the porch. "I thought for sure that you would have stayed overnight."

"Your share is twelve dollars for booze and steaks."

He's turning the thick red slabs that he's traded for some captured NVA booty. Whenever we can, we go to the Da Nang Navy Base, Camp Tein Sauh. It's not too hard to find an old Navy Chief willing to trade a box of steaks, or two, for a captured AK-47 or some NVA web gear. Who knows what they get for it when they deal with their fellow sailors on the ships that bring the cargo into Da Nang port? We get all the war souvenirs we'll ever want or need from CCN but for a sailor who's only time in Vietnam will be volunteering to unload a LST at Da Nang harbor, any booty that's NVA or rumored to be NVA, is the second thing he's looking for after arriving on the docks. With the chance, more likely the sure thing, that the Chief has several cases of booze stashed somewhere and at a few dollars a bottle they can become property of the Griffins, the trip to Da Nang becomes one you can bet we'll jump at.

"Don't let Fred out. Fucker's been trying to get at these babies since I unwrapped them."

I open the door and jam my foot inside. Pushing Fred back I ask over my shoulder, "Jimbo, you need a beer?" Then not waiting for the answer I know he'll give, I enter the hootch.

After the door slams shut Jim yells, "Yeah bring me a couple."

Throwing my equipment into the faded yellow lawn chair, I walk down the narrow aisle toward the front of the hootch and the small community area. I open the platoon refrigerator. It's a large one that was stolen from some other unit when the Griffins first came to Camp Evans. Several layers of paint, in varying shades of green have been applied over the years, but the Kid has just finished a complete, and very neat, paint job this past week. Inside I see it's filled with beer, sodas, and other assorted boxes of goodies that Jimbo's procured on his day off.

Others are undressing, grabbing their shower gear, and

leaving the hootch with a trademark slamming of the front door as they go. Heat, humidity, and the added hot CCN mission made this one very sweaty day.

I take three beers and kick the door shut. Walking to the back door, I'm surprised how quickly the hootch has emptied. I open the door while trying to keep Fred inside and throw Jimbo two beers. Closing the door, I quickly pop open the last one and gulp half of it down while standing before my cubicle.

I know that one of the beers Jim took will be used for his method of seasoning. Whatever he's cooking, whether steaks, deer, pig, or even a stew, you'll find him pouring generous amounts of beer into the meet. One night while we were still with the 108th Arty, Jimbo cooked us a stew. As we watched him put ingredients from one can of meat after another into the pot, we knew we were in for a treat. But after he had put the potatoes and a few other veggies into the pot, he ordered a couple of beers and quickly dumped them into the steaming pot as well. We all thought he was nuts. Several even had the nerve to say so. But Jimbo just ignored them and started stirring. After what seemed like an eternity, Jimbo finally proclaimed the potion ready to eat. Everyone took a canteen cup full and proceeded to eat, though I'm sure some, including me, had our doubts if it was going to be palatable. It was delicious. I myself had three or four helpings and would have had more but the large pot was quickly emptied. Later when I asked him for the recipe, he told me there was none. Just throw whatever you have into the pot, heat till it boils, then add beer. Once the beer boils off, it's ready to serve. Nothing fancy is all he kept repeating, nothing fancy. I've never forgotten it.

It's all part of the image that Jimbo presents to you. His good looking features with the sense of humor that is infectious, throws you off to some of his talents. I'd be one of the last who thought of him as an accomplished cook, or maybe even chef. But he is. In talks I've heard him tell over and over how this is one of the quickest ways to a woman's heart or other parts of the anatomy. As he says, invite them to dinner, but surprise them and cook it yourself. Not just steaks, hell anyone can do this. But put together a total meal and then present it under candle light. Jimbo says, and I believe him, that this makes a date into a sure thing.

Jimbo, who's Texas raising would not be considered a good one for being a fine cook, was started early. His mother and father were away from the home, so that meant that many meals were prepared by the oldest, which was Jimbo. His two sisters are much younger, so Jimbo became the unofficial head of household. This, once he got over the ribbing that the local boys dished out, gave him a chance to learn how to cook. He also can wash his clothes, and iron, but he's said that he'll never do those chores again. But in the kitchen he was able to experiment with cooking and the end result is he's accomplished. With us, both here in the Griffins and while with the Sneaky Whites, he's the official cook whenever the platoon decides that the mess hall isn't going to receive their presence that night. He has also been invited to several other units, not only because he knows the pilots, but because they enlist him into cooking for their event.

After a cold, but quite refreshing, shower I put on faded blue Bermuda shorts and the flowery Hawaiian shirt my wife bought when she met me on R&R in Hawaii last year. The R&R was probably the last good time we'll ever have together. It was a hassle to get the arrangements made, and to me it wasn't a place I want to go, but it was a concentrated effort, at least on my part, to rejuvenate our faltering relationship. Staying at the Scofield Army Barracks Visiting Officers Quarters for those few days was enjoyable. I felt that I got a feel of the times spent by officers in post-World War I Manila, or maybe the Canal Zone in Panama. What a time it must have been, not only for the beauty but the general military operations at those posts. It was an era I missed, and would never get a chance to live it as it's time has passed. But Hawaii let me imagine what the golden years of foreign duty must have been like. But if I had my choice, I would have given anything to have been a China Marine. Those marines stationed with the 4th Marines, especially in the 20s and 30s really enjoyed foreign duty. Even my stint in Okinawa could never compare to those days. Now this shirt is about all I'll carry out of my marriage and several times I've felt like discarding it in order to rid myself of the reminder. Worst case, I could give it to Fred, and let him use it to lay on rather than my poncho liner.

Hanging my flight gear on the appropriate nails, I listen to the chatter from the two newest warrants. They're aging quickly—too quickly. Whatever they're talking about is drowned out when Double D enters his cubicle and turns up his tape recorder. Double D's into rock 'n roll, and right now Jimi Hendrix is his favorite. To me the guitar playing doesn't make sense, just noise being blasted. Whatever happened to good music. I enjoy opera and classical. I really like some of the country music that is being played. And I enjoy Frank Sinatra and the Mills Brothers but here in this unit I'm the only one. The noise from Double D's cubicle is not something I want to listen to anymore tonight.

As I pick up my lawn chair and several beers, I look across to Mask's cubicle and see him engrossed in the small stack of letters he received this afternoon. I push open the door and step out onto the pride and joy of Second Platoon, our porch. Fred, for some unknown reason, has elected to stay on my bed, even though the aroma of Jimbo's cooking has permeated the area. The porch has been rebuilt three times since I've been here. What started out to be a four-by-four landing grew into a four-by-twelve porch when Doc Holiday decided he needed a place to lay out and get a tan without people walking over him constantly. Doc, who's father is a high priced lawyer, was raised with the notion that a good tan was a sign of healthiness, therefore, his concern for having an undisturbed tanning area.

When Cool arrived he expanded it into the typical California beach home rear porch. Now it's eight-by-twelve with seating built into the railings. Using old wooden rocket boxes and assorted pieces of plywood that were either stolen or swapped from the SeeBees on the north side of the airstrip, our porch has become the envy of the unit, if not the base. With the help of the unit electricians, Cool put in a couple of strings of overhead lights that use the small multi-colored Christmas tree bulbs sent in by his family. The lights give it a flavor of a Mexican bordello, a real cheap one at that. Normally, the evenings spent here at the hootch, rather than the club, are at some point moved out onto the porch. It's size allows visitors to come and not crowd the place. This lights offer enough glow that allows you to write a letter, or read a book as long as the print is large enough. With the layout of the other flight platoon hootches to either side and the enlisted hootches further down the hill it gives intimacy to a normally nonintimate surrounding. Each of us has staked out a small area that is our own, and when going to 'The Porch', we know just where we will be sitting and where everyone else will be sitting.

Cool has now come up with a new idea, which he is working into a set of drawings and then hopefully into actually building. It's a mini shower. The shower is not for showering, at least this is how he's explained it, but for delivering light mist for the sun bathers to use. Jimbo has twice nixed the idea, but Cool is still working on it. It means a 55 gallon drum will have to be placed either on the roof, above my cubicle, or on a stand built for it next to the porch. Then through a set of hoses, some with small pin holes punctured into them which are mounted in a circular fashion, one could stand below the hoses and receive a gentle spray. We have questioned where he thought up this hair-brained idea. Cool tells all of us that in California this is the latest rage. I, one on one to Jimbo, expressed my worry about all the water that would collect on the ground beneath my corner of the hootch. I already have Malaria and the thought of more mosquitoes in the area upsets me. Then the thought of my corner being subjected to all the spray will mean mold and everything else in my cubicle. Jim's agreed with me, at least so far, but it's not stopped Cool from working his plan.

In the center of the porch is a grill, which divides the area into two large sections. It's a 55-gallon drum cut down length-wise, then four steel legs welded to the bottom. The legs are made of angle iron and are much stronger than the porch. But as with all metal in Vietnam, they are rusting quickly. Within a month after installing the grill, Jimbo had to have holes drilled in its bottom so the rain would flow out, otherwise it would have rusted through in no time. For a grate to cook on, someone scrounged up pieces of steel re-bar that were welded together. Though large pieces of meat can't fall through Jimbo still has to use a metal plate for the smaller ones. This grate is effective but weighs over thirty pounds and the whole thing probably weighs several hundred pounds. The day it was delivered, it took all of Second Platoon to lift it over the porch's side railing and muscle it into place. Jimbo, who it was made for, had input throughout its manufacture. Even its height is set just for Jimbo, so he doesn't have to lean over to barbecue. Since it's arrival, I've not seen anyone use it other than Jimbo. He takes time to prepare the fire to ensure the coals will be evenly spaced, as well as a section on his left that will only have a few coals used for keeping whatever warm without further cooking. From its location, Jim can not only tend to the fire and the meal he's preparing, but he can hold court with all who are on the porch. With the gradual falloff toward the enlisted hootches, he can also have a clear view of the common area behind all the officers' hootches as well as the front areas of the enlisted men's living quarters.

Scattered on the porch are several lawn chairs from DEROSed pilots. These are not only left out permanently but many of them have become the property of Second Platoon members who use them whenever outside. I'm not one of these guys, as I have my own chair. It's low slung and I've built two beer can holders on each side of the armrests. Using large peanut cans with old socks stuffed into the sides and bottoms, each holds a beer can and keeps the beer cold for a few minutes. It saves me from getting up and making trips to the refrigerator. I wait till someone else goes toward the rear door, then ask if he'd bring me whatever number of open cans I need to reload my chair. Also, located on the ends of the porch, are two 55 gallon cans we use for trash. It's become a game for the younger warrants to chuck the empty beer cans at the large cans like a basketball player would. Problem is Jimbo has to force them to clean up the mess every few days.

Looking over at Jimbo, it's obvious he has almost everything set up, and with Klien helping what isn't done will soon be. I throw my chair down to the left of the barbecue. Two groups are divided formally by the grill and invisibly by the friendships and alliances. On our side is Cool, Double D, E'Clair, Killer, and Randy Hunt. The empty chair next to Jimbo's must be Klien's, so I push them apart enough to get mine in between.

On the other side is Scoop, deeply engrossed in a pocket book and oblivious to life around him. Though he's on the other side, his loyalty spans both groups. He's not paying attention to the food preparation or the arriving pilots banter, but is seated with his legs up and hanging over the railing and his head focused downward. Wearing a sweat-stained OD green shirt and his flight pants means he's passed up the cold shower and will probably try for a warm one later. Scoop is known to avoid the rush to wash the Vietnam filth and sweat off, and will wait hours if necessary to take a leisurely shower.

Lieutenant Jonathan "Skip" Verdine and Lardo, still dressed in his sweat stained flight suit with his pistol belt on, are together. Lardo's chair is pulled close to the railing and facing toward the enlisted hootches. This accounts for Second Platoon except Nix, who I am sure is still down at maintenance.

"Steak's ready. Rare on the front. Well to the back and medium in between."

Jimbo takes the first dripping steak off the grill and balances it on a flimsy paper plate not large enough to hold the thick, light brown slab of meat. While it hangs over both sides, he adds a very liberal amount of homemade steak sauce shaken from an old whisky bottle. The sauce is another of Jimbo's culinary secrets. His mother, the hometown Post Mistress of a one-room US Post Office, sent the recipe for him to use while we were up at

Dong Ha. Her instructions included the pointed message not to share the ingredients with anyone. He says it's been in the family since they first settled in Texas, back in the 1870's. Though he couldn't get all of the ingredients here in Vietnam, at least this is what he's told everyone whose asked him about it, it's still about the finest concoction I've ever tasted. It's gained a bit of a reputation with other units, including our Battalion staff. Once, while at Battalion, down at Camp Eagle for a "Hail and Farewell", there almost was a fight over who was going to get the last of the mixture. At the last possible second Jimbo stepped in and produced an extra bottle he had hidden in his flight suit, and for a while this kept peace.

I stand up and slowly make my way to the grill, though there is a short line before me. I reach over and get a plate and stick my K-bar knife into one of two steaks in the corner that look uncooked. These are for me, as no one else in the unit likes their meat raw. Another trait I was given by my mother. As she use to say, just let the cow walk through the flames and singe her hair, that'll be fine. I was raised on red, dripping with blood, meat. And I still partake in the family tradition of taking a piece of bread, or a roll, after the steak has been devoured and sop up the blood and juices left on the plate. Then, and only then, is the steak fully consumed. When Jimbo first saw me do this he asked if I was from Texas. I'm not but my mother is and the Texan way of eating beef has carried through. After sitting back down in my chair, Fred jumps up at my legs trying to get into my lap, and of course my steak. Fred has snuck out when someone opened the door.

"Kid, put Fred back in the hootch before you get your food," I say to Jimbo's assistant for the day.

Klien is standing toward the end of the line, making sure that everyone has what they want. Though this meal is simple. Only meat, red meat. No vegetables, no salad, and no dessert. Some meat, some beer, and that's it. But for us it's easily a five star eating establishment.

Leaning over to Jimbo I ask, as he's busy cutting his dinner.

"Got any extras?"

"Yeah, should be. Two for everyone and a couple of extras is what I laid out, why? You're not thinking of giving that mutt any are you?"

"Nah... I owe Rick one for today."

"Bullshit! I heard what you did." Shifting in his chair to face me directly, his mouth full. "After all this time don't you know the difference between a fifty-one and a Zeep? Well, don't you?"

Seconds pass before he breaks into a smile, then he shoves another large hunk into his mouth. His black mustache has collected some of the homemade Texas sauce and it's now dripping onto his shirt and shorts.

I wonder what Clarke Gable would say, looking at his likeness dribbling his food down his face and into his lap.

"What the fuck do you expect from a Marine?" E'Clair joins in.

Skip gets up to get a second steak, then shuffles back next to Lardo. These two ought to get along really good. Verdine doesn't fly CCN. Though assigned to our platoon as number two in command, he spends most of his time working as the Battery S-1 Officer, and helping Jolly Roger when needed in Operations. He'll make work for himself, doing any possible job, rather than fly. He flew one CCN mission, that I can remember, and hasn't been back since. He also flew a couple Two-Minute Hot Status days and no longer does those flights either. On the Two-Minute Hot Status flights, you have no idea what your going to be asked to fly or what you'll be asked to do. Also, these flights usually end up with some night time operations. He's got to where he's permanently on the Fifteen-Minute Hot Status, which means he'll be the last to launch and it also means he'll only get about ten hours flight time a month. These ten hours are more than enough to meet the requirements for his flight pay. With ten hours a month for a year, he'll go home with three or four Air Medals and that will be plenty for his career advancement. It's all part of the Career Officer Ticket Punching Program. Get the right tickets punched and move on, at some point you pass go and retire as a Lieutenent Colonel. Really simple for the guy who doesn't make waves, and goes along with the time honored system. For those that want to make a change, or who feel that they don't want to be part of this charade, they will be identified, then marked, then moved out. You're just not a team player, though I wonder if we're all on the same and right team.

Klien stumbles out the back door with two cases of beer and a couple bottles of Mateus wine in his arms, then announces, "Called Nix, he'll be up in five." Then glancing over at us, "Should I put on his steaks?"

"Yeah," I mumble with a mouth full, "if you know how he likes them."

"Where's your gas mask Randy?" I ask the young warrant who's attacking a steak with such furious movements that already he's pushed it out of the plate and onto the floor once. He rubbed the dirt, if any, off and added more Texas sauce, then reattacked it with vigor. The paper plate is now useless, and if I were him I'd just grab the meat and eat it with my hands. After all we're with friends aren't we?.

Grinning, he turns and raises his bushy eyebrows in a comical way. What is missing is a cigar and some glasses, then he could pass, poorly, for a Marx brother. "Didn't you know? Your Fred ate it?"

"Shit! No wonder he's got the runs and keeps farting so much."

"Why do they call you Sneaky?" Klien interrupts for no reason at all.

He's asked me something that, though I'm proud of, I don't like talking about. Everyone gets a nickname while with the Griffins. They are based, somehow, loosely on a personality trait, a physical look, or some action no matter how dumb that the man has done in his short career. It's understandable to wonder about the names if, and only if, the nickname isn't something obvious. Sneaky isn't an obvious nickname. While in the Marines, 'The JAW' was, it's because of my large protruding jawline, as well as my ability to stick my jaw, or nose, into other peoples' affairs without being asked. But Sneaky is a name that needs, though I don't think so, some explanation. Klien has probably been put up to this, but his natural curiosity is understandable, but why ask here and now. No, he's been goaded into this, but the question is, by who? I look around trying to see who has a smile that gives him away.

I ignore his question, hoping it will just go away. Then Double D and E'Clair start on me, telling me that as a senior warrant I have a responsibility to help new warrants with any questions they have. Then Klien asks again, with eyes almost pleading with me to open up.

"Listen kid, it's a long, very long, story. If you want to hear it, I'll tell you later when we have time."

Klien's eyes show disappointment, until Jimbo nudges me, and shakes his head. With Jimbo pushing the matter I really have no choice. Why Jimbo is involved in this I don't know. Hell, he was there and he's the last one who needs to hear the story told again.

"Well, before I came to the Griffins, I used to fly LOHs up at Dong Ha for the 108th. It was a semi ash and trash unit that several of us were allowed to expand into a mini hunter-killer unit with a couple of aircraft. Along the way, I had the opportunity to fly the Deputy Commander of the 1st ARVN Division. The General is one of us, a true killer. Been fighting since '37 or so. First the Japs, then the Viet Mein, and now the NVA. He's been decorated several times by the US Government and holds a Silver Star, so he's got balls. Plus he knows where the enemy is, and likes a good fight. So over a few months I got to know him and if a warrant can become friends with a General, I have. Anyway, among his many official duties, he also has the ability to take visiting VIPs out to dinner, and good times in Quang Tri, or Dong Ha."

"Don't let him fool you kid, there is no such thing as good times in Quang Tri City," Killer interjects.

"Anyway, if you don't mind Killer, otherwise you can tell the story. So, the General put the word out in a couple of local whorehouses in Quang Tri and Dong Ha, that not only am I to be made welcome, but I don't have to worry about the bill. So of course I have, on occasion, taken the General up on his hospitality."

"Not the whorehouse!" Killer is going to screw with me throughout this.

"Listen up, I was there and it's true." Jimbo gets their attention, at least the new warrants, with his serious tone.

"Anyway, if you don't mind Killer? I was the maintenance officer as well as one of the 108th General's pilots. One night I decided to go to town and get a piece of ass."

"Sure you did." Still razzing me.

"Fuck you!" Turning to avoid Killer's look. "I also took my Tech Inspector, a Spec 6 named Piffer. Great guy. Piffer fought with the Germans during World War II as a fourteen year old, then was adopted by an American and was raised in the States. He's all Army, US Army. Anyway, I hitched up my trailer and we drove my jeep to the main gate. That night we happened to be under Red Alert, so when we got to the gate it was closed and very well guarded."

"I'm sure that didn't stop you, it's never stopped you before."

I lean to Jimbo, but before I can say anything to him Klien speaks up. "Shut the fuck up Killer!" The Kid's interest is now evident.

"The Officer of the Day told me I couldn't go off base because of the alert. I told him I was the General's pilot and he could call the General if he wanted to confirm permission to allow me to leave the Dong Ha Combat Base. I went on to explain that the reason I had the trailer was that I had to pick up an engine for the Genera's aircraft at Cau Viet. That without this engine the General's aircraft would not be able to fly in the morning and therefore someone would be in big trouble. Now, if I wasn't allowed to go get the engine, who was going to get blamed for the lack of the aircraft's ability to fly. Remember Kid, when all else fails, you dazzle with bullshit, it works every time"

The older pilots are chuckling, knowing Cau Viet is a Navy outpost just north of Dong Ha on a small tributary of some small river. It's about the size of a volleyball court and the last place helicopter parts would be kept. Not only by the Army but the Navy as well.

"And the poor OD was conned by an old warrant." Double D's shaking his head. Though he's heard the story many times, he still thinks it's one of the best he's heard in Nam.

"So the Second John was afraid to call the General, and disturb him, but he ordered the gate to be pulled back and off we drove into the dark."

Looking around, while I pause for a gulp of beer, I see I have the undivided attention of those on the porch, even Lardo's looking over his shoulder at me.

Still smiling, I continue. "We drove straight to one of the houses I know and parked right out front. After going in and having a few drinks, I went into one of the back rooms with one of the girls, who the mamasan told me was her best. In no time, at least before I really get into what I had come for, the mamasan starts yelling 'MP! MP!' So I grabbed my pants and pulled 'em up."

Jimbo and Marty are shaking their heads in agreement, as they seem to be co-signing each part of the tale. Every so often Klien looks past me toward Jimbo, then back to Marty St. Clair for reassurance that I am telling the truth. Scoop has put down his book and turned on the bench to watch, though he has to bend a bit to see around the grill.

"Hearing MPs asking where the GIs are, I proceed to bail out of the little window in the small room. Without saying goodbye to the girl, I had grabbed my gear and headed out as fast as I could. Upon landing outside, I saw before me, in a glow of fog shrouded lights, the back to Dong Ha Combat Base. In a way, strange one at that, it was a welcomed sight. So I said screw it, and started walking toward the concertina wire."

"How many beers?" Nix asks, as he climbs the stairs going for the back door, though not waiting for answers as he knows there's a dozen of us.

"So I keep walking toward the wire, until I finally am able to make out one of our bunkers. I start hollering toward the bunker hoping the GIs inside can hear me. I told them not to shoot as I'm an American. I even have my flight jacket inside out, with the orange side out, waving it like mad. Would hate to be shot by one of our own."

"Damn! We had our chance."

"Fuck you, Marty," though I know Marty is just joking.

The laughing continues as Nix comes out with beers in hand. He leans down, first at Klien, then makes a wide circle including me next, then Jimbo, and on. When he leans down we each take one out of his arms, I took two as my beer ammo cans are needing refilling on my chair. Slowly he makes his way around until all of the pilots have received a beer or two. He lets the last couple slide out of his arms onto the railing then turns toward the grill. He hasn't changed his flight suit though it isn't as sweat stained as ours were. Typical maintenance officer appearance. Just enough hydraulic and engine oil to appear you've been involved in doing something, but not enough to ruin your flight suit. I've seen it for years. First with Marine maintenance officers, then with the Army maintenance types. I'd bet it's in all the services. Part of the position is your appearance, and though not school trained, Nix has the appearance. But today, along with Lardo and Scoop, his dress is out of place. We here gathered on The Porch in a makeshift array of casual clothes that some of us would not be caught dead wearing in the States. Since my stay, not brief enough, in maintenance, Nix and I have come to a working relationship. I hope never to be stationed with him again, but probably will. But I can see that at times, he's like me. If I were transferred down to the 1st CAV, I'm sure I would have my hands full learning their style of flying. Their style works for them in the southern AOs, so it's not wrong. But it would take some serious training on my part to understand it, and then agree to fly like that. No, Nix is not one of the bad guys, just one of the guys from a different school of thought. Hopefully he understands that I'm no longer his enemy, especially since he's moved into a maintenance position until he can work out a transfer.

"My steak?" Nix asks Jimbo.

"On the grill, if Mask didn't burn it," Jimbo points.

"Beautiful, who got them?" Nix, arms finally empty, walks to the grill. He grabs a paper plate thrown by Mask and quickly loads his plate with the two steaks.

Mask thumbs toward Jimbo.

"Excellent *mon Capitan.*" Bowing his head in recognition to Jimbo for buying them.

"Your share is twelve dollars for the booze and the meat," Jimbo replies with mouth full.

"Anywaaay . . . The guards let me climb through the wire. A damn bitch I might add. Ripped my fucking flight suit in several places. I promised them a bottle of hard stuff if they don't tell anyone. But they wanted weed." I look over to Cool and the old timers laugh.

"After going to my hootch and returning with the booze, I passed out."

I stopped to take a couple of bites of steak. Fred's out again, because of Nix, and going from hand to hand looking for any leftovers or any meat that has yet to be devoured.

"Next morning, at the General's Mess, my usual seat by the back door is taken. The Old Man has me sit next to him. Hell, I smelled like a barroom outhouse, and looked like death warmed over."

"Mind if I join you?" Sweet Griffin says coming up the stairs.

"Come on up. Sit down. We're listening to a Sneaky story. Klien get him a steak."

Jimbo is a most gracious host. The southern gentleman exudes from him. You never know if he likes you or not, but he can sure make you feel at home. It's the beauty of southern charm, with a bit of Texas thrown in.

Klien takes a cold, well-charred steak off the corner of the grill and gives it to Rick with the nearly empty bottle of sauce. He sits between Jimbo and me up on the railing.

"Anyway, the Old Man doesn't say a word all day or, for that matter, several days. I fly him all over the DMZ and he never once says a word about the incident. Then one night he comes into the club and calls for attention. In his hand is a hat with a W2 bar on it. He calls me front and center, and presents it to me. Then, tells me to find the owner. Everyone knew about it, but nobody had asked if it was me. I guess they just took it for granted."

"Shit, no one could believe you did it is why," Jimbo interjects. "When I heard about it, I didn't believe it."

"Finish the fucking story. I want to go to the Club." Marty is standing up, waving his hand for me to finish.

"I take the hat, which happened to be the one I left in the whorehouse, and the General says, 'I'm going to call you Sneaky from now on. 'Fuck that', I tell him and I ask him why. He say's that whoever owned the hat and, yes, I'm sure he knew it was mine, had walked through a minefield to get back onto the base."

Both Klien and Hunt lean back into their chairs with looks of shock on their faces. In Army aviation there's many stories that are true, and some that are not so true, so this has them guessing. What starts out as a minor incident becomes a very large story as the years go by, with the help of the pilots repeating it a little more colorfully than before. New warrants are easily led down the path of many a tall tale, but these guys are getting wiser, so they're thinking, "Is it, or is it not, true?"

They both look over to their platoon leader who they know would never lie. Jimbo waits, letting the story sink in before he nods his head affirmative.

"So when the next SOI came out, our call-sign was changed to the Sneaky Whites and I was . . .

"Of course you were." Marty interrupts.

"Fuck you Marty. I am, get that! I am the original Sneaky White, or Double White. The name has stuck since. We changed our unit patch from the Black Maria's to Casper the Friendly Ghost."

Glancing around, I catch Lardo twisting his head to avoid eye contact. He and Skip both shake their heads in amazement or maybe disgust. Fuck them. What difference does it make what they think?

"You really walked through a minefield?" Klien asks, his mouth agape.

"Yep. And I wouldn't advise it for young W1s to try. Need to get some time in country before you're that experienced." Still they're not sure if this was a story story, or a truthful story.

Marty puts his foot out and stamps it on the porch. "Yeah, typical Marine mine sweeper."

It breaks the seriousness and everyone laughs. The ice is broken and although the newbies are not totally sure, they try to fit in with the other pilots and laugh in exaggerated displays. Cautiously however, their eyes dart between the pilots, looking for a sign that they're being kidded.

"Let's clean this place up and get to the Club." Double D is ready to get drunk.

"Attention!" Laughter continues. "Attention! Tonight is the last night Bob Nix will be with us," Jimbo announces. It's a surprise, heads turn toward him, "Tomorrow he becomes the 2nd Brigade Commanding Officer's pilot. A Brandy Flight pilot. Congratulations Bob!"

Marty stands up and asks, "They have whorehouses in Phu Bai?"

Pilots grumble among themselves as they like Nix, although I have nothing to say. We'll meet again someday.

"Fuck it. Let's go to the Club and party!" Marty's throwing the last tidbits of steak to Fred, begging in front of him. He catches them in mid air and without chewing swallows the meat whole.

Cleanup is done in record time. All scraps are thrown to the floor for Fred, paper plates and empty beer cans into a fifty-five-gallon trash drums. Full, and half full, cans are carried, sloshing, into the hootch. Bottles of Mateus, now empty, are taken inside to become candle holders.

"Sneaky, you wearing your dress flight suit to the party?" Killer asks.

"No! I wear it only for formal occasions and this isn't formal."

Referring to the Artillery Red flight suit I, Sweet Griffin, and a couple others, had custom made in Thailand. Form fitting with all the standard pilot pockets and zippers. The different patches we have gathered in our flying careers are attached like baubles. Embroidered into my epaulets are the CWO-2 bars. On the upper right breast is a Griffin. Over our heart and below our silver Army Aviator Badge are our names. Above the wings, a big round red and white peace patch with the words FUCK COMMUNISM encircled around it. I don't have my Marine Combat Air Crew Wings, CIB, or novice Parachute Badge embroidered on. This is worn just for aviation gatherings. The short sleeves are filled with patches. On our left are three by five inch American, Vietnamese, and Thai flags sewn vertically. On the right we wear a 'Laotian Highway Patrol' patch. From afar, it looks like a California Highway Patrol patch but California has been replaced with the word Laotian and there's no 'Eureka' in the center just a big gold star. Rick has a 'Yankee Air Pilot' flag below this. Below our names, we have two patches. The outer one is an 'Over and Back' patch, signifying trips over and back into Laos and North Vietnam. It's Snoopy leaning against a dog house which is shot full of holes. The patch to the right is the 'KILL - SO OTHERS MAY LIVE' patch. On the other side of the full length zipper, we have the 'Southeastern War Games' patch. Then a 'Ski Mugia' patch, which represents the toughest valley in Southeast Asia. It has peaks that top out at five-thousand three-hundred feet and allow NVA gunners to fire down at you when you fly through to enter North Vietnam. Air America crews get paid big bucks for these flights.

Below these patches, Rick and I vary on the patches and the placement of them. On mine, from outside to the zipper sown tightly together are patches from HMM-262 Flying Tigers, 282nd AHC Black Cats (though I was assigned to the maintenance unit called the 484th TC) and the Sneaky Whites. Below these are a Jungle Expert and Cobra patches. We wear the suits with our highly shined black boots and around our necks, a white silk scarf with the CCN emblem embroidered on it. Standing together we look like a pair of overly decorated Christmas trees. Rick hopped an NKP Black Bird to go over to Thailand to get them. When we got them, everybody snickered, but now we're the envy of the unit. One night we went down to Camp Evans for the monthly Battalion "Hail and Farewell" party dressed in them. We caused a stir. Later the brass relayed orders that unauthorized uniforms would not be tolerated. I wonder if they think we fly in these red zoot suits. Good idea, but no, we only break them out for special occasions.

One at a time, the pilots leave for the club and the hootch stills. Lardo has not said a word to me even though I caught him glancing over several times while we were on The Porch. No acknowledgment of each other's presence have been made since our return late this afternoon.

At the custom chair in my cubical, I sit in front of two Sanyo fans. I direct the air flow so the heavy damp air will hit me, not my bunk with Fred full of steak perched on it. Reaching over, I turn up the Teac 6010 reel to reel I bought last year. I play long hair music that no one likes, finding it easy to escape my present reality while listening to Mozart's Piano Concerto #21. The strings smooth the turmoil left from this morning's encounter with the reaper.

"Turn that shit down!" Marty, a true Motown consignor, has never liked me playing classical music.

I plug in my earphones and slide them on, then lean back. Last night's hang over was cured by noon, but my new one will be starting in an hour or so. Reaching under my bunk into the duffel bag, I pull out a bottle of J&B Scotch. These pilots don't drink much hard liquor, and none of them like Scotch. This has it's advantages because I'll drink anything and I don't have to worry about platoon members getting into my private supply. I take swig after swig straight from the bottle, no need to impress anyone here. Another gift my mother gave me through years was the knowledge that Scotch is bruised when mixed with water or any other liquid. Pouring it over ice is the worst you can do to perfectly good Scotch. So drinking it from the bottle or, in front of company, from a water glass, is how I've become accustomed to enjoying it. After each swig, I take a small sip of beer to wash it down. Yeah, I'll be drunk early tonight.

Chapter 13

Fred wakes me. His tail wagging excitedly at a good one-to-one vibration. My watch shows it's eight-thirty. God, I've dozed off. I pull off the earphones and throw them on the bed. Capping the large green bottle that's resting in the crook of my arm like a baby's bottle, I slip it back into it's hideaway for the night. Not fully awake I pick up the warm beer and stumble to the front of the hootch. No one's here, it's quiet except for muffled sounds of Strauss's Emperor's Waltz coming from my over amplified earphones. Turning on the light over the bar, I see the place is cleaned up. Since we got the Kid, the place never seems to be in the turmoil it used to be. Everything is where he's neatly arranged it. There's a place for everything and everything's in its place. His handy work is exhibited on opening the refrigerator as well. Cans of beer, Mateuse wine bottles, sodas, and water jugs are neatly lined up. Taking a jug of water, I step out the front door. I pour the cold fluid over me while standing on the front steps. It shocks me out of oblivion and becomes refreshing, as it tingles over my open sweaty pores. I ought to go back in there and rearrange everything in a mess to remind the Kid he's still a newbie in this platoon.

Walking back to my cubicle, I throw the jug on the Kid's bunk. Let him fill it when he gets back. I need to brush the rancid taste from my mouth then get to the club and see what I'm missing.

On the back porch, I brush my teeth, without tooth paste, and rinse my mouth out. I come back in and turn the fans back toward my bed, then turn off the tape player. With Fred at my heels I go for the front door. Stepping out, I look straight out and westward. Vietnam sunsets are the most beautiful I've ever seen. Even Cool admits they cast a spell on you. Reds, violets, and deep purples born somewhere over Laos or Thailand are given to the Vietnamese to witness and to us Westerners to savor while visiting. Truly spectacular. Several nights I've set my Nikon up and taken pictures for several hours, as the vast palette changes its kaleidoscope of colors. Such a beautiful country to be so brutally torn apart. Are we part of the fix or part of the problem? In all my years over here, I've vacillated between those thoughts. There's times we have done good in helping the common Vietnamese. Then there's times we've lost control and become part of the problem, with the destruction of their country and I too have at times fell into this trap. As it's been said and repeated often in the Fourth Estate, "We'll destroy the Hamlet to save it." Somehow I just reason with that kind of logic, or illogic. Are we good or are we bad? It has to be one or the other, doesn't it? Isn't life black and white? Or are there grays, and those grays are viewed differently by opposing sides? At this point, I'm not sure, but if you listen to the press, we're on the wrong side. But from what I've been taught, the press could never have its freedom to do its job if it was with the bad guys. Hell who knows, and more importantly, who cares. When you're a spec of sand on the beach, you sort of get missed by glancing eyes. Maybe I'm just a spec in this war, probably am.

I thought about where I'm going to retire. It will not be back to Connecticut. I've had it with snow and I don't want to live in the shadow of my father. North Carolina would mean I'm with my wife, and at this point, I don't see that happening. Plus, I just don't want to live around a military base. After all these years I've come to understand why people loath the military. So North Carolina is out of the picture. I really think, if I live long enough, that I'll settle here. My girl friend, Twit, is in the Hue area in the small roadside village of Houng Ca with our son. I am sure I could live quite well off my retirement with the cost of living like it is.

Maybe I can even get a job with Air America and continue flying. I need to look into this. As long as there is an American presence here, you can be sure Air America will be operational.

The though of Twit warms my heart. Though a girl friend, our relationship has gone a lot further than this. If anything, we are more man and wife than what I am experiencing with my legal wife. It's not only having a son, though he can pass for me except for his black hair, which is from his mother's genes. He's being raised under the thumb of his grandmother, and her views are slanted toward the Vietnamese ideas. Twit's a beautiful Vietnamese-French mix. Her father, the French side, was killed in some unnamed skirmish near An Khe years ago while he was serving with the French Army. To me, the French have never had an army, but I give them credit for putting on a slick parade. But Twit is very proud of her father's service and sacrifice, so quickly I learned to keep my feelings about the French to myself. Her mother moved her and two brothers up to Hue, to be near her family, after the loss of her husband. The brothers are a strange lot. One, is serving in the Vietnamese Navy. He's based out of Da Nang Harbor on a small patrol boat. When he gets up to Hue, which isn't often, he seems more willing to take from his family than to bring. In our two meetings, both over dinner, it was made clear that he wasn't happy with Twit's relationship and he was down right rude to me. The other brother I've never met. In fact, I didn't know he existed for some time, till I asked about a picture Twit had on a wall. She tried, at first, to say that she thought he was dead. But after some more questions, she then said he just left one night in 1965. When I asked if anyone had heard from him since, the verbal answer did not correspond with her facial one. I've come to the conclusion, not based on fact but more on the lack of facts, that he's probably a VC running around the jungle trying to do his best to kill Americans. One night, after a few too many Cognacs, I made that statement. It got me a far from playful slap and a cold shoulder for the rest of the time I was in Houng Ca. At this point, I don't give a damn either way, but I do care about Twit, so I'll leave the subject alone.

I'm now accepted by her family, and extended family, at an arms length, but it's proven to be hard on Twit. Of course we've compounded this with our son. I can't comprehend it, because of Twit's Eurasian heritage, it should, if anything, allow a peaceful joining of Twit's and my feelings toward one another. Unless the resentment against Americans is more prevalent than those against the French. The major issue with me is Twit. I know of her feelings toward me. It's not prostitute yourself to get money or gifts, if you can call it gifts. No, it's become love that has allowed us to overcome some of the problems that arise when two cultures become entwined. I see it in her eyes, and words do not need to be spoken. For me, it's a wonderful feeling that not only am I enjoying but I feel is lasting.

It's nights like this one when I wish I wasn't here but instead wrapped in Twit's arms. If I was based in Hue, I'm sure it could happen more often. For me, being with Twit is more enjoyable than going to a thirty-by-fifty foot club with a bunch of drunken warriors. My Griffin tour will be up in February, though I've been thinking of going back to an Aero-Scout unit. Maybe I'll extend for something at Da Nang. The only two units I would consider are the Black Cats, which I have already had a very short stay with, or the XXIV Corps Aviation Section. The 282nd Black Cats would be the better choice, not only because of the aircraft they fly, but being based at Marble Mountain Airfield would make life sweeter on the nights I couldn't get downtown. Going over to Corps Aviation might be a good move to have my ticket punched, but I know I would never last long with all the stuffed shirts around. Plus a VIP unit really isn't my calling. There is a large maintenance support unit at Red Beach I might be able to get into, but there I would be doing maintenance all day long. I bet their pilots don't get thirty hours a month and none of it combat. No, I've got to think of something else. I need the kind of unit that I could get off every few days so I could spend a few nights with her, rather than the once a week I'm getting now when I'm lucky. I also need to be at a base where when I leave it doesn't draw as many stares as I presently get. And where leaving with a few boxes of Tide soap powder and a couple bottles of Cognac stuffed in a helmet bag isn't considered a sin. It's gotten to the point that the Griffins have even given me looks of contempt when I leave and I'm sure they don't know about my child. They know I go to Phu Bai and they suspect that I'm spending the night with a Vietnamese, but that's it. I've tried to keep the Americans from knowing of our liaison, and not from shame, but because of the questioning I'd have to endure.

Americans in Vietnam have never taken the time, or interest, to seek the beauty of the Vietnamese people and their culture. Instead, they have shown destain toward them, calling them slopes, gooks, or slant-eyed motherfuckers, as if we were so almighty superior. I'm sure for some it's a carry over from boot camp, and all the military schools they have been paraded through, but it's still not an excuse. We're living up to the Ugly American image that at home we'd all deny. I have asked the question; why do we go fight a war for people in some far distant land, that most can't find on a map, if we don't like them? To this day, I've never received a plausible reply. For me, I feel at home here. I've found an inner peace and I feel it's beauty. It's not just during the daylight hours but through the time. I know to be happy, I must stay. Like a comfortable shoe, even when not needed you want it around, handy, just in case you need it.

The din of the club sweeps into my head.

"Come on Fred, let's see what's going on."

Turning, we go by the 1st Platoon hootch. Facing us, between the Admin/CO's hootch on the right and the Supply hut, is our club. By Army war zone standards, it's about average. Though I enjoy the club for atmosphere, some units use it as a status symbol. Spending thousands of dollars and time to spruce it up. The Phoenix club over on the other side of the runway is one like that. It looks like a whorehouse out of the 1880s. Also, I've been down to Da Nang several times to Gun Fighter Village and the

Air Force must have spent a million dollars on their club. It's carpeted, air-conditioned, with teak wood work and furniture throughout. The chairs are richly upholstered in velour, not old rocket crates as we have. Lighting is indirect, while ours is fourteen bare overhead one-hundred watt bulbs hung by the same wire carrying the electricity. But we do have an assortment of Playboy centerfolds on the walls and, if the breeze is blowing, we lift the upper wall panels and get a rush of air, though not air-conditioned or fresh.

In Gun Fighter Village if you go to the latrine, or head as I still refer to it, you walk into a tiled men's room that would be fitting for Grand Central Station. For the Griffins, it's down the stairs across the dusty maintenance road and pissing into an angled one-five-five canister shoved into the ground. Usually the rusted screen is holding freshly captured cigarette butts like a spider's web. The area around the tube base is water, or urine, making the act of urinating a challenge unless you don't care about standing in what you're discharging. The smell depends on the time of the year, time of day, and usage. This one's a stinker. Something about beer and the bladder allows us to dispose of the liquid as fast as we can drink it. And one tube has proven no match for the Griffins' many overfilled bladders.

Further down the maintenance road, off to the right, is the four holer, resting next to the Officers' forever cold shower. If you need to use it, carry plenty of matches or a lighter, the smell is totally unbearable. Not only from human waste that's resting in honey buckets located below each hole, but droppings piling up that have missed the twenty-three inch diameter containers. Added to this is the kerosene smell that is used to ignite the holdings of the buckets, which are burned each day. I'd give a year's pay to have the dumb son of a bitch who thought up the idea of burning shit with kerosene fuel in my grasp for five minutes. What a sick fucking mind. I'll bet he's never been to Nam. Probably at Fort Sam Houston treating the nurses to his gentlemanly charm before they go off to tend to the poor wounded boys in Vietnam.

I open the Club's back door to see it's packed. Letting Fred run in ahead of me is one of the few privileges Fred knows is his. All three platoons are represented tonight. I walk along the bar until I get to it's end where I throw a wrinkled twenty cent military payment certificate on the bar, and without a word, a cold Crown is opened by Sergeant W.E.L. Jones. Jones, the 2nd Flight Platoon Platoon Sergeant, and I are friends and he knows that with no scotch in the house I'll only be drinking beer.

"Sneaky, there's only a case or so of cold beer left, rest are warm."

From Washington State, he's been in the Army for seven or eight years and is considered a 'lifer'. At first, he and I were at each others throats when he found out that I helped Wee Willie change a main transmission one night. Then when he found out it wasn't even my aircraft, he when through the roof. When he got to me, he was beet red with anger. He'd never been around a warrant who got his hands dirty. He couldn't figure out why an officer, though only a warrant officer, would help a crew-chief work on an aircraft.

Jones had been in aviation since he joined the Army so he'd been around many officers. Until his assignment, he'd been assigned to slick or Charlie Model gun units. So being in Cobras, for the first time, did present some new problems for him. The first was that the crew-chiefs didn't fly with the aircraft, which meant a bit lower moral for the unit. But with Hueys, the pilots, and especially the warrants, would help keep the bird clean. It was more the rule than the exception to see a warrant cleaning his window or dusting the console between pilot's seats. So then he hears that a Mr. White helped change a transmission in one of his aircraft, and it was not his, during the wee hours of the morning, and then to top it off, this warrant officer then had the nerve to sign the work off as if he knew what he was doing. But after inspecting the safety wire job on the chip detector and being told by several of his men that yes, the warrant officer did that wiring job, he wanted to meet me.

After feeling me out about my abilities, I informed him that if he checked the wiring job again, he'd notice that it wasn't done with safety wire pliers, but the old hand over hand method. To me, as I explained to the now calming Sergeant, it was the better way to safety wire, and if I had my way safety wire pliers would be forbidden in the Army. He left, still a bit PO'd but calmer. Wee Willie told me that he had gone straight back down to the hanger to reinspect the chip detector. Wee Willie was cleaning Zero-Two-Seven when he watched Jones go into the next revetment and open the doors to perform the inspection. From there Jones, who at the time had been in the Griffins less than a week, asked Wee Willie what he knew about me. I can only guess what he was told, but within days Jones and I became friends.

"Wilham, I need a couple cases for Wee Willie. Zero-Two-Seven took it in the shorts today."

As the platoon sergeant he'd know just how bad I took it. He'd witnessed my landing and the outburst with Lardo so I was sure he and Wee Willie had talked.

"Damnit! I almost forgot, I need to give the sheet metal mechanics a couple of cases as well."

"Gave Willie three cases after dinner. He said two were yours and he paid for the third. I didn't know about the other two cases," he looks over to the stack of beer against the wall, "I could send a couple of warm cases down there. They can get them cold how they want." He's referring to the frowned on, if not illegal, practice of using a fire extinguisher on the cans to instantly cool them down. If not careful, you freeze them solid.

Unzipping my lower right calf pocket, I pull out a wad of MPC. It looks like Monopoly money, and when drunk you give away twenty dollars thinking it's five. I throw a twenty and a ten on the bar.

"That's for his beer, the guys in the hanger, and I want what's left of the cold now."

Jones reaches for the colored crumpled bills and lays them

on the damp bar. Then with great care, he rubs them flat then slides them into the metal ammo box that is being used as the till. Then he searches for change, until I wave him off.

"Keep it and take of a couple of the cold ones for yourself."

Nodding, he turns and opens one of the three refrigerators lined up on the back wall. If they have already gone through the cold beers then I am really late for the party. But the noise at the tables is not of the party nature, more of individual talk among friends. Wilham starts stacking up cold beers on the bar. Grabbing three or four in each hand, I walk over to the table in the corner to my left. It's near the back door and has Killer, Scoop, Mask and the Kid sitting around it. I make the trip several times until we have all the cold beer on our table. Before finishing the last trip, I ask Jones about Zero-Two-Seven.

"Don't worry. They're not going to work on it tonight. Wee Willie said not to come down, he's at his hootch." Jones knows I'll go over there after a while and have a few beers with the crew-chiefs, whose company I enjoy.

The Kid moves his chair back as I sit down, allowing me to lean back and still be in sight of everyone. Small talk is going on at each of the seven tables. Lardo's at the other end of the club sitting with Jolly Roger and Sherrily, probably trying to figure how to get a medal for today's action. Surprise asshole! No medals for CCN missions. The Griffin warrants have an unwritten rule not to make a big deal about our actions during CCN flights. What the hell is the citation going to say?" On such and such a day, so and so flew a Cobra in support of classified missions in classified area so and so. While flying, such and such happened, and so and so did this to protect so and so when this happened at this classified location. Then, who'd sign it? Shit! CCN is flying for the thrill of it, not for dog and pony show awards. We're part of the toughest operation in Southeast Asia and to me, that's honor enough. To be accepted by the likes of Captain America, Billy Washburn, Blaster, Valentino, the Recon Team members, as well as your fellow Griffins is more then we need. If medals were given, all the brass would go out to get one or two or whatever the market would bear. If we did what we did for CCN on regular ARA missions, we'd all be laden down with baubles and trinkets. Or, we'd be in Long Bien jail awaiting court martial. It depends on who saw what and who reported it to what superior.

"Sneaky is that true about the pig?" The Kid has asked a no no.

"Not the fucking pig!" Jimbo, two tables over, hears the word pig and the thought of hearing the story for the hundredth time aggravated him as well as me.

"Come on, tell the Kid." Double D has probably got the Kid into this, like the Sneaky story on The Porch.

I should get up and leave. I'm welcome at Wee Willie's. Or, maybe I can get a jeep and try to get on the road and go to Hue for the night. The drive is too long and you never know on QL-1 at this hour, but I'd sure try. But I'd never get past the gate. This isn't Dong Ha and the 108th.

"What about the pig?" asks Mask sitting across from me.

I lift Fred onto my lap and feed him a stick of beef jerky from those laying in a pile in the center of the table. I start to tell a story that could have been the end of my military career.

"One day I was flying a re-supply mission out to a radio relay site at the west end of Happy Valley. It's west of Da Nang overlooking the Laotian boarder. I had just made AC and this was one of my first flights. Because it was our slack day, we started about nine in the morning and the crew was hung over to the max."

"When have you ever not been hung over?" Marty's remark gets laughs from the other tables, but not this one.

Ignoring the chuckles, I go on. "I was flying an early D Model. My crew-chief, an old timer on his second or third tour, was Buck. Because we had a late start, Buck was still drunk from the night before. Come to think of it, I've never known Buck to be sober."

"Perfect crew-chief for you," yells Cool, who's sitting across from Jimbo.

Sweet Griffin is holding court with older AC's at his usual table diagonally across from us in the other corner. Should have sat with them, then this wouldn't be happening.

"Any fucking way . . . I was hung over . . . hell we all were hung over. Some old snake eater unloaded his jeep into our slick, making sure that everything was checked off on a manifest I had to sign for. After we were loaded, we took off. Now this was during the old days at Da Nang Airfield, before the Marble Mountain air strip down at China Beach. When you took off by helicopter, you had to do a tight orbiting climb directly over the field 'til you got to three-thousand-five-hundred."

"You've never been that high in your life," Marty is still trying to end this story.

"You get a nose bleed?" Jimbo has joined in with the jabs at my story. Then rolling his eyes, he and Marty laugh.

"Fuck both of you gentlemen," as I hoist a can of beer in their direction.

"Go on, what happened?" Mask asks, leaning forward in his chair. He is trying to block out the other pilot's chatter. He's engrossed in this new and unheard story about Sneaky.

"Well, we climbed up to altitude and flew to Happy Valley and landed on site. The site was sitting on the pinnacle of a mountain and you could only put one skid down while loading and unloading, something like Hickory. Buck threw everything out quickly, and I peeled off diving down the mountain's side. A couple minutes off the pad their RTO called. Said we forgot to give them the pig."

Mask opens beers for the six of us at the table and hands me a fresh one. "Here."

"Thanks. Anyway I told the RTO that we forgot the pig at Da Nang. Hell, I didn't know where it was or even if we had brought one. When I asked Buck, he said we'd left it back at Da Nang. So I promised the next time I was out in the area, I'd make it up to them plus throw in a case of beer."

"Why do you do everything based on a case of beer?"

Jimbo and Marty have moved their chairs to our table. Cool leaves Nix sitting alone as he stands up and goes through the back door. He's going to find a few crew-chiefs to smoke grass with. With that, Nix moves to our table as well.

Lizard, Yo Ho, and Dancer slide their table next to ours spilling a multi-tiered pile of empty beer cans. The comotion causes Fred to jump up in my lap, almost spilling my beer.

"Any fucking way!" I want to finish this before the night gets too much further along.

From my seat, I look directly at the corner table with Lardo, Sherrily, Jolly Roger, Crane, Stahel, and Verdine sitting around sipping beer. Lardo's still in his sweaty flight gear, pistol belt, and SOI chain, that's visible around his neck. Hell, he hasn't even gone back up to the TOC. Their table is bare of beer cans, which are stacked high on other tables. They seem to be observing the behavior habits of warrants rather than having a good time of their own.

"Ah. . . when we land at Da Nang and hover to the front of the line shack, there are several jeeps with Air Force brass milling about. After shutting down, my CO tells me to come to the hot shack, ASAP. While getting out of the Huey, one of the Air Force Majors starts yelling at me. Says he'll have my wings and that I'm a disgrace to aviation."

Stopping to take a long swig of beer, I observe that now I have the full attention of the other pilots and the room is quiet. Spider, Sweet Griffin, and several First Platoon ACs walked up to the circle, each holding a beer or two.

"So I ask Buck what the fuck happened?"

"Just before we get to the Hot Shack, he says, 'Mr. White as we were climbing over the airfield the pig stuck it's feet through the wicker basket, and shuffled to the door. Hell, I didn't know what was going on. So the fucking pig looks out the door. Looks back up at me, then winks."

"Winks!" Mask's mouth is agape. Sweet Griffin is shaking

his head. The others, who know the story grin. Those who don't, look about questioning.

"Yeah . . . Winks like this!" Marty is winking at Mask. Then, turning he winks at each of the gathering. "Everybody understand?" His animated gestures cause smiles.

"Do it a second time for the Commissioned Officers. I'm sure they might have some difficulty." Killer's remark has everyone laughing but the Kid, Yo Ho, and Mask.

"Let me finish the fucking story, okay? Anyway, Buck says the pig winks at him. Then the pig shuffles out the door and free falls about two-thousand feet."

Laughter starts again as the newbies think about the pig winking, then falling.

"It's not the end of it. Tell them what happened," Marty is now into this story as much as I am.

"Well the pig fell, without auto-rotating, until he crashed on, no I guess I should say in, the wing of a VNAF DC-3. That's why the Air Force was pissed. Sixty pounds of free-falling pig does a lot of damage to metal. Goddamned lucky he didn't kill anybody. Anyway there was no Board of Inquiry or Review. Our CO made a deal that we would help fix the damage and my name was mud in the Black Cats."

The new pilots and some of the older ones, that hadn't heard the story, are doubled up with laughter. Sneaking a glance over to Lardo's table I see they're not laughing, just sitting stonefaced in the corner looking at the warrants.

"Jones! Get the house a round!" Yelling above the noise of the laughter.

"Sneaky, it's only warm. Will that do?"

"Yeah, it's free. These bastards have no manners or morals."

"Got it."

He opens a refrigerator door decorated with a collage of photos of past Griffin pilots. Most show them in different stages of inebriation and doing antics that would not be considered proper conduct for an officer and gentleman. Yo Ho brings over a dozen beers in his arms, holding them like a young school girl with school books held tightly to her newly blossoming breasts.

"That's six-twenty Mr. White."

I pull out a ten and throw it at Yo Ho. "Put the rest on the bar."

"Tell them the rest of the story. It ain't over," Double D interjects.

"There's more?"

"Well after I got the Old Man calmed down and I knew I wasn't going to be hung by the balls, I drove back to the unit with Buck. I asked him for the truth because I was sure he threw the pig out. Once again he told me of the pig shuffling, winking, and jumping." Laughter again, though not as hard as before. "But Buck adds, 'Mr. White, I looked out the door and the pig was waving his legs like he's trying to fly'."

I stand and demonstrate with my arms fraying at the air. The younger guys now are doubled up and telling me to quit it, because it can't be true.

"Last thing Buck said was, 'Hell, I thought all Special Forces types are suppose to be jump qualified.' You've now heard the true story of the Special Forces pig on his first HALO jump and his arrival at Da Nang Airfield."

Looking at the younger men before me, who are laughing, I watch as Mask and Yo Ho stand facing each other waving their arms in the air.

Marty sees a chance to get one in. "They got a new dance called the chicken. I think we ought to send Sneaky and you too, Dancer, to American Bandstand to do the 'pig'."

Laughter gets out of control as several others stand doing the new dance Marty has named. Killer chokes while drinking and beer runs out his nose. Seeing this, we all become almost hysterical with laughter. It's become contagious. Killer swings the can around spraying me and Double D. Neither of us move, too tired and wet from sweat already.

Sitting with "Doodle" Woodruff is Dale "Bones" Collier, a twenty-four year old ex Air Force Medic. He's a lifer and his new wife is a college student going through nursing school in Maryland. Bones, though a lifer, has a great sense of humor and chides, "Sneaky lay off the Air Force."

"Come on Bones, you know the Air Force is a bunch of stuffed shirts."

"Fuck you, Jarhead!"

The laughter still hasn't died down. I get up and walk over to the bar to get another beer from the dozen or so stacked up on the counter. While I'm standing there, Lardo approaches.

"*Dai Uy*, want one?"

"I'll buy my own." The surly tone in his voice is easy to distinguish.

"What the fuck, afraid to take a drink from an Aggie?"

Snapping his head around he looks at me with indecision.

"Lardo, how the hell did you ever end up in Oklahoma? The Rio Grande was never dry enough to let you get your fat ass across it."

The laughing stops. The hanger incident has been discussed throughout the unit in whispered tones. Battle lines are clearly drawn. Warrants know flying into Laos takes guts and unorthodox methods to survive. Unfortunately some, mostly commissioned officers, are more worried about their Officer Efficiency Reports and then there is the idea of not being the last American to die over here. Enlisted will side with the warrants. Not because we're right, just that we're less wrong than the commissioned officers. A couple of the senior warrants will side with the commissioned, but in their heart they know I'm right.

"Listen asshole! You had the guts to cross the Rio Grande, at least have the guts to quit flying CCN if you're yellow." I turn away from him in disgust and open a fresh beer.

"I'll show you who's yellow!" Yelling, even though it's deadly quiet in the hut.

Feeling something poking at my left temple, I try to turn my head to see it. As I move my head, it stays pressed tightly against my skull. All I see is the outer side of a cylinder and the two heads of bullets inside of the chamber of a pistol.

The quiet is becoming deafening. I stand still, and though I can't move my head because of the pistol barrel, I know that I need to. This is no drunken prank! Looking into Jones's eyes, I see fear that he's never before experienced.

Rolling my eyes to the left I can see thirty-eight caliber bullets. I know this might be the end. Taking a deep breath, my mind gets fuzzy and time seems to stand still.

I'm propped against the door on the club's back porch with several warrants around me. Jimbo pushes the screen door against my back, making room for his large frame and steps outside.

"You'd better go to the hootch and sober up."

He's given me an order, not a friendly remark. I've known him long enough to comprehend the tone.

"I'll take him."

Klien grabs an arm and pulls me up, then drapes me over one of his shoulders. He has one of my arms swung around his shoulder and his arm around my waist. We do an uncoordinated dance, more of a shuffle, away from the club. I don't know what happened and I'm not ready to go to sleep. Fuck these guys that don't want to drink. Stumbling along, Klien half drags me, half supports me, toward our hootch.

"Fuck it! Let's go to Wee Willie's." I'm always good for a drink in his hootch.

"Captain Mitchener said to take you to our hootch."

"Okay let's go in the front, grab a six-pack, then out the back."

"I don't know. He's mad. He did give you a direct order." Youth is blindly innocent.

"Fuck you! Fuck his orders! What's he going to do, send me to Nam? Fuck all you bastards. I've got more time in country than all of you. So don't tell me about somebody's fucking orders."

"I don't know, Sneaky?"

"Fuck you too. Either grow up and take charge of your life, or let your mother . . . Jimbo . . . Lardo, or any other stupid son of a bitch tell you what to do."

"Okay, I'll come just to keep an eye on you," then stopping in his tracks and adding as an after thought, "but I won't drink."

"Fine, don't drink. More for the rest of us. Fucking pussy!"

He opens the front door and while I'm leaning over the bar, he pulls out a six-pack from the noisy refrigerator.

"Lets go, goddamn it! You're slower than shit."

Out the back door and off the porch, I stumble down the three small steps. Trying to grab me, he drops the beer, but still misses me. Hitting the ground, I lay there for a moment then stand, only because of his help.

"Goddamn it! Don't shake the fuckers, asshole!"

The beers are picked up by Klien.

We enter Wee Willie's hootch without knocking. Music is blasting and huddled to the right are forms hunched over an open case of beer. Empty cans litter the plywood floor like the back of a one-five-five howitzer after a heated fire mission.

"Yo . . . Sneaky." An armorer gets up to give me his chair.

"Thanks Rog." I say plopping down next to a speaker reverberating Ike and Tina Turner's, "Rolling on a River".

Hell of a great song, it's just that in my ear, it hurts. As helicopter pilots get older and get more flight time, they began to lose their high frequency hearing. It's because of all the noises generated by the helicopter. Most pilots have small plastic vials hanging from their helmets, with two rubber ear plugs inside. When putting on the helmet, they first put in ear plugs to help save their hearing. After thousands of hours flying, both as a door gunner, crew-chief, and now pilot, I know I should have worn them.

In the old days, with H-19s and H-34s, hearing the engine sounds and other assorted moans and whines was critical for a good crew-chief and pilot. You could tell by the sound what was going on inside the machinery hiding their parts and their woes. Once, as an H-34 crew-chief flying from New River, North Carolina, on a cross country flight to Quantico, Virginia, I told the pilot there was a strange new sound coming from the big R-1820 nine-cylinder engine. The pilot, who didn't fly my plane often, told me we'd look into it after we returned to New River. After shut-down at Quantico, I went over every part that I thought might be causing the noise. The new sound, a low noise, put the symphony out of tune. Finding nothing, I buttoned up the clamshell doors and headed to Washington, D.C. to party hard. Two days later, on our return flight, after refueling at Norfolk Naval Air Station, we leveled out at six-thousand five-hundred feet and the noise grew worse.

I asked my pilots if they heard or felt anything, and would they look for any changes in the engine instruments. Their "negative" answer was quick and irritating. Five minutes later, we sucked the number three intake valve, which lead to a complete engine failure after ten or so more revolutions of the Pratt and Whitney engine. After radioing maydays and relaying our position to the Elizabeth City, North Carolina Coast Guard Station, we proceeded to crash in the Great Dismal Swamp. We came to rest in two and a half feet of water, mud, and goo. Days later, after changing the engine in the swamp and flying the bird home, the maintenance officer asked me if I had any indication that something was amiss. He'd already inspected the log books and noted no written indicators. I told him that engine frequency was lower and about the new sound. A Master Sergeant sitting with us during our talk looked at the Major and said, "Well he's a real helicopter mechanic now." A rite of passage in my aviation life.

Now whenever I fly, I listen. Listen to the low basses of the main rotors and the main transmission, and to the altos or mid range sounds of the tail rotor, tail rotor shaft, forty-two, and ninety degree gear boxes, and then to the beautiful soprano whine of the turbine engine. When flying a Huey, your body will tell you if things are out of adjustment or balance. If you have a tail rotor our of track, by resting your feet lightly on the pedals they'll become numb quickly. To check a main rotor blade track, especially on aircraft with just two main blades, you hold a pencil by the point while you rest your elbow on your knee. If it doesn't bounce in sync with the rest of your body and the aircraft, then you have a beat. A beat can be a one-to-one which would be one main rotor blade tracking at a higher or lower plain then the rest. Nothing highly technical about it, just some good old Yankee intuition. So in time you and your body become part of the aircraft, feeling each new beat, knowing if it's a good one or a bad one. Pilots, in their own special way, are conductors keeping all the parts from flying off on their own, and trying to keep them working together.

"Kid!" In new territory his awkwardness shows. The enlisted men will take my cue on how to initially treat him. They know I'd never bring a jerk here. They also know if he treats them like shit on the flight line in the morning, someone will tell me not to bring him back to their living quarters. "Go up to the hootch and under my bed in the duffel bag is an open bottle of Scotch."

"All right . . . Good shit!"

"Shit hot!"

"Pass those beers around before you leave. And get a six-pack out of my box,"

I blink, trying to focus my eyes, then counting the half dozen men sitting around the low table between the two bunks. On the table before them is the torn open box with empty crushed beer cans strewn about.

"How bad's the damage?" I scream at Wee Willie.

The others stop their imaginary drum and guitar playing. Michaels turns down the music. "Said it might be ready late tomorrow, but I don't think it'll be flyable 'til Friday," he says looking to his right at the shirtless ebony skinned specialist sitting next to him.

Don't know his name as he's been in the unit only a couple

weeks, but the word is he's one of the best metalsmiths in Battalion. He asked for Griffins, so that he could be here at Camp Evans where some distant relative is stationed or maybe just to be far away from headquarters.

"Might have it day after tomorrow." He's talking to other crew members and purposely ignoring me, then turning he continues. "If I can get the stringers repaired. If that takes a lot of time, then everything's going to take a lot of time."

He's talking belligerently and with contempt toward me. I've got no idea if it's because I'm an officer, white, or the one who got Zero-Two-Seven shot up.

"Fuck it. I need another day or two off." Gulping down the now warm beer. A knock reminds me of the Kid on his booze run.

Entering the hootch with the Kid is Sergeant Jones carrying a case of beer and a large bag. The Kid didn't tell him I was down here, judging by the surprised look on his face when he sees me.

"How you doing?" he asks while everyone shuffles on the cots, either to the left or right, giving the two new drinkers room to sit.

Before I answer, he shakes his head. "You know I thought for sure the Captain was going to shoot you."

Shit, I remember now. No, I don't. What happened?

"After Captain Mitchener got you out, Captain Rogers took Captain Lardo to the Old Man's hootch. The Exec called right after that and told me to close the club down." Shaking his head. "Hell I can't believe what you said."

Neither can I. What did I say? Thinking at this stage is difficult. Can't remember what happened while I was at the club. There was music, I bought beers, I sat with second platoon guys, and I swapped a war story or two. Hell, what could I have said to get the club closed? Glancing over to Klien, I see him questioning the remark by the now unemployed bartender. If he doesn't know what happened, then maybe I'm not involved.

"What'd I say?" I ask, needing to prepare myself in case the Old Man calls me in.

"Hell! Sneaky, when he pulled the gun and stuck it to your head it got so quiet in there I couldn't believe it. I didn't know if it was loaded or not, 'til afterwards. Damn thing had all six rounds in it. Fuck, you stood there so calm, I thought I'd shit in my pants. Then you say, 'Well *Dai Uy*, either pull the trigger or put the thing away cause I can't stand here much longer.' Well, I didn't know whether to laugh or pee. I mean it. Looking in his eye, I didn't know what he was going to do. How did you? He could have shot you anytime he wanted to."

This explains some things. Now to figure out why he pulled the gun. My big mouth I'm sure. Shit! Can't remember a damn thing. Klien's expression tells me he doesn't have any answers either.

It's quiet, except for the hi-fi, with looks being traded from side to side and across the bunks. Some are in disbelief, some in awe. The black metalsmith's wrinkling his forehead to show his dissatisfaction at having officers invade his domain.

Grinning, Wee Willie breaks the silence. "A toast to Sneaky, the gutsiest pilot I've ever known."

All but the black and Klien raise cans in a salute to Wee Willie's toast.

"Thanks."

"Fuck Lardo." Wee Willie starts a conversation I shouldn't be part of. "Other ACs are complaining about him. Mr. Holiday said he overrode the controls during a rocket pass, while out in the A Shau."

First I've heard of this. "Knock it off! It's history!" I've got to change the subject. Klien, looking no longer like the young babe in the woods, as the premature aging process has started to catch up in his face, walk and mannerisms, is eyeing me. "I'm here to drink, listen to music and parrrttty."

"Alllll right . . . Lets boogie"

"Frenchy, turn it back up."

Janis Joplin is now raising into a crescendo as she sings Kris Kristofferson's "Me and Bobbie Magee." Wonder if they know

Kris was a helicopter pilot. Hell, he was also a West Pointer. Now this would cause a good argument trying to convince this drunken crew about Kris's background. Plus I think his dad was a 2 star General in WWII.

Heads are rocking back and forth to the music. Hands are drumming, picking the phantom instruments, feet are tapping out the beats. Janis has captivated these tired and overworked youth in this small plywood and tin building six-thousand miles from Janis' South Texas home.

Letting my eyelids fall down, I picture Twit's beautiful light golden brown body. I should have tried to go down to Hue but returning late from CCN screwed that up. Tomorrow my plane will be down, so I'm going there first thing. I'll hitch a ride on some vehicle traveling down QL-1.

Voices disrupt my thoughts. It's the off key sounds of the kids trying to get as far from Vietnam as possible, even if it's sitting in a car with Bobbie Magee listening to the windshield wipers keeping time.

Twit's now before me. Her long black hair hanging with all it's silkiness to mid-thigh. She lets me brush it for hours after I've relaxed and forgotten of war and flying, of Khe Sanh, A Shau Valley, and even of CCN. Her large almond eyes with the small thin black eye lashes, flicking away to gather my attention. The tantalizingly cute mouth that she has learned to use in ways that drive me crazy. My wife would never consider this a form of love making, only something a whore would do. My wife has her idea what being open about sexuality is all about, and it's only the missionary position that God gave her which is correct. Everything else is sinful and perverted. Twit's newest surprise is waking me up with her tongue flicking on my most sensitive extremity. Not quite a hundred pounds, she's very well proportioned for her four foot-three inch frame. Her skin is not typical Vietnamese but a lighter shade of olive brown that she takes pride in and keeps covered whenever in direct sunlight. When we first met, she would wear makeup but I've stopped her, explaining that I'm not interested in her trying to look American. So out went the push up and pinch in bras, most of her western style clothes, and her little containers filled with western cosmetics.

When dressed in traditional *Ao Dia*, she's the picture of Vietnam. Simple, vibrant, dainty, pure, but with inner strength. Vietnam's inner strength is proven again and again as one after another invader tries to influence it's culture. Whether with the Chinese invaders or centuries later in the 1600's with a Jesuit priest who didn't like the sing-song Vietnamese language and felt that he should change it. Vietnam is still resisting the change being exerted from many directions by the outside invaders, whether it is China, Japan, France or, like now, the United States. She's held to the simple ways that have served her people so well for thousands of years. And for me, their simple ways are part of her beauty.

Twit's eyes are rounder than most Vietnamese and her mouth is slightly larger which adds excitement to our lovemaking. A beauty to look at, which I try to remind her of when I call her my Orchid. She's dainty, fragile, but the strength is her power that bursts from her inner being, just as it does from her homeland.

She has a body that's firm, narrow at the waist, and hips that have not spread even after bearing our son. Her butt is round, not flat the way most end up. I joke about her pubic hair, or lack of it, but I actually enjoy the almost void area with its fifty-six black hairs that I've counted many times. She reminds me that westerners are hairy and asks about western women. Sometimes I think I ought to have some big blond Amazon women stand next to her and let her compare, then maybe we could get on with our lives. Her stomach is flat and has no stretch marks. Her breasts, though small, are firm and the nipples are deep brown with a slight upward tilt. The areola is larger then other Orientals and as we've learned, are very sensitive to the touch or kiss. When first together, she didn't like me to caress them, but as time has gone by her feelings have changed about sexual matters. No longer is it mechanical. Now it's an event that we both look forward to eagerly.

One night after coming home from a multi-course dinner at the small cafe near the main Hue Catholic church, we were laying entwined in each others arms. Idle talk returned to the subject that punctuates most of our talks after the lights are out, whether or not she was physically good enough, complaining of lack of big tits, pubic hair, and so on. She told me for the first time she had felt an orgasm though she didn't know how to explain it. Giggling, she whispered that I gave her this special gift. It was a gift we shared and I knew that may be the only time in my life I'd have those feelings.

"Sneaky!" I'm being pushed. "Another beer or Scotch?"

"Scotch."

Squinting, I see nothing's changed but the music, now it's The Doors. The room, still dark, is as I left it before entering my dream moments, minutes, or hours ago. Vietnam to these men is work, geting loaded, sleep or passing out, work, get up, sleep or passing out, and so on. It never changes, it just runs on and on, until the three-hundred and sixty-five days are completed and DEROS has arrived. This is their Vietnam, not mine.

Klien pours brown fluid into a rusted and dirty canteen cup. He has a beer tucked between his thighs. He too has succumbed to the gentle persuasion given in war. You're either flying or getting drunk to forget about flying. War does this to you slowly and after a year or two you don't know where time went, what you did, or who has entered and left your life. He'll find this out much too soon. Already aged in physical appearance, he's no longer the spit shined boots, freshly cleaned flight suit, young virginal warrant trying to learn everything and please everybody. No bright and crisp patches; now they're faded and frayed. The flight suits have a musty smell that all our clothes end up with after several months in Vietnam. His hair's too long, and I see he forgot to shave, but then he could forget several mornings and no one would take notice. He tried growing a mustache but the ribbing got to him, so in a drunken frustration one night it was whacked off.

With only a dozen whiskers under your nose there's no need to let them run wild. I cut off my handlebar mustache several weeks after he joined the unit, so he knows what a good mustache looks like.

The change inside has been the most dramatic. I'm sure Mother would not like her baby boy, Buff, now. Not only did he age too quickly, though by Vietnam helicopter pilot standards he's normal, he's also drifted in a direction she may not agree with. Sometimes his answers are a bit too surly and quick. He's been known to snap back when pushed. It has come time to regard normal human life as a passing phase we go through while becoming gun pilots. Handing out free passes for another day and then on other days taking away the right to breathe. One day, while flying in the DMZ, a Dustoff took fire from a bombed out school house. We flew over to provide some protection and after a couple passes the remaining NVA scurried out the back and ran down a rice paddy. Turning in on one we were less than a hundred feet off the deck flying at one-hundred and twenty knots when I fired a pair of rockets. The rockets converged on the black pajama sprinter and after impact only a hole was left in the dirt dike. Pulling out, Klien, my front seat begged me to fly over the hole and it's pieces, parts, scattered limbs and pajamas, so he could get some photos. A sign of callousness creeping into a virgin. It's said one small wiggly sperm can get a women pregnant and look at her size after eight or nine months. One small ride in a Cobra, and look what happens a few months later.

In a far off land, in northern India, is an area called Ladakh. Ladakh is located in East Kashmir along the Tibetan boarder at an altitude of over 15,000 feet. Very few people live in this remote cold desolate wind-swept high desert. Plant life is sparse and animals are rare and dependant on each other. This is the home, and the only place in the known world of the Griffin Vulture. The largest of all vultures and known for it's flesh eating habits. Are we Griffins named after those vultures or for the mythical creatures that are brazened onto our patches?

Or could the ride in the Cobra start a growth, which like the pregnant woman becomes a large growth. Is it cancerous, does it extend life, or take life?

I knew he was infected with the cancer after a CCN mission he flew. The 'yards brought back four bodies, not bodies, just heads. Klien, and a few others also infected with the cancer, took turns taking pictures of each other holding the heads by the hair. Two per hand and grinning like they had personally gone out in the deep dark jungle and done the deed themselves. Shirtless and standing in front of Cobras, they held the fruits of their labor. Does his mother, or society, know what they are going to get back when his tour is over? This business is for the warrior, not for a loving mother's son. Buff's cancer has grown out of control and I wonder if we all will become infected ten or twenty years from now. Will we be callous, will life be just a passing fancy? For some I hope not. For others, maybe we ought to stay in Vietnam and not go back to America to spread the cancer in the clean pure western society. This is why I'm different. I feel the cancer and I have seen it grow. I know I can't go home and give it to others. As a leper, I've found a new home, away from western mankind.

Also during the years, I've grown to respect the NVA. This has caused many arguments. No longer do I look at myself as a soldier. Now I'm a warrior. A warrior has a mission, and the job is nothing personal. I go out and complete the mission. If you give me a mission to fly and fire rockets or if a target opens up on me, it becomes a test of my warrior status. I'm not doing it 'for God and Country'. Not fighting the red demons. No, it's a test of my status, my warrior status, and it's the obligation I owe. Medals don't mean shit. Those are for guys who want to impress other noncombatants or wannabees. The medals we get are intangible, it's respect within the section, flight, platoon, battery, battalion, by the men we help out, and by other warriors who are honor bound. I have found this far more satisfying than going to some dog and pony show, listening to some blown up lie about how we risked all to do this mission. Shit, I don't risk anything. It was an honor to serve my fellow warriors. I love it and having everybody shake my hand saying what a fine guy I am is bullshit. Pure bullshit! I'm not a nice guy. I don't socialize well. When a major or colonel tells me I'm an asset and good for Army Aviation, I think of just what men, old men, will say or do to push younger men to their deaths. As with Samurai, we warriors here in Vietnam know the difference between us and the much be-medaled career soldiers who are here for their mandatory one tour to get some unseen ticket punched that will allow them to advance a rung in the military complex.

"Sneaky! Sneaky let's go."

Looking around, the music's lower, bunks are empty except of their curled residents. Klien and I sit alone.

"Yeah we got to hit it."

Wee Willie says as he plugs in a head set with the earphones hanging over his pillow. "See ya."

I stand, unsteady, and give a final wave to the now still hootch. Small glows in several cots, as mechanics try to get a quick cigarette or joint, before falling off into oblivion.

Klien still trying to support me, helps me up the slope to our back porch.

"Was that true, about the pig?"

Now alone, he hopes to get the truth.

"True my lad, very true."

Not knowing that in several years while flying for Air America I'll hear the story again, this time with a water buffalo being slung under the aircraft, being told by men who don't know that I am the Sneaky and it was only a pig.

Entering the hootch, I stumble still clothed onto my bed. Air blowing from repositioned fans makes it bearable. Boots dropping on the floor and a grunt or two following is all the good night I get from Klien. Fred rearranges his head which is now resting on my calves, and we both fade out.

Chapter 14

"Let's go! You're flying."

Jimbo's up, and it seems as if I only just got back on the late 5th Trans. log run. Spending time with Twit those two days has given me relief and time for Captain Lardo to be gracefully transferred to Battalion Headquarters. Our confrontation with the pistol several nights ago has caused a shakeup in the platoon and battery.

The next morning, the Old Man had me in his office with my heels locked. After one of the greatest ass-chewings I've ever received and threats of multiple charges under the UCMJ, I was given time to allow things to be sorted out. The warrants came to my aid, as did those who had flown with Lardo. They were adamant about him not staying in the unit. It wasn't only his attitude, but several came forward and told of their controls being overridden by the captain. The issue of the controls was the no-no that sent him packing. The surprise was Captain Crane's and the XO's responses. Though not in my corner, they felt Lardo's actions were totally unbecoming of an officer and gentleman.

Warrant officers are not real live officers. They're just a mistake the Army had been lulled into in its need to quickly build up its aviation corps. Some feel warrants are overpaid and over promoted truck-tank drivers. My experience is that commissioned officers on flight status are a waste of money and it's proven when they decide where, when, and how the warrants are to fly missions. A four or five hundred hour commissioned officer telling me about flying, when I've got several thousand rotary wing flight hours, plus the fact that I've been raised around airplanes all my life, is not only asinine but a complete waste of the manpower that the generals are always crying about not having enough of.

I was born in England, where my mother was working for the United States Embassy as an executive secretary. She met my father, a German going through English medical school, and the rest, as they say, is history. When I was two, the Germans had started bombing England, and my father sent us to the safety of the States. He stayed on, joining the Royal Navy as a flight surgeon in a submarine patrol squadron. Because he was a Jew, the RAF assigned him flight duty on anti-U-Boat patrols flying 'loaned' American PBYs from Reykjavik, Iceland across the North Atlantic to Nova Scotia. Mom and I first lived at Quonset Point Naval Air Station in Rhode Island, but moved to Floyd Bennett Field in New York City so she could work for the US Navy Department there. Every few months we'd take the long train ride to Nova Scotia and see my father who'd lay over for a few days. By 1943 he was the squadron commander, unusual for a flight surgeon, but his flying abilities coupled with the horrific loss of RAF pilots flying on the Eastern Front won out. This allowed our trips to become more and more frequent.

With the war ending, his last official naval act was to supervise some paper shuffling at the Alameda Ship Yards, as the British gave back some of the hardware they borrowed while in the Pacific Theater. We lived in Richmond, California, and I attended my first non-Jewish school. Going to public school while in California was a shocking experience. Upon his discharge, it was decided we'd stay in America. All my father's family, and extended family, had been marched off and killed at Treblinka concentration camp. The Germans were a thorough bunch, not only was the family gone but so was the little Jewish village my ancestors were from. People, property and even buildings, were flattened and the land turned into 'productive farm land for the Third Reich.' The loss of his family changed my father, as I am sure it did for thousands like him, forever.

We moved back to New York City where my mother worked as a manager for Longchamps Restaurant, while my father struggled nights at Children's Hospital getting board certified so that he could practice medicine in his new home. In no time, he passed and opened up a small practice in Harlem. We moved from the Hotel Teresa uptown to Fort Washington Avenue with our new wealth. After buying our first car, the family goal was to buy an airplane. By '48, we were doing well.

Our first plane was a silver Navion which, for its day, was considered large. It could carry four comfortably and five if you had someone who was small squeeze between the two in the back seat, though there was no seat belt for the fifth passenger. We'd fly to upstate New York or to Martha's Vineyard for weekends. Once a year, we'd make the winter treks to Florida, which allowed me weeks of planning the flight. By thirteen, I was able to command the whole flight. From a very thorough preflight, to the start-up and take-off, in route flight, and then ending in a smooth landing. As father's practice expanded, and money flowed into the family accounts, the aircraft grew proportionally. By fourteen, I was licensed to fly a single engine, land, fixed-wing, receiving the FAA license on my birthday.

The only problem that grew with time was the conflict of priorities between my father and me. I wanted to fly, and fly all the time. He felt, as did my good Jewish mother, that I should be a doctor and leave the flying as a hobby. This meant, in their eyes, study, study, study. To this day he still hasn't figured out why I want to fly a helicopter that is forever trying to kill me.

"Get up Sneaky!"

"Shit, I got in late. Let me sleep." I kick Fred, who's become a nuisance at my feet.

"CCN today, so let's hit it."

Those who'll be airborne are moving in the dimly lit hootch. The others will sleep in. Each lighted cubicle is a sign of a job assignment for the day.

Mask staggers toward me, not fully awake. "I'll preflight

Zero-Two-Seven if you bring me coffee."

"Asshole, you'll preflight the fucking thing anyway. Go get your own coffee, I've got to go to the TOC," I bitch as a swing my legs off the bed and put my head in my hands.

I could use a shower, but no time. The days off were great. Being with Twit is relaxing even though her betel-nut chewing mother spent time with us. I took them to dinner at a local snake restaurant overlooking the Perfume River. Twit wore a brightly colored *Ao Dia*, with freshly washed white pants underneath. She looked stunning. Taking the bicycle taxi, rather than one of the older Mercedes taxi cabs, was the roughest part of the night. Exhaust smoke from the taxis roll through Hue like a Cape Hatteras fogbank. The dinner was great, We had eleven courses served over several hours. After getting home, the night was fabulous. The next morning her mother gave us many strange looks. So what if Twit and I were noisy the night before. I just smiled back, hoping that whatever her thoughts were she understood that Twit meant the world to me.

Getting dressed slowly, I yell to Jim to pick up my SOI and give it to me when we get up to CCN. I just don't want to be around the brass this morning.

The preflight is completed when I get to the revetment. Wee Willie is not saying much even though he and Mask were having an animated talk before I arrived.

We lift off the pad, and in a long straggle, fly to Quang Tri. Jimbo has Double D in the back seat. Though Jimbo's the Section Leader, he's letting Double D act as lead today. He'll learn just how busy and demanding the job can be. It is only a matter of time before he's made a Section Leader.

Next in order is Doc with Scoop, then us, with trail being flown by E'Clair and the Kid.

On landing, we find the place looks like a deserted ghost town, with four Hueys squatting on the pad. We shut down, and go to the Operations Hut to get ready for the day's operations. Billy explains that we won't be inserting until late in the afternoon, just before twilight. The only flying until then will be a re-supply flight to the radio relay site, Hickory.

The flight to Hickory is done with two slicks and two Cobras. Jimbo again lets Double D have the back seat and act as Section Leader for the flight, as part of his training. Doc does the same for Scoop, though he's not an AC, it lets him get back seat time with a senior pilot on a hopefully non-combat flight. E'Clair and I stay back. Mask and the Kid have joined in a card game with several Phoenix pilots. E'Clair stretches out, looking very uncomfortable on folding chairs, and falls right off to sleep. The way I feel I should do it too but I know that in the 'yard's hootch there's food and a cot. I wear a bracelet, given to me during a formal ceremony at the Mai Loc Relocation Camp. It may be my greatest honor, because it can't be bought or traded for. Few in Nam wear them, and most are Special Forces advisors assigned to work with a specific tribe for a year or so. It's a sign of respect and high regard given by the Montagnards. The thin brass bracelet is engraved with a design according to each tribe's style. For me, it's a badge I earned in '67 flying for the FOB out of Khe Sanh. That, along with surviving Khe Sanh, were highlights of that tour. When thinking of the losses of friends during that tour, the good times are few and far between.

The hut, a mixture of 'yard culture and American combat equipment, is a disaster area. Each 'yard has his own area but it's a sterile area. No pictures of home, girl friends or wives. Everything is OD green, and marked or smeared with black paint to give it a camouflage effect. They wear, but not when on missions, brightly colored T-shirts and boxers. These men get paid by who, what, or where the mission takes them. They have no say in the matter, they're part of a team and if the team draws a mission in Hotel-Nine, they go. I've never heard one complain or say no to getting on a helicopter, though I wouldn't understand it anyway. Though small in stature, they're damn good fighters. Looking like a rag-tag army dwarfed by the weapons and packs they carry, they're devastation to foes. In a fire fight, time and time again they prove their mettle. If the South Vietnamese could only field an army made up with the spirit of these men. They're dark skinned, both from natural pigmentation and deep tans from years spent outside. Their wiry frames carry no body fat. Their small taut muscles always seem ready to explode. Framed by their black hair and deep black eyes, their smile overwhelms you. You can't tell by looking at them their age, time in combat, or their guts. Out here the first time one fails it's shame on his whole family, and in this culture family means everything. Maybe we, the rich, powerful, and smart society, should take a look at these simple but very honorable and friendly people. Yes, we might learn something.

Entering their hootch I'm greeted by a mob going out to play volleyball. In a few hours they'll be starting a seven to ten day odyssey that might mean the ultimate sacrifice. But for now, they're a jovial group going to play this American game taught by advisors years before. I go to the back of the tin structure and see the old one. He's leaning over several pots and directing a large spoon from one pot to another, like a conductor's baton, as he prepares the meal.

He flashes a warm, toothless smile. Pointing for me to sit on the bamboo rug is his method of communication that tells me that he'll make sure I eat well. The meal, in it's many small courses, is surprisingly good. It's amazing what can be done with LURPS, the dehydrated Army meal used on the long range patrols. After eating, with no words spoken — just smiles and informal signals given for approval. I back away, rubbing my stomach as I indicate to him in rudimentary sign language, that I'm full. Taking the can of Fresca offered, though I can't stand its tart taste, I find an empty cot and stretch out. Sleep is just what I need. With a full stomach, I'll go to sleep quickly. If I get run down any more I'll have another malaria attack. It's not something I enjoy, but so far I've been able to combat it with the help of Twit going to a pharmacy in Hue for quinine. The Army's prescription is to tell me to stop drinking, get plenty of sleep, and with luck, get sent back to the States. Who needs the Army's help with this?

I'm shook out of a deep sleep by a grinning 'yard dressed in camos with his face covered in green and black pigment lines. It's time to go. He calls me "*Dai Uy*," not knowing that I'm nowhere near being a captain. Getting up, I kick over the still full Fresca can. The hootch is a bee hive of activity with voices raised, not in fear but in anticipation. They're getting ready, and I must leave the hive and go to the Operations hut.

Entering the Ops hut through the rear door, I catch the briefing, then stroll to my aircraft. Mask is kidding Klien about the money he won. Fuck it. I'm ready. I put on my stabo rig, survival vest and pistol, and pull the heavy chicken plate over my head. Climbing into the cockpit, I see all the pushes have been neatly rewritten on the left front canopy window. Klien must have done this. We get the turn up signal and launch to Quang Tri POL for fuel. Refueling is quick and efficient. The flight out to Laos is quiet and uneventful. The team is inserted in an area of gentle rolling hills, nearer to Techpone than I've ever flown. As the weather has gotten better, we've extended our range to the maximum our fuel loads allow. All missions now are executed without the luxury of much station time. Fuel has become the most important controlling factor.

The Hueys of Phoenix are emptied of their heavily burdened camouflaged men. Quickly, the wavering elephant grass spreads apart and consumes the dropping forms, then waves back with no sign of its new intruders. This is a nine-man team and the three slicks quickly move off and start an orbit to the east of our location. Eagerly they anticipate word to release them back to Quang Tri and the much needed fuel pits.

Covey finely releases them for their arduous trip home. He also asks for us to stay on station as long as possible. Though we've received the double squelch breaks from the team and their insert is considered not compromised, things have been known to change in seconds, once the overhead escort has left.

"Magic Man Lead. Black Beauty Four-Four, over." This call

from Covey should be releasing us.

"Go Four-Four," Double 'D' answers, though Jumbo is now in the back seat.

"Ah . . . Moon Beam Sierra seems to be quiet for now, you're cleared to return and refuel."

"Ah . . . Roger. Magic Flight is returning to the Red Palace."

Jimbo steeply banks to the east and the long brown track, QL-9, which will lead back into the arms of friendly civilization.

"Magic Man Lead. Freight Train Lead at Khe Sanh."

The Phoenix slicks have made good time. Phoenix One-Four is a good friend of mine who flew with the 282nd Black Cats while I was in their gun platoon. A second tour slick driver, he's another one waiting for his time to be over so he can go to work for an airline.

We're flying a hundred feet above the gently rolling hills on the north side of the valley that leads from Techpone to A Loui which is captivating in it's beauty. The view to our right is breathtaking, with the valley climbing quickly on the other side of the Xe Pon River. Underneath the lush mosaic of green is a limestone base that was formed millennia ago. Wars have been fought here for centuries. The Americans are not the first foreigners that have, for one reason or another, tried to influence the gentle mountain people, or their brothers the farmers. Rice is what it's all about. Rice feeds Asia. Vietnam grows more rice than it needs which gives it hard currency that's used for the few modernizing projects going on.

The railroad running along QL-1 is an example of money spent, or misspent. Though only one set of tracks with steam operated engines pulling old rickety cars, it provides a method of moving heavy cargo in the area. The rail system is probably slower and more unreliable than the road. The roads are paved now, thanks to the war, because they're used by the large American military complex. Otherwise tracks are dug into the earth, which in the summer are hard and windblown, and in the monsoons, impassable because of mud and mire.

It leaves the smart Vietnamese entrepreneur the only other method to accomplish movement. Boats, large, small, and in-between. Powered by sail, paddle, and motor. Sails are usually dirty colored and multi-patched, and would be considered very primitive, except for their efficiency. Motors range from simple two-stroke from mopeds, blue smoke belching, noisy contraptions, to the slick five cylinder Mercedes motors on the larger junks that ply far out in the South China Sea, going from Cau Viet at the northern border all the way around the southern tip of IV Corps. Families eke out livings for generations on the boats. Whether it's fishing, hauling cargo or people, or the nightly silhouetted boats carrying aid and comfort to the enemy, they provide livelihood for families that never set foot on the land. From birth, through adolescence, into maturity, and finally at death, their feet plod on the wooden decks of creaking hulls that support them, as it has supported ancestors before and will support their children's children in the future.

Before the Americans, the French, the Japanese, the Chinese, before time remembered, it's been a land of turmoil for independence and self rule. Now, depending on whom you talk to, it's said to be a civil war like we had during the 1860s. I don't know. Politics are so confusing, and slanted by the person your talking with. I've given up. A warrior doesn't care about the politics.

"Whoa . . . What's that!"

Snapping me out of my thoughts, I see Jimbo in a tight right-hand turn.

"Dinks! In the open!"

"Where?"

"Mark 'em!"

"Don't see nothing."

Jimbo climbing in a steep spiraling tight attitude and is now above his target. We can't see whatever he's seen but he's trying to keep it in sight.

I fly with the others in a larger orbit around Jimbo,

searching the ground for the telltale movement that means the enemy, or the white flashes that signal we're taking fire.

"Got him. It's a panel being flashed."

"I see it, it's next to the dead tree."

"That's it."

I'm searching now, looking for the dead tree. Flying over the bottom of the clearing, I see it. Next to the tree, in a low crouch is a green object, quickly flashing one of the twelve by eighteen orange panels we use for marking our team's location.

"Black Beauty Four-Four, Magic Man Lead."

Static fills the air, then a scratchy voice comes up. "Go Lead."

"Four-Four, we've got a target over here that may be friendly, can you come over."

"Roger. Where are you?"

"Four, we're about twelve klicks west of A Loui, just north of QL-9 by two klicks."

"Roger, on the way"

"What do you think?" Mask asks me.

"Don't know. Keep alert with the turret, this smells like a trap." My mind is running in circles now, as I think back to our morning briefing by Washburn. "Jimbo, there were no teams near here were there?"

"No! Ah . . . may be a civilian who's lost." Though the CIA would never admit to owning an agent stumbling around in Laos, and Nixon has repeatedly stated there are no Americans in Laos, this little man could be one of ours, or at least on our payroll. But it's highly unlikely.

All four of us have tightened up our orbits, though not in a set formation, but weaving in and out of each other's way, trying to confuse what may be on the ground waiting for us.

"Magic Man Lead, Four-Four, over."

"Go Four."

"Lead, would you give me a quick count, so I can get a fix?"

"Roger Four . . . One . . . Two . . . Three . . . Four . . . Five

. . . Six . . . Seven . . . Eight . . . Niner . . . and Ten." There's a pause and hearing no reply from Covey Jim asks. "Did you get us?"

"Roger I'm crossing QL-9 now . . . Ah . . . I don't have you in sight."

"Ahhhhhhhh. We're on the trees, let me climb up."

Pulling in a sharp nose up attitude, he climbs a quick five or six hundred feet, then dives back down.

"Got ya . . . Now what's the problem?"

"Got a body down here flashing a panel. Don't know who he is."

The Covey comes in above us, and we break our orbit up and get in a staggered trail following Jimbo. Though dangerous, we need to let Covey know who's in charge.

"In the clearing to my nine, there's a dead tree at the south. Just below the tree you'll see the panel, when I flew over it, he would open and close it. So, who the fuck is it?"

"I'm coming down."

The silver and white O-2 rolls into a steep bank and plummets towards the earth.

The little high-wing aircraft is a pusher-puller and flies overloaded all the time. Usually, there is just an Air Force FAC on board but at times one of the CCN staff will go out to observe, direct, or run an operation. There's no armament other than one rocket pod, containing seven Willie Pete rockets for marking, and the pilot's 38 caliber pistol. Several years ago CCN team members gave the Covey pilots several CAR-15's, but in order to use them, it would mean they were on the ground, and this is the last place he wants to be. One day, a Covey had taken a hit in the front engine and had to fly back with only its rear engine operable. Problem was, he wasn't able to climb, just barely maintain altitude. So we escorted him back to Quang Tri through the valleys just clearing the ridges he had to cross. The next time we were in Da Nang at the Gunfighter Village Club, drinks were on the Air Force.

"I see him!"

The little plane now starts a steep climb back out of any hidden surprises that may be lurking below.

"You tried to contact him?"

"Negative Four-Four. Don't know where to start. There's no beeper, no one up Guard. We don't have anyone out here do we?"

"As far as I know we don't. Ah . . .   sometimes NKP will insert and we won't have it on the maps for a day or so." Climbing higher. "Hold while I make some calls."

We now go back to our regular, irregular pattern, flying around the clearing. Jimbo comes up, "Keep your eyes open, not at him but for other surprises."

Squelch breaks are quickly given. We're alert out here, no day dreaming, no AFVN, no picture taking. The ACs will have the controls and I'm sure just as Mask has his turret ready so do the others. In Jimbo's aircraft, he has taken control of the situation from Double D. This flight will not be a training one anymore.

"Red Palace, Beauty Four-Four, over."

"Go Beauty Four-Four." It's not Billy, and I don't think it's Milo either.

"Palace, come up secure."

"Roger Secure. Switching now."

The two switch over to the secure system on the radios. Cobras don't have it installed, and with the number of helicopters lost in this war I can understand why. All you hear is a tone in the headset when they talk. The radio takes the voice message and scrambles it in a method that is inaudible to others on the same frequency. The teams we insert on the ground have the same capability, though if captured it would take a stroke of luck to have it set properly to allow a transmission to be overheard by the NVA.

"Magic Man Lead, Four-Four, over."

"Go."

"Can you get down there and get a good look at the target?"

Christ, that's asking for a lot. What the hell does he want us to do, land and pick the bastard up?

"Yeah I can get a good close view of him if they don't shoot the hell out of me." Jimbo knows this could very well be the last mission he ever flies. "Okay guys, here's the game plan. I'll go in and fire all my rockets to the north end of the clearing, then do a quick one-eighty and see if I can get close to him. Watch the east and south side."

Squelch breaks are the only assurance he'll get that we understand what he's going to try to do. A rocket run to the north, overflying the tree sheltering the unknown person. Clearing the tree, he'll fire all his rockets at the northern tree line, then execute a tight one-eighty and fly close to the tree. We'll all be gathered north of the clearing and after he expends his rockets we'll escort him through this turn and into the clearing. I do not like this at all.

"Doc, I've got the west side, you take the east. E'Clair lay back and if there's fire, you go to it."

More unspoken replies on squelch.

"Lead be careful. This could be a trap."

Covey seems to feel as apprehensive as we do. It's getting dark, and out here when it starts to darken there's not much time left, it's like someone turning off the switch.

"Jimbo keep up your airspeed." Doc knows, as I, this could end disastrously.

Jim breaks out of our orbit and flies southward setting up his approach back into the clearing. We move to the north, adrenalin pumping. This is against everything I've ever been taught, or heard about. It's getting dark. We have no radio communications. There are no known losses in the area or possible MIAs. And, we're deep in NVA territory.

"You guys ready?" Jim asks, as if we needed to be asked. The question should have been if he, Jimbo Mitchener, was ready. He's the one flying into the mouth of a mighty big lion.

"Roger we'll swing around," Scoop replies for Doc.

"If he takes any fire, shoot the fuck out of the bastard," I say to Mask on VHF instead of ICS. All the others know how I feel about the next few minutes. Then releasing the radio/intercom button one notch, I add on intercom only, "and any targets you see."

"Inbound." Jim's voice is no longer a carefree one, but now stern and business like, and much deeper.

The lone Cobra starts it's roll in, heading toward us. Firing pair after pair into the tree line in front of us. The rockets come out in a continual explosion with only a short lag, as Jimbo changes over from his outside pods to his inside. He's spraying the tree line from west to east. We're at less than five hundred feet, and watching rockets go below us is a weird feeling.

"Breaking!"

His nose jerks up and a pedal turn is executed at the same time. At this attitude, any gunner within sight has a free shot at the vulnerable green machine hanging a couple hundred feet in the air.

Damn, what a maneuver. Lost all his airspeed, got a few hundred feet altitude and is now going right toward the tree.

Leaving his radio switch on, Jimbo gives a running commentary of what lays before him.

"Dug up clearing . . . No fire . . . Grass about two . . . ah three feet high . . . God it's quiet . . . He's a couple hundred feet in front of us . . . If the bastard fires shoot him . . . " Must be saying that to Double D. "Shit the bastard's running toward us . . . If he has a gun shoot him . . . "

"Get out of there Magic Man!"

Covey's left-hand orbit is a tight one above us. He can see what's going on but surely doesn't have the close up view as Jim and Double D are now experiencing.

"Shit, he's going into a hover."

"It's a gook! What the hell do you want me to do?"

He's right up next to him at a hover. Then without a word the Cobra lowers to the ground. Is he hit? We watch in astonishment as the front canopy opens and the faded green Nomex arm points to the ground. Unbelievable!

The small body climbs into the front seat.

"What the fuck's going on down there?"

"Get out of there Jimbo!!"

We're all yelling now, and without knowing what is taking place, we all must assume the situation is getting worse. Darkness is now no longer creeping up on us, it's now rushing around us. Time has now joined the NVA as our enemies. Shadows in the tree line are extending deeper into the clearing, and the dead tree looks ominous, towering above and over the slender eel-like green helicopter with its blade's white stripe rotating like a dish in the LZ.

"Coming out. I can't get him out of the front seat."

Can't get him out of the front seat? He's in the front seat? What the hell's going on?

Jimbo's aircraft lifts slowly, avoiding the tree, and he does a pedal turn to the southeast, and starts a climb away from the clearing. Double D's canopy window is still open with a set of bare brown legs dangling out of it. Whatever's happened is unbelievable.

"What's going on?" Again Covey is asking the sixty-four thousand dollar question.

"Ah . . . We got him aboard. 'yard I think. Nothing but his shorts and that panel. D tried to point down to the ammo bay door but he just climbed in, and I wasn't going to stay there any longer."

"Red Palace, Red Palace, Black Beauty Four-Four, over."

"Go Four-Four."

"Palace, we need you to launch a pair of Freight Trains to meet us at Vandy. We have picked up the package and will meet them for transfer."

"You picked up what package?"

"Ah . . . Palace, come up secure."

"Going secure, over!"

"Goddamn he's heavy. And does he smell." Double D must be really having a hard time with the little man, whoever he is.

"Magic Man Lead, Red Palace, over."

"Go ahead Palace."

"We're launching a pair to meet you. They'll be up this push in a minute. Be careful."

"Ah . . . I've got to hold it down to about fifty knots, otherwise I blow the shit out of the front seat."

We now start the trip back, with one lone Cobra flying slow and climbing, while three others circle below him as if sharks awaiting to start a feeding frenzy on any tidbit taking a shot at our Lead.

His climb to several thousand feet is slow, and the time seems to take longer as fear has us all within it's grasp. With fear, time seems eternal.

"Lead, I'll be coming alongside . . .   This is something that I'll have to have proof of, otherwise they'll never let me into the Club again."

The O-2 approaches Jimbo from the left rear, with flaps extended and its spindly landing gear hanging down. Being this dirty in flight will slow his airspeed down to well under a hundred knots.

"Ah . . . I'm at your seven . . . Ah . . . Please smile . . . Ah . . . "

"Thank you for the great pictures. I'll make sure you get some copies." He retracts the gear, and the flaps are sucked up into the wing. Diving down and we hear, "Red Palace, Four-Four and flight with package at Khe Sanh."

"Roger Four-Four. How's he doing?"

"Palace, he's doing fine, but you better have the slicks ready it's getting dark."

"Magic Man, Freight Train Lead, over."

"Freight Train Lead, this is Black Beauty Four-Four. Go ahead."

"Roger we're about five out of Vandy, state your location."

"Lead orbit Vandy 'til we get there. Our flight is slow because of the package. ETA about one-five. Don't land 'til we're all there."

Looking down from our perch in the sky we see the evening

shadows are now sneaking into the cracks of the valley floor. Hopefully we'll be at Vandy before it's too much darker.

Vandy, or the renamed LZ Stud, is situated on the southwest side of a large mountain and has a small valley rolling to it's west. It should allow us to have some extra light, no matter how dim it may be, that we can use in the transfer of the little person now resting in Double D's lap. The flight takes more than fifteen minutes, and the darkness is now going to add to the danger of the transfer.

"Train Lead we've got your beacons in sight. I'm turning on my landing light." Doc now extends his flight toward the two small circling aircraft above the abandoned firebase. "Sneaky, let's clear out an area for them to land."

"I'm on you. E'Clair stick with Jimbo."

Doc now starts a dive toward the last area still clearly visible at the base of the hill. "I'm firing nails to clean out any surprises."

"Go. I'm with you."

We both fire most of our outside pods, in a general spraying pattern, trying to either kill whoever maybe lurking down there, or invoke a response from any NVA that may be dug in.

"Come on down Train Lead, land where those nails go. Jimbo, can you get close to him?"

Jimbo's now starting a very long and gradual approach. When breaking from my pass, I see the Phoenix Lead now on a short final to some unmarked spot on the ground. Several sets of legs are dangling over the Huey's side, and the door gunner is looking out his well for any hidden dangers that my be lurking in the shadows.

"Lead's down."

Coming out of both sides are six men loaded down with weapons, getting clear of the plane. No 'yards here, these are large men, all Americans from the MLT. No doubt Billy is there, but I can't make him out in the darkness.

"Tighten the orbit. If there's a problem, it's going to happen now." Covey has stayed with us all the way back and is still directing the show.

"Short final." Then a bright spot light appears. Jimbo has turned on his landing light as he hovers toward the slick. "Damn, no fucking flat place to set down."

"Griffin, move over to our other side it looks flatter there."

"Roger."

Jimbo is now hovering in a severe nose down attitude, with this body half way hanging out his left nose. It looks like a tongue of a dog, panting for fresh cool air.

"We're down."

The landing light is extinguished and quickly darkness takes control of the small area where only two rotating beacons are spinning their now telltale sign of man-made objects resting on the ground.

The large blurry forms are running to the Cobra. They grab the little object as it backs out of the open canopy and carry him back to the Huey. The front canopy closes.

"Coming out."

The big green Cobra lifts without a hover check and assumes a steep right-hand climb. Without the weight of a full load of fuel and rockets that were expended a half hour ago, it leaves like a very light, high performance helicopter. Jimbo's now flying a sports car. Getting rid of his extra passenger is added incentive to raise quickly out of the darkened shadows and crevasses at max power.

"Phoenix lifting."

It didn't take a minute, clearing the LZ, slick landing, Jimbo's landing, unpacking the body from the front seat, Jimbo lifting, and the Huey with the added passenger raising. You'd think we had this planned and well rehearsed for just a day like this. No. Never have I heard of an operation like this.

Next year while flying for the 2nd of the 17th CAV I'll be shot down flying LOHs. Standing procedure in the Condors is that when a Cobra lands you open up one of the ammo bay doors and you lay on it for the ride out. It's been so well perfected, all the troop's

Cobras have old seat belts inside the ammo compartment just for this emergency. During Lom Som 719 next year, an Assault Cobra crew will come out riding on its wingman's rocket pods. Immediately after their rescue and before they could get back to Khe Sanh, the lone Cobra had to cover a C&C Huey making a rescue of a downed LOH crew. The Cobra pilot was afraid to fire his rockets with two crewmen sitting on them so his front seat used only the turret to protect the C&C aircraft. The story told by the A Troop pilots later was, that while rolling in and firing the turret, the two rescued pilots were firing their 38 caliber pistols. What do you expect from the Calvary? For over one-hundred years they've ridden in and rescued people in distress with pistols blazing, so it appears nothing will ever change.

Chapter 15

"Let's go! Starts in less than five!"

"Be right there Jimbo."

`For some reason I'm caught up in his rush to get a front row seat to the briefing that Jolly Roger has laid out for us. Hell, it'll be like all the rest. "Here's the suspected enemy, we are here, we want to interdict them and make sure the area is safe for the Vietnamese," etc, etc. Yeah, all bullshit. These briefing types are getting to believe their own junk. They ought to get out in the real world and get shot at once in a while.

Putting on a fatigue jacket, I make sure I have the one with all the patches sewn on it. Might as well give the REMFs something to look at.

"Fred you can't go." I mutter, kicking at him as I go out the front door. "You get seen by these bastards and your gonezo, understand?" He doesn't, but to keep him I'll have to keep him out of sight for the day.

I walk across the small cleared area that serves as parade ground for award ceremonies, volleyball court, touch football arena and now a parking lot for the several jeeps in front of the mess hall. Entering the mess hall, I see it's full. Once again I'm the last to show up. The group is mostly officers, though at one table there are several senior NCOs, looking uncomfortable and out of place. In the front of both of the long tables are chairs replacing the benches. A few are still empty and seated in others are men whose faces I don't recognize. Behind them in the first row of benches are faces of recognizable staff members from our Battalion headquarters. Those in the front row, and the few Battalion types, are all decked out in crisply ironed and starched fatigues. Reminding me now, as I squeeze between the two tables and walk to the back of the room, that their appearance is worth far more than any substance they might have to offer this group of seasoned gun pilots. Each of these Captains has proven this on at least several occasions. I wonder why they're here? To screw us again?

Before getting to the rear table, I pass Rick 'Sweet Griffin' Frier sitting at a table with his map spread out in front of him. No telling what they've talked him into, but it must be good to take his attention away from CCN. At the last table, I see several newbies have left room for a couple more bodies. I stand at the end of the bench 'til the younger pilots shuffle toward the wall and allow me room to sit. Having once been sent to a briefing at XXIV Corps Headquarters, I know how the game of musical chairs is played. During the XXIV Corps briefing I was the junior officer present, and if I remember right the only officer under the rank of Major, but then General Westmoreland was being briefed and we all knew it would be good for our careers to have been near his holiness. After most of the others had given their briefings, I was called forward for a "keep it short" synopsis on the enemy situation in the area west of Khe Sanh. I stood up and quickly said there were a lot of enemy out there, and that I could go into some of the units and strengths later under a more secure setting. Or as I put it, "those with the proper security clearances and who have a need to know." I quickly left the podium area, stepping down off the wooden platform onto the thick plush carpet.

Sitting to the right of General "Holiness" was the Deputy Division Commander of the 1st ARVN Division, Lieutenant General Lam, whom I'd known for several years. I had, on occasion, flown Scout missions with him as an observer. His valor under fire was legendary, especially because he was a high ranking Vietnamese officer. He had earned an American Silver Star and several Air Medals while flying with me. He was one of the true anti-communists. I found out he had been fighting in wars since a teenager against the Japanese, Viet Minh, and now the North Vietnamese. A true patriot in the same vein as Patrick Henry or Paul Revere.

He stood up and introduced "his old friend Sneaky" to "his holiness" and indicated to the United States Army Colonel, full chicken at that, sitting to his right to move over so that I might sit next to him for the rest of the briefing. This caused a musical chairs shift of the officers to the right, then each row behind us. Some poor Lieutenant Colonel, whose date of rank was the latest, ended up having to stand during the rest of the dog and pony show. I could feel the stern looks from frosted eyes boring holes in the back of my head throughout the rest of the briefing. I couldn't wait to get out of the room when it was over. Not a word was said to me. The looks were the only message I needed to be reminded that I was only a warrant officer.

"Attention," SFC Kaiser calls while entering the now converted dining room.

Major Stafford, our XO, the Battalion XO, and battalion intelligence and operations majors are tagging behind our Battalion Commanding Officer in a gaggle. Last to come through the door is an unknown Lieutenant Colonel with a Captain carrying several rolled up maps.

Several of the Captains in the front row have started the shuffling process allowing higher ranking Majors seats in the front row. I've never figured it out. Why not let the guys that have to fly the mission have the front rows so we can see what the fuck we need?

The chatter dies down and Major Stafford says in his Commanding Officer voice, "Gentleman, please be seated."

Noise again as the audience shuffles onto the wooden benches, then scraping them on the plywood floor to get into some sort of comfortable position for what promises to be a long briefing. In my experience with the Army, you don't bring this many pilots, staff paper shufflers, and NCOs together for a five minute chat. WO Folsom leans over from the other table and hands me a cup of coffee. The cup appears to already have been used several times, but what the hell, there's no disease here that I haven't had. Folsom, looking older, than the young man he is, from being in country for several months, eyes me as if we've been stickmates or wingmen for thousands of hours, when in truth I've never had him in my aircraft, or on a flight with me. I nod, an informal thank you with someone I'm not yet comfortable with. Sitting to my left is another new warrant, Stockman, from the State of Washington. We've already given him the name of "Big Foot". With size 14's he should have known it would be the only name he'd ever be called. His sitting in the front seat of a Cobra is a sight. We've already told him he can't fly with Jimbo, for the aircraft even without fuel will surely exceed the 9,500 max gross weight.

"Gentleman I'd like to introduce you to some of our visitors."

Major Stafford has taken charge of the meeting and from his experience knows there's no use in stretching it out. Say what must be said, and then let's get on with it. Helicopter pilots get antsy after twenty-five or so minutes. Gun pilots need to find a target to hit otherwise things get out of hand.

Looking over the visitors I see no Special Forces patches, only 101st ABN. These are division types, which probably means a change in our mission and I know this will not please some of us, especially me.

"Lieutenant Colonel Daggard."

At the mention of his name, a tall thin man stands. He turns and faces us, with a stern face he nods to the forty or so pilots seated before him. His hair, shortly cropped, is showing a receding hair line and the sprinkle of gray at the temples. His combat patch is from the 173rd, which, in my opinion, is a good sign. Incompetence in that unit was quickly transferred out and, luckily for the "Herd", far away.

Major Stafford goes on, "Colonel Daggard is the Commanding Officer of the 2nd of the 506th, based at the Currahee Pad across the strip."

After the Colonel sits down, Stafford quickly goes through

the process of introducing the other visitors, though not as formally. The niceties are over and I see my coffee cup is dry.

"Captain Jorgenson, 06th Operations Officer."

When he stands, you know he's served his time in the field. The tan and tightly packed body means the fat cat life of a battalion staff officer flying around in a C&C Huey aircraft has not yet gotten to him. His 101st combat patch, if properly worn, means he's already done one tour with the 101st and he's either on an extension or he's into his second full tour. I'll bet it's an extension. Why would a grunt Captain extend in Nam? Even with an early out he's not going to go fly for an airlines, so what's in it for him? Must be career.

The introductions of our ARA Battalion staff are more a formality than an introduction. We know who they are, though a couple are not that recognized. Captain Lardo is with them which is not a surprise, but looking him in the eye proves uncomfortable for him. Upon mention of his name he stands and glances around the room looking for some friendly home of refuge, a place that he can look or turn to when necessary. You can't study maps and charts all meeting. I wonder when he was told he was coming up here? Obviously he didn't volunteer, and I can't fathom what he could offer in the form of expertise or sound intelligence information. A man without a mission, sitting before the very people who proved that he couldn't cut the mustard. Humiliating I'm sure. Maybe Lardo's job was to fly the Battalion Huey with its priceless load of staff up here.

Captain Pratt, our Assistant Battalion Operations Officer stands after Stafford turns the meeting over to him. He's a second tour pilot and served as an advisor to an ARVN 105 Artillery Battalion in the Delta before arriving up north with us. He's due to be promoted to major soon and the scuttlebutt is he wants to command the Griffins. Though young in appearance, he's not. He served three years in the 82nd Airborne as an enlisted man before leaving the Army to go to college. After graduating, as the ROTC Distinguished Graduate of his class, he came back home to the

Army as a second lieutenant in Artillery. With the aid of the GI Bill, he had obtained his FAA commercial pilot's license and then convinced the Army he was what they were looking for in a young career military man who could transition from NCO to Officer, leaving behind enlisted friends and acquaintances. Once flight school was completed, he was able to get assigned to the 11th Air Assault. It was a new concept, and behind his back many of his NCO ex-friends hoped the move would be bad for his career. The 11th Air Assault changed over to the 1st Air Calvary. The now first lieutenant found himself in Vietnam flying a B Model Huey as a platoon leader. He knew he had made all the right choices. Others thought he must have friends in high places to pull it off but the lieutenant knew better. He had a vision of what the helicopter could do for the Army, and he had followed his vision.

Pratt and I get along very well, though at arm's length. I met him the first time at a "Hail and Farewell" party and found him a bit too formal. Seeing my Marine Corps patches, he waited until I was alone at the bar before approaching me. Standing next to me, he closely inspected the patches on my brightly red colored dress flight suit. He asked about the HMM-262 and HMX patches. Quickly I informed him they were from my Marine days. He continued the conversation by asking what I did in the Marines. I told him I was a crew-chief. Hoping to cut him off and get back to the table with the round of drinks I was buying, I mentioned I had been an enlisted man. Surprisingly, he told me his father had been in Marine Corps aviation and retired after the Korean War. He used to go down to the HMX hanger area, as he had been raised on Marine bases and spent many years at Quantico. In the brief talk, we found common ground which might have ended there except for one night a month or so later.

Twit and I were in a small restaurant in Hue not normally frequented by GIs. In the many times I had been there I'd never seen a round eye in the place or, for that matter, in that part of town. As we were finishing the meal and I was drinking my second Cognac, a group of South Vietnamese Officers came in with an

American who I first thought was their advisor. It's common for advisors to spend many hours, both formally and socially, with their counterparts. It turned out it wasn't their advisor but Captain Pratt. As we started to leave, he called us over to his table and after formal introductions asked me if I came into Hue often. I explained that Twit and I shared a small house on the north edge of Hue and I tried to get down to see her and my son as often as possible. When we left him, I wondered if I would be brought up to Battalion to discuss being in downtown Hue and being attired in civilian clothes.

Several days later, while the Battalion Huey was shut-down on our Hot Spot, Captain Pratt came to my hootch, and though refusing a cold beer and opting for a warmer root beer, he told me how surprised he was to see me that night. I told him of my relationship with Twit, of our son, and my general feelings about Vietnam and my love for the people and the country. The more I talked, the more relaxed I felt. He knew and understood what I was saying. It was then that the field phone rang to notify him the flight was ready to leave. On the way back up to the Hot Spot, he told me of his love who was living in Da Lat. As we walked up the hill he explained the desire they both had for her to move to be near him. When he left that day, I knew I had met a man I admired and respected. Not for falling in love with a Vietnamese, but for falling in love with Vietnam. He was not the type I would pal around with as I was still a warrant but he could be a distant friend. In the Army, distant friends can help you better than your pals. Just before he climbed in the Huey I moved to salute and he put his hand out. We shook hands, not as captain to warrant, but men who share a mutual love. As I walked down off the Hot Spot and headed to my hootch, I knew that, like me, he would never want to go home to the land of the big PX.

Pratt started the briefing with good news, at least for most of us. "Gentlemen, MAC-V-SOG has requested the Griffins remain as the primary Cobra support for their CCN operations. We, the 101st, are going to honor their request."

Several cheers and whistles come to life as the real gunnies expressed their satisfaction of the 101st brass using their heads properly. The Griffins are the best at flying CCN and to change now would cause a possible weakness in CCN air operations while they had to find and train new Cobra pilots, all the while not losing recon teams during the transition.

He continues with what I always think of as the good news - bad news scenario. Or as most call it, the 'kiss before the fuck.'

"The change in the Griffin's mission will be that you, C Battery, will no longer provide general ARA support missions to the division. Your alert status aircraft will be entirely OpCon to the 06th, and their mission for the next few months. I'll let their staff explain this in detail later, but here's the overall concept." Pratt glides, in his old NCO manner, to the map that's been propped up on the food service line and appears from this distance to be of A Shau Valley.

If this is true, we're going to be doing a lot of flying over the next few months and it isn't going to be easy. The Valley. The place doesn't belong to the Allied troops. It's Indian country and just happens to be located on maps within the boundaries of South Vietnam. If it was up to me, I'd redraw the map and give it to the Laotians, or whoever wanted it. Those who've not been in the Valley are in for a big surprise. I'd rather fly ten CCN flights than one A Shau flight. Too hard to get to, though nearer to Camp Evans, and too many enemy. This elongated valley could hold a division or two of NVA and they wouldn't be crowded. Hamburger Hill, A Shau Special Forces Camp, O'Reilly, Bradley, are names that remind me this is not the place to be, even in the good weather. What might be good weather here, may not be in the Valley. It has a micro-climate which causes problems of its own and whatever the weather is, it can change in five minutes. Too many pilots and crews have died just trying to go out, or come back, from the Valley without a shot being fired. Fuck the Valley!

"For some of you who have flown the Valley, ah . . . "
Looking over the room for specific faces. "Ah . . . Sweet Griffin,

Captain Mitchener . . . ah . . . Sneaky in the back, and a few others . . . ah . . . You'll know what a tough one this will be."

He turns back to the map and, with a pointer, jabs the north end of the map in one of the red circles placed in the stair step formation of red circles.

"From this fire base the 06th will branch out and conduct patrols, doing reconnoiter . . . missions . . . your basic NVA hunting. So far we've met sporadic resistance. We've been using a troop of the 2nd of the 17th to provide gunship support and their aero scouts to feel out the area south of this area."

I've flown aero scouts and will fly them again. But, I don't want to fly scouts into A Shau.

"Your sister unit, Toros, has been providing the coverage up to now. Effective the day after tomorrow, at 0000 hours, 17 March 1970, C Battery will assume this mission. On the 17th, Griffins will provide four aircraft to MAC-V-SOGs CCN mission each day. The remainder of your operational aircraft, ah . . . , at least eight, will go to the 06th for their operations. The 06th will have a liaison here with Captain Rogers to coordinate the missions. If there's a shortage of aircraft or the need to launch more, Toros or Dragons from our Battalion will supplement the necessary number to meet the commitment of the particular mission."

Striding back and forth he looks across the room for questioning faces.

"Before I turn this over to Major Westerly of the 06th I want to impress upon you newer pilots that though this is in South Vietnam, believe me . . . ah . . . ask some of the more experienced ACs..." Pointing out to the men he'd already named. "Ah . . . the A Shau is a tough area. Keep your heads up these next few months."

He stops in front of the Major and hands him his pointer. The Major, now standing, looks like the banker I borrowed the money from for my last car.

"Thank you gentleman, Major Westerly, the S-3 of the 2nd of the 06th will continue."

"Gentleman, as you may or may not know, troops of the 3rd

Brigade of the 101st along with ARVN soldiers from the 1st Regiment of the 1st ARVN Division have been operating in the Valley for the last several days."

A short compact man in his early forties, Major Westerly has closely cropped hair. His moustache is one that I'm sure he'll shave off before he gets on the Freedom Bird home to his next stateside assignment. If not for the Army appearance standards, then surely for his wife who will demand it to be cut off before she slips between sheets with him.

I'd bet he's on the Lieutenant Colonel's list. This assignment is a stepping stone for Majors. He wears no ring from the Bastion on the Hudson, but he has the West Point look. A voice that is forced as if he has to push each word out. Patches show he's been through the basic ticket punching classes: Rangers, Pathfinder, Senior Parachutist, the Infantry CIB and surprisingly the Vietnamese Parachute Badge. He wears no combat patch, but I think this was done on purpose. He must be on his second tour. As he starts to talk, I find his voice irritating. Just what we need, a long drawn out briefing by a talking head.

"Intelligence tells us the NVA 803rd and the 29th NVA Regiments are operating with impunity in the Valley. Their exact location is presently not known. We expect to find, identify and root them out with this operation."

Shit! Not one but two NVA Regiments. To me this means more than that, especially with the Laotian boarder being less than a days forced march to the west. The NVA Division Headquarters must be near. NVA might let a Regiment operate independently, but not two of them in the same area. Plus, with the freedom of movement in the A Shau, what better place to set up a large base camp for your operations in the northern I Corps area? It doesn't take a military strategist to figure this out. Why don't they just admit it?

"On 5 March, the 3rd Brigade and the ARVN 1st Regiment started Operation Chicago Peak. The initial plan was to insert 2nd Battalion of the 506th into the Valley. Here."

Swinging around he points to the southwestern red circle.

"Everyone see this?" he asks, looking across the tables to see if all heads are directed toward his pointer tip. "Because of weather we were held up until the morning of the 13th."

Noise picks up as the pilots move restlessly about. Getting the newbie's, Folsom's, attention, I point to my now empty cup then push it to the end of my table. The young warrior leans over and picks it up, then slides it down his table toward the large coffee urn at the end. Might as well get a refill. This appears to be a long, dry briefing.

"This is Hill 902, which we were going to insert A Company of 2nd of the 06th. The Air Force waved us off the hill because of enemy activity and we inserted onto the secondary LZ. Ah . . . Here." The pointer moves a couple klicks north and a klick to the east. "Hill 970. From here on it's Firebase Ripcord."

The circle is nine or ten klicks south of O'Reilly, which means they will be able to receive supporting artillery fire. One of the lessons learned in some far off war and still practiced today, which the French didn't know or care about at Dien Bien Phu, is each base should fall under the covering fire of another. The best case would be to have it fall under the umbrella of artillery fire of two other bases. This means they can mutually support each other and they don't live and die, as did the French, on the use of air power and good weather.

"On landing, Alpha Company was met with intense small arms, recoilless rifle and mortar fire. Within several hours we directed them to move off the hill." Looking closely at the map, he points to an area east of Hill 970 and continues, "to the east, along this high ground."

The 101st really wanted to get in this area if they aborted the primary landing zone because of enemy movement and then landed on the secondary, with its intensive fire, and moved off this LZ as well. One of my rules of combat is to multiply enemy fire by three from insertion to extraction. If you take one round going in, count on three coming out. Using Sneaky's rules of combat means the LZ, now called Ripcord, will be hell getting out of.

"In the early hours of the 14th, members of the 1st ARVNs captured some documents that lead us, ah . . . the Division . . . ah to believe the 6th NVA Division Headquarters is located in the Ripcord area."

Whistles are sounded and heads look around. Young pilots are thinking of the kills they'll be able to get. Us old timers know it's a lot more than that. It means a lot of slicks and medevacs are going to have a hard time going in and coming out. We also know that with a division there, it means large guns and more organized resistance. No matter what Presidents and Generals say, the NVA are damn good fighters, and when organized and able to fight on their terms, they'll give us a hard time. The newbie sets the stained coffee cup, with the steaming heat lazily rising from it, back onto my table.

"Gentleman," The Major is trying to settle the pilots down and get on with his briefing, "back to the business at hand. This morning we are in the process of extracting all units from the Valley, so that we can utilize the Air Force, Navy, and whatever artillery fire we can to bomb the Valley's hot spots. We are planning to reinsert the 06th back into the Valley on the 17th at 0600 hours."

Noise picks back up as many small whispered conversations are heard. Some from those that have flown into the Valley, others wanting the misguided opportunity to have the chance to say they've been in the Valley. The thought of these young men trying to rush off to get killed amazes me. It sure makes the politicians' and Generals' who don't get maimed and killed by this madness, jobs a lot easier. Someone wrote a song about what are we fighting for and let's go to Vietnam cause we're all going to die. Hell, this is a song about youth, not the air-conditioned C&C high flying senior officers. I bet it would add a new wrinkle to modern warfare if there was a rule that said wars could only be fought by men over sixty-five. But then who could find politicians to pass such a law, it would be their death warrant?

Major Westerly is finished. Looking out across the room he asks the big question. "Any questions?"

None are asked. Though he doesn't know why. The newbies will want to ask the older ACs. The older ACs will play each mission as it comes down. We, the older ones, know we're in for a hard few months work.

With no questions asked and Major Westerly sitting down, Major Stafford stands up and says. "If there are no questions gentlemen, this briefing will come to a close." He looks around and then calls, "Attention! Meeting's dismissed!"

I missed the last few minutes of talking, thinking of a far off world where warriors all had gray hair. Gulping my coffee down I hope not to get caught up in any discussions with the younger pilots about the theories of A Shau Valley warfare. Having flown the Hamburger Hill fiasco, I know what's ahead.

"Captains McMullen, Mitchener, Crane, ah . . . Lieutenant Frier and Mr. Morris, Woodruff and ah . . . you too Sneaky . . . ah . . . that should do it, don't you think Captain Rogers?" Our XO seems to have something more for us planned.

"Yes. That should be all we need, Sir."

"You gentleman, stick around for a minute."

We gather around Rick as he finishes plotting the locations of what has transpired in the Valley on his map. Then he folds it, so the Ripcord area is on the facing page.

"This will only take a minute."

Major Stafford has returned from escorting the visiting officers out to their respective jeeps, and on their way back to their darkened holes to try to out think, out plan and outmaneuver their NVA counterparts holed up under the thick mountain rain forest that blankets the Valley floor.

"Captain Rogers and I have discussed this upcoming change in our operational mission and we've decided to treat all flights into A Shau the same way we would a CCN flight. This means Section Leaders. We will try to send at least four aircraft per flight and an AC in the back seat of each plane. No, repeat, no ACs in the front seat giving the peter pilots back seat time. Understood?" He looks at each of us. "We would like to have most flights with two leads, and no, I repeat gentlemen..." Again looking each one of us in the eye, "No single ships going to or from the Valley. It means you ACs and Section Leaders will have a lot of flight time, so keep a close watch on each other."

Looks of indecision appear with this new revelation not mentioned during the formal briefing.

"This is the way it's going to be. If you have trouble with high hours, fatigue, anything . . . understand . . . anything, let me or Captains Westrock or Rogers know right away."

Major Stafford cares for his men and this decision, though maybe not too popular with some of the older ACs, will mean we all have a better chance to survive, and this is what it's all about. Surviving the war to go home walking, not in the black thick vulcanized bag with the heavy duty zipper. Stafford's concern about us is what sets him apart from many of the commanding officers I've served under.

"Any questions?" Captain Westrock now asks.

With no questions, he follows the CO out the door with Jolly Roger bringing up the rear. Leaving us standing with the added responsibility of knowing we will all be stretched to our limits during these next few months. We all leave the now quiet and deserted mess hall with the map boards still set up. Going out the door we see the S-2 Spec 4 standing by waiting for us to leave so he can take the maps back to the TOC. Now each of us, silently and in deep thought, walks directly to our hootch and the security of our cubicle to contemplate the new mission of the Griffins.

Another page in the Griffin history, or diary, of the unit that so many of us love. What this next page holds for us, though now unknown, might prove to be an emotional roller coaster that we never thought we would ride. But it's too late to change the ticket now. All we can do is strap in and hold on.

Chapter 16

"Let's get going." I say to the Kid, who's still struggling with his equipment in his dimly lit cubicle.

"Lets go!"

"Coming."

It's a good thing most of us went down to the pits last night and carefully went over our aircraft. We won't get a good preflight in this darkness. Ripcord has become a royal pain in the ass. Not only for us, but also for 2nd Battalion of the 506th. The times I've gone over to the Currahee Operations hut and listened to the latest briefings, I've come back knowing I was right on target with my assessment of the A Shau Valley. Why do commanders want to operate there anyway? It should be a free fire zone with LRRPs running some patrols and letting the United States Air Force do their thing with five-hundred pound bombs. Less risk to the men, at least the ones that matter, though I'm not sure our commanders care about them. All I've been asked about is how many bodies, how many crew served weapons, how many this, how many that, did we take out? If there was a way we didn't have to send grunts out in the field and just send numbers back up the chain of command, everyone would be satisfied. Give the numbers to the commanders, but save our boys. This Valley isn't worth it.

"I'll get coffee," E'Clair calls as he goes out the front door.

"You better be ready when I get down there," I reply gruffly to the Kid, though he knows we've become friends.

He's no longer the stumbling, trying to please everyone, kid that arrived months ago. At a distance his mother would still see her baby boy, Buff. But closeup, we all see the metamorphosis. Eyes sunken back into the head, which now continually dart within the limits of their sockets. His hearing, though constantly being eroded by high frequencies, is keen. He is always on the vigil, alert for movement, sounds, the feeling that tells you something is not right. Just as the coiled Cobra in his element, always at the ready, Buff Klien has become a predator. Now he awaits the opportunity to strike out and smack down what he perceives as wrong, unjust, or out of place. He's become a part of the aircraft that encapsulates him every day. The Cobra, waiting, watching, coiled and at the ready.

He doesn't write Mother as much as he did when he was an FNG, and his eagerness to fly deeper into Laos separates him from his adolescent high school chums far away. He's not the fair-haired boy the neighbors thought was so sweet. No, he's grown into a killing machine. When coming home from flights without kills, he now vocally expresses how it was a wasted flight. Several times he'd ask if we could fire left over rockets into areas he thought there might be enemy lurking. The most telling sign for me, and Jimbo noticed it as well, was turning down R&R so he could stick around for the A Shau Valley operation.

"I'll be there and ready, Sneaky."

I know he will be. Nothing keeps him from a mission and the possible opportunity to have his rendezvous with destiny. Going out the door with survival gear hanging off one shoulder, and my helmet bag and chicken plate in the other, I know he's not his mother's baby boy anymore. I'm partly responsible for his metamorphosis. He's flown with me every chance he's had, requesting to change with other co-pilots, so he can be in my front seat. He's become a shadow watching what I do, asking the right questions at the right time, and not forgetting the lessons learned. Though I've never met his mother, she's sent me a few cards and a package of home-made cookies arriving in crumbs after the United States Post Office handled them. I know she'd be angry at me if she knew that I, Sneaky White, had changed her darling sweet

Buff.

"Better like it black. Couldn't find any sugar or cream."

"So long's it's hot." Shifting my survival gear to my other shoulder, I take the steaming cup from E'Clair. He's getting short and has been using all his free time to study everything he can get his hands on for the FAA fixed-wing ATR exams. "You're too short to be out here."

"Yeah I know." While readjusting his gear, we start the climb to the TOC. "Taking a Lead slot sounded good at first. I figured I'd rack up more time. But shit, this is too much time."

Marty and several others were made Section Leaders right after we undertook the Ripcord Operation. Flying two Leads per flight means that most of us top out on flight time quicker than normal. He was reluctant at first and I'm sure sorry about it now, but Jimbo and I had impressed upon him the advantage of the added flight time before he got out of the Army.

He flew with Jimbo's flight his first few days. When we didn't launch into A Shau on the 17th of March as planned, he flew Lead with Jimbo as a wingman on our CCN rotations.

The Griffins' first missions into A Shau were April 1. April Fool's Day as it turned out, fooled no one, especially the NVA. Bad weather had prevented the combat assault on the 17th and every day we heard "Be ready to go," until the 1st of April. If the rest of 1970 is going to be like this, we're going to have a hard year.

B Company of the 2nd Battalion 06th was lifted onto Ripcord for an April Fool's Day surprise. The trouble was, the surprise was on B Company. By 1830 hours they'd been evicted off the hill. Moving east seven hundred or so meters along the same finger that A Company had traveled two and half weeks prior, until joining up with A Company. The new location was eight-hundred and fifty meters high. This meant they'd given up high ground to the NVA. Though no one mentioned it during the briefings, Rick and I had noticed how many hills were higher than the ones the 06th was trying unsuccessfully to occupy. Though I'm not a believer in the rule that we must have the high ground, in this area the NVA were using the peaks for accurate spotting posts. Their communications have proven excellent and enemy units are working in well orchestrated movements to confuse us as well as to accurately set up effective ambushes.

"Good morning Sneaky, Mr. St. Clair."

Captain Rogers has made an effort to be pleasant to me since the transfer of Lardo to battalion. Rumor has it Lardo made a few comments down at battalion about Rogers' lack of flying and it got back to him. Then my short recuperation assignment with maintenance helped put me on better terms with the "REAL LIVE OFFICERS." I've made an effort, just as with Captain Shirrley, to get along in some strained fashion with Captain Rogers. It's been hard, but I understand I must. But with all the bullshit aside, it's really more important for pilots to fly the Valley, as well as CCN missions. Some of the pilots who didn't fly CCN didn't want to fly the Valley either because they thought it was just as bad. This made scheduling difficult for Rogers. One thing about me, he knows I'll fly, anywhere, anytime. Just hand down the mission.

"Morning *Dai Uy.*"

Niceties over, I check out an SOI. I then go over to the newly planted First Lieutenant from the 06th, now occupying a desk that once had weather info strewn about. He has two radios on the end of the desk, and the new radio operators we have in the TOC belong to him. There's a 06th jeep outside, but from what I understand the grunts have been spending most of their time over here, taking meals and bunking in whatever spare space they can find. Their hours have been long and, judging by their appearance, the toil of the operation is being felt even for these men in the rear.

"What's scheduled for today, Lieutenant?" asking after E'Clair has joined me.

One of his radio operators, a tall black man with a larger than regulations allow Afro, comes up to the table. Black officers in the Army are rare and for him to see a black warrant officer aviator will be something to tell the bro's back in the 06th.

"O'Reilly has been taking everything the NVA can dish out. Ah . . . let's see . . . as you know . . . it's the 31st straight day of incoming." He's turning a map around so we can look at it. "Same shit, mortars, recoilless rifle and sporadic small arms." Looking down at the map with its grease pencil marks of both American units and the neutral players, the ARVN. "A Company will be lifted out of O'Reilly to this small LZ." Moving his dirty finger from the large red circle to the east-south-east a couple of klicks. "Hill 805." Then moving his finger to Ripcord. "B Company is still here. Into their fourth day of hell. Charley seems to be throwing everything in the world at them." Looking up he sees E'Clair nodding. "C Company is here, at Churrahee pad, getting ready for insertion back into the Valley. The winds are up already . . . ah . . . last report was gusting to 45 knots which will make things difficult for everyone."

Shit, another hot, windy day. Those guys on the ground must be tired as hell. The A Shau Valley has given us delays because of bad weather. If not fog, it's low clouds, rain, or the high winds. The enemy has used the weather very effectively in their chess match with our commanders. The idea of having FSB Bradley reopened to provide artillery support was scrubbed after the 06th Battalion CO flew over it to check it out. His report at first was taken as one of hysteria, but when the C&C Huey pilots spread the word at the Club and we got word of it, we knew the A Shau was hopping. It seems all the time the C&C bird was flying over Bradley it was taking NVA artillery fire from Laos. After the number of rounds, and their location was discussed, it was felt the NVA gunners were registering their guns for the anticipated combat assault of the 06th onto Bradley. If the 06th had gone, it would have been a meat-grinder for those that survived the initial landing.

"Let's go down to the aircraft. Thanks Lieutenant." I smile at him, but it's a hallow smile, and he looks too tired to notice.

He hands me a small piece of paper he's prepared with the pushes and call-signs that we'd be using today. I start to walk away while the black RTO nods at E'Clair. It's with respect in recognition of someone breaking the Army's invisible color barrier. Being promoted to more than a motor pool sergeant as a black must be an accomplishment, in an Army that still practices racism in very subtle ways.

Our walk down to the revetments is done in quiet. Each of us are into our own thoughts about what the day might bring. Except for the occasional stumble on the worn down path the only noise is the cranking of aircraft from revetments across the runway. Looking to our revetments, we see beams of light being aimed by unseen hands as crews make ready for their day into the mouth of the cat. In minutes, we join them not only for the ritual of the preflight but for the flight out to the Valley, and the long day of flying in orbits, then being called to wisps of smoke that sometimes, and sometimes not, rise from the thick triple canopy of trees that hide our brothers. Also hiding below the canopy and lurking behind the many natural cracks and crevasses are little brown skinned men of the NVA Division who's job it's become to protect their Valley. It's their Valley and visitors are only welcome as long as the enemy wants us there.

This day, like all the rest, will be one of flying out to the Valley, getting a fire mission either from our TOC or the 06th Arty Forward Observer, flying to the vicinity of the company or one of its patrols, then requesting smoke. Waiting for the smoke to, with luck, ooze up through the trees and not be dissipated. Then hopefully, we can get a location of the friendlies, do some shooting of rockets and the short ride, at least compared to CCN missions, home. Refueling, then repositioning to the Hot Spot to rearm and then the cycle starts over again. Some of the trips are less than an hour, others require time to find the friendlies which adds to over-extending our bodies again.

Some of us have been getting in night flying as well and this is when things get confusing. For us to fire at night means the friendlies are in big trouble. This is not like CCN where we don't launch a night extraction. No, out here we go. On the nights I've gone, the A Shau has given further aid to the enemy with its low cloud cover. Though beautiful at a distance, once you get down low to set up your rocket run, the beauty changes to horror. Under the thick canopies, tiny but powerful strobe lights are invisible or appear for only milliseconds as we fly by. Several times I've asked the grunts to fire a short burst of tracers straight up into the air. Then I'm able to get a fix on an approximate location. After this, the RTO will guide us in by the sound of our aircraft.

The flying is draining and it shows in all our faces, including the men not flying but supporting us. Fatigue lines are forming on the normally tight skinned faces. Eyes seem to be receding further into the skull. Dark skinned bags, now rising in front of the eye sockets, add to the haggard and haunted look. Conversations are crisp and to the point. Little things bother us and usually, as with life in general, we take it out on the ones we care about. I've caught myself a couple times yelling at Wee Willie for some insignificant maintenance problem. War does this to you and no matter how much of a warrior you are, the time adds up.

For me, and I'm sure for some of the others, the day our rotation for CCN comes up is anticipated with relief. CCN hasn't slacked off, in fact it's pushed to the very end of our flight envelope. But between flights we can lay down and nap, and an hour or two stolen here or there is welcomed. I now know how the Huey pilots feel when I see them slumped over their controls after they shut down. Too tired to get out and lay down. Just close your eyes and let nature take over.

The MLT's crew has been more than helpful with our slack time on CCN. Not only in giving us a good meal, which for me means eating with the 'yards, but the relaxed atmosphere around the camp is something that draws us up there for the peace and tranquility from the go-go flights of the Valley. Their missions are still tough, but they don't panic. Things are thought out and well planned. The execution of a CCN operation is why we have such good results. Every third day that I get with them is like escaping from the rigors of being beat up by a heavyweight boxer. It's like a breath of fresh air in a crowded, smoke-filled room.

One day, during a CCN flight coming back from Laos, I was letting the Kid fly from the front seat and I was relaxing and enjoying the scenery. North of QL-9, I spotted what appeared to be something hidden under a group of trees. Grabbing the controls, I quickly turned back around to the site, while calling my intentions to the flight. I dove to within fifty feet of the ground trying to see what was under the camouflage. The Kid was looking left then right. Just as I saw what appeared to be a vehicle, he yelled that we had a bulldozer under the trees. Without thought or comment, I started firing pair after pair into the massive rusted steel vehicle. Though we'd used most of our ordnance on the extraction, I fired what I had left, letting the rockets bore into the machine hiding under the trees.

We called Covey to have him get the location and I reported the small fire started by my rockets impacting the fuel tank. Covey would not give me a confirmed kill, but said if the bulldozer was there in the AM, he'd go ahead and credit it to us. When he bet me a case of Mateuse wine that it would be gone by the next morning, I jumped. For here was a left over Worlk War II Japanese bulldozer that I surely had caused extensive damage to, and I knew the Mateuse was mine. The next morning's fly over proved 2.75 inch rockets failed to stop it's use and probably only slowed the crew down an hour or so in their repair of one of the many roads running through the area. A case of Mateuse was lost, as a 2.75 FFAR is no match for a steel bulldozer.

This incident reminded me of the stupidity of the war. With a President, Congress, and even my own mother saying they didn't want us extending the battle into the enemy's safe refuge of Laos. If my mother only knew I was flying here. Hell, the NVA have extended the war into Laos, not us. When we all signed the Laotian Neutrality Act years before, including Russia, we all knew that the paper was worthless. Within ninety days Uncle Ho commanded his troops to build what is now known as the Ho Chi Minh trail. It seems to me that I'm fighting a war for democracy with one hand tied behind my back. Is it worth it? Is it fair play, Marquis-Queensbury Rules and all, that the United States government is worried about? Ask the families of the black vulcanized rubber bags slipped neatly into polished aluminum containers for the trip home. Full pieces of bodies going off to a clean, sanitized, neat war. Then the bits and small pieces coming home, from a dirty Asian war. Such a beautiful tranquil land to have so much death and destruction laid across its fields. And let's ask the MIA's families!

I realize now, that I can no longer fight as an American soldier helping a small country battle communism. No, I'm in love with Vietnam and when you do something to my family, my children, my love, then I fight back. It's become personal.

The loud ringing of the canvas encased field phone irritates my sleep. The hootch has been very quiet as if it's lost one of its occupants. The Griffins have not lost a pilot in over two years, and most of these men don't know the eery feeling that comes over you with the death of one of your own. It's not only one of your friends you are grieving for, but the turmoil in your heart, for you know it was better for him to die than you. If a slick or scout pilot entered our hootch now, he'd think we'd lost a pilot. The stillness is that evident.

The ringing is still continuing and no one has stopped it. Maybe they too have run out of energy. Now it's stopped. Either it was a dream or the person on the other end gave up.

Usually after flying I'm in the club getting drunk, or down in Huong Ca with Twit for the night. But not with Ripcord still raging. Last night, after a cold meal of greasy hamburgers, runny instant potatoes, and a mixture of Jello and Kool Aid that was served both as a drink and as desert, I came back to the hootch and laid down. Fred immediately jumped up and laid between my legs, and we've been here for who knows how long. In my exhaustion, I didn't strip off my Nomex pants or unlace my boots. I flung my still sweaty Nomex shirt over the lawn chair just before I collapsed. I reached over and pushed the ON button of my reel-to-reel and the headphones started playing a tape of Strauss. I've been in a state of suspended animation since I laid down. Though needing a hot shower, or at least to flush off the sweat that covers me, I couldn't raise my body off the bunk and take the walk to the shower.

"Get up!"

Is someone talking?

"Sneaky! Get up Sneaky!" an unknown but familiar voice says.

"What?" I mumble to the far off sound.

"Get up! We've got a flight."

It's dark and I have to squint my eyes into focus but I still can't make out who's standing over me. Is it Jimbo who's entered my dreams? Why would he do that? It's my dream, not his, and I'm with Twit at the Da Nang Hotel for dinner.

Someone's tugging at my leg. Raising up with a start, I squint through my sleep encrusted eyes and leave my dream of Twit being close to me.

"Jimbo?"

"Yea. Get up and get your gear. We got a flight." The large darkened form now turns and leaves my cubicle, stops and turns to add, "Meet you in operations in ten minutes."

"You nuts? Is this some kind of joke?"

"No joke. Rogers just called and it's a priority emergency. So get up!"

I try to let my eyes focus in the soft glow of the light radiating from the front of the hootch. I'm not the only one up. I hear others complaining. I raise out of bed and stumble to the platoon bar and see Jimbo bent over his bunk gathering his flight gear.

"Ten minutes, you got that?" Jimbo turns and opens the door but before it swings shut he sticks his head back in and adds, "Make sure Doc and Killer are with you."

Squinting my eyes, which are still not completely focused because of the brightness of the stolen one-hundred watt light bulb dangling by thin electrical wires over the bar, I see Doc and Killer are both sitting on the edge of their bunks though only dressed in their boxer shorts. It's obvious that neither of them is awake either. Ripcord operations have drained the strength out of us. Not only 2nd Platoon, but all the Griffins. The pilots have flown every hour they could and maintenance people are putting in long shifts to keep our aircraft mission ready.

"For Christ's sake, what time is it?" Killer asks.

"I don't know. Fucking Jimbo said we got a flight," Doc stretches and moans and then, as he stands up adds, "Shit, that sure didn't feel like eight hours of shut eye."

"Wasn't." E'Clair is sitting at the bar fully dressed and drinking a beer. "It's a little after ten, ah . . . at night, in case you really need to know. I'll go down and help you get your planes ready."

"What the fuck is going on?"

"Killer, the shit has hit the fan out at Ripcord and you're launching," E'Clair says without emotion.

He's the only one that's fully awake. Marty has been trying to take every third day off as he eagerly awaits this week to pass so he can catch the Pan American Freedom Bird home to the land of the big PX. I can't blame him for not wanting to fly out to Ripcord in his last week in Nam, especially at night.

"You're shitting me."

"No way, Killer. Tonight's your night to find out if you, the great Griffin Nine-Two Alpha, can kill dinks in the dark."

E'Clair's not joking nor is he rubbing in the emergency night flight Killer's been asked to fly. He's just stating the cold hard facts that all Griffins must face at some point during their tour in Nam. After all Marty's been through during his tour and a half, he's made up his mind he's had enough and just wants to go home.

"All I want to do is fly Pan American 707s, for the big bucks".

"Fuck that!" Killer says in disgust, throwing his flight gear onto his bunk.

"Let's go. Least we can do, is go up to the TOC and see what they're asking us to do. Then I'll let you tell Jolly Roger it's his night to earn his flight pay." I say as I walk, now more steadily, back to my corner of the hootch. I glance down at my Rolex but my eyes still are not ready to focus on the dial.

I snatch the Nomex flight shirt. It's still damp from today's sweaty flight.

"Fuck it," I mumble and put it on, zipping it half way up.

I reach for my survival gear hanging on their appointed nails. It takes just moments to have everything hanging on me. I pick up my M-14 and helmet bag and look down at Fred, who has gone back to sleep. Lucky bastard I think to myself.

"Let's get going and get this over with," I say as I pass Killer, who's still fumbling with his gear.

Doc has the front door open, and he's finishing putting on his gear. I turn and look back at Killer, as Doc and I both pause at the door waiting for him to catch up with us.

The walk up the darkened path is done purposefully slow. Each of us is engrossed in our own thoughts about the possible request to fly out to Ripcord tonight. We all know this could be the only reason to get us out of bed. I'm sure each of us is pissed that someone, probably Captain Rogers, has accepted this mission. Thinking about it, I remember it's the 3rd Platoon's night on two-minute hot status. I'll bring this up to Rogers as soon as I get into the TOC. This is bullshit! 3rd Platoon has pilots that can fly night missions. Hell, with Sweet Griffin, they have the best Cobra pilot in the battalion, if not the Army.

Entering the darkened TOC, the soft glow of red lights lulls one into a misleading calm until we hear all the radios crackling. Having spent hours in the TOC, I've never heard this much radio chatter so late at night. Usually, after the sun goes down and the grunts are dug in for the night, it's quiet and the red glow of the overhead lights add to it's warmth. Not tonight, something big is up. The NVA, in their push to overrun Ripcord and throw us out of A Shau Valley, have reached over twenty miles into the Griffin's warm cozy TOC and upset the placid respite that we have come to enjoy.

I ease up behind Jimbo who, with Captain Rogers, is looking down at a map. I notice Major Stafford is here also and he too is bent low over the map looking for something in particular. In a semi-circle around them are others looking over their shoulders. Whatever it is, it's captured the attention of more non-flyers in the Griffins than I've ever seen.

The group moves back to allow the three of us to come next to the table. Looking up, while I drop my gear on the floor, our CO sees my rumpled appearance.

"Evening Sneaky. Sorry you were called but we've got a problem. Captain Rogers will explain." Looking over to Rogers, he gives him a nod to start the informal briefing.

"Gather around," Jimbo says as he moves over and lets Doc and Killer squeeze in close to me around one side of the waist high table.

"About an hour ago, 3rd Platoon launched four aircraft to try to provide fire support for Ripcord."

"Why did I know it was going to be fucking Ripcord again," Killer says under his breath, although we all hear it above the static and crackling of the radios.

Rogers ignores Killer's remark and continues. "At the present time Ripcord is under a ground attack from the north and west. Fast movers can't drop close enough. The weather's closed-in with dense ground fog. All that can be done now is for us to fly out there and keep a cap over the firebase and fire whenever there's a break in the weather."

"Are we on Hot Status?"

Killer's showing his contempt. He knows that 1st Platoon should be called up as they are on five minute alert this twenty four hour period.

"I specifically assigned each of you for this flight. After conferring with Major Stafford and Jim, they both agreed that you're the best crew we could send. I expect at least half the flight to be under instrument conditions and this is why you were picked. Any problems with this?" Jolly Roger asks as he rolls up his eye brows and looks directly at Killer.

"Hell Sir," Killer turns to Major Stafford and disregards Captain Rogers question, "I'm beat and I don't know if being this tired I can fly safely." Killer is putting his feelings out before the group. He's speaking for us all now.

"I know, that's why there will be four Aircraft Commanders up there. You will watch over each other. So whoever is the co-pilot is also AC rated. Now, any questions for Captain Rogers?"

We each answer no, as Major Stafford looks at us individually waiting for an answer. Killer is the last to reply, and it's like pulling teeth to get him to finally say "No sir."

"I asked Jim to send down two ACs to help you with the preflights." Then turning to Jimbo asks, "You send them?"

"Yes Sir. St. Clair and McIntyre are in the pits now. They should be going over the aircraft and they'll be ready when we get down there."

"Get your SOIs . . . ah . . . each one of you check one out and I'll drive you down to the pit."

Once again Major Stafford has proven his concern for his pilots is genuine. Not many COs would get out of bed and come down to the TOC to oversee the briefing, and then drive the crews to their aircraft. I don't ever remember a commanding officer having other ACs help with the preflights in order to save time and I expect to have another set of eyes, though tired, inspect the aircraft.

While we pile into the jeep, Jimbo hands out the assignments. I'll fly with Jimbo in the lead aircraft, and Doc will have Killer as his front seat.

During the bumpy ride down off the Hot Spot, Major Stafford reminds us not to get complacent, and to talk to each other during the flight to insure we are awake and alert. The drive off the hill from the TOC and Hot Spot goes to the northwest. Then as we make the looping right turn to the east along the dusty maintenance road to the revetments located in the Griffin Pit, the Major pulls off and drives up to the back of the mess hall. Before arriving he taps the horn a couple times.

Coming to a full stop under the dim light the back screen door opens and Captain Westrock comes out with Specialist Dozer in tow carrying four thermos bottles. Hell, I don't know where they got 'em but I couldn't be happier. Dozer, grubby as ever and his hair looking like he hadn't combed it in a week, hands each of us an aluminum thermos and two paper cups.

"Sorry, it's only black. But it's hot and it should help." Westrock must be doing this on the orders, or a very pointed suggestion, from Stafford. "If you need more when you come in to re-fuel, call the TOC and we'll meet you at POL."

After grinding the jeep's gears, Stafford backs away from the door while Jimbo, Doc and I join in unison to say thank you though we all really know, it must have been Major Stafford's idea.

The ride to the aircraft takes less than two minutes along the maintenance road past the Griffin living quarters to our left and the smelly four-holer and officer's showers to our right. As we pull up to the revetments, Stafford reminds us once again to talk to each other and double check the instruments. He repeats himself several times, saying he doesn't want any accidents.

"Double D, how's it look?" Jimbo seems more awake and animated than I.

"Just fine Jimbo. I've double checked all the fluids and I did a radio check with the TOC. Everything is working as far as I can tell."

Double D ignores me as I start to quickly go over the aircraft. It's not that I don't trust him, but in the dark things are missed that would normally be easily spotted during daylight inspections. A flight like this, bad weather, into A Shau, and Jimbo and I being tired, needs all the eyes it can to check everything out. As I walk down one side of the aircraft, Jimbo is inspecting the other side. With me, is a mechanic with two flashlights. He waves them in directions trying to anticipate what areas I will be inspecting. When my light stops at a particular area, he immediately shines his lights on the same spot trying to give me as much light as possible.

On reaching the tail rotor, I meet Jimbo and the crew-chief. Though no words are spoken, each of us is trying to delay the take-off until we become more awake.

"Let's do it." Jimbo is as ready as he'll ever be and it's his flight. I'm just in it for the ride, and hopefully it will be a safe one.

For one of the few times while in Vietnam I follow the Army approved, and ordered, check list. Calling out each line item and getting the appropriate response from Jimbo. My flight school IP would be very proud of me now. If ever there was a flight that should be done properly, we both are hoping this will be the one. After Jimbo has gotten us turned up and we're lightly bouncing at flight idle, Major Stafford climbs up next to Jimbo and talks to him. The Major then comes around to my side and climbs up to give me his last words of encouragement. Before we request clearance to take-off, both Jimbo and I watch, in silence, as our concerned commanding officer goes over to the next revetment and repeats the same messages to Doc and Killer. Hopefully Killer is a bit more civil now. Killer hasn't served under a real son-of-a-bitch that wouldn't give a damn whether you died or not, so probably doesn't appreciate Stafford's concern.

Our take-off is done under visual flight rules although it's dark. We have several hundred feet of ceiling here at Evans. There's no telling how the weather is out in the A Shau. Jimbo maps out his flight path to Doc, and then explains what he wants done if we get separated or enter clouds and have to fly IFR. A radio call to the 3rd Platoon flight brings us bad news. Sweet Griffin advises us that Ripcord is still being attacked and the situation is not getting any better. Then he adds the weather has closed in, and ground fog has now started to envelope the beleaguered firebase. The weather once again has worked in favor of the North Vietnamese. I wouldn't be surprised if the NVA have a machine that they can dial in to get the weather they want in the A

Shau Valley.

The flight out to A Shau and the change over with Sweet Griffin and his flight goes smoothly. I'm not at all surprised to hear that the four aircraft contain all eight of 3rd Platoon's ACs. Major Stafford has not let a plane launch tonight that didn't have two ACs in it. Rick says he'll be back in an hour or so and if anything comes up to let the TOC know right away. One thing about Rick, he surely didn't ask to have us launched. He's never one to pass a tough flight to another crew unless there's no other way to provide support for the ground troops.

The TOC, specifically Captain Rogers, has been making radio checks with all six of the Griffin aircraft that are now flying.

We've flown out to the south of Ripcord and now turn north. Jimbo has set up a large orbit to the southwest of Ripcord away from the incoming artillery fire that Bradley and O'Reilly are hurtling into the area to help the ground troops. We watch as the ground fog continues to roll in from the west. It's nice and puffy white, even in the moon lit darkness, though for us and the men of B Company and B Battery who are dug in on the figure eight shaped firebase, it's not a welcome sight. From our high and out of the way perch, we watch the flares as they gently swing down suspended by the small parachutes. The lights dissipate quickly in the fog bank from our overhead view and I'm sure the flares provide very little light for those on the ground until just before they land. The Air Force has provided a C-130 flare ship for the operation tonight, though with the number of flares they're dropping I would be surprised if it will last another couple of hours. Relief will be needed for that crew.

"Griffin Nine-Three Charlie. Griffin Nine-Three Charlie this is Rockslide Romeo, over." A voice transmits on FM radio.

"Rockslide Romeo, go ahead this is Griffin Nine-Two." Jimbo answers the unseen infantryman.

"Griffin Nine-Two are you presently on station?"

"Roger Rockslide. We replaced Nine-Three Charlie." Jimbo now has officially committed our flight.

"Ah, Roger Nine-Two we have a fire mission, over."

Shit, a goddamned fire mission in the clouds. I can't believe I'm hearing this.

"Go ahead with the mission Rockslide."

"Roger Nine-Two. To our Whiskey, we have Charlie in the wire, can you provide some fire? Over."

I now interrupt. "How the hell are we going to see the area to shoot at?" I ask looking down at a fog covered area with glowing yellow balls seemingly suspended in the gray-white mass.

"Hell, I don't know but maybe the fog will break for a few minutes. And Sneaky, turn down your panel lights," Jimbo replies on intercom.

The red glow of our instruments appears brighter, though it's really because our eyes have become accustomed to the night's darkness. One of the design problems of the Cobra is that during night flight, the co-pilots instrument panel lights reflect up onto the front plexiglass windows causing problems for the back seat aircraft commander.

I reach down and turn the lights down very low. All I need to see is the altitude, airspeed, and turn and bank indicators. If we fly into fog, or clouds, I'll then go to watching all the instruments on my abbreviated instrument panel. Jimbo is one of the better instrument pilots in the unit. The 2nd Platoon's best, E'Clair, is no longer flying. He's too short for a flight like this, though I'm sure he'd go if asked. In our flight of two aircraft, we have over 7,000 combined flight hours, which should be more than enough experience to complete the mission safely.

"Rockslide Romeo this is Griffin Nine-Two at the present time your area is in the fog and we can't see to fire, over," Jimbo tells the ground commander, though I'm sure everyone on the ground already knows you can't see a damn thing in this weather.

"Nine-Two we're in big trouble down here. Is there anyway you can you put some rockets down here, at least in the general area, over?" The desperation is clearly evident in his voice, and the background noise is punctuated with weapons fire.

"Romeo, ah . . . if you can give me an accurate location of the friendlies we'll see what we can do to help you." Jimbo is trying to calm the grunt, knowing under the cloud cover any rockets fired would be very dangerous for the friendlies..

"Nine-Two will do, over."

In less than a minute the fog covered location down below us erupts into a huge white-lighted glow. In the center is almost a small sun with the halo being formed around it from all the moisture in the fog.

"Nine-Two, Romeo. Can you see that, over?"

"Roger Romeo we have the large lighted area. Is this your location, over?"

"Nine-Two if you will fire two-five mikes to the two-eight-five from that center location you will hit Victor Charley, over."

"Roger, two-five mikes at two-eight-five, we're rolling in hot so get your heads down."

Jimbo starts to trade our airspeed for what little bit of altitude we can get under the present weather conditions. He then calls on VHF, "Doc, I'll shoot and you cover me."

"Roger Jimbo. Ah . . . can you see anything?" Doc's concern with the present weather and now a possible fire mission is reflected in his questioning response. Doc doesn't want a friendly fire incident either.

"Negative but if that's their location, and we shoot to the west, we should be safe and maybe kill a few Charlies. I'll only fire one pair and see what happens. These guys seem to be desperate."

Jimbo now switches back to the FM radio to talk to the ground. "Rockslide Romeo this is Griffin Nine-Two inbound hot. Ah . . . get your heads down." As I feel our aircraft start it's nose over, Jimbo says, "Sneaky read out the altitude, I want to pull out at three-thousand seven-hundred."

"Three-thousand seven-hundred. Got it!"

Then looking out of my front windshield I see we are aimed slightly to the left of the bright white glow. Jimbo decreases our power until we're at thirty pounds of torque, then fires a pair, after telling me to close my eyes.

I start the count down of our altitude softly so Jimbo doesn't have to concentrate on the instruments and keep his head looking in the rocket sight and the red glowing pipper. "Four-thousand... ah three-nine . . . three-eight . . . ah three . . . "

The flash of the rockets leaving the tubes and shooting past me is a shock though I knew he was going to fire, and had my eyes shut.

"Breaking hard right," Jimbo calls as the aircraft jerks us both into a slow climbing turn to the south.

"Jimbo, we hit three-six before we started to climb." I advise.

"We're on you Nine-Two." Killer's call is a secure feeling.

"Nine-Two, Romeo over." The grunts are calling.

"Go Romeo," Jimbo answers as we are climbing through four-thousand six-hundred feet still flying on a one-eight-five heading.

"Excellent shot. Could you cover that area and to the one-eight-zero? Also you can come in closer, by two-zero mikes, over." The grunt wants us to bring the rockets in closer without realizing the fog has eliminated any chance for us to shoot with pin-point accuracy.

"Roger on the one-eight-zero area. Ah . . . Romeo we will only fire two rockets per pass because of the friendlies, and you're going to have to keep the place lit up. Understand?" then Jimbo says on VHF, "No way I'm going to shoot any closer."

"Roger Nine-Two," comes across the FM from the ground commander's PRIC 25 radio.

I can't believe we're shooting rockets at targets we can't see because of the forty or fifty feet of ground fog. This is not something any of us is trained to do, or for that matter wants to do, but the men below us are in dire straights. It's missions like this that we appreciate being helicopter pilots rather than grunts.

"Doc, on this pass follow me and fire just to the west of my rockets." Then Jimbo adds, "I would advise to wait until you're under four-thousand to fire, and pull out at three thousand seven hundred, understand?."

"Roger Jimbo. What heading are you starting at?"

"Ah . . . I would say for us to use one-zero-zero. If we fire too far west, it will miss Romeo. Then pull a tight one-eighty with a steep climb out and keep your airspeed up. Do not go below three-thousand seven-hundred. You got that?" Repeating the altitude he wants Doc to pull out.

Before he answers we start our exchange of airspeed for altitude. If I live through this I will know I've done it all. I know Jim is cautious when shooting around friendlies. The Griffins have only had one friendly fire incident, and that was years ago when they were flying Charlie model Hueys. One rocket into the hill top will defeat this whole mission.

"Romeo, Nine-Two and Two-Delta will be inbound hot. Keep your heads down," Jimbo calls for both of our aircraft.

"Go Griffins." The ground commander voice is now raised in anticipation of the rockets that will be raining down on the enemy. But to me, the din of combat in the background isn't reassuring for me.

Jimbo starts our dive again and I now concentrate on the altimeter rather than look at the fog encased hill top. "Four-nine..." as we start to gather airspeed, "four-five . . . ah. four-two...."

"Griffin Nine-Two, this is Three, over."

Before I can answer for Jimbo, Killer comes up on the VHF and advises our TOC that Jimbo's in a rocket pass.

"Nine-Two..." just then a bright flash passes by my front seat from the outboard rocket pods. The bright light ruins my night vision. From now on I'm going to cup my hands over my eyes to save my night vision.

"Breaking right." Jimbo's call is followed by, "Griffin Three, Nine-Two, over."

"Griffin Nine-Two Delta's inbound." Doc calls to the ground on FM.

I'm still watching the altimeter as we are climbing. At the same time I listen to Jimbo explain to Jolly Roger and a TOC full of Griffins, both pilots and enlisted, of our shooting rockets into the fog shrouded firebase.

Just as Doc calls his right hand break, Griffin Six comes up on VHF wanting to know if what he just heard is correct. That his flight, from 2nd Platoon, is shooting rockets at targets unseen because of the ground fog.

Jimbo informs Major Stafford of the firing passes we have made and reiterates that we have not hit any friendlies. As he finishes Jimbo calls back to Rockslide Romeo to announce we'll be in for another pass.

As we go through this pass and the thirty or so more, I sit and watch the altimeter climb then fall, then climbing through for another cycle, as Jimbo fires all our rockets. I'm in a sweat and adrenalin has rushed my body. My mouth is bone dry. I've not had the time to drink the coffee, and to be honest, I would never try. A fear that I have not experienced before has caused my stomach to knot up. I know I'm not alone.

After an hour of this, we've expended all of our rockets into the unknown abyss of ground fog. As we are on one of our last passes, Sweet Griffin, with CWO Jack "Crusty" Garrett on his wing, arrives. They join up with us on our last two passes, then we break to the east for the short fifteen minute flight back to Evans, and hopefully to the comfort of a warm bed.

As we leave, Rick calls to us with his assessment of our shooting rockets into the fog shrouded hill. I am too pumped up to listen and only catch his closing remark of, "Shit-hot Nine-Two."

Shit-hot is not the half of it, this flight has scared the hell out of me and we didn't take a single round of anti-aircraft fire. Just the bad weather, the unseen target, and the fearful knowledge that I'm flying out of my element.

Chapter 17

"Let's go!" I yell as I run past Mask in the Hot Shack toward Zero-Two-Seven.

I'd been sitting in the air-conditioned TOC monitoring Ripcord's radio traffic while its extraction started. I know this day will be one I remember for a long time. Especially after the three trips I made out to Ripcord last night as Jimbo's co-pilot. Firing rockets into the fog and praying that we would not hit friendlies. The good news is, after fourteen Griffin flights and firing rockets into the Ripcord perimeter last night, we ended the missions with no friendly-fire incidents. The NVA have been getting ready for the extraction for days. Though I think we ought to call it an abandonment, rather than an extraction. The loss of a Chinook on the 18th, that crashed onto Ripcord, shows that the NVA are more than ready. It's obvious with the amount of news coverage that the Generals and politicians don't want this to turn into a victory for the North Vietnamese.

Five days ago when a CH-47 from the Pachyderms took heavy fire while flying into Ripcord, it ended up crashing onto the 105mm ammo dump which caused massive destruction. Though only two were killed, the resulting secondary explosions caused the destruction of five 105mm howitzers, two 106mm recoilless rifles, and a lot more associated damage. The one 105 left, though damaged, was not able to be used because of the loss of all the 105 ammo that blew up in the dump. If there was a message in this incident I'm not sure the military strategist saw it, but I did. But then I've lived through the siege of Khe Sanh and it makes me not only a minority but, to me more important, a survivor.

For the Griffins, today's operation started about eight o'clock last night and just continued. We've been flying steadily since this latest attack started.

It was planned for today to use fourteen CH-47s to pull out the artillery pieces of B Battery, 2nd of the 319th Arty. It was to start at 0545 but we all knew it would not happen on time because of the weather. Chinooks are scheduled for twenty-two sorties. They will pick up the one 155mm howitzer battery with its six tubes. Then they are to lift out the two M405 bulldozers, the one M55 Quad-50 from the G Battery, 1st of the 65th Arty and the remaining damaged 105mm howitzer left over from the incident on the 18th. After all this is completed there will be a sortie or two for the assorted Conex boxes used as TOCs or artillery fire direction centers.

The plan, presented in a briefing yesterday afternoon at the 06th Operations hut at Currahee, revealed the losses of equipment from the July 18th downing of the CH-47. The men from the B Company 2nd/506th were supposed to be lifted, by Huey, off Ripcord after the completion of the 'hooks lift of the usable artillery pieces and men of the B Battery, 2nd Battalion of the 319th Arty of the 101st Airborne Division. As the military jargon goes, we're suppose to have the show on the road, H-hour, at 0545. Last night in the club, in very somber tones, all the ACs expressed doubt on the judgment of the commander who thought up these plans. All it will take is one SNAFU, as they say, and the time table will be thrown to the wind.

I've been holed up in the TOC since 0515 hunched over the radios, drinking coffee with Captain Rogers and a few other ACs, waiting to hear how things were going. After my three trips into the Valley last night, I know I couldn't go to sleep until today was over. The appointed H-Hour arrived, and passed. First the weather held us up and when it broke the winds picked up. The NVA waited for the weather to clear to start another day of intense 60 and 82mm mortar fire. The early reports we are hearing indicate their aim is very accurate, and they are firing in waves that must be coordinated from a central command location. The NVA have waited for this day and now it's arrived. They are very well disciplined and intend to control the outcome of this battle. Even if we get everyone off unscathed, the NVA have forced us into this decision, not some Army commander in a bunker at Camp Eagle.

Now its 0745, on July 23th, 1970, and all hell has broken loose on Ripcord. At 0620 the first Chinook is able to start the extraction of the artillery pieces. As each 'hook goes in, it's being fired upon all the way from multiple locations. It's a real shooting gallery at Ripcord. They have all taken many 12.7mm hits, and so far, two of the CH-47s are back here at Evans down with major battle damage. The hour we have been gathered around the radios has been one of solemn introspection because we all know that our turn in the Valley is coming shortly.

We all listened to another 'hook pilot on his approach, radio the amount and direction of 12.7mm fire he is taking when all of a sudden he announces he is going to crash and would try to make it onto Ripcord. If he doesn't land on the firebase he'll be in big trouble, for I'm sure the hill is now surrounded by NVA. We have four Griffins out there from 1st Platoon, but as soon as the Mayday is called, we launch everything we have. Before Jolly Roger opens his mouth, I'm moving to the exit with Doc Holiday in tow. We're running as fast as we can, knowing that Jimbo and E'Clair are right behind.

"What happened?" Mask asks as he joins in our run to the plane.

"Let's get going!" I say while climbing into the back seat. Ignoring his question for now, he'll know soon enough the situation that we will be flying into.

Mask unfastens the main blade and swings it free. Then he climbs into Zero-Two-Seven's front seat.

As he's climbing in, I yell, "A Pachyderm's down on Ripcord."

I engage the starter button and the process has started. Within two minutes, we'll be lifted off from our small oil soaked pad and moving southwest. Slipping my helmet on, I hear confusion begin to flood the air.

Jimbo's calling Evans Tower with an emergency departure and instantly we receive it. The quick clearance allows us to be airborne within ARA's two-minute time frame.

It's a short flight and on the way I brief Mask as to the facts as I know them. The radios are cluttered with different pilots relaying the coordinates of the active anti-aircraft gun emplacements they've spotted, and the attempt by a C&C to rescue the downed 'hook crew. This day is turning into a real goat fuck.

Ripcord is still taking mortar fire, and I'm sure they hope to score a direct hit on the wounded Chinook. If it landed hard, I'll bet it's a total loss already.

Once getting out into A Shau Valley we're directed to contact a small patrol from A Company of the 06th that suspects they have a positive location of one of the active NVA mortars. The weather isn't helping with a low overcast sky forcing us to fly lower to get under the fast-moving clouds. With all the aircraft up, the chance for a midair is now my biggest worry.

"Keep looking out for other aircraft," I remind my co-pilot for the day.

I was supposed to have the Kid with me. We have flown together the last six days, except for last night's flight. But, with E'Clair flying, Jimbo put them together. E'Clair has only days left and if we didn't need ACs so bad, he'd be back at the hootch, or in the club, missing all this excitement. This, he told me a couple hours ago, will be his last combat flight in Vietnam.

"Hell, look at all the helicopters," Mask says as he scans to our right.

To the north I see the Chinooks in a large orbit with several Hueys flying in and out of the 'hooks formation. I would expect that some of the Hueys are trying to find a chance to swoop in and land. Firebase Ripcord is a carved out figure-eight shaped complex on top of Hill 970 that's surrounded by thick vegetation. Though they have cleared away a lot of the scrub to allow for good fields of fire, any NVA with a rifle can take a clean shot at helicopters coming and going into the besieged scrap of land. Half of the debris cluttering the firebase appears to be ablaze, indicating the CH-47 must have crash landed on the south side. Time and time again small light gray plumes rise throughout the barbed wire enclosure. They're still taking heavy mortar fire, and it's coming from more than one tube. This is going to be a difficult extraction and I hope we can get it done in one day, otherwise the men left over night will be in for a long hard fight to stay alive.

"Be advised. All Chinook aircraft in the Ripcord area return to Evans."

This announcement is a surprise and it's not a good one. Either the higher-ups have decided to abort the extraction, which means the men are in for a rough time getting off the hill, or some commander has made the decision to bomb the hell out of the area. Hopefully, for B Company of the 2nd of the 06th and B Battery of the 2nd of the 319th Arty it's bomber time. Having survived the siege of Khe Sanh I know what hell is like and Ripcord could very well become hell for the men left on the ground. B Company cannot leave the firebase until B Battery has been extracted. So these men have a tough fight ahead of them.

"Griffin Nine-Two, Delta Zulu, over," a voice from somewhere on the floor of the valley calls.

"Go Delta Zulu."

"Roger Nine-Two. We're at the same location as yesterday and we can hear a tube firing, over."

"Roger Zulu, we're about over your location-pop smoke, over."

Then knowing the smoke will be almost completely dissipated after it clears the trees, I follow Jimbo's swing into a right-hand bank in the general area of one of A or D Company's patrols. For most new pilots in Vietnam all the green foliage looks the same color. With time you learn to recognize the differences of the many green hues and tints and it becomes easier to pinpoint locations. If you have a good idea what the shade is of a green tree, then when you roll back into it you'll find yourself looking for that one shade of green. Though many trees may be of the same shade the mixture of lights and darks, with shadows adding to the hues, allows the area to develop its own fingerprint. Most gun pilots have a hard time recognizing this because of the speed we're moving. I learned the trick while flying scouts. I've told my fellow Griffins that while flying scouts you may be hovering only twenty feet or so above a trail. When you're this close, you can follow a blood trail easily after just a little practice. It's the ultimate form of hunting the smartest animal in the world, man.

"Got goofy grape at two," D.D. McIntyre says, while Jimbo does a tight turn toward wisps of purple smoke rising out of the trees.

Looking back to my five I just barely make out the purple haze coming up through the trees. It's not in a vertical plume, but spread flat across the tops of the wind blown trees. The lower canopies have worked for the NVA and have dissipated the smoke.

"Mask, keep watching the smoke," I remind my co-pilot.

With the Kid I had gotten out of the practice of asking for this to be done. Klien not only kept the target in sight but, as I would roll in on it, he would call out it's location as we flew closer. With Klien as a co-pilot, my job was easier.

"Ah . . . Zulu, we got goofy." Jimbo now starts his search for the possible enemy location.

"Roger Griffin Nine-Two. From our location, heading zero-one-five, approximately one-zero-zero mikes is the tube."

"Roger Zulu, zero-one-five at one-zero-zero mikes. Ah . . . we'll be firing from Echo to Whiskey with a break over your location Zulu."

We only have seventeen pound rockets on board because nails can't be fired in this close to friendlies. Several hundred meters to the south of this patrol is the mother company.

Switching to VHF Jimbo advises, "We'll roll in from the east with me and Doc firing. It will be a south break and overfly the team using a left-hand pattern. Keep the team in sight. Sneaky, you and E'Clair will not fire. Just cover us. There are too many fifties out here. Fucking valley is full of them, so keep your eyes open. After we make several passes we'll switch positions."

This means E'Clair and I will do a high cap, though in this overcast cloudy weather it won't be too high of a cap. While we're orbiting around, Jimbo and Doc will be making their passes and firing their rockets at the suspected enemy location.

Squelch breaks confirm the orders as we now over-fly the area that is thought to be harboring the mortar tube. It's densely thick with lower growth trees, but there are several places that a tube could fire though the canopy. The NVA have positioned themselves in a good location, set between Ripcord and two American units patrolling one and a half kilometers to the south. The word has been passed down that after the completion of Ripcord's extraction both A & D Companies will be lifted out and returned to Camp Evans.

I break into a tight three hundred and sixty degree climbing turn to allow Jimbo to set up on his pass and get some altitude between us. Looking back over my shoulder I see E'Clair has extended his turn so that he will be able to observe both Jimbo and Doc, as well as me. Jimbo starts his break back toward the target knowing the necessary interval between all of us will be completed by the time he rolls in.

"Zulu, Nine-Two is inbound hot."

Jimbo pulls the nose up, trying for some more last minute altitude, then rolls it over into a shallow dive, firing rockets as he approaches the blanket of trees.

"Griffin Nine-Two, excellent." The RTO's soft voice is louder now that there's Cobra support above.

Because of the low level passes we are forced to use, we can't fire as many rockets per pass as we usually would.

Then Jimbo calls, "Sneaky join in behind Doc on his next run in." Then with a short pause says, "Doc, follow me out and we'll cover them."

Double squelch breaks are the only answers on VHF.

I now pull the Cobra into a tight turn rolling in behind Doc's aircraft. As he starts his pull out I let my collective down until the torque meter shows thirty pounds. Checking the turn and bank needles I see I'm in trim.

"Sneaky's inbound."

"Roger . . . ah . . . Sneaky?"

Zulu's RTO is calm considering he's been walking up and down the valley floor for what must seem like years. I remember Marines in Okinawa wearing custom jackets embroidered on the back with a map of Vietnam above which, in fancy scroll, was a saying about being "The Meanest Mother In The Valley." As far as I'm concerned anyone who walks in A Shau Valley and survives is both lucky and, under the conditions, a mean mother-fucker.

As I fire the first four pair I call out, "E'Clair get an adjustment." Though it doesn't need to be said, I just want to get this mission over and get back to Evans without any battle damage or problems.

"Delta Zulu, Griffin Nine-Two Kilo. How was that? Any adjustments?" E'Clair asks as I start my break.

"Kilo, could you add ah . . . Two-five on your next pass, over," the still calm RTO advises.

On VHF I call, "Breaking left."

"Got it Zulu. Add two-five, Ah . . . Zulu, Kilo's rolling in hot." Now the Kid answers for E'Clair.

I'm climbing back up and have a good view of E'Clair's rocket run out my left canopy. "That's the area Kilo," as I see E'Clair's first pair slithering into a darkened hole in the undulating trees. Marty keeps firing pair after pair quickly now that he's got the enemy's position. "Great shooting Kilo. You got them! They've stopped firing." The voice now seems excited with the knowledge that the enemy, the fucking little slopes, are getting killed.

"Kilo's breaking."

The Kid is still on the radios. I wouldn't be surprised if he's flying this pass from the front seat. Though very difficult, with practice it can be done and I've let him do it several times while on CCN flights.

Most of the 2nd Platoon ACs know Klien's ready to become an AC. Jimbo and I have talked to Rick about giving him a check ride but because of the Ripcord operation we haven't had the time or aircraft to spare. Everyone's being pushed to his limits. I'm sure when E'Clair leaves in a few days the case of Klien's check ride will not have to be made again. Right now I'm at one hundred and thirty-five hours flight time for the past thirty days. I, like most of the other ACs, am flying on an okay from the Flight Surgeon. If I remember right, he asked me if I felt okay, at the same time he was signing the papers to override the high-time flight limits of the one-hundred and twenty flight hours per thirty day period. I'm sure I didn't see him for more than thirty seconds. In fact, he saw seven of us in less than five minutes, then got back in his jeep and drove off in a cloud of dust. So much for the Griffins being fatigued.

The Army has a regulation allowing commanders to get around the flight time limits. It says during an emergency the Commanding Officer can waiver our flight time caps. Major Stafford has been more than visible during the operation. He sees, talks and quizzes each of us every day. He's found in the mess hall early in the morning and late at night. He's at every briefing given. He's in and out of the TOC as the flights leave and return from missions. I've seen him down in the Griffin pit talking with the maintenance crews several times. Several of the pilots commented on the radio that he carried rockets to their aircraft when they were doing a quick turnaround to go back to Ripcord. Even Wee Willie mentioned that the Old Man was down at the revetment asking how he was doing and if he needed anything. He knows what is at stake and he cares for his men. He'll do whatever he can to prevent any losses from fatigue. It reminds us that he hasn't forgotten about us which makes each of us feel like we belong. But he still sends us out. Stafford knows what each man is capable of and he drives us to meet these expectations.

Watching E'Clair break left and start his climb out, I've slowed down and tried for the last little bit of altitude before swinging the nose around and starting another roll in. As I fire the first set of rockets, Jimbo comes on the air.

"Sneaky, make that your last pass." Then switching over to FM, he checks with the patrol, "Delta Zulu, Griffin Nine-Two, over."

"Go Nine-Two."

"Zulu has that taken care of the tube?"

"Roger Nine-Two. It's silent now. Ah . . . we heard yelling so we think you got 'em. We're going to try to get clearance to recon the area, over."

"Roger Zulu we'll orbit overhead if you want."

"Roger Griffin. It sure would be appreciated." Then the radio operator tries to contact his company commander on the same frequency. "Delta Foxtrot, Delta Foxtrot, this is Delta Zulu, over."

"Delta Zulu go ahead."

"Foxtrot, Alpha Romeo Alpha has silenced the tube. We want to do a BDA, over"

"Roger Zulu, as long as you have Alpha Romeo Alpha overhead you may proceed to the area and do a quick recon, over." They must be happy knowing they're going to have the chance to see the damage inflicted by sixty-four seventeen-pound warheads hitting the small firing pit. "Griffin, did you copy that last transmission?"

"Roger Delta Zulu. We'll hang around."

I scan down to the eight-day clock and see it's 0830. The planned lift of B Company by the Hueys didn't start at its scheduled time of 0745. The delay seems not only to be due to the Chinook's demise into the firebase, but the continual 60 and 82mm mortar fire Ripcord is still receiving. The talk is the Huey lift will start in another hour. It's a bad day for the home team, or are we the home team? I guess one would call this a road game, though for us who have to travel, it's not much of a game.

"Sneaky, you and E'Clair head back and re-arm and refuel. If these guys run into trouble, I want continuous coverage."

"Roger Jimbo. Let's boogey, E'Clair."

Double clicks tell me that E'Clair monitors and looking back, I see he's broken away and climbing to get in behind me.

The trip back to re-arm and refuel goes smoothly. We're flying light and pulling full power which allows us to make the trip in short time. We reposition from the POL pits to the Griffin Hot Spot and we're met with a swarm of shirtless men holding rockets for the quick turn around. Not only armorers and crew-chiefs, but pilots as well. Griffins have a surprising amount of team spirit considering the crew-chiefs don't fly with their aircraft. Everyone knows this is a big operation and they also know the trouble the 06th will be in if we don't get them extracted in one day.

As the re-arming is completed, Captain Rogers emerges from the TOC. I close my window and receive the takeoff clearance from the tower. Looking back to my left, I see Jolly Roger standing in the rotor wash with one hand holding his hat, and the other with a thumbs up. There's no doubt he's glad we're out here flying and he's inside the air-conditioned TOC listening to the radios. But over the past week or so Rogers has not once corrected me when I used my Sneaky call sign rather than Griffin Nine Two Gulf. I need to cut Jolly Roger some slack.

Flying straight through the valleys to get out to Ripcord could be a hazard. I'm surprised the NVA haven't put a few .51's along the valleys to and from A Shau to add excitement to our trips. There's no enemy fire after leaving the valley, which makes for an easier trip, especially after fighting the weather problems in the A Shau. The weather is nothing like what was taught in flight school at Fort Rucker or, now, at Fort Walters. Here, micro-climates allow all the normal weather conditions to be thrown out the window, and this means the weather could be anything from bright cloudless sunny days, to zero-zero and heavy rain. This change in the weather can happen in less than half an hour. If the NVA could have requested bad weather, I'm sure that is what they would have wanted. The mornings and nights are foggy or misted in. This leaves a small window of opportunity each day for flight operations such as re-supply, troop movement, or medevacs. Repeatedly the Dust Off pilots have proven they're not going to be kept from their appointed rounds by some inclement weather. Several of the stories we've heard have been amazing. Like the pilots of DMZ Dust Off, Eagle Dust Off goes the extra mile to save a life. Nothing bad can ever be said about the medevac pilots flying in Northern I Corps. I never have a problem buying a few rounds of booze for these guys.

As we enter the valley, I hear on UHF that a flight of Hueys is going to try to extract B Company, 2nd of the 06th. These guys are really going to have their hands full with this extraction. The Griffins have four aircraft from 1st Platoon flying with this extraction flight, as well as four pair of Cobras from the Redskins of D Company, 158th Assault Helicopter Battalion of the 101st ABN. Everyone knows it's going to be a hot extraction.

I call on VHF, "Griffin Nine-Two, over."

"Go ahead Sneaky. Where are you?"

"Just entered the valley, how you doing?"

"Still quiet on the ground, but we're low on fuel and the weather sucks."

"Go ahead and break. Tell Zulu we're inbound."

"Roger."

"Delta Zulu, Griffin Nine-Two Indio."

Jimbo's front seater, Chief Warrant Officer 2 Donald "Double D" McIntyre, is making the call. Double D just came back from emergency leave for his father's funeral, so Jimbo has him flying with him for the first few flights into A Shau, then he'll pick up some of the time other 2nd Platoon ACs are flying.

"Go Indio."

"Zulu Nine-Two is going to re-arm and refuel. Our wingman will be on station in four or five, call-sign Nine-Two Gulf."

"Roger Nine-Two Gulf. Thanks Nine-Two for sticking around and great shooting."

"Roger."

"Bingo, Nine-Two at ten o'clock." The Kid, on VHF, is on his toes.

"Delta Zulu, Griffin Nine-Two Gulf and flight will be overhead in a few minutes, do you copy?"

"Roger Two Gulf. We're just starting to enter the clearing where November Victor Charley was firing."

"Roger that, Zulu," I answer.

On VHF comes Jimbo. "Sneaky try to get a BDA from them. We'll be back as soon as we can."

"Roger. Call the TOC while you're at POL and they'll give you a quick re-arm turn around."

Double squelch breaks are heard, and I see Jimbo wave as we pass each other.

"Zulu, Gulf approaching at 1400 feet," I answer.

"Roger Gulf, we hear you. You want smoke?"

"Negative. Ah . . . negative on the smoke. Once we fly over you, give us a mark and we'll set up an orbit around you." I look down into the vast green tide of trees moving as the winds have still not let up.

"Mark! Mark! You're over us now Griffin."

Jerking the cyclic hard to the left, we turn in a tight oval and below us we see a small cleared out area with shapes just barely visible. "Got you Zulu."

"We got 'em." The Kid seems to have taken over his aircraft, which I personally don't mind.

"E'Clair let's keep a one-eighty around them."

Double squelch breaks.

We continue the orbit for several minutes, waiting for the patrol members to make a bomb damage assessment and then head back to their company to the south.

"Griffin Two Gulf, Delta Zulu, over."

"Go Zulu."

"Griffin, you have got one eight-two mike mike tube destroyed, six Kilo India Alphas, all November Victor Charlie, and four Alpha Kilos damaged. My initials are Juliet Alpha Sierra. Do you copy?"

On VHF the Kid calls, "Got it Sneaky." Which I can imagine he has written in his typical neat form on the front canopy plexiglass.

"Roger Zulu. Thanks for the kills," I reply, happy that this Griffin flight will have some kills. At least I'll not have to listen to the Kid bitch tonight. No doubt he'll rush back to his cubicle and sit down and write in his diary the BDA we got from his mission. I'll bet his diary is more accurate than our unit diary, plus I know it will be neater.

"Thank you Griffin. Great shooting."

"Break, break, Griffin Nine-Two this is Delta Alpha, over."

"Go Delta Alpha."

"Griffin, could you stick around while Zulu heads back to our location?" the Company commander asks, then adds, "also, he might find some more targets for you."

"No problem Delta Alpha, we're here."

Really I'd rather stay here than go over Ripcord with all the aircraft weaving in and out of each other's flight path. This has to be safer at the present time.

"Delta Zulu, Delta Alpha, over."

"Go ahead Alpha."

"Roger Zulu. Oscar says to rejoin our position, over."

"Roger Alpha we're on the move. Griffin, did you monitor that last, over?"

"Roger Zulu, be careful and call if you see anything."

On VHF E'Clair calls, "Sneaky, I've been up on Uniform and the extraction has been put off to 0930, and I bet it's not going to start on time then. Shit, what a mess is going on to the north. It's going to take two or three hours to get it completed and that's with this weather. If the weather gets worse, we're all fucked. By the way, they are still taking mortar fire all over Ripcord."

"Bet you're glad you're over here," I interject.

"I'd rather be at the Club sipping a cool one. Hell, I'd settle for a warm one right now," E'Clair quickly answers.

"How many hours you got this month?" Asking the question that each pilot knows to the minute because of our high numbers.

"I've got 127 to 130, depending on today's total. At least I was spared flying last night. I don't know how you are making it."

"The next time the Doc comes over tell him you can't take it any more. You're too short for this shit," Masks adds to the conversation.

"I thought of that already. But I don't want to flake out on you guys." E'Clair knows none of us would stop flying when being needed like the AC's are now. But I know today is his last day up.

"I wish you would flake out so I can get my AC check ride." The Kid can't wait to become an AC.

"How the hell do you know if you can pass the ride?" Mask asks, then laughs.

This causes the radios to light up with comments, and Klien stubbornly defends himself. For the next fifteen minutes, as we fly in a tight left-hand orbit, we tell the Kid why he'll fail his ride. And just as vigorously he defends himself with reasons why he's the best.

"Sneaky, we're in the Valley," Doc Holiday calls out on VHF.

"Roger, we're flying a cap on the team. They are moving Sierra. Ah . . . they gave us good BDA."

"Call it in to Jolly Roger," Jimbo interjects before I can go any further.

I pull into a climb to get some altitude to make the call back to our TOC. The climb's restricted by the cloud cover, but I think I can get enough altitude. Glancing down I see the Rate of Climb indicator now at one thousand feet per minute. The gray clouds are quickly approaching as I level off, while still in an orbit around the location of the patrol. E'Clair hasn't climbed so we are looking out the left windows down on him. His one rotor blade is painted white on the top, so we see the pale dish formed from it's 230

RPM's through the air.

"Griffin Three, Griffin Three, Sneaky, over."

"Go ahead Sneaky this is Griffin Three Mike."

"Roger Griffin Three Mike we have a BDA for you to copy, over."

"Griffin Nine-Two Gulf, use your proper call-sign, over," Jolly Roger orders. This comes as a surprise as the past week he's never said this.

"Ah . . . Griffin Three Mike, you're coming in garbled, over." Then switching to VHF I say, "Just like him to be official when he knows the whole world is monitoring. They all know me as Sneaky, not fucking Nine . . . Two . . . Gulf . . . " I wonder, maybe the old man is there and he feels he was to do this.

"Get the call off Sneaky and quit fucking with him." Jimbo, on VHF, has been listening to all this.

"Ah . . . Griffin Three Mike. Sneaky with BDA as follows. Six, I repeat six Charlies KIA. Four AKs damaged. One eight-two mike-mike tube destroyed. Initials are Juliet Alpha Sierra. Do you copy all that?" Then before an answer can be given, "Griffin Three Mike, you're garbled. Sneaky, QSY at this time."

"That's telling him Sneaky."

The Kid has started to hate Jolly Roger as much as I do. I know he has a job to do and he is a good Operations Officer, just a rotten scared-shitless pilot. But the Kid's becoming more and more outspoken to the pilots that don't fly hard missions. Some of this is my fault because he sees how I act and say things. He doesn't realize that I pick and choose my remarks. Plus, there's no doubt I'll fly any mission that comes up. And the Kid, is just that. His total time in the Army is less than mine in combat. No matter how much the RLOs dislike what I say, and my attitude, they know I've been through it and continually come back for more. Klien will have to temper his remarks, at least till he gets several tours under his belt. It 's possible, though I do not think so, that Jolly Roger would make an example out of him to send me a message. As much as I hate Jolly Roger for not flying, he's a damn good operations officer, and you need a good ops officer to make the unit run smoothly. Maybe I need to talk to Jolly Roger and tell him I'll slow Klien's mouth down a bit, sort of preventive maintenance. I hate to see Klien get in trouble.

The extraction of the units from the top of Ripcord takes longer than anyone planned. It's one helicopter in at a time. Each extraction aircraft is going in and coming out under heavy, concentrated anti-aircraft fire. It becomes a test of who has the most ammo. The NVA gunners are shooting everything they have at the extraction aircraft. We, the good guys, have diverted everything we have to the area. At any given time Cobras are rolling in from two or three directions firing their rockets at the enemy. When a known .51 caliber emplacement is found, the Griffins go after it. The Griffins are a form of airmobile artillery, which is why we fall under artillery sections and are called Air Rocket Artillery. We do not carry wing mounted mini-guns or have aircraft equipped with the newer 20mm cannon firing from the left-hand stub wing. All of our aircraft are equipped with the XM-159 rocket pods on all four stub-wing mounts. It's also very seldom that we use our turret weapons.

It quickly appears the NVA gunners and mortarmen are not impressed that the Griffins are flying against them, though our business cards have been thrown out the cockpits, fluttering down to the earth, or most likely to the tops of the trees. Whoever picks up the cards will see a picture of a Griffin in the center. Underneath the four color picture of the fabled mythical creature are the words, "Death From Above, Wire GRIFFIN, APO 96383." In a semi-circle above the Griffin is embossed the saying, "Love By Nature, Live By Luck, Kill By Profession". But today the 803d and 29th NVA regiments don't seem to be impressed with our business cards or our motto.

By 1214 we're all released to go back to Camp Evans. Ripcord is now vacated. The number of aircraft hit by 60 and 82-mm mortar fire, the fifty-one caliber anti-aircraft and small arms fire is surprising. Though we have tried to knock out those weapons, we have failed today.

On short final to the Griffin pit, Jolly Roger orders the Griffins to leave their gear in their planes and get a ride to the mess hall for lunch and a quick briefing before we go back out to the A Shau.

"Why are we going back?" Mask asks, thinking the mission is over for the day.

"We got to pull out the other two companies to the south. You wouldn't like to be left out there over night would you?" I say spitefully.

"Shit no!" Mask now understands that our day might just be starting.

After landing and hovering into the revetment, I allow the temperatures to cool down for the required time before I start the engine shut-down process. As the blades are slowly coming to a stop, Wee Willie jumps out of the back of the jeep driven by one of the Operations NCOs.

"How's the bird?" my crew-chief asks as he reaches up to grab a rotor blade.

"No gripes. I think we'll be going back out in an hour or so," I say as I fill out the Dash 13 maintenance log.

"You'll be taking off at quarter 'til the hour, so I need to get you up to the mess hall right away Mr. White," a new member of Jolly Roger's Operations crew yells over to me.

I climb out and disrobe from the chicken plate and survival vest, dropping them on the open ammo bay door. Mask comes around the nose of the aircraft without his gear.

"Well let's get up there and find out what the fuck we've got to do," I say while watching E'Clair and Klien walk toward the jeep from their revetment next to ours.

The drive up the dusty maintenance road is done in quiet. We all know that we still have two more companies to pull out of A Shau. Now, because of our first flight this morning, we also know the enemy is close at hand. The slicks were only able to extract the men off Ripcord with one aircraft at a time. Also, I'm sure we'll be using only a one ship LZ for this afternoon's extraction. Our luck is it will be a hover hole and the slicks will be taking fire in and out. Hopefully, the weather will hold.

As we pull up to the mess hall, Lieutenant "Skip" Verdine is standing out in front with Jimbo.

"Marty! Skip will be taking your place this afternoon," then with a big grin coming across his face he adds, "from here on out, you're grounded!"

E'Clair looks surprised at the good turn of events. Then after pausing and thinking for an answer he says, "Nah, I'll finish today's flights."

"No, the Old Man says you're grounded. Go grab a cold one for me."

Then Jimbo turns and opens the right-hand door to the Officer's and Senior NCOs side of the mess hall. I follow him, with Mask grabbing the door before it slams shut.

After sitting down and trying to consume a pressed dry mystery meat and dry bread sandwich, and a cup of coffee, our attention is diverted to the door as Captain Rogers and the 06th Lieutenant enter with an unknown Spec 4 struggling with a large plywood board with a map attached.

"Gentlemen, may we have your attention." Captain Rogers says to the dozen or so pilots before him.

Jolly Roger is going to hold this briefing himself, which ought to prove very interesting. He's never been into A Shau and to the best of my knowledge he's never even seen pictures of it. But I'll try to pass on making remarks this afternoon.

The specialist props the acetate covered map up on the first table, then stands behind it as if he were a leg to an easel. His hand out steadying the flimsy contraption.

"The evacuation of Ripcord is complete. We are now going to extract the two companies from an area south of Ripcord."

Then turning, Captain Rogers points to a blue circle about a klick and a half south of the now abandoned firebase.

"Jimbo and his flight have been operating out here this morning for members of . . . " then looking over to the grunt lieutenant for help.

"A and D companies, Sir."

"Yes, A and D companies."

Now looking back and gathering his thoughts, he is interrupted again with the sound of voices coming though the door. When the door finally swings open, it reveals Major Stafford and Captain Sherrily.

"Carry on."

Stafford doesn't want to interrupt the briefing, and he and Captain Sherrily walk behind Captain Rogers and go to the far wall next to the two large coffee urns.

"Good afternoon sir." Jolly Roger is being more formal now that the CO is in the room.

Stafford replies with a nod of the head.

Captain Rogers continues with, "As I was saying, Captain Mitchener's flight was working in that area this morning. They were able to get a mortar tube knocked out and some confirmed KIAs . . . ah . . . so we know the area is hot. Because of this, we'll be sending out Captain Mitchener's flight first. The scheduled extraction begins at 1300 hours. I want Captain Crane and his flight to follow at a twenty minute interval to provide relief for 2nd Platoon." Then looking to the back of the room at Jimbo he adds, "Jim you can direct 3rd Platoon to the location."

Rogers looks bewildered and appears lost for words when Jimbo doesn't reply. He looks over to Major Stafford. Nothing ever looks worse than a very large man with a pointer in his hand, who's supposed to be in charge and directing a briefing, lost for words.

"I've got nothing further. Just fly safely. I expect there will be a lot of aircraft and you need to stay alert." Then without any fanfare the CO nods back to our Operations Officer.

Looking down at his large, probably Rolex, watch Jolly Roger announces, "Gentlemen it's twenty minutes 'til launch. I think you better get to your aircraft." He finally regains some sense of authority.

Without much talk the crews stand up, some gulping down the last of their cold coffee, and start heading for the door.

As Jimbo walks by Jolly Rogers, he says, "Skip will be flying instead of St. Clair."

Rogers snaps his head back looking at Jimbo passing behind him and asks, "Why's that?"

"Major Stafford has grounded him," is the last thing Jolly Rogers hears as Jimbo exits the door with me close on his heels. Truthfully, I feel for Rogers right now. He's been bypassed in a command decision and he knows it. I know Jimbo talked the old man into this without saying a word to Jolly Rogers.

I climb into the back of the crowded three-quarter ton truck and in minutes the 2nd Platoon flight crew is deposited on the PSP matting a couple revetments away from our aircraft.

As I walk toward it, Mask comments, "That sure was nice of the Major to let Marty have the rest of his time off."

Mask is a new kid in the military and doesn't realize what war does to men. Though he's not changing as rapidly as the Kid, he too will go home much different from the young naive lad who came to Vietnam, after a recruiter told him of all the glory and great times he would be having as a dashing helicopter pilot. Problem is, most recruiters are not combat veterans, but usually administrative types that get jobs in their home towns to convince young impressionable boys of the value of going into the service, then going to war. And yes, in some cases even dying for your country. Why else would they give recruiters a large emblem to wear as if they had been on the field of fire? Hell, they probably have used all the skill and cunning needed to fight an enemy just to get some of these kids into the military. If necessary, a recruiter will help alter a high school diploma, or go down to the local court house and plead with a judge to release the wayward lad into his care and he'll ensure the military will straighten him out. The courts get rid of the hellraiser and the recruiter makes his quota.

Someday, this will come back and haunt the military. But like all errors in the military, it will come back far too late for many bright-eyed young men.

When I joined, out of anger toward my father because he wouldn't buy me a new car, I tried every branch of service and failed each until the Marines. I was a hundred and twenty-five pound kid with a very bad case of acne. Though I would max the written pre-entry test, my problem was the physical. During the first two physicals, Air Force and Army, I had been truthful on the questionaire and checked the boxes affirming that I had infantile paralysis and a cleft palate.

After realizing the infantile paralysis was getting me rejected, I didn't check it but still checked the cleft palate box during the Navy and Coast Guard physicals. Another problem was I was going to the same pre-induction center in New Haven, Connecticut, each time. Quickly, they got to know me.

As a last resort I entered the Marine Recruiting Office in the Hartford, Connecticut, Central Post Office 3rd floor military recruiting center. I stood before a sergeant, of some sort, for what seemed like ten minutes while he continued to read his newspaper and never looked up or acknowledged my presence. Finally I leaned over and placed my hands on the immaculately clean oak government issue desk and announced once again I was wanting to talk to someone about joining the Marines. Without ever looking up he stated, "Get your fucking hands off my desk, maggot."

I was stunned. Who the fuck was he to say this when I, Robert Bryan White, was here to enlist in the Marine Corps? After he put the paper down, I looked into the steel gray eyes of a very determined and hardened older man with sprinkles of gray in his thin and closely cropped hair. His uniform was perfectly pressed and though I didn't know what was right or wrong in his appearance he looked like the poster of every Marine I've ever seen. I told him that I wanted to join the Marines and further explained that I had already taken all the tests but was having trouble with the physical. Quickly he called the other recruiters and found what my problem was during the physical. For whatever reason, though I think it was because it was the end of his recruiting quarter and he hadn't made his quota, he gave me in-depth instructions on how to fill out, and conveniently omit, certain facts in my physical form. Because I'd been to New Haven so many times, he then had me scheduled to go to the Springfield, Massachusetts, pre-induction center for the physical. From there, after passing with flying colors, the rest is history. For the old grizzled sergeant, I filled a spot on his monthly body count. For me, it changed my life.

As Mask and I walk up to the aircraft, I continue the talk about commanding officers and those that are good or bad.

"There are very few COs that really care for their men. Most are in it to get a promotion to the next level. You, as a warrant officer, are not looked upon too kindly by the RLOs." Then, seeing his questioning look, I continue with, "We are only flying because the Army wants to save money and time getting helicopter pilots to Vietnam. Never forget that."

I walk up to Zero-Two-Seven as Wee Willie unties the main blade and swings it free.

"Is it ready?" I ask, knowing I will not be preflighting it for this next hop and if there was something amiss either Wee Willie would have already fixed it, or he would have notified me so that I could have preflighted another aircraft.

"She's all ready. I put some hydraulic fluid in the primary," he says as he takes his hat off and stuffs it into his back pocket. "I can't seem to find the leak." His eyebrows raise up.

I stoop down and pick up my survival vest and call out, "Let's go Mask!"

I zip up the vest and grab the sweat stained chicken plate off the ammo bay door and pull it over my head. Then I take the two dangling velcro strips and pull it snugly around me. Upon climbing into the back seat, I look over and see other 2nd Platoon ACs are in their aircraft.

"Clear!" I yell as I start the Lycoming engine.

The smell of the JP burning has always excited me. The difference between AV gas and JP is its smell, and of course the flash point. I look down and watch the needles of the engine and transmission gauges climb as we slowly go up to flight-idle RPM. Pulling my helmet on, I feel the sweat left over from the earlier flight has now cooled but it's still wet. Though my hair is long by regulation standards, it's still matted down to my skull. The helmet's two ear pieces have left large dumbo-like impressions around my ears. The top and back of my head have flattened surfaces from the foam padding inside the helmet pressing tightly on my wet hair.

"Two's up," Jimbo calls on VHF.

After a quick scan of the instruments, I roll the throttle up to full power while I make the call to Jimbo that I'm ready. With no wasted moves or radio calls, the flight backs out of our revetments and glides, nose low, to the center of the pad. Jimbo's call to Evans Control Tower is answered quickly by the harried controller. He gives us clearance and advises us to be alert for the Phoenix flight of Hueys taking off from north of the active. I'm sure he knows where we are all going. Ripcord has not only commanded the services of Griffins, Redskins, and the numerous slick units, but all the support units based here at Evans. We've all had to work extra duty to provide aide to the grunts of the 506th.

My takeoff, in position number three, is smooth as I've waited twenty seconds in order to get separation from Jimbo and his wingman. The DA has climbed and old Zero-Two-Seven needs clear air for takeoff. As I'm lifting, the Kid, flying in the trail position, calls to the Griffin TOC that the 2nd Platoon flight of four has departed. Then he adds the change of AC flying with him.

"Sneaky have you ever served with a CO as good as Major Stafford?" the inquisitive Mask asks.

Though our flight out to A Shau will only be a ten or fifteen minute trip, I had hoped it would be in quiet. One of my traits, probably from my father, is the need to have silence. I'll pass on idle chatter for a few minutes relief of total quietness.

"Yeah, I served with some good COs and a number of assholes as well. It seems you really don't know what to expect 'til you are with them under fire. But that goes with everyone. Until the bullets start hitting the aircraft, you just guess the guy you're with has what it takes." Then thinking back to my Marine days I add, "I was with Lieutenant Colonels 'Wild Bill' Shadrick and Greg Corliss, who were both great COs. But I also served under Dwane Eddy Tilger in the 1st of the 17th with the eighty-deuce who was a flaming idiot. At least I never had to fly combat with him."

I reach down and turn the UHF frequency off the Evans tower and to the assigned push for this mission. I make a quick "Sneaky's up," call, then continue my conversation with my front-seater.

"In my short, ah . . . very short, grunt tour, we had a great battalion commanding officer. But my company CO was a jerk that was with E Co, Int/6th, 198th Light Infantry Brigade."

Thinking back to my captain, whose four plus years spent at West Point taught him nothing other than to push his men at any cost so he could get the credit of being the best, the first, and the greatest of anything he remotely thought the battalion commander might desire. Just thinking that men like Patton, Stillwell and MacArthur had gone through this same school and came out so much better has made me wonder what has happened to the ivy covered school overlooking the Hudson River.

"In the 108th, Jimbo and I were under Major Buddy Kibby, who without a doubt was the dumbest man I've ever met."

I reach over to re-adjust the air-conditioner vents slightly up to allow the stream of condensed air to hit the darkened visor of my helmet. With the repair of Zero-Two-Seven's air-conditioning unit, I've been in a lot better mood while flying. And because of this, my remarks to Shirrley, and Rogers, have not been as stinging or numerous. A little bit of cool air sure makes me a happy camper. Who needed those weeks of hot sticky air blowing on me.

"If you could fly for anybody, who would you fly for?" Mask seems bent on carrying on a conversation today.

Thinking for a minute, I give him an answer that will shut him up for the rest of the flight. "I'd go fly scouts for 2nd of the 17th Cav under Colonel Montinelli. If there's a CO in Nam with brass balls, he's the man."

"Shit you'd fly scouts again?"

Thinking I'm kidding him, Mask pushes for a response to what he must consider a dumb answer. He looks up at me, and through the mirror I watch him pull up his tinted visor and look me in the eyes.

"Don't get me wrong, I love the Griffins. But before I go home, I'm going to extend a tour to fly scouts with the Condors of C Troop." Though I've thought of this, it's the first time I've said it.

"You're fucking nuts, Sneaky." He again looks up into the small three by five mirror to his right and catches my eye, "Fucking goddamn crazy. That's just what you are. Fucking goddamn crazy." Then he jerks his visor down.

Then it's quiet. He'll think about this for the rest of the flight and I wouldn't have to be bothered with his pesky questions. For me, this might just be the answer to where I should go.

For the next hour we, and members of 3rd Flight Platoon, provide support as the Hueys go, one by one, down into a hole blasted in the trees by carefully placed C4 charges, to pull out the members of A and D companies. Though there's sporadic small arms fire during the extraction there's no incoming mortar fire. For the slick crews this must be a good mission as no major damage is incurred. Shortly after 1400 hours, seven minutes to be exact, we're told that the extraction is completed.

For the next few hours artillery fires CS gas into the valley and from a higher than normal Griffin flying altitude, we fire into areas that are inundated with the gas. If any NVA are on the ground, the gas will have driven them out of their protective bunkers. Then our rockets will kill them. So much for A Shau Valley and the NVA who own it. We, and this means everyone, has spent far too much time in, over, or supporting actions in the

Valley. I'm glad as hell I'm out of here. Give me some good old CCN and Laotian Highway Patrol flights.

Chapter 18

A briefing has been called. It will be the after-action briefing from our last thirty plus days of playing around the A Shau. I'm not one to get excited about after-action briefings and am thankful that the Griffins are not part of the system that presents them after every little skirmish.

Entering the mess hall, which I've been in lately more as a briefing room than to sit down and try to gulp down the meals being served, I see we have all the Headquarters Battery people with us here tonight. Shit, when will the fucking operation end?

I walk to the back side, near the stainless steel urns, where there is a short line of warrant officers lined up to get a cup of hopefully hot coffee.

"Sneaky, I got you a cup," the Kid gets my attention and waves while spilling the black liquid from the filled cup.

I nod toward him while squeezing between the tables. Sitting by him, without looking at him, I say, "Thanks."

"No problem."

Then he opens an oil-stained bag and pushes it toward me. While leaning back against the back wall, I peer into the darkened opening. Though the mess hall is dark I'm able to make out vague round objects stuffed in the bag.

"Go ahead. I swiped them." Klien has a devilish smile on his face as if his theft is one of his great accomplishments.

The Kid, because of his lowly rank within the unit, has been assigned several collateral duties. In his case, one of them is the Food Service Officer. I have no idea what that entails, but I do know he's made himself a good friend of the Mess Sergeant and several of the cooks. The food hasn't gotten better, but our platoon's issue has gotten larger. Though usually it's food that he brings in late at night and stuffs into our refrigerator and ultimately ends up in Jimbo's beer stews.

Reaching in I feel hot donuts, their aroma now starting to reach my nostrils. I pull out one, then in typical Marine fashion, reaching back into the darkened bag pull out a second donut. "Thanks."

Klien then grabs the bag and carefully rolls it into a ball and slips it into his half unzipped nomex flight shirt.

"Men, may I have your attention." Our Commanding Officer has stood up. Looking out to the men before him he asks, "Captain Payne, are all your people here?"

The 1st Platoon Leader immediately stands up and takes a quick survey of who's present. While he's finishing his head count, 3rd platoon's Captain Crane stands and looks about to see if all his pilots are present.

When Payne finishes his head count he reports to Stafford. "Sir, 1st platoon is all present."

Stafford nods his head and looks over to the urns where Jimbo is standing, coffee cup in hand. "All here except St. Clair," is said before Major Stafford has the chance to ask. Jimbo's casual nature is directly opposite of Payne's and I bet Crane's as well.

"He's excused. By the way, tomorrow there will be a going away party for Mr. St. Clair for those that want to attend." Then glancing toward Westrock, he asks, "It's at eight, right?"

Westrock gives a thumbs up in reply.

"Dave, all your people here?"

Captain Crane still standing from his count, comes to attention and replies, "All present, Sir!"

"Shit, doesn't he ever quit." I murmur too loudly, because several of the pilots from the tables in front of me turn around. Most are smiling, though two of the Lieutenants give me a look of disgust. "Fuck them," I think, given time they will be just like

Crane.

"I'm going to have Captain Rogers quickly cover the results of the Ripcord operations. These are not pleasant numbers, but we made it out with no losses. I'm proud of how you men completed your missions. The 06th has sent us a well done, and several of the platoon leaders and company commanders want to come over and buy us a few rounds."

With that, murmurs of, "Here! Here!" are sounded throughout the room.

"Also, we have heard from the Division and General Sid Berry, Acting Division Commanding General, as well as our battalion headquarters, who all send us a 'Job Well Done'."

Then several more "Here! Here!" are called out, though without the enthusiasm of the first set.

"Once again I personally want to thank each and every one of you for a job well done. Because of this, I have cleared it with battalion to have a stand down tomorrow. But before you get ready to party, there will be a CCN flight. I'm sure some of you won't mind flying the CCN run tomorrow."

Chuckles rise from the room with the thought of someone asking you to fly a CCN mission on the only stand down any of us have ever taken while flying with the Griffins.

I watch the Major as his eyes sparkle with the announcement of the stand down. This is his last command and if it was up to me I'd let him have it for as long as he wants. True, he may not be fitted for a higher command, but, as an ARA Battery Commander, he's the best.

I look over to Sweet Griffin sitting at the table in front of me. I nod my head and point my thumb at myself. Rick Frier, like me, will be flying tomorrow. He nods in return as I elbow the Kid, hitting him in the area where his bag of freshly stolen donuts is resting.

Leaning over I ask, "Want to fly tomorrow?"

"Damn right," he answers quickly, too quickly..

Still looking at Rick, I nod my head toward the Kid and Rick gives me a thumbs up. We are set for tomorrow.

"Before I give Captain Rogers the floor, there will be a Battalion Huey to shuttle those that want to go over to Wonder Beach. It will run every other hour after 0800. Don't get too drunk. We will be operational again the day after tomorrow." Then facing the large form seated in the front row, he says, "Captain Rogers, the floor is yours." The Major has turned over the briefing to Captain non-flyer himself.

Rogers stands up, wearing freshly ironed fatigues, and shuffles several papers from one hand to another.

"Gentlemen this will be short and simple."

Looking down he starts reading the prepared synopsis of the activities which will go down in history as the battle for Ripcord.

"On the 17th of March, 1970, we, the Griffins of C Battery, were OPCON'd to ...." and his briefing starts. I've been through too many of these to listen to the numbers. My mind wanders trying to avoid the words being spoken that in reality were men's lives being tallied. "Aircraft losses, ah . . . UH-1s. Thirteen minor battle damage, ten major damage, and three destroyed in the A Shau. LOHs used were only OH-6s, with one minor damaged, four major damaged, and one lost. The CH-47s got it the hardest with, ah... five minor battle damaged, three major damaged, and of course the two total losses on top of Ripcord." Then, looking around the room, he adds, "It should be noted that during today's extraction over sixty aircraft received some sort of slight battle damage, including our three aircraft."

For some of the newbies, this is the first time they have been in a briefing where the numbers are thrown about so carefree. It's possible that lives lost during Ripcord were classmates in flight school. I remember the first classmate that I knew had been killed. It was a shock, for though I had been in combat, I didn't expect any of my classmates to die. It was the other warrant officers that died, not those from the 3rd WOC's class. Then when I learned that our class' first death was due to a training accident and not because of enemy fire, I was really shook up. It's bad to hear about one aircraft going in, but the next day is just that — the next day. You don't add up the grand totals of lost souls. It takes a briefing like this to drive it home, and for some of these kids it will scar them for the rest of their tour if not for their lives. They're learning the hard way that life isn't guaranteed. For helicopter pilots with less than a half year life expectancy in combat, the only guarantee you have is death. We don't have to pay taxes while in Vietnam, so the Grim Reaper is the only paymaster awaiting our toll. I'd never compare our job to a line grunt. But our losses have been high and just like the grunt, the losses become personal. Who needs to enter Vietnam with the knowledge that we average 180 days before death.

"The losses of artillery pieces on Ripcord included five 105mm howitzers . . . "

I drift off again. Get the goddamn thing over with Rogers. I need a drink. I stuff the second donut in my mouth hoping the noise from my chewing will cover the raw information that's being sent out by the overweight Operations Officer.

"Total losses from the 06th are 68 KIA," before the Captain can continue, he realizes just how quiet it's gotten when the losses of life are mentioned.

The briefing has now turned to the American soldiers lost. These were men. Yes, they may have only been eighteen or nineteen years old, but they were men in every sense of the word. We tried to fly cover for them for so many days. Looking around, it's become uncomfortable for him. He sorts through his papers to see how much longer he'll have to stand before the pilots that flew into the valley and didn't hid in the TOC. After a moment, he continues, "Ah . . . 443 WIAs. During today's extract there were 3 KIAs and 20 WIAs." Then he stops and searches for something to say. Finally, after far too long of indecision, he genuinely adds, "We are all grateful the number was so low due to the amount of gunfire out there."

Fuck him, how would he know about the gunfire out there, listening on the radio with a cup of coffee in his hand? Every time

I get to the point I can stomach him, he steps on his dick with his attempt to be 'one of the boys'. You're no warrior, so leave it alone Rogers. I can accept you if you can accept yourself. This is the difference between you and Shirrley. Shirrley has the guts to know who he is.

"On a sad note, I want to add that today the 506's Commanding Officer and S-3 were killed during the downing of their C&C aircraft . . . "

Why did I come here? Not to hear this! Another set of names to be listed on one of the back pages of the Stars and Stripes. Somehow we have to stop it. My vote for General Curtis LeMay in '68 went for naught. He had the right idea. Pull out all the Americans and drop the bomb. Yes, the big bomb. But he's one of those old guys who says we should never fight a ground battle in Asia. I wonder what else he knows? My parents couldn't believe I voted for him because he was on the same ticket as George "The Racist" Wallace. But they don't understand what a quagmire we're in over here. If the people at home are not going to support us, then I don't see a good ending. But with my love of Vietnam, where do I fit? Do we have to destroy the whole country to save it? Maybe my vote for LeMay was wrong. Did I vote to kill my love?

"Ah . . . confirmed enemy losses were 422 KIAs. Also, 6 NVA POWs were taken. Ninety-three weapons were captured, as well twenty-four crew-served weapons. Griffins are credited with taking out eight .51s and three active mortar tubes."

The whoops and hollers of the pilots congratulating themselves overcomes the voice of a captain scared to fly. Come on, *Dai Uy*, let's get this over with. I need to get drunk.

"One last item of note. Several Griffins have been put in for awards,"

Captain Rogers is now trying to appear as a good guy by putting in for some awards. He doesn't understand that most of us don't give a damn. I've not met one warrant officer who's flying over here to get some piece of multicolored ribbon to hang on a uniform, and then have some State-side inspecting officer ask you how, what, and when it was earned, then ding you because it's discolored, frayed, pinned on crooked or, Lord help you, in the wrong order. Who the fuck cares? At some point they lose their luster and the reality of what happened when the medal was earned sinks in. I remember my Dad telling me how he received his Distinguished Flying Cross from the British. As a pilot of a PBY Catalina patrol aircraft flying over a German U-boat, he got a bit too close and what happened to him may put him in the history books as the only pilot ever shot down by a submarine. I used to laugh, but my Father's loss of a flight engineer and one of the waist gunners when they ditched into the North Atlantic wasn't a laughing matter. Now that I've been through the rigors of combat I know there wasn't anything funny about his mission. I've learned about war, and the blood, guts and sheer horror of death. Both sides of war see it, but being a Cobra pilot gives me the chance to inflict more than my fair share. But then, getting shot down by a U-boat who surfaced just to shoot the lumbering patrol aircraft down, really is funny. It took a very determined U-Boat Captain to make that decision.

My father has never asked me about my flights, my losses, or my tours. At first I thought he didn't care about me or what I did. Maybe he was still mad at me for joining the service rather than finishing college. But I've learned. It's the losses one has endured that are guarded so tightly and he, having been through it, understands as well as I. Combat is a very personal time and we warriors don't walk around beating our chests Tarzan-like. Men who hold emotions close, hold the horrors of combat very close.

"Gentlemen, if there are no further questions," Captain Rogers looks around the room, then over to Major Stafford who shakes his head no, "You are dismissed."

The rush to the door and to the club has started. I hold back, not wanting to join my fellow pilots tonight. I have a fifth of J&B in my duffel bag and two six-packs of rusting cans of Crown beer in my refrigerator, so I'll drink alone. Hopefully I can fall asleep easily, though without booze in my blood, I don't know how I could ever do it. I need peace and quiet, the silence to escape.

My walk back to the hootch is done alone. Once in the hootch, I complete my task without any interruptions. The bottle of scotch is quickly inhaled with a beer or two used as chasers. The only noise is the whimpering of Fred and Patsy Cline songs gracing my headphones. Though needing silence, Patsy's voice brings me relief till I pass out. No shower, no getting undressed, boots still on, just drowning in a black bottomless eddy of confusion, fear and relief. Fuck A Shau!

"Good seeing you Sneaky," Milo says as he opens the MLT Operations hut door for me. "I bet you're glad the Ripcord mess is over?" Knowing that the area was totally evacuated yesterday.

"Got that right. That place is not for us, let the fucking NVA have it," I reply to the aging NCO.

Entering the darkened room I see movement near the back next to the oversized map. Walking up, I find Billy Washburn bent over plotting the latest gun emplacements along QL-9. Looking back over his shoulder, he gives me a grunt of recognition and continues his work. Several team's members and a couple of the MLT team members, Blaster and Valentino, are looking over the map. Blaster and Valentino have more experience walking the trails of Laos and North Vietnam than most grunts have in the field after their Vietnam tour is complete.

"We going out right away?" I ask, hoping that we will have an easy schedule today.

The bottle of scotch has left a residue in my mouth and my head is pounding. I have cottonmouth and no matter how much water I've consumed this morning it hasn't helped.

"We may have an insert later this afternoon, but I want to re-supply Hickory once the cloud cover burns off," Billy answers without turning his head from the map.

The front door is again opened as other pilots start to enter the cool recesses of the hut.

"Good, I'm going back with the 'yards and grab some chow."

Looking at who's entered I notice Sweet Griffin has not joined us. I guess he's probably going to see the MLT-2 Team Leader, Captain Stanton.

"Sneaky if you're going to eat with the 'yards, I'll join you," the newer Chief Warrant Officer 2 from 1st Platoon says as he catches up with me at the back door.

"Let's get going Crusty, otherwise they'll figure out a way to have us flying." I open the door and let the senior warrant exit first.

Crusty, as we call him, is on his second tour as an aviator. He doesn't make much of it but some of us know he did two Vietnam tours as a Special Forces grunt before opting for flight school. Like most of us, he wears only his flight wings on his Nomex suit. I also know he has Thai and German parachute wings along with a CIB. He wears, as a combat patch, the 1st Aviation Brigade patch from the days he flew Cobras in '69. Once when I questioned him why he didn't wear the SF, his answer was that too many people asked questions. I agree with him, too much on your uniform gets the nosey-bodies asking far too many questions. He started out in 3rd Platoon, flying with Rick, but the need for an experienced AC in 1st Platoon prompted his transfer. I sure wish he'd come over to 2nd Platoon, he's my kind of guy.

"I hope they have something cooking. I could eat a horse."

Jack "Crusty" Garrett got his nickname from me, with the help of Gary Gluth, after I realized he was older than me. Most guys in the unit don't know how old I am and my baby face helps disguise the few years I have on them. Though at times, behind my back, I've overheard them talk about the old Marine bastard. If they knew I had two sons, ages eleven and four and my new Vietnamese son, and a two year old daughter named after Christy Michele, the Playboy centerfold who appeared the month she was born, they would have call me Crusty long before Garrett ever checked into the Griffins. My tours in Nam have not aged me like it has a lot of others, though my mother would argue that point. She thinks her baby boy has aged considerably. I don't think my eyes have sunk back into my head like many who have spent years in combat situations. But then I don't study the mirror either.

We both enter the recon team hootch that the Montagnards have staked out as their domain. I see there are only a few laying on the cots. Each has it's green mosquito netting rolled up onto the thin wooded slats above the six-legged cot. Some of the younger 'yards are getting their gear together, which means these are the ones that will be going on the slick out to Hickory for a thirty-five day stay on top of the rain and fog shrouded mountain. In the back, the make-shift kitchen is empty except for the old 'yard who's the unofficial cook. Turning, he sees us loping toward him and immediately the big warm grin appears on his face. Though his teeth are about all gone and those left are dyed blue-black from the betel nuts chewed constantly, his smile is a sign of approval. The Montagnards are some of the friendliest people I've ever met. They will give you a smile that you can't help but return. Their warm open faces quickly thaw any distrust that you may have when meeting them for the first time. Their hospitality is extraordinary and legendary. We, as a civilization, could learn from them.

Before Crusty and I can get to the thin bony elder statesmen of the kitchen, he has put his hands up, palms together as if praying, though we know it's a form of Buddhist greeting. After we exchange bows, he waves to the plywood floor in the direction of a makeshift bamboo table. The use of a small bamboo mat to sit on is common in the Far East. Though no words are spoken, he knows us both and how we appreciate his good food.

Crusty and I engage in small talk as the old man serves us several small bowls containing different concoctions that not only taste good, but smell incredibly good. This is the kind of meal that you want to smell before you savor it's taste. My father has a large wine collection, but I never understood the practice of smelling the aroma of the wine before drinking it. I usually gulped it down like water. After eating with the 'yards, I've learned that some things have more than one dimension. The old man has shown me that his delicacies are valued for more than their taste. They are a dining experience. My father would be proud of this education I've received.

"Sneaky, you back here?" Sweet Griffin yells from the front door of the hootch.

"Yeah," I answer with my mouth full of steaming hot rice smothered in a wild pig sauce that I've been shoveling down for the past five minutes.

Rick enters the hootch, walks to us and looks down at the two of us eating. We haven't looked up at him.

"We're going to re-supply Hickory as soon as the fog breaks. How about switching Klien with Yo Ho? Then I'll take the front seat for the flight out to Hickory and let Klien get some back seat time."

"No problem, you want me to fly your wing?" I ask, as I expertly work the loaded chopsticks into my mouth.

"Yeah." Then turning, he heads to the door. Before exiting he hollers, "I'll let you know when the fog clears."

Neither Crusty nor I acknowledge his departure as we keep the thin wooden sticks in motion. Our brown-skinned cook hovers around us like a mother hen to ensure no bowl gets too empty. In his native tongue he yells out to one of the younger 'yards sitting on one of the cots watching the two round-eyes devour the meal. Instantly the barefoot 'yard jumps up and runs to the door.

Before long, the young warrior wearing bright orange shorts re-enters the hootch holding cans of beer. As he approaches, the still jabbering old man, he pushes four cans out in front of him. The old man snatches two of them out of the young hands and opens them. The spray from the hurried bouncing trip spurts across Crusty and I, and though we look up, we don't stop eating.

"This is the best I've eaten in the past couple of weeks," I mumble with a mouthful, thinking of the times I spend with Twit and how she prepares meals for me when I'm down in Houng Ca. I need to get down there now that Ripcord's over. Maybe we'll go to one of the snake restaurants for a small celebration.

Crusty grunts and shakes his head in reply to my assessment of the late breakfast.

"Thank you, thank you," I say as I'm handed a beer to wash down the hot meal.

Crusty hasn't been that friendly with me though I'm sure under the right conditions we could become good friends. He, like me, Rick, Jimbo and a few others, is committed to doing this mission to the best of his ability. Where I differ from the others is my love for Vietnam. There is no doubt that I'll try to stay as long as possible, and should the right occasion arise, I will stay here as a civilian. I've talked to several high-ranking ARVNS about possibly joining the VNAF as a helicopter pilot, though it would cause me great difficulty with the United States government. But then, as long as Air America is operational, I'm sure I can find a home here.

In all my tours in Vietnam, the short four months spent as an Army Sergeant was the only time I disliked being in here. It wasn't because of being a grunt, but because I was mad at the Army for sending me to Vietnam instead of flight school. The SNAFU, as the Army conveniently called it, started at Fort Polk after my transfer from the Marines. When returning from the battle at Khe Sanh and checking into New River Marine Corp Air Station, I immediately requested, and got, an inter-service transfer to become an Army aviator. At first, the Army tried to send me to basic training and I proceeded to tell everyone up to the Chief of Staff of the Louisiana base that being a former Marine meant that I didn't have to go through any other service's basic training and that included the Army's. The Colonel agreed with me. While trying to decide what to do with me while I was waiting the three months for my scheduled flight class to begin, I suggested I wouldn't mind going through Fort Benning's parachute school. I'm sure he saw a chance to get me out of his hair, so off I went. Though I thought it was a good idea, it started a series of events that I couldn't stop for five months.

After finishing the torturous three weeks and having my "blood wings" imprinted over my heart, I found out I had been put on the levy for Vietnam as an 11 Bravo, or your basic infantryman. I was shipped out before I could convince anyone at Fort Benning that I was just killing time when I went through jump school, and I was supposed to go to Fort Walters for flight school.

After my family contacted our local United States Senator, and had the problem explained to the Army through political channels, the Army said they would bring me right back to the States and assign me to the next flight class.

It took one-hundred and thirty-one days for all this to happen. Meanwhile, I learned, and not willingly, that life for an infantryman in Vietnam was tough. I came out of the experience in better shape than I had expected, though the three weeks at Benning toned me up for the short Vietnam tour. I had a good case of crotch rot, and the skin on my feet would roll off with a little rubbing. My malaria had resurfaced, but I had no new Purple Hearts. Prior to leaving the brigade, the Commanding Officer had a very stern talk with me regarding using political influence to correct a wrong that the Army would surely correct once I had finished my year long tour as a grunt. Then he wished me well on my aspirations to become an aviator, with repeated suggestions that I could apply for infantry OCS instead of taking the flight school.

The surprise was that my unit, 1st Battalion, 6th Infantry of the 198th Light Infantry Brigade attached to the Americal Division, presented me with a Bronze Star with Combat V, an Army Commendation with Combat V and Oak Leaf Cluster for meritorious service, and the much coveted CIB or Combat Infantryman's Badge during the last couple days before leaving Vietnam. I know why I received the Army Commendation, or green weenie as it's called, for valor, but the one for meritorious service was unwarranted because all I did was my job. The Army goes overboard in the issuance of babbles, badges, ribbons, and medals especially for doing one's appointed assignment. I wear the CIB only when standing some specific formations because I'm embarrassed when asked about earning it. It was earned because of an Army fuck up, not because I wanted it. I see the day coming in the Army when you will get a ribbon for graduating boot camp, finishing AIT, and each duty assignment you're posted to. Any service that gives a badge for being a truck driver or shooting a BAR or throwing a hand grenade surely is only a step away from issuing ribbons and medals for just being somewhere and breathing. I can never see myself in the same room with guys like Stanton, Blaster, Valentino or Billy Washburn wearing a badge that they have earned hundreds of times over. It's said that I'm crazy, or loose, but you can bet I'm not stupid. The Combat Infantryman's Badge is one that I know is difficult to earn, and those who wear it are to be respected. For me, the time spent under conditions to earn it are times I have no desire ever reliving again. I also wear the Navy-Marine Combat Air Crew Wings, which can only be won in combat. These are my pride and joy and I know I earned them.

I, like Crusty, have gotten to the point that I wear only certain badges or patches depending on who's going to see them and the mood I'm in. Here, in the Griffins, there is no need to get decked out. When you are with the best, you don't need to remind those around you how good you are. They know how good you are, otherwise you won't be with them. Our reward is being a Griffin, and the black, red, yellow and gold Griffin patch we wear on our left breast pocket. But there are times when we need to make a statement to some non-combatant who thinks he knows it all and is superior to a warrant officer, which rarely happens here. This is when Crusty and I and a few others get dressed up.

The Griffins may drink too much by other's standards. We may swear too often by other's standards. But very few in the Army fight as we do and have the commitment to the grunts that we have. The Marine Corps makes a big issue out of their tradition and *esprit de corp*, but here in the Griffins, the Marines couldn't hold a candle to us. Though a lot of my Marine friends would argue this, having been with both services gives me the authority to voice my expert opinion on the matter.

"That was good." Crusty says after we have both expelled several belches.

"You bet! I could come up here for a couple of days and relax." Then, thinking of Twit, I add, "but I'm going to take a day or two off and go to Hue."

I don't think he knows about Twit and, though Crusty has several tours, he's not the type to decide to make this a home or go out and find a permanent female companion.

"You go down to Hue quite a lot." He stands up and stretches. Then continues, "You got a broad down there?"

Surprised by his question I act like it's a joke and I answer, "You know me, after the whorehouse in Dong Ha, my reputation with the ladies has flourished."

Then bringing up his time spent in Thailand, he asks. "Ever get over to NKP and get hold of any LBFMs?"

"Shit yeah, best thing going for a short R&R," replying to his use of the LBFM, or Light Brown Fucking Machine, that some GIs named the Thai women years ago and has deservedly stuck.

In my travels, there is the one question you can ask in a room and find out who's been to Thailand. 'Have you got hold of an LBFM?' Then after that will be the praise of the perfect one that the GI found and how there could be none better than her. I personally like the Thais but their food has too much curry in it and about kills me. The country is beautiful and it's a peaceful American-loving kingdom, but I like Vietnam more.

We both laugh as I get up. The old 'yard is all smiles, and we both raise our hands in the Buddhist tradition and bow our heads, while thanking him in English. Though he doesn't understand the words, I know he's aware of our pleasure from his excellent meal.

As we go out the door, Rick steps out of the back door of the Operations hut. He hollers over to me, "Let's go." Then, while twirling his right hand over his head, "Time to saddle up and get out to Hickory."

I walk around the Ops hootch and Crusty, still belching, goes toward it's back door. The meal will sit heavy in our stomachs but is an added reward for flying CCN today.

Walking across the grass of the CCN pad, I see the Kid and WO1 Howard Christian swapping their flight gear to their newly assigned aircraft. Klien sets all his gear on the open ammo bay door of Rick's plane, waiting for the seasoned check pilot to come get his helmet and gear and move to the front seat.

Walking up to Zero-Two-Seven, I observe my new co-pilot for this mission stowing his gear sloppily in the front seat. He's not like the Kid.

"When we going?" I ask, though not sure he'll know the answer.

"Mr. Frier told me to be ready in a couple minutes," he answers formally.

Yo Ho Christian is the youngest, and newest, 3rd Platoon pilot. Though he's been with the Griffins for several weeks, he hasn't got much flying in because of the Ripcord operation.

Rick gave him the nickname Yo Ho because he always answers with yo. Rick, whose father is in the Air Force, says the tall, black-haired, muscular kid is a service brat.

I turn around to see 'yards coming around the Operations hut loaded down with filled ruck sacks and equipment. Milo is with them carrying two large and full dirty gray mail sacks. Several other 'yards are straining with the large ammo boxes carried between them. They are not walking in sync. After a few steps they put the boxes down, yell at each other, then pick them up again. This is repeated several times before they get to the first Huey.

A half a dozen pilots come out of the front door of the Ops hut and join the group moving toward the two lead Hueys. Finally, Sweet Griffin comes bounding out the door with a paper in his hand waving it at me. I walk over to meet him halfway to his aircraft.

"You ready?" he asks, knowing I'm still hung over.

"Yeah, let's do it," I answer, while taking the paper from him. I see it's the radio pushes we'll be using for the flight.

"I'm not going to do any emergency procedures during the flight because we're too heavy," he says, standing with his hands on his hips. "But, I'll have him lead the whole flight." Then Rick looks over his shoulder at Klien and adds, "You have any thoughts?"

I look past Rick and see Klien going over Rick's aircraft in an abbreviated preflight. "No, he's ready. Though a bit gun happy."

Rick laughs at this offhand remark. "Aren't we all? Aren't we all?"

I look back over to the Kid, and say, while I start walking toward my aircraft, "Most captains aren't, at least the ones I know. By the way, when are you supposed to make captain?"

"Fuck you, Sneaky!"

"Let's saddle up," I yell over to my new co-pilot.

He unties the main rotor blade and swings it free, then opens the small nose compartment and puts the blade tie-down strap inside. He quickly climbs into the front seat and straps in. I walk up to his side of the aircraft and hand him the paper with the frequencies and call-signs on it,

"Get these up on the window."

Without waiting for a reply, I walk around to the other side of the Cobra and put on my survival vest. Looking around, I decide it's too hot for the chicken plate. We're only going out to Hickory and return, so I take it off and stuff it up behind my seat in the small space where a never-used first aid kit is snapped to the bulkhead and the seat ventilation hose comes through the firewall..

I begin my startup procedures, ignoring the new addition to my front seat.

Chapter 19

"Sparrow Hawk, this is Morning Star, over."

The Kid makes his call as we overfly the abandoned Vandegrift fire support base. His call to Quang Tri with a flight of four, two Griffins and two Black Widows, went well. After our re-fueling and take-off from Quang Tri, we slowly climb in altitude trying to reach five thousand feet by the time we get to Khe Sanh. My front seater, WO1 Christian, has been quiet for the trip and I turned up the ADF so we could enjoy some rock and roll. Several times, I've noticed Yo Ho has taken pictures of the different abandoned bases and the two Hueys we're escorting out to Hickory.

Hickory is a radio relay site used by CCN for monitoring the recon teams' radio transmissions and, in the case of very bad weather or at night, an extra set of ears to pick up any emergency transmissions. With the mountains in the way, line of sight transmissions are not possible between our recon teams in Laos and Mission Launch Team at Quang Tri.

The site is located in the northwest corner of South Vietnam sitting on top of a mountain peak, at approximately 4,500 feet. It's coordinates, XD855451, are embedded in my skull. This peak offers line of sight radio transmission and provides a natural security fence because of the shear drop off on its perimeter. They do on occasion take sniper fire and once in a great while a mortar round or two will land somewhere on the peak, but duty there is relatively safe, though boring and tedious. The added bonus is that during clear weather it's an excellent observation platform, providing a good view of the valley floors to the south and west.

I'm sure the North Vietnamese find the site a thorn in their side with their operations in the tri-border area, but its inaccessible location prevents them from doing anything about it. Not only does the physical shape of the peak help protect them in the event of an attack, but our aircraft could fire at the base of the mountain peak and easily root out any enemy trying to climb its sheer sides.

"Good morning, Morning Star. You out in the area for a resupply of Hornets Nest?" the O-2 Covey pilot asks, but I'm sure he's been expecting us. Also we would not have launched unless he had given Billy, back at the MLT, a weather clearance.

"Roger Hawk we've got two Black Widows with us and are presently just west of Vandy headed your way." The Kid sounds very professional in his new roll as a lead pilot.

"Roger, ah . . . call when you get to Khe Sanh. I'm checking out several teams to see how they're doing."

The Covey pilot is making his morning, though late, check out of all CCN teams that are on the ground in our section of southern Laos. It's done at least twice a day by the FACs. He checks first thing in the morning, then, usually at dusk, when the FAC is making his last flight out in the AO before he heads back to Gun Fighter Village at Da Nang Airbase.

The FACs will call each team and find out if they have moved since their previously confirmed location. He will get a team okay if the mission is going smoothly. In some cases he will be given information, which once relayed to the proper MAC-V-SOG intelligence personnel, may be used in the planning of future bombing missions.

The little O-2 aircraft will not directly fly to the team's location once communication is made. The FAC will, by using his map, figure out the team's exact location. He'll fly a zig-zag route that will pass over the team but will not look as if he's looking for something important. As the FAC approaches, the team will use either a small mirror to reflect light into the cockpit or the team will flash an orange marker panel as the low flying aircraft flies overhead.

The Covey FAC's other duties include checking out possible future sites for inserts and extractions of teams and general aero-observation. When targets of opportunity are found, the FAC will direct the fast movers in on their bomb runs. They try and do a low level bomb damage assessment after the bombers have expended their racks of ordnance. Sometimes, flying in the Covey will be an intelligence NCO from CCN with a camera snapping pictures of possible future insertion sites. In many MLT briefings I've attended, pictures of the landing zones that the slicks were going to use were passed around before the flight. The advantage is the pilots knew what to look for and usually the direction of entry and exit were planned using these photos.

"Sparrow Hawk, this is Morning Star at Khe Sanh with the package. Over,"

No answer for a few moments, but rather than Klien calling immediately back, he waits, figuring that the Covey is talking to one of our teams.

"Star Lead I hear you. Go ahead and start to Hornets Nest Sierra. I'll be over there in five or so," the Covey answers softly with a lot of background static. He must be low looking at something.

"Roger, we're on our way." The Kid pauses for a moment, then adds, "Flight, did you copy?"

The squelch breaks are affirmatives to his question.

"Hornets Nest Sierra, this is Morning Star, over."

"Go Star," comes a strong quick reply.

"Roger Sierra, Star at Khe Sanh with a package for you."

The Kid has now sped up to pass the pair of Hueys that are slowly inching their way north of the deserted Marine base by three klicks.

Then Rick comes up on VHF with, "Sneaky stay with the package. We'll do a quick cruise around the site."

I answer with double presses of my radio transmit button.

"Sierra, Star has a flight of two Blue Birds for you. They're up this push."

"Roger Star. Break, break! Blue Bird Lead, this is Hornets Nest Sierra. Over." The Special Forces NCO calls from his underground living and working quarters atop the mountain now looming before us.

"Sierra, we have you five by five. We are inbound with a package. Do you have your package ready to go?" asks the Black Widow Lead AC.

"Roger we do. I'll pop smoke when you're ready."

"Sierra, this is Star Lead." I hear as I see the green Cobra coming around the mountain from the western side and is now flying toward us. "It looks fine to the north. Let's get this show on the road whenever you're ready."

The Kid has so far handled this flight like he's done it a hundred times before.

"Ah . . . Star," The background noise of the Black Widow's rotor blades popping almost engulfs the AC's voice. "We're ready on final if I can get some smoke." Then switching to FM from UHF we hear, "Sierra, go ahead with the smoke."

"Roger, understand smoke."

On the top of the ragged mountain, we can make out the wisps of yellow smoke being swirled around by the wind blowing up the sides of the steep cliffs.

"Tally ho, banana," a pilot calls.

"Morning Star, this is Hawk. I'm at your Whiskey at six thousand."

The Covey pilot has now joined the package in its delicate maneuver to exchange personnel and quickly resupply the eighteen man Montagnard team led by the five Americans. We'll only change one third of the men on the site today, then in ten days or so another flight will come out here and do the same.

As we orbit over the jagged mountain, I look down to the team's home for the past thirty days. Small pockets of poncho covered areas are scattered atop this jagged peak. The landing pad was built from twelve-by-twelves that were lifted in by Marine CH-46As three or four years ago. Though it's not really a large pad, the Huey is able to land in the center of it using the often taught pinnacle landing procedure.

Quickly we watch the clean uniformed team members jump out of the AC's side of the aircraft. Though having only a partial instrument panel, the right seat has become the home of the helicopter ACs after too many crash landings with the main rotor blade slicing through the left-hand side of the cockpit killing the left seater. So, years ago, some smart AC decided not to sit in the left seat like fixed-wing pilots. Let the co-pilot sit in the seat that has had more than its share of decapitated men after crashing.

While sitting on Hickory, the aircraft's co-pilot, or peter pilot, overlooks a fall of several hundred feet onto jagged rocks. The rotor blades grind the smoke into a swirling vortex that prevents it from escaping through the main rotor. The smoke quickly envelops the squatting green aircraft. The men moving to the aircraft are in uniforms dirty from weeks of wear. There's no extra water up here to wash or shave with. Usually when it rains, the team members lay out their clothes and fill whatever pots they have with the water, hoping to take a bird bath and a quick shave later.

"Blue Bird Lead is lifting with three," the Black Widow pilot calls.

I look over at the lifting green helicopter, with the legs of the escaping team members dangling out the door as they sit on the floor, and watch it come up to a hover then quickly glide off the pad. As it clears the pad, it loses the transitional ground effect and starts to plummet toward the valley floor. The nose is rolled down and, with the quick rise in airspeed, the aircraft is able to level out in the exchange of newly gained airspeed for the much needed altitude.

"Blue Bird Two is inbound."

"Roger, smoke's out."

"Roger, goofy grape," the slick pilot on final answers.

The scene plays again. There's no difference other than the color of smoke being captured by the rotor blades and quickly dissipated. Just as quickly as the first slick exchanged it's contents the second one has completed it's exchange.

"Two's lifting with three."

"Go ahead Two," Klien answers as we both continue our orbit around the mountain peak.

Once again I watch the Huey struggle to take-off then, dive its nose toward the ground to the southwest of the peak. As it continues to dive, Black Widow Lead comes up on FM. "Sierra, we're clear. You have a nice few weeks and we'll come back for you."

"Roger that. Let's hope the weather is better. I can use a sun tan."

"Morning Star, this is Sparrow Hawk." The Covey has been silent during our transfer of personnel and equipment.

"Go Covey," the Kid answers on UHF, not using the formal call-sign assigned for the day.

"Star, your flight is cleared back to Dancer's Sword."

Then, as if giving a wave goodbye, the little white and gray painted pusher-puller aircraft buzzes by our flight and climbs out to the west. I'm sure he's going to look for targets of opportunity.

"Roger, we're RTB."

"Griffin, let's low level, we might see some deer or wild pigs," one of the slick pilots suggests.

There's a pause before an answer, caused by the Kid checking with Rick to see if it's okay. "Roger, let's get down and dirty. Ah . . . Sneaky, lag back in case of a one-shot Charlie."

"Got it," I answer while diving to catch up with the three aircraft flying below me at my ten o'clock position.

"Sneaky, you were here at Khe Sanh weren't you?" asks my young exchange pilot from 3rd Platoon.

"Yeah."

I reach down to turn up the ADF hoping to drown out any possible conversations regarding my prior tours.

"Can we go low level over the strip so I can get some photos?" asking though he knows that we're not supposed to have cameras with us during CCN operations.

I've never known anyone to get in trouble for it, though it states it's a no-no clearly on the forms that we've signed before being allowed to fly MAC-V-SOG missions. In big letters if I remember correctly it says, NO CAMERAS ARE ALLOWED. But then what the hell are they going to do, court martial us and send us to Vietnam?

Upon reaching the western perimeter of the old firebase I dive down to less than twenty-five feet. Quickly I line our flight path down the center of the old PSP strip. Checking my airspeed I see we're at one-hundred and ninety knots. He will not get many photos taken on this flight. Closing in ahead of us at a hundred feet altitude are the two Hueys with the Kid flying at five hundred feet or so above them.

"Get your camera ready. Coming up on the left are the helicopter revetments used during Tet 68," I announce, though not slowing down.

I look down to check the power and I'm at the top of the green. We're motoring down the long since inactive bombed out runway.

Just as we pass the revetments, I look in the mirror and see him facing left with his camera mashed into his helmet opening.

Then I announce, "On the right will be the ammo dump that blew to hell. See the road on the right . . . ah here . . . there," saying as the road goes by in a blur, "Down there is where I lived for seven months."

"Must have been a hell of an explosion!" he remarks, now seeing the damage, not only from the gigantic hole left in the red laterite dirt, but also the torn up PSP matting that was never repaired and now has started to rust in grotesquely tangled shapes.

As soon as we finish going down the old runway, I tell him to get ready to take a picture of the small waterfall located at the northeast end of the perimeter. As we cross the perimeter, which is now overgrown with large green foliage, I yank back and to the left on the cyclic and our Cobra jumps into a steep left-hand climb. G forces are tugging at us as I point out the small stream below us.

"There it is. I'll try to orbit over it."

"Beautiful isn't it?"

He's excited now. The falls' natural beauty is surprising. One would never expect that only a few hundred meters from the war ravaged area of Khe Sanh exists such a scenic, peaceful setting.

I explain to him that, although beautiful, it's been the location of several deadly ambushes sprung on unsuspecting warriors from both sides of this war.

I look around searching the sky for the other aircraft and see, to our south, Klien and Rick orbiting.

"Griffin, we've got a couple a boars down here."

While talking, the background is flooded with the sounds of M-60 machine gun fire. The door gunners must have found an easy target.

"Roger Black Widow, I see you've hit a couple. Wait 'til Sneaky gets over here then you can go in and get them."

The Kid knows the program. At least every month or so we are able to kill either a wild pig or one of the light brown, almost golden, small deer that graze usually unmolested here on the plains of Khe Sanh Valley.

"Roger Griffin. Ah . . . Widow Three-Four you make the pick up. I think you're lighter."

"Roger."

"Go ahead Three-Four. I'm almost over you," I announce as we have now reached the area next to the abandoned road that is overgrown from inactivity.

We're about a thousand meters northeast of the old Khe Sanh village adjacent to QL-9, right near a small track that leads to the east and small coffee plantation once operated by a French family, the Poilane's. The family and the Montagnards that lived in the area were moved out in early 1966 when the enemy activity became too frequent to be able to provide adequate protection for them. I join up with Rick in a circling pattern and watch as the Huey starts to flare and pick up the makings of a big feast for the MLT tonight.

As the Huey lands, the Hickory team members jump out and lift the dead carcass into the aircraft. Then climbing on the skids and holding on to the overhead bulkhead, the team members ride while the Black Widow AC hovers twenty feet or so over and the cycle is repeated. The low growth grass is easily moved by the rotor wash from the slick's blades. Fifteen to twenty feet around the main rotor blades the grass is invisibly beat down to form a saucer.

"Three-Four lifting with three and two dead hogs."

As the Huey lifts off from the ground the squelch cracks acknowledgment to his call.

The flight back is quiet except for my asking Christian what his father did in the military.

"He's a Chief Petty Officer stationed in the Mediterranean aboard a DE. Ah . . . that's a destroyer escort." he answers.

I press him for his fathers rating, or job skill.

"He a snipe, which means . . . "

"I know what the fuck a snipe means," I interrupt. Then wondering why he joined the Army instead of going into the Navy, I start to ask.

"You know why I came in the Army? " answering before I can ask, "because I didn't want to be gone six months of every year and finish twenty years with no formal overseas tour but years away from home floating aboard some rust bucket." Then looking up into the mirror, he puts two fingers into his mouth as if trying to gag himself and adds, "Plus I get sea-sick."

Looking away to watch the lumbering Huey loaded down with it's approved and unapproved cargo, I take a quick glance back up at the mirror and he's smiling at me. The Huey is following the narrow overgrown road north at a low level trying to gain the airspeed necessary for his climb out.

"You going to stay in the service?" I question.

"Sure, why not? It's a good life plus I'm a pilot which is really great," he answers with the enthusiasm of a small child just finding a new toy.

"What's your Dad say about you being in the Army?" asking as I fly to the east of the Hueys while watching the Kid ease to the west of the flight. We now have good separation and are in position to blast anyone who makes the mistake of shooting at our charges.

"Pissed at first because he never thought I would graduate. Especially when I was held up for a couple weeks between Walters and Rucker when I got pneumonia. After that I did really good, and he got over it."

"Black Widow Lead are you planning to low level back to Quang Tri?" Klien asks, knowing that, as we start to go through the passes from the eastern part of Khe Sanh Valley and follow the snaking QL-9 through looming hills until we're clear of the mountains around the Rockpile, we are all vulnerable to a One-Shot Charlie taking aim.

"Griffin we'll be starting our climb out if you want," the lead AC answers.

"Roger, let's get some altitude," Klien answers, which surprises me because normally he's the first to bitch if we're flying too high.

I see the Kid in a new perspective now that he's responsible for the flight. I'm sure it also has to do with Sweet Griffin sitting in his front seat giving him this check out. The real test will come when Sweet Griffin and I are not flying with him.

"Your Dad come to your graduation?" I ask, remembering that my wife pinned my wings on me.

Later that day we went out the front gate of Fort Rucker and bought a shiny black Corvette with the 435 horse-power engine. Although I was still paying on a Chevy II and had three children to feed, she wanted to have that new sports car. And like a fool, I signed the papers.

"Yeah, he got permission from his ship's Captain to fly back and pin my wings on. Mom and my five sisters were there as well."

"You've got five sisters?" asking in shock, having never heard about this.

"Yeah, I'm the only boy," he replies as he aims his camera at the pair of Black Widows flying at our eleven o'clock and now starting their climb from the valley floor.

The Hueys are full with the tired and dirty team members huddled up toward the center of the aircraft trying to stay out of the wind swept doors. The one aircraft has the boar carcasses being held by several sets of dirty green fatigue covered legs draped over the dead animals.

"Don't tell the guys in your platoon about them. They'll be wanting introductions right away."

Laughing because I know how helicopter pilots, single or married, are always looking for a sympathetic ear to tell our wonderful, though slightly exaggerated, war stories to. Not to mention wanting a roll in the hay after the story as a reward for living through the event and to prove that we're the greatest warriors to have ever fought in combat. As the saying goes, real helicopter pilots go down in some hairy places, and I'm sure this has absolutely no meaning relative to Vietnam.

The rest of the flight back goes quietly. As we cross over the jagged ridge called the Rockpile, the Kid makes his call to the MLT.

"Dancer's Sword, Morning Star, over."

"Go Star," a quick reply is returned. Though I'm sure the new team at Hickory has notified them of the change over and the departure of the flight after hunting for game on the Khe Sanh Valley floor.

"Dancer, we'll be dropping off the team, then the slicks will refuel."

"Roger, ah . . . we've notified the 'yards you're bringing in a couple of guests for dinner." There is a pause with a chuckle heard in the background of the Launch Site's radio room, then followed by, "They'll be waiting to meet you, over."

"How the hell did they know we got those kills?" Christian asks.

"On one of those slicks is the One Zero and he'll have a Prick-25. So I'm sure he's called back."

The returning team One Zero has not only advised the MLT of the incoming dead pigs, but has probably requested that the team be delayed a day before they return to CCN's Da Nang Headquarters. They do not need to be immediately debriefed by intelligence types as they were not out on patrol but sitting on a mountain top for thirty-five days. They'll want to enjoy the feast that will take place tonight up here at Quang Tri rather than the meal served in a mess hall at Da Nang.

Whether its hog, pork, pig, boar, I bow to the custom of eating it when served by my hosts. Though I try to practice my Judaism while in the military, it's difficult at best. I've never been in a military unit that had a Rabbi. If I wanted to go to schoul, I have to go to one of the Regiments or to one of the larger support units. As far as eating kosher, my love of shrimp has really blown any pretence of being a good practicing Jew out the window.

At home in Snead's Ferry, North Carolina, I've been known to drive down to the docks and buy shrimp fresh off the small boats at twenty cents a pound. After getting home with ten or twenty pounds and peeling the shells and heads off, I throw one in my mouth for every two I put in the pot. So, after coming to Vietnam, I figured if shrimp could be considered possible kosher, at least by me, then when protocol called for it, the eating of hog, pork, pig, or boar, would be as well. Anyway, after eating monkey meat and, while in the Philippines, a few dogs, who would know what is kosher anyway? Hell, this is war. But I never open a can of pork and lima beans, that's just too blatant a violation of the talmudic religious law.

On landing, I shutdown while watching the 'yards wrestle the two large dead carcasses from the still turned up Huey. It's comical as they try to move around each giving orders to the others on how to carry the large brown-speckled animal off the plane.

Though these wiry men are strong and can carry a large amount of weight for their size, carrying the limp forms with each trying to go his own way and not being able to find a good hand hold is funny. Yo Ho has climbed out of the front seat and is snapping pictures of the event while our blades slowly come to a stop. All this is being done under the watchful eye of the old 'yard.

After climbing out of the aircraft and securing the main rotor blades, I walk over to Klien.

"Well, how the hell did you do?" asking though knowing Rick would not have given him the check ride if he hadn't been ready.

"No fucking problem."

The Kid grins, though it's easy for me to see he's lost the once youthful appearance that he had months ago. They grow old much too quickly. And with this loss of innocence comes the bravado of a bull fighter.

I walk over to Rick as I see they're not changing their gear, which means Rick will fly with him for the rest of the day, at least as long as it's quiet. I stop in front of Rick as he is hooking the blade strap onto the end of the blade. Then we both walk around to the aft of the plane so he can tie it to the tail skid. Looking over the tail boom I see the Kid has started to walk toward the Operations hut with Christian in tow, he appears to have a new swagger to his step, and Christian seems anxious to learn how he did.

"How'd he do?" I ask, eyeing Rick.

"He's young and inexperienced, but I think he'll make a good AC. I'm going to sign him off as soon as I can do emergency work and touch and goes at Evans." Then readjusting his hat, he adds, "Though, he's got a long way to go before he makes section leader."

Hell I knew that. But at least we can get him into the back seat as an AC which will help all the other ACs in 2nd Platoon. Every one of us has too many hours and we need some time off.

Stopping by the Operations hut, I see the other pilots lazily spread out on the hard wooden benches trying to catch some shuteye. Fuck it, I say to myself and go out the back door and walk to the 'yard hootch. At least here I'll get a nap.

Before getting to the hootch I see the 'yards, now under the direction of the old man that served Crusty's and my meal, getting the two large boars ready for slaughter. I pass them by, and the old man smiles at me and gives me the thumbs up, as an approval of the catch that I'm sure he wasn't expecting. I wave back, enter the now deserted hootch, and lay down on the first empty bunk I find. In no time, the noise of the excited 'yards getting ready for a festive evening cookout is lost in my dreams.

Chapter 20

"Wake up Sneaky!" I hear someone yell.

I open my eyes to the bright sunlight that has now filled the hootch. As I rub my eyes, I hear it again.

"Get up Sneaky! We've got a Prairie Fire!" A voice that I recognize now as the Kid's.

"What's up?" I ask as I stand up and stretch.

Looking down at my Rolex, I see it's almost three o'clock. Smelling the air, I notice a hint of burning wood and an aroma that wasn't there before I went to sleep.

"Come on, everybody's waiting!"

Klien is impatient with me, as I stand, stretch and try to get my bearings.

I move quickly toward the door and, at a trot, head the ten meters or so to the back of the Operations hut. Entering, I pass Milo and several others bent over the radios listening to the crackling static that now is blaring through the two OD green four by four inch speakers mounted on the bookshelf above the radios. Not stopping, and with Klien on my heels, I enter the large room, brushing past Billy, who is at the large, wide-open map, feverishly writing down grid locations and frequencies on the plexiglass map face.

I don't have my knee pad with me, so as I sit next to Rick, I snap my fingers and hold out my hand. He rips off a sheet from his pad and hands it at me. The Kid slides in on the bench behind us. Looking across the aisle to my right, I see the Black Widows are now seated and waiting for Billy to finish his writing. It looks as if all the pilots are here.

I hear the front door open and slam shut behind me, though I don't turn around because Billy has started his briefing.

"We have a problem with a team out in this area," he says, pointing to an area east-south-east of Techrone.

The team shown as a large black "X" is on a ridge line that traverses east-west, west of Co Roc Ridge. This is south of QL-9 and the Song Be River in an area we usually don't work. Most of our inserts are to the north of the river. I start writing the frequencies that are plainly visible above Billy's head.

Billy reads from a small crumpled piece of paper, "Xray Delta Three-One-Seven Four-Two-Six is where they are right now. The team was hit about twenty minutes ago and they've got three injured and one KIA. They're in the corner of a little clearing that was under cultivation. But since the monsoons, we've had no activity in the area. Da Nang has given the okay to Prairie Fire the team."

The noise from the right side of the room, where the slick pilots are sitting, is clearly heard. If it was just a mission to help a team break contact, we'd be going out with only two slicks in case of an emergency. This means an extract and we all know we'll be under fire.

"Copperhead is a three American, four 'yard team and they have been out for five days. They're up three-three six-zero on Fox Mike. Ah . . . call-sign Dark Wind Hotel. Covey is presently out there and has plenty of station time. Covey's call-sign is the same as this morning, ah . . . " then looking back on the plexiglass behind him, "Sparrow Hawk and he's up two-four-five point one-five on UHF. He's reported the weather is clear and Hillsborough can get fast movers if we need it. Spads are on station now and will probably expend before you get there."

Billy looks over our heads to the back of the room.

"Our two *bac si* will be going out with you. Ah, in the lead and second aircraft. They will be up the same Fox Mike and using call-signs."

He holds his hands open in a questioning manner.

From behind us I hear, "Plasma Charlie and Victor."

I turn around to see who said this. Standing by the door, dressed in sterile cammos with their faces and hands painted with green and black grease, are the two medics from the launch site. They're twins and not many can tell them apart. The Wilson brothers are named Ty and Randy, though I've never figured out which is which, so I just call them Doc or *Bac si.*

Though they're primarily trained as medics, both have been crossed trained and have the secondary MOS of small weapons experts. The few times I witnessed them in action, I was taken by their amazing courage when trying to get to those needing help. Behind their backs it's been said that both would rather kill, especially with a knife, than save a life. But this has never been proven. In one instance, I watched them jump from a slowing helicopter at about ten feet off the ground and then wave the bird off until they could assess the situation before recalling the rescue bird. Every time I've seen them on the ground, they were always the last to get into the final departing rescue helicopter.

The Wilson twins are from western Pennsylvania. The town, in a rural small coal mining area, allowed the boys to grow up with hours spent alone together in the woods. They brag how they each had killed their first deer, and then dressed it out, before they were nine. They also remind those, that will listen, that Pennsylvania deer are a whole lot larger than the deer most of us are used to. I've been able to get a few digs in about the deer in Vermont that I've bagged, so this has kept them at bay with me. Their father worked the mines, and now has a lung problem which all but has him bedridden. Their mother, a nurse, not only takes care of their father, but also works in a small hospital, which as the crow flies is only thirty miles away, but by the state road is just under sixty miles. Those miles are slow miles as well, twisting and turning around each hill and dale.

For the twins, it was a perfect family. Papa, a man of German stock, taught them how to hunt, live off the land, and take care of themselves. Their mother, Helda, not only pushed them through formal school, demanding they study and get good grades, but shared some basic nursing skills with them. When the day came, of their rite of passage into manhood, meaning their father got out the fifteen year old run down pickup and drove them to the Army recruiter in Pittsburgh, the twins, who were the All-American boys, scored not only high on all the tests but both showed a surprising amount of knowledge in the medical questions. One might say this was because of their mother, and it surely helped, or another might say it was because the boys were always out hunting and then dressing their game.

The recruiter quickly found out that he didn't have to sell the Wilson's, including Papa, about the advantages of military service. The only issue is what they were going to do while in the Army. This decision should have been easy, but turned into a several hour project once the boys started asking questions about this field and that. The recruiter knew these two fair-haired boys were going to become medics, whether they wanted to or knew about it now. But just before he got them, with their Papa's signed approval, to sign the papers one, then quickly the other, noticed on a back wall a poster with a Special Forces trooper just landing after a parachute jump. This caused several rapid fire questions, and it meant the recruiter had to start his sales pitch all over, this time geared for the gung-ho work of Special Forces, who the recruiter thought, was a bunch of bullshit and a passing fad. But that day was the next to the last day of the quarter, which meant everyone was trying to meet their quotas, so the SFC spent time to tell how wonderful it would be for them to go into the Army together, and become Special Forces medics together.

For the boys, the ride home was a quiet one. When their mother arrived home from the hospital, she didn't cry, but everyone knew later that night behind the bedroom closed door she would. Papa would comfort her and tell her everything would be just fine, and they would probably end up going to Germany, as the recruiter, who would never lie, had mentioned several times he would make a note in their enlistment papers that they wanted to go to Germany. This was how it all started. What happened next was not how the recruiter had reassured them it was going to happen. It was not how papa had envisioned and surely was not what Helda had hoped would happen to them.

After basic and Advanced Infantry Training, they were quickly herded off to Fort Benning for Jump School. They graduated number three and four in the class and were chosen, after requesting it, for Ranger School. Then, before their first leave home, they found out that they would be assigned to the 82nd Airborne Division at Fort Bragg, North Carolina. After thirty days home, where their papa and mother could not shower them with enough attention, or figure out why they were with the 82nd rather than being sent to Germany like the never-tell-a-lie recruiter said, they drove them to Pittsburgh and put them on a plane for the quick flight south. It took less than a year for them to not only impress the unit commanders, but to get picked up for Special Forces training. After schools for almost a year, they got to go to Fort Sam Houston, where they took the Special Forces Advanced Medical Training Course. They not only excelled in the course, but during the Dog Phase, where they lost over half of their remaining class, they pushed their grades to the very top of the class.

Upon graduation and a quick return to Fort Bragg, they went home again but this time the talk was not of Germany, but of Vietnam, which their orders read. Their mother was beside herself with grief that she might lose one or, God help her, both of her children. Their papa, though now ill and unable to work, was very proud of his boys. He spent much time consoling mother that they would be just fine and back in a year. It didn't work out like that. After getting assigned to different A-teams, and completing eight months of Vietnam duty, they went on R&R in Hong Kong. While there, they decided to extend their tours if, and only if, they could get assigned together. When they returned to Nah Trang, they confronted the 5th SFG re-enlistment NCO, probably the easiest job in the whole Army, and told them what they wanted to do. At first he said it was no big deal he would handle it and get back with them. But after a month, it became a big deal when no paperwork came to them to sign.

After getting a few days off, and meeting together again down at Nah Trang, they found that no one wanted a pair of brothers, much less twins, in the same unit, for fear that they would have to write not only one, but two letters home to the same parents to tell them how sorry they were for their sons' sacrifice. But lady luck was on their side that night. While brewing over their options, which included leaving Special Forces and going to the 173rd or 101st Airborne units, a Sergeant Major overheard them. Without their knowledge, he got on the radio and made a few calls. The rest is history. CCN Headquarters, at Da Nang, suddenly got two new medics. Within months they were attached to recon teams, though not the same ones. Then after another eight or nine months, and more than proving themselves under fire, they were asked if they would want to be assigned together up at MLT-2. It meant they were no longer on a recon team, but they would be together, and they would get out into the field whenever there was a shit sandwich, which in the SOG business happened a lot. They jumped at the chance.

The only drawback was going home on leave. They could not go home together anymore. One had to stay behind. The first time this happened, their mother though that something had happened to the other and really was never at ease while the one took his thirty days leave. But that was quickly fixed when two weeks later the other long lost twin arrived on the front porch. Neither of them told their parents what they were doing and where they were doing it. They both, after a discussion prior to their first thirty day leave, decided to tell them they were working with the hill people, the Montagnards. They had plenty of photos to show, and this pleased their mother as she didn't want her boys in any firefights. Little did she know that the two medics are a couple of our best fighters.

Now, as I see them loaded down with ruck sacks, medical

bags and ammo draped across their shoulders, one would never realize they're medics. Their mother, and I guess papa too, would be taken back seeing the twins loaded down with gear, most of it for killing, not healing. One, Ty I think, always carries a Swedish K for a weapon. They don't socialize with the other MLT team members, which isn't unusual, but I think it's because they're young.

Billy continues with his standard briefing. "Copperhead is in the northwest corner of the LZ and so far the only fire has been from the south side of the clearing where they were ambushed. We feel the NVA will try to encircle them at some point, so we need you to get out there right away." Looking down at Rick and me, he asks, "Questions?"

"Yeah." The Black Widow Lead, a chief warrant officer on his extension, sitting with a captain who's probably his platoon leader flying as his co-pilot, inquires, "Can we land in the LZ or is this going to be with strings?"

"At last report," then Billy looks over his shoulder through the door to Milo who's still hunched over the radios, "Ah . . . Milo! Are they at the same location?"

"Yeah, they can't move with the wounded and the Spads are working the southern tree line," Milo yells over the crackling sound that's heard out in the briefing room.

"You heard? It looks like a set down LZ"

Then reaching into a briefcase at his feet, Billy brings out several black and white eight-by-ten photos of what must be the LZ that the wounded recon team is holed up in.

"Here are some pictures, although they're two months old. As you see, no rocks or large trees, but it's a tight LZ."

Then Billy passes them to the Black Widow Lead AC.

One of the Wilson's asks, "Who's Lead and which one will be Chalk Two?"

The warrant, sitting next to the captain, answers as he stands and passes the pictures several rows back to another warrant looking much older than his years, "I've got Lead and

John will be in the second slot." Then looking over to Rick, he asks, "Ready?"

I interrupt before he can answer, "Rick, who's flying with whom on this flight?" I'm sure Rick will lead the flight and let the Kid fly my front seat.

"You lead it with Crusty on your wing. I'll have Klien in by back seat with Goose on my wing." Then looking over to Klien he asks, "That okay with you?"

Klien doesn't hesitate with his answer, "Noooo problem."

Klien's eyes sparkle. He knows that he hasn't had the official AC check ride, yet he's made the grade and will now be flying as an AC. What's left, beside the paperwork, is an hour or so at Evans doing emergency procedures.

"Let's do it!" Rick says as we walk past the standing Black Widow pilots.

The slicks are already topped off with fuel and only need to load up the medics and start their trip into Laos. Because of the small CCN pad, the Cobras will have to top off with fuel. If we landed full, we could never take-off. When loaded, we need a running take-off like a fixed-wing. We will have to fuel quickly and catch the slicks, hopefully above Carroll or no further than Vandy.

I get to my aircraft and begin to strap in while watching the front seaters unhook the main rotor blades and turn them to ensure that they're free, then quickly climb into their respective aircraft. The sounds of ignitors popping and the smell of the raw fuel now fills the air. The whine of eight starting aircraft is all that can be heard. The beat of the blades has started my heart and mind into a tempo that will carry me through the next hours.

I quickly go through the startup procedures and look out my open window to see the other Griffins turning. As I close the right-hand plexiglass window-door, I see the Wilson brothers make their way to the slicks. Both of them are fully loaded and ready for the mission. Each of their ruck sacks is filled with the tools of their trade. The one headed for the lead slick has an AK-47 and a shotgun hanging off his shoulder. Though the shotgun is not a common weapon used in this war, for those on missions into Laos, it's a weapon most like to have along.

Tagging along behind him is a 'yard, carrying what appears to be several Nightingale rigs, rolled up like small throw rugs. The rigs are among the more clever weapons designed just for this war. It's a piece of three by four chicken wire, rolled up for easy carrying. Several dozen small fire-cracker like devises are attached to it. When ignited, they sound much like the small arms we use and create a sizeable distraction. Basically, once the plunger is pulled, all hell breaks loose. It's dipped in a dark green wax-like compound to ensure it's water resistant and the noise can last ten to fifteen minutes.

We use it generally when making a false insert. The helicopter will go in and land, and while the pilot counts to five to simulate the off loading of a recon team, a member of the MLT riding in the cargo compartment will pull the plunger and throw the nightingale into the LZ. The Huey then lifts from the vacant LZ, and after a few minutes the NVA in the area will hear the sound of imitation gun fire. Of course, the NVA will head for the LZ thinking they will find the Americans.

Then two things can happen. First, if it's done in several LZ's within close proximity of each other, we put the team in the target LZ without Nightingales. We hope the NVA will think no one has disembarked and they will run toward the sound of the gunfire, instead of the LZ the recon team has been inserted into.

The second method, though not used often enough in my opinion, is to allow the Nightingale to go off for five minutes or so, then have Cobras, or a flight of Spads, come in from nowhere and dump as much ordnance onto the LZ as quickly as possible, with the hope that by then the NVA have arrived on the scene and are caught out in the open. Why we have Nightingales on this mission, I don't know.

The second Wilson, which must be Ty because of the Swedish K, is walking toward the aircraft parked right behind the lead Huey. He's dressed just like his twin. A dyed OD green scarf tied around his head, the paint across his face. His uniform is sterile with black streaks painted on it to break the solid color. His ruck sack is full and his web gear is weighted down with canteens, small packets holding who knows what, and grenades freely and conveniently hanging. His sleeves and pant legs are taped tightly around his arms and legs with black electrician's tape for some unknown reason. I think it's either to prevent snagging in the brush or to keep curious critters from seeking a habitat next to their sweaty flesh, or maybe both.

When I was in the 198th, we didn't tape our uniforms like this. We did tie our trouser legs to keep crawling things from entering. But then, my time as a grunt could not be remotely compared to the experiences of these men. That's another reason I would never wear a CIB on a uniform up here. These guys have more than earned their CIBs. My three months spent patrolling around rice paddies and the few small villages is nothing to stick my chest out about. I only saw action four times, and those were over in less than five minutes as the enemy hit, then recoiled back into the dark folds of the surrounding tree lines. We all dove behind the dikes that surrounded the paddies. Other than those incidents, the only action our company ever saw was the constant booby traps that, no matter how careful the men were, would be set off. Limbs, especially legs, were lost at a high rate in our company, battalion, and the division as well.

As a last gesture before climbing into the aircraft, each Wilson gives the other a wave, then it's business. They are loaded and have to back onto the turned up Hueys butt first.

"Sneaky's up," I call on VHF.

Quickly the squelch breaks follow as I'm switching over to make the radio call on UHF. Looking up I see Christian is starting to write the frequencies and call-signs on his right window, although still not as neat as I'm accustomed to.

"Quang Tri tower, Griffin Nine-Two Gulf with a flight of four snakes at CCN for emergency reposition to POL," I call out as I pull up on the collective and we become light on the skids.

"Roger Griffin, your flight is cleared for take-off with an immediate left-hand break and then direct to POL. Altimeter is two-niner eight-four with winds at three-two-zero at eight. Present DA is, ah . . . six-four-zero. Call on short final."

"Roger tower, Griffin flight is lifting," I reply as I start my take-off to the southeast with a sharp turn as soon as the airspeed hits 60 knots.

Flying heavy, low to the ground, and with very little airspeed is the most dangerous time for us. We are out of the envelope of safety in case we have some type of emergency or failure. From the first days of flying, helicopter pilots are taught that low and slow equals death. Though while flying LOHs I found this didn't apply. If you crash in an OH-6, all you do is roll into a little ball. The design of the Hughes egg shaped aircraft has saved many lives.

On VHF Rick calls, "Crusty, we'll switch positions at POL." Letting me know that Rick has taken off right behind me and Crusty is now third in the line of Cobras now approaching the busy, paved two lane QL-1.

Looking down to my left I see the 5th Mechanized Division's PX with its red dusty parking lot. The roof of the large tin building has the 5th Mech insignia painted on it, and it's now covered with dust carried by the winds of Quang Tri. Dirty forms walking to and from the PX look up at the heavy armed helicopters flying overhead. Several of the men are aiming their cameras up at us. It's a chance to get a good photo of the famed Cobra gunships that bring death and destruction upon the enemy.

"Quang Tri, Griffin's flight is on a short base with four, systems cold."

"Roger Griffin, your flight's cleared direct to POL."

As the controller finishes, I hear, "Quang Tri tower, Black Widow One-Five with a flight of four slicks at CCN with a scramble to the west, over."

As we land our Cobras next to the open POL points, I look out to the right and see a heavy pink team from the 2nd of the 17th Cav hovering out of the way to the north. They're waiting for us to finish our topping off and departure. Our rotor wash is causing havoc with the small OH-6s, who are bouncing around like fat bumblebees trying to land but having a hard time doing it smoothly.

I call on UHF, "Ah, little bird we'll be right out of your way. Just need a taste."

I remember a year ago when I was in the LOH and was being beaten to death by the larger helicopter's rotor wash at POL. Then, looking over, I see all our front seaters have returned the long hoses from the big black bladders in front of them and have climbed back into their respective seats.

"Quang Tri Tower, Griffin Nine-Two Gulf with a flight of four snakes at POL for take-off. This is a scramble and we have the numbers," I call, knowing the tower operator understands there is an emergency after the call by the Black Widows.

"Roger Gulf, your flight cleared direct to three-six. Call when you're clear of the field."

We lift off from the POL spot and slowly make our way to the active runway. Quang Tri is a single strip running north-south, with a standard northern take-off. As we move, we slowly start to gain speed and just when the airspeed needle makes it's jump to the forty knot line, the sound of the change in the rotors blades tells me we've entered translation lift. The aircraft drops down from the slow-moving forward hover and we are in flight. It's slow but we are now airborne and headed north.

As I break to the northwest I hear, "Quang Tri tower, Griffin flight is clear and we'll be QSY at this time." It's First Lieutenant Daniel "Goose" Baker calling as I switch frequencies to two-four-five one-five and try to contact the Black Widows.

The flight to Khe Sanh was uneventful. We caught up with the slicks above the Rockpile and slowed down so we could provide the vulnerable Hueys with an armed escort. Over Khe Sanh, I make the call to Covey relaying our position and he replied that there is still some sporadic fire, but he feels the Spads have prevented the situation from getting totally out of hand. The old World War II Douglas A1-Es are now raking the area with their twenty millimeter cannons after having expended their bomb loads. When we get there, they'll stay above, flying a high cap until a replacement flight of A-1Es can arrive on station. This mission, because of the distance from Quang Tri, is about at the end of our usable fuel envelope. We won't have time to dally around and make sure everything is proper. It will be one of getting there, quickly assessing the area, and going in to get the team. If someone goes down, we'll be in a tight spot trying to recover them because of the low fuel.

"Sparrow Hawk, this is Morning Star Lead, over," I call as we now pass over the invisible border between war torn South Vietnam and supposedly neutral Laos.

"Go ahead Star Lead."

"Roger Hawk, we have the package and expect to be in your area in fifteen," I call, while scanning the sky ahead of us, looking for any telltale signs of the aircraft.

"Roger Star. Dark Wind Hotel is ready for pickup." His voice is muffled by the noise of the fixed-wing's straining engines. Then he adds, "Give me a call when you have us in sight. We want to have you come in from the Whisky with a November-Echo departure. Hotel has movement to their November and Sierra, over."

"You copy Blue Birds?" I ask the Black Widows who will go in for the extraction.

"Roger, we copy," one calls with several squelch breaks following.

Then another Huey pilot asks, "Is the Lima Zulu level?"

The Covey, who's monitoring both the frequencies of Copperhead's team as well as ours answers, "Roger, it's a good Lima Zulu, though I expect you'll take fire from the Sierra during the pickup."

"Roger Sparrow Hawk." Then after a pause, a Black Widow asks, "Everyone hear that?"

After several squelch breaks, I reach down to tighten up the light grey straps that hold me in the seat. The Cobra and I have become one — joined through the seat but not noticeable to any outside observers. I give the instrument panel a cursory inspection, checking to ensure all gauges are in the green range signifying smooth operation. I reached down to readjust my air-conditioning vents for one last time before action.

"Tally Ho," comes a call that must be from one of the slicks because of the amount of background noise. "Fixed-wing at ten."

Everyone now scans the sky to our ten o'clock position, looking for the aircraft that will be diving and climbing at some nondescript ridge line along the two-thousand-foot escarpment that we've been flying adjacent to since leaving the border, passing by the mysterious and threatening Co Roc Ridge. This escarpment overlooks the Song Be river and QL-9 with views of the gently rolling hills extending to the north for what seems like hundreds of miles. Though some small areas are cut and burned to provide small farming areas, not many people live out here. Those that do are either in the North Vietnamese Army or are natives that have become sympathetic to the NVA because of necessity and survival. I've found that the further away you get from the government and the war, the less interested are the natives in what goes on in Saigon or Hanoi. They don't give a damn about politics. All they want is to farm their small piece of land and try to exist on the meager crops that they're able to grow. To the south, the escarpment seems to stretch for miles, though I know that it gradually tapers off. This area to the south is one that we stay away from, though members of CCN's MLT based out of Phu Bai are inserted into this area.

"Morning Star, I've got you in sight," Covey calls having spotted us, though I've only been able to spot two Air Force Spads working the ridge line.

From this far out, we have not seen any explosions or smoke from the area to help us establish where the LZ is.

"Extend your flight to the Whiskey and get a good

separation. When I call, bring your flight around to the Sierra and line up on a zero-nine-zero heading. This will start your approach to the clearing."

I call, using VHF, to our flight, "Kid, you and Goose stay with the flight I'll go over and see if we can get a good positive on the LZ and the team." Then as an afterthought I add, "Crusty, watch to the Sierra, I expect a few fifties to open up once they see us."

"Roger, we're on you," Crusty answers.

I turn our Cobra around to the left while reducing power so that we are able to lose the extra altitude we have prior to reaching the escarpment. Now, looking at the area that the Spads are diving on, I can make out the small clearing where we will be extracting the team. It's rectangular shaped with short light green growth blanketing its southerly banked opening. The trees around it, though not triple canopy, seem higher than normal which will aid the enemy in this extraction. To the south, I can see freshly burned out areas that are remnants of the napalm dropped in the past hour.

The Spads are flying their pattern from west to east with a southern break. We will be operating in the same direction with a northern break. The Spads should keep the NVA's heads down during the extraction, at least those to the south of the pick-up zone.

"Dark Wind Hotel, this is Morning Star Lead, over," I call down to the recon team that after five days, eagerly awaits their ride home.

A whispering and muffled voice responds, "Go ahead Morning Star."

"Ah . . . Dark Wind if you're ready we'll bring the package over and get you the hell out of there." Before he can reply, I add, "I'll be flying over you and will need a location."

Though we have been briefed on where they are supposed to be, it's generally not where it's been marked on the map. Also, I want to be able to talk the slicks right onto their location. It will save valuable time if a slick doesn't have to hover around, trying to find the team.

"Roger, we have a panel out."

I fly over the tops of the trees to the clearing's north side, searching out the right canopy for the orange panel that I hope will be easy to see.

"There!" Christian calls out.

I see panels laid out in a large X with small green forms gathered around it. They're hiding in an old over-grown bomb crater which offers them some protection from any ground fire that the NVA have surely laid down on them. I'm certain that the Huey will receive enemy fire from the southern tree line when it makes the extraction.

"Mark! Mark!" I call, as I sharply whip the cyclic to the right and overfly their location then jerk the cyclic back to the left to start a steep climb out in a northern break.

"Star, you're taking gunfire from the eastern side of the clearing," the team's One-Zero calls.

I hear the crackling, but I don't think we have taken any hits.

"All right Sparrow Hawk, if you're ready let's do it," I call to the Covey. Then on VHF, I say, "Crusty did you get a good mark on them?"

"Roger, Sneaky."

"Roger Star Lead, bring the package over." The Covey is high overhead and will have a front row seat to this hot extraction.

"You hear that Kid? Let's get 'em over here." Then as an afterthought I announce, "Blue Bird, you'll need some good separation. When you come out, break left. There's some small arms at the eastern side and I expect they're waiting for you."

"Thanks!" The Huey lead responds as the sound of his rotor blades is heard distinctly in the background of his radio.

I approach the flight that is coming out of the northwest. They have started their gradual descent and separation is being gained as they get closer.

"Blue Bird Lead, I'll talk you in. They're in a bomb crater that's covered with brush in the northwest corner of the Lima Zulu. As soon as you clear the trees, start your descent and you should see them, they have panels out."

I start to swing around so I'm in position for the slick to come up on my left.

"Crusty, stay to the south of the slicks."

Looking over my shoulder, I confirm that Crusty has slowed down so he'll be ready to start his roll in when I break.

"Hotel, this is Blue Bird Lead. We're inbound. Put the wounded on the first bird."

"Roger Blue Bird. Do you want smoke?"

"Negative on the smoke, just keep the panels out."

I've let the lead Huey pass me and watch him as he skims along at tree top level headed for the clearing. We are flying six or seven hundred feet above him, ready to pounce on any enemy anti-aircraft fire that might pose a threat to his approach.

I watch the Huey's attitude start to change as he slows to land. Though still at tree top level, he has no way of seeing the location of the team. The spot he wants to touch down on, to ensure a quick pick up and departure, is blind to him.

"They are at your one Blue Bird. Start your flare." I direct him from my location using the clock for directions and he knows that the LZ is just before him. "That's it . . . Ah, slow down you don't want to overshoot them."

"Taking fire!" Yells one of the pilots. "Fire at three!"

I immediately drop the collective to under twenty-five pounds and push in right pedal and fire two quick pair of rockets in the general direction of the unseen enemy fire.

"We're at your twelve!" Someone yells on FM.

The Huey's tail is low and shudders as it sinks unceremoniously to the ground. The rotor wash is whipping the loose dirt and grass up and it engulfs the Huey in a brown turmoil of wind and dirt.

Looking over my left shoulder, I start a tight left-hand three-sixty break to quickly get in behind Crusty who's now the only protection the Black Widow Lead has.

"Breaking left!"

Damn, he's been on the ground a long time.

"Lead lifting with three WIA and one KIA," The long awaited call finally breaks the tension.

I'm swinging in behind him, in front of the next Huey racing in at tree top level being guided by the Kid. Though the Kid hasn't seen the team, he was in position to watch the lead Huey settle into the LZ.

"I'm breaking," Crusty calls.

"Got 'em!" I answer.

I'm now the rescue helicopter's protection as he climbs out of the dusty clearing. I swing to his right and fire several rockets to the eastern side of the clearing for good measure. The rockets whiz past the right-hand side of the shuddering Huey with its right-hand door gunner spraying the southern tree line with the red tracers from his machine gun.

"Taking fire from the trees," the lead calls again.

I'm not able to put in rockets so I yell, "Shoot, goddamn it!"

In an instant, our front turret opens up with the slow methodical thump of the 40 mm. It's sending out it's small golden headed cylinders of destruction.

I then call to Crusty, "I've got Lead. You go back with Chalk Two," knowing the extra Cobra escorting the last aircraft in will help.

Lead now clears the escarpment and the Song Be River valley is falling away from us, allowing us to have more distance from any small arms.

Klien calls, "Start your flare. They will be right in front of you when you break the trees."

He sounds like he's in charge though he still hasn't seen the team's location. His confidence will help steady the nerves of the Huey crew.

"Flaring," then as if on cue, "Taking fire! We're hit! Shit!"

I hear Rick radio from his front seat position with the Kid, "Pull collective! Break to the left!"

After what seems like an eternity of silence, I hear the dreaded news, "Two's down!"

Another voice breaks in, it's Rick's take charge tone. "Two's crashed in the LZ. He's on his side. Get another aircraft over here!"

Covey now calls to the other two slicks left over the Song Be. "Blue Bird Three and Four we need you over here right away. Two's down in the LZ." Though I am sure that both of the slicks knew what was happening.

I call knowing that not only is the enemy against us, but time will now be working against us. "Blue Bird Lead I'm braking and will escort Three and Four to the LZ."

"Roger. We'll orbit over here," is the answer, though I'm sure the AC is trying to communicate on his unit VHF frequency to find out the condition of his wingman.

"Star Lead, Dark Wind Hotel, we've secured the aircraft."

The aircraft must have crashed near the team in order to get that quick of a response. Already the three remaining team members have rushed over to the crashed helicopter and are trying to put out covering fire while the slick's crew gets out of the downed aircraft.

"Hotel, this is Star Three. What's the situation down there?"

Rick has taken over radio communications from the Kid. I'm sure the Kid didn't want something like this on his first CCN back seat mission. If we have to refuel and come back, I'm sure Rick will be in the back seat.

"Three, this is Plasma Charlie, get in here and get us out, we've got everybody."

"Roger Plasma. I'll call when Three's on short final. Get ready to pop smoke." Rick must have his hands full now leading the operations and probably flying the Cobra from the front seat.

"Roger smoke."

"Ah . . . Sneaky bring the flight over to the November. We'll have to do an east-west approach because of the mess on the ground." The mission pickup flight route has now switched 180 degrees.

"Roger, Sweet Griffin." We have given up our mission call-signs while quickly making decisions that will determine life or death.

"Sparrow Hawk, this is Sandy Three-Nine Alpha, over."

"Go Sandy."

"We're on station if you need help," the pilot from the replacement Air Force A1-E Squadron announces. Having the extra A1s will help, especially if we need to go back to refuel.

"Roger we have a downed bird and will be trying to extract them. If you would join with Spad, ah . . . on TAC One. He'll direct you to join with his runs. Use only twenty mike-mike, over."

"Roger only twenty mike. Spad flight go TAC One," he answers.

Rick calls the Huey that is flying in the third position and who normally would not have had to land on this extraction. Now, because of the loss of his wingman's aircraft, he will be going in to make the pickup of the downed crew.

"Chalk Three can you carry out eight?"

I know what Rick wants to do. He can see that any more aircraft going in and out of the pick up zone will increase the chance for another aircraft to be shot down. If we can get them all out in one pick up, we'll all be better off.

"Ah . . . I think I can."

The answer is from an uncertain pilot who wants to do it but knows he'll probably have to use every trick in the book to lift out with the eight, especially from the cluttered landing zone with the green metal chopper laying over on its right side. The once roomier clearing has suddenly become crowded and will be a tight fit for the slick pilot to get in, make the pick up, then climb out over the crashed Huey and clear the high trees in front of him.

"All right, here's the plan." Rick has had a few moments to figure out the best way to get in and out of this mess in the least amount of time. "We'll be coming in from the east. Three, you land in front of the downed bird. Ah . . . you'll see a crater to your right. Everybody's in the crater. Once you lift, break to the northwest and fly low level until you hit the valley."

"Got it."

Rick continues as he joins up with us, "Goose and I'll take the slick in. Sneaky, you and Crusty lay to our left and blast the hell out of the southern part of the LZ." Then as an afterthought, he calls to the Covey, "Sparrow Hawk, hold up on the Spads 'til we get in and get this crew out."

"Roger," is the answer from the Covey whose orbit has allowed him a perfect view of the whole operation including the crash. "Spads and Sandys, you copy?"

"Roger, we copy," one of the Air Force pilots responds.

Crusty and I answer with squelch breaks on VHF while Rick's talking to the Covey. I reduce the collective and pull back slightly on the cyclic to get the separation as Rick has now picked up the Huey for his escort into the LZ.

On FM, "Hotel, this is Blue Bird Three, pop smoke, over. Pop smoke!" The voice is excited but not screaming, and the pilot has not lost control, though he appears on the edge.

Watching the fat green helicopter start its flare, I see yellow smoke rise clearly from the LZ. Though close to the downed Huey it will not affect the pickup as the crashed bird's rotor system has been ripped out by the impact. One blade is now stuck into the ground with part of it bent over at an angle representing a broken cross. Missing is the main transmission with its rotor mast no longer attached, and I can't see where it ended it's flight out of the aircraft.

"Three's down!" Comes the first of the two calls we have been waiting for.

I, with Crusty at my seven o'clock position, fire rockets into the southern tree line. Then on VHF, I direct him to fire rockets into the southwestern trees, remembering that the slicks had received ground fire from this area on their approach and could receive some on their departure.

I start to break from my rocket run. Not wanting to break to the south where all the bad guys are supposed to be entrenched, but I have no choice with the Huey landing and our other two Cobras to my right.

"Breaking left," I announce as I sharply pull the cyclic back and to the left.

I pull up hard on the collective hoping to outdistance any possible gun fire from this area. Our climb goes quickly, though we hear the sharp crackling of small arms fire directed at us.

"Yoooo!" Yo Ho calls out, then adds, "We took a hit."

Just then on UHF, the Huey calls. "Three lifting with eight." No sooner than he finishes his call, we hear from both of the Huey pilots, "Taking fire! I'm hit!"

Then the continued call from one of the pilots, "AC's hit, ah . . . at our nine taking hits." The background noise of the radio is the sound of gun fire and screams. It sounds like he has a hot mike or maybe in the excitement he's let his right index finger clamp down on the cyclic communications button.

I drop collective and push in left pedal and start a rocket run from the now unfinished climb out of our last pass. "Sneaky's inbound to the LZ."

On VHF I hear, "I'm breaking Sneaky." Crusty has started his climb out.

"Get out of the way Sneaky. We're inbound." calls Rick who's now coming in behind me from his tight right-hand break after passing the Huey.

"How you doing Three?" The Kid asks.

"We're hit hard but everything's in the green." The pilot has to scream over the background noise that must be from the confusion in the aircraft. "Got eight!" He adds.

"Breaking left!" I yell over the other radio transmission and, as I start my climb out, I see Goose's aircraft passing by in front of us.

Rick calls, "Hawk, the LZ is clear. You may go ahead and

destroy the Huey and clean out any enemy."

"Roger, the LZ is clear and you have twelve on board." The Covey needs to ensure that all are accounted for before he lets the fury of the bomb laden Sandys roll in.

The lead Black Widow calls, "I've got four."

Then after a few seconds the third Black Widow calls with his count. "We have eight. Three, and five from the downed bird. We have three WIA's."

"Roger, the LZ is clear and you have twelve." Then again on UHF the Covey makes the call that will raise havoc on the ground. "Sandys, I have a clear Lima Zulu. You are free to destroy the downed aircraft."

With that statement goes the loss of another $250,000 aircraft from the Army's inventory and the United States taxpayer's pockets. Though it will never be officially reported as lost in Laos, we who are out here today know it went in with no chance of being recovered to be repaired and flown another day. The salvage process would probably cost human life and possibly the loss of another aircraft. As they say in fishing, sometimes it's worth it to cut the line, forget the bait, and come back another day. Today, we have cut the line, a large crumpled green metal machine that will never take young warriors to the heavens again.

We all join up and start the trek home, though we are one bird less and three more injured from the downing of the Huey. The flight back is silent. We're all thinking what it would have been like if we had gone down or were wounded while in the LZ. Or, what if Black Widow Three went in? No way the fourth aircraft could have picked up twelve and flown back.

As we approach Vandy, several of the ACs, including me, announce the presence of the blinking low level fuel light. The first few times it comes on, it lights up the Master Caution Panel. We have to reset the MCP's yellow light to ensure that if there are other warnings, it will light up again. When the fuel sloshes in the tank it goes off, then reappears. Each time lighting up the yellow MCP light. Within two to three minutes, it's a steady glow and the MCP light is disregarded.

The calls are made to the MLT to notify them of the wounded and the need for security to be waiting. Though the third and overloaded Black Widow has been hit numerous times, the pilot elects to land directly at 18th Surg, rather than complete a precautionary landing at the Quang Tri. His AC has been shot in the right arm, the gunner is gut shot, and the crew-chief is slightly wounded.

Our landing is done with much fanfare. We'd notified Quang Tri that we were inbound, low on fuel, and had several ships shot up. Two are going directly to 18th Surg, which alerts everyone that the Americans have had a bad day. Everyone knows that we have been to the west. It's only in their minds that they can imagine just how far west. The pilots and tower operators know it's been in Laos, but others look at the flight as just another shot up group of aircraft.

As we nose up to POL, all four Griffins and the lone uninjured Black Widow Huey land in front of the thick black JP hoses. The sighs of relief are heard across the UHF tower frequency. We have arrived, though on fumes and with the help of someone watching over us.

After the refuel, we takeoff and land at CCN. The Huey has topped off, but the Griffins have not. As we shutdown, Milo is unseen, but one of the supply NCOs comes up to each ship and reaches from a ruck sack to hand out cold beer. It's been one of those days and it's only early afternoon.

After climbing out, I walk over to Rick. I want to ask about the mission and the Kid's performance. I hope that Klien didn't blow anything, but if he did I can understand. It's his first day in the back seat and on a CCN mission that goes to shit.

As I walk up to Rick, his beaming smile telegraphs that things weren't that bad, though flying a mission like that from the front seat would have been a pain in the ass for me. Sweet Griffin is a natural instructor and has spent hours in the front seat guiding some new AC, or some old forgetful one like me, through some procedure that needs to be refreshed or refined.

"I saw the slick hit the trees with his tail rotor on short final," saying before I can even ask. Then, continuing on, "Klien did okay but I had to take over once we lost the aircraft." He wasn't saying it as an excuse, and I would have done the same thing.

I'm wondering if Rick will sign him off for CCN flights. "So what's the verdict, is he going to be an AC or what?"

"Yeah, I'll give him an AC check ride tomorrow and then I'll sign him off."

Dropping his chicken plate and survival vest on the open ammo bay door, he turns to grab the slowly turning main blade. The front of his nomex flight shirt, like mine, is stained dark with the perspiration that the last hours have oozed from us. But like always, Rick is smiling and optimistic. I'll bet he asks the Black Widow Lead how long will it take to have replacement Hueys up here, so we can be ready for another mission.

Chapter 21

Almost all of the pilots are in the club when I walk in and most are on their way to a heavy hang over. Several of the new W1s are sitting in the corner. They're bright red from too much booze and from passing out under the sun during the last few days of good weather we have had. The Griffins are now back on track from Ripcord operations several months ago and have settled back into the groove of normal operations. The sun will not be with us much longer and everyone is trying for one last good tan.

The celebration, for no formal reason, is in full swing. I throw down a wad of crumpled up funny money, and Sgt. Jones gives me two beers. Jones has just extended his tour for another six months.

"What the fuck, no Budweiser?" I ask, knowing that if we had any, the Sergeant would have given them to me rather than these rusted cans of Crown.

"No Sneaky. I guess the Division needs Budweiser more than we do," he laughs, reminding me that in any Division Headquarters club at Camp Eagle there is Budweiser. Those of us up here at Camp Evans get what the others don't like. At least it isn't Black Label or Ballentine.

I walk over to the table where Sweet Griffin is holding court. As I get to it, I throw one of the Crowns to Rick. Normally the Kid would have jumped up and given me his chair, then gone and found one for himself. Now that he's an AC, he has assumed the status where others get chairs for him and he doesn't get up for anybody. The mindset of being an AC has set in. He doesn't know that if he went back to the States tomorrow and checked into a unit, he would be back at the bottom of the pecking order. True, he will be a Chief Warrant Officer soon or certainly one once he returns to the States, but then that's all there are in the units back in the States. W1s are only for Vietnam.

"Here you go Sneaky," W1 Folsom says getting up so I can sit at the table.

As one of the junior warrants in the unit, he quickly found that though he was now an aviator and a Warrant Officer, he's still considered at the bottom of the pecking order. He's started growing his black hair long. His moustache is starting to extend below his lip though he hasn't started to wax it into a handlebar. His personality is one that drives him to be accepted and this extends to flying, playing, or drinking with the older pilots. He arrived just before Ripcord and though in the unit, didn't get much flying time till it was over. But since then, he's like the rest of us, flying all the time. In time he'll become a good AC, but he has to learn it will take time. This is the problem with all new Warrants. The most dangerous thing in aviation is a freshly-minted pilot, who thinks he knows all, and the that wings pinned to his chest are a testament to his great wealth of knowledge. After a thousand hours or so, he'll learn that he really doesn't know that much. I pity those who have to fly with them until they build up the hours. Folsom cannot help but fall into this trap. I did and most other pilots have.

"Thanks," I answer. Looking at Klien, I add, "Apparently the junior AC doesn't realize he's still a WO JUG and must never forget that."

There are a few chuckles at Klien's expense, who's ignoring us. Folsom comes back with a chair and, after some shuffling, we are all able to sit around the table.

"Where you been, Da Nang?" Rick asks me as I gulp down the cold, watered down beer.

"Na, in Hue."

"Sneaky, you got a girl down there or what?" W1 Stockman

asks.

Before I can answer, Crusty speaks up. Sitting there with his squared face, I can picture him living a hundred years ago. He's the type who looks like he just got off a horse after a long hard dusty ride. Some say he's a bit weathered, others might call him ruddy complexioned, but I look at him as one who's been in a couple of hard fights and is not afraid of the next opportunity.

"Sneaky's been with his old lady." He slurs as he talks, indicating that he's probably been drinking all day.

"You got a nurse or something?" Stockman asks, inquisitively.

"Fuck, Sneaky can't spell nurse and after he was tied to the bed at 18th Surg you know damn well that no nurse would want the son-of-a-bitch near her," the Kid gets his licks in. Since becoming an AC, the metamorphosis that will transform him into a bonafide helicopter pilot has sped up.

"I'll have you know that I once was in love with a nurse," I answer defending my honor as a horny helicopter pilot and trying to change the subject from the past two days I spent with Twit.

The group around the table erupts with laughter.

"You can't spell nurse and couldn't find one with both hands on your dick," Crusty slurs.

While everyone is laughing, I stand up and grab my crotch announcing, "I'll have you know that the sexiest nurse at Fort Eustes was a blonde captain named Eileen Kelly and everybody tried to date her." Then shaking my crotch I add, " . . . and your's truly, Chief Warrant Officer White, was the only one whoever got her to go out. And the rest, as they say, is history."

"Bullshit!"

"Sit the fuck down. I can't take any more of this," Rick joins in.

"I'll have you know that she and I still write and I'll go get the letters to prove it."

I now am defending my prowess as a lover. Though the truth is that Eileen is probably the sweetest girl I've ever met. She is a graduate of the University of Maryland and upon her entry into the Army was promoted to captain. She was very standoffish when I first met her. I quickly found out it was because of the many officers at the club hitting on her for a quick roll in the hay. She's got a body that won't quit and after setting my sights on her, I bet the other members of my AMOC class that I would be dating her before I left.

Eileen's long blond hair, deep blue eyes, and warm smile drew stares everywhere she went. She didn't drink and I quickly found out that she was a devout Catholic. She lived in the BOQ across the street from me at the western end of the Fort Eustes Officer's Club parking lot. One day after seeing her in her stiffly starched whites, waiting for the shuttle bus to take her to the base hospital, I offered her a ride. Though the first few rides were quiet and very formal, in time we started talking about a variety of subjects. One thing led to another, and I was taking her to dinner.

I was able to collect the several hundred dollars in bets that I wouldn't be able to bed her down, without doing it. One night she and I stayed up very late in her quarters listening to Rod McKoown records. She read to me from some of his books and we both fell asleep in chairs. Although nothing happened, as I left that morning I was observed by two of the warrants in my class and the word quickly spread that I had thawed the "iceberg". It wasn't true, but I never denied it and collected the money that the stag club bartender was holding.

After finding out that she didn't drive, I offered to take her up to her mother's home in College Park, Maryland, on several occasions. Her father was dead and her mother was very protective of her only daughter. When I got my orders back to Nam, Eileen cried, promised to write, and put in for overseas duty. Hoping for Vietnam, she was disappointed when ordered to a Korean Army hospital unit. We write once every month or so. I understand she and I are very different and will never be together. I know that our time together will always be one of my fondest memories. She's like a sister, one I've never had and can only imagine how it would be.

The Kid pushes the subject further, "Sneaky you got an old lady here?" Then spreading his arms open he continues, "If she isn't the hootch maid," then looking around the club for the young girl who works in here during the day, "and if she isn't the club girl, who the fuck is she?"

Everyone at the table is now asking. The Kid has started something that I don't want to talk about. I haven't been back from Houng Ca for more than an hour. During my time with Twit, she told me that she's pregnant again and was beaming with pride in anticipation of having another child. For me, it is a feeling both of elation and of pain. Until I can figure out how to stay in Vietnam during the withdrawal period, or weasel a transfer over to Air America, I'm in a spot. I know that as soon as I get home, I will file for divorce. Although I have children there, I can't see myself being happy in the States. I need to talk to someone, though I don't know who, about this problem. The guys I trust have no experience in this field and the others wouldn't understand. I'm sure someone would put a letter in my file regarding my relationship with a possible enemy. It seems the Army has a problem with it's soldiers going too native. I know of many men who were stationed in Germany and have married *frauleins*. They have their own homes there and, whenever possible, they return to Germany for a tour. It's another one of the double standards found within the military.

"Come on asshole, tell us who she is." Crusty nudges me now that I'm seated in the folding lawn chair next to him.

"All right you bastards. Yeah, I got me a girl. She works in a restaurant in Hue."

Telling this lie should slow the conversation down. It might delay the hundreds of questions that would be levied at me if they knew the truth. She is by no means a girl. If given the chance, she would show them how wonderful she really is, but she'll never be given this chance. They do not see the Vietnamese as I do and will never give the people a chance. It starts in basic training, goes on in flight school, and manifests itself here in country. American GIs hate Orientals just as the Marines did during the China Rebellion. The sneak attack by the Japanese fueled the fire, and Korea reminded us that China was always ready to support a war against the round-eyes. Now we are here, another dirty little Asian war. We have born and bred a society of Oriental hating people and they are now all around me.

"You SOB," Klien says. "You got a broad working in a restaurant so you can eat that stinking food for free."

Laughing uncontrollably, the others now think they know why I have a Vietnamese girl friend.

"What's the restaurant, so I can get a free meal next time I go to Hue?" Klien asks.

"Yeah, what's the restaurant?"

"Fuck you all! I found her and she's mine," I say, knowing that I now have a way of ending the conversation.

"I wouldn't piss Sneaky off if I were you," Sweet Griffin says. "Remember he does get even. Don't you Sneaky?"

"Who me?" I reply, grinning as I now see the conversation shift away from my private life.

"Tell 'em about the Marine Sergeant."

"What's this about a Marine?" the Kid asks, trying to keep the heat on me.

I would rather talk about the Marine than talk about Twit because these men, young men at that, would never understand my love for her.

"Well it happened years ago when I was in the Marines."

"Anything that happened in your life happened years ago," Crusty says as I start my story.

Sweet Griffin calls for a round and pulls apart the wet and soggy bills of MPC laid out before him. He'd been using them as a coaster for his can and they have absorbed the condensation and spilled beer until they have become matted into one thick wad.

"Well any fucking way, while I was with HMM-262 in '66 I was a crew-chief and this Master Gunnery Sergeant named

Crisman was my boss. For over a year he fucked with me every day."

As Jones brings the tray of beers over to the table and puts one in front of each of us, the Kid interrupts my story with, "I'd love to see someone who could fuck with you, especially for a year. The son-of-a-bitch has to be nineteen feet tall, hairy knuckles and a pea of a brain. A typical Marine!"

While the laughter from Klien's remark goes on, I continue, "The guy stayed on my ass every day from sunup to sundown. His claim to fame was that he had fought in the real war, flying in DC-3s 'over the hump' during WW II."

I stop and empty the can of beer in front of me, then grab the new cold one that Jones has just had delivered.

"So when I was back in the States on leave this last time, I thought I'd look him up. I went up to HMX-1 at Quantico, Virginia and saw a good friend of mine. He tells me Crisman is the senior Marine Instructor at NAS Memphis."

"What the fuck is at Memphis?" 'Big Foot' Stockman asks.

"Well it's really at Millington, Tennessee, just north of Memphis. It's like the Army's Fort Rucker for helicopter mechanics and crew-chiefs." Trying to ignore the interruption, "I see Master Sergeant Otis Felton who was stationed at HMX-1. He tells me his brother-in-law Big John Ableman is an instructor at Memphis. So I call Big John, who at one time was the heavyweight boxing champion of all WestPac for the Marines. Big John and I ran around together when we were both buck Sergeants."

I stop to open the cold beer I've been holding. It sprays it's white sticky foam across the table before I can get it to my mouth to suck it in.

"I'm due to come back to Nam in a few days so instead of getting a direct flight from Washington, D.C. to Seattle I get one to Memphis and spend the night with Ableman and his wife. The morning after I arrive, Ableman's wife, Mary, drove me to the base during the morning break at the canteen truck. I was dressed in the Army full class A uniform with every ribbon, badge and other bullshit do-dad I've ever been awarded hanging from me. Hell, I looked like a Christmas tree with the dark green uniform and all the little colored things hanging off me." Chuckles are heard around the table. "I walked up to the roach coach right after I see Crisman walking toward it. He had gone to the head of the line, exercising his military rank, and had a cup of coffee in one hand and a donut in the other. Upon seeing me, he didn't recognize me at first and said, "Good morning, sir." Then I looked him in the black pits he has for eyes and asked him if the Marines still saluted officers. The shock in his face was evident the moment he realized who I was. Seeing me, dressed in an officer's uniform was almost more than he could take. He stammered for a second. I then repeated the question in front of all his fucking Marines, 'Do the Marines still salute officers?' This time loud enough to be heard several rows deep in the group of privates and young seamen pushing themselves next to the opened sides of the white stainless steel truck."

The guys around the table are laughing, knowing that I don't believe in saluting and all the protocol involved in a formal military setting.

"So what the fuck did Mr. Marine do?" Klien asks knowing how brutal I can be with those I don't like.

"Well, he damn near dropped his shit and snapped to attention, ah . . . like a good fucking Marine."

Everyone is laughing hard now. Folsom stands and gives a salute like the British, palm out. Which brings hearty laughter to the group seated before me.

"I waited before I returned it. While all those privates were looking, I said, 'For the benefit of those who don't know what the fuck is going on, you may carry on Sergeant. But, I would advise that you not fuck with someone that may one day be your CO!"

Gulping in a mouthful of the cold Korean beer, I let them think about this before I finish the story.

"I then returned his salute, did an about face, and walked to the parking lot. Big John's wife drove me to the airport."

"That's it?"

"Can't be. You didn't punch him out?"

"As an Officer and a Gentleman, I provoked no violence. I just left and flew to California to spend a day with some guys at Santa Ana. But, by the time I got to California, Big John had called and reported the incident to all the Marines who hated Crisman. Hell, I couldn't buy a drink in the NCO Club for the two days I was there."

Everyone is laughing really hard when Captain Rogers comes noisily through the seldom used front door. Looking around the room until he sees Rick, he strides up to our table.

Not completely under my breath, I say, "What the fuck does this asshole want?"

Before anyone comments or replies, Jolly Roger tells Rick to come up to the TOC right away.

Looking up at Rick as he stands, I remind him not to volunteer for any hair-brained half-assed idea.

Rick leaves the Club with Jolly Roger leading the way. The conversation goes to the many possible reasons why Rick would be summoned to the TOC. It's 1st platoon's Hot Status day but then maybe it's a CCN mission or maybe something to do with an accident somewhere. Who fucking knows and cares? I'm going to get drunk.

"Jones!"

"Yes, Sneaky?" Jones answers with my nickname, though when around the higher-ups he will use Mr. White.

"Bring over ah . . . " Then quickly counting heads at the table, plus adding one for Rick whose return I expect soon, I say, "Ah . . . seven times four is twenty-eight plus get yourself a couple." Then I stand up to pull out several crumpled bills.

In the small talk going on around the table, I ask Crusty, "You know my tour will be up in February and I think I'll extend again. Can I extend for a year?"

Crusty answers with what I already know. "Nah, just the standard six month extensions. Hell, you should know, you've got three or four of them."

"Fuck!"

I know if I go back to the States and immediately put in to return to Vietnam I might not be able to get back over here. Somehow I need to extend this tour again and try to remain stationed in this area or at least in I Corps. Maybe I can go back down to the 484th with the Black Cats if they need a maintenance officer. Maybe get an assignment working with the VNAF helicopter squadrons now accepting the aircraft and equipment being left by the quickly departing Army units throughout Vietnam. I'd have to get a Huey IP check ride to add to my present maintenance MOS to ensure that they would accept me for this type of duty, but no problem.

"Why don't you go back to scouts?" Klien asks, knowing how I liked flying the little birds. "Shit you told me months ago you wanted to go to the 2nd of the 17th." Then looking around the table, he adds, "Remember?"

"Yeah I know I said I'd go up there if I could fly for Colonel Montinelli," knowing that Lieutenant Colonel Robert Montinelli had command of the 2nd of the 17th Cav Squadron for the 101st Airborne Division. Montinelli is my kind of CO. A no-nonsense type who looks for the enemy, and upon finding them, leads his men into destroying them quickly and efficiently. I'd follow him to downtown Hanoi if he asked. They broke the mold of straight forward leaders when he was born.

Rick comes though the door and quickly calls out several of the 3rd platoon AC's names. Without further conversation, he points to the back door and walks out. The looks of surprise are not only on the faces of the pilots singled out, but everyone when Rick says, while going out the door, that he's got an emergency CCN flight.

"You need me?" I shout as the door slams.

He sticks his head back in the door and says to no one in particular, "We've got this one covered. It's some mission that has got all the higher ups asking for volunteers but not knowing what we are supposed to volunteer for." Then he's gone as quickly as he arrived.

Several pilots, both those he'd called and other 3rd platoon members, rush out to follow the dean of the Griffins.

"Fuck it. I'm getting drunk!" I say to no one in particular as I raise the beer to my lips and without stopping, gulp the almost full can dry.

As the night wears on, I get drunker and drunker. We party hard. None of us knows what tomorrow brings.

We're on short final to the CCN pad. The Lancer slicks have arrived before us, and I'm sure they've topped off as I see crew-chiefs and several recon team members securing the thick green nylon ropes to the aircraft's floors. The daily cycle has started. The arrival of the aircraft, preparing them for the special flight operations that they must fly, briefing the crews, and the waiting. We're waiting for the fog to lift in the area of insertion or extraction to get the flight off the ground. We ride the flight out, with the terror of anticipating the eruption of gunfire. And then at last, we watch the last slick leave the landing zone and make the long flight home. For some, this simple everyday mission, though mundane, can be satisfying. For others, after they're notified they have a CCN flight, their stomachs cramp up as the fear slowly creeps in. For them, it will be like this all day until they're back in their cubicles and a few beers gulped down.

Why the Army in its infinite wisdom has not assigned a set of crews permanently to CCN flights is beyond me. The value gained would be immense and, at some point, life saving. Those that work day in and day out together become a team or, as a well-known Chicago Mayor once said, a well-oiled machine. You not only know what you're going to do, but you understand in advance what the others around you are capable of and when they're going to do it. Surely it isn't because the Army doesn't have the men and machinery to assign permanent flight crews. It must be some West Point educated commanding officer who doesn't want his assets delegated to Special Forces. The jealously between Special Forces and regular Army is unbelievable. When you add the secret missions of MAC-V-SOG, then it really comes to a head. The battle is said to date back to the beginning of Special Forces, when the Airborne community didn't want to relinquish control of these hand picked men. The requirements are tough. Not only physical but mental toughness is important. According to Army regulations, to become a commissioned officer you must possess an IQ of 110, though this is waivable. To go into Special Forces, whether as enlisted or officer, you must possess an IQ of 120 and it's not waivable.

There is the issue of the coveted Green Beret that would never have been approved without President John Fitzgerald Kennedy. The story of its approval is popular folklore in the Army, as well as one of antagonism from the Airborne community. Since Barry Sadler's top selling song about the Green Berets, they've become the unchallenged best in the military, especially by those who know nothing about the armed forces. A legend was started when the beret was authorized, and the song has romanced the image into an unbeatable fighting machine. The day will come when everyone will claim they were a Green Beret, though most couldn't have filled out the request for interview or transfer to Fort Bragg to start Q Course. Even the Air Force has gotten on board by letting their Air Police wear berets, though to compare an Air Force AP with an Army Green Beret is like comparing a high school basketball team with the Harlem Globetrotters.

I'm in the process of shutting down when Milo comes over to the aircraft with a clipboard in his hand, the clamped papers flapping in the rotor wash of our slowly turning blades.

"You talked to Sweet Griffin yet?" He asks, while I'm pulling off my helmet.

"No," then thinking, he wouldn't have asked me this unless there was some important reason. Rick left with a flight of four late last night for some sort of CCN emergency. Though I haven't seen him since he got back, the word is not to ask what happened, where it happened or who was involved. But I'm sure Billy will tell me today. "What the hell happened?"

Milo shrugs his shoulders and replies, "Can't say, but it was a hot one." He abruptly walks off toward the aircraft in front of me. This isn't like Milo.

I catch up to Jimbo as he walks past the Lancer aircraft. Once out of hearing range from the other crews, I ask, "You hear anything about Rick's mission last night?" I'm sure if he had, he would have said something during our walk up to the TOC this morning.

The tall good-looking Texan turns to me with the most serious look I've ever seen on him and says, "Don't ask anything about it. It was some kind of CIA mission and they have all been sworn to secrecy. I heard it was an assassination team that had been out for over thirty days, and they went through hell to get rescued." He quickly walks away from me.

I can't let this go since I know a lot of the teams we put in are Agency planned and controlled. Catching up, I question, "So what the fuck is new? Why is this one so special?" I'm pressing Jimbo, who must know more than he's telling. Shit, I shouldn't have gotten drunk yesterday afternoon. Then I ask, "What team was it?"

MAC-V-SOGs Command & Control branch falls under an Operational Plan 35. The command is broken down to three sub-units located in three areas of Vietnam. The southern most, is CCS, for Command & Control - South. CCS teams ply their trade along the many waterways of the Mekong that flows lazily though Cambodia. A lot of CCS's teams are manned by Navy SEALS.

In the middle of Vietnam, men operate out of CCC. These teams, from Command & Control - Central, who are headquartered in the Central Highlands, are named after States. Their area includes the northern part of Cambodia and the southern tip of Laos.

CCN is headquartered at Da Nang and our area of operation is Laos, the DMZ, and, of course, North Vietnam. There are reports, denied and totally unconfirmed, that teams have infiltrated into southern China in the search for intelligence or some covert activities. CCN recon teams are named after snakes such as Python, Anaconda, Rattler, Viper, and so forth.

I have a friend in CCC who was running as the One-One, or the second in command, for RT Illinois until a month ago when he became the One-Zero of Team Indiana. On occasion, CCN will have CCC teams temporarily assigned to them for special missions. As CCN teams go further and further north, it means the teams from CCS and CCC must cover larger areas to their north. I'm sure the teams all have difficult areas to operate in, but there's no doubt that CCN is the more difficult of them.

James "Red" Tramerling, who's now the One-Zero with RT Indiana, has told me several times that he'd rather do two CCC missions than one CCN mission. At least they can get into the area. A lot of the insertions into the CCN operational area get blown out before the helicopter can land and drop off the team.

"Well, what RT was it?" Knowing that this will give me some information I can use to find out about the mission.

Jimbo, now visably annoyed, stops, turns to face me while sticking a finger in my face, and growls, "Listen Sneaky, the word is the mission and Rick's flight never happened, understand! Is this clear enough for you?" Then starting to turn toward the Operations hut he, adds, "It wasn't a CCN team. They were called Five Fingers, or something like that, so your guess is as good as mine where they came from, but they were CIA and the rumor is they came down from China." Then opening the door for me, he adds, "I mean it, forget about this."

"No problem *Dai Uy*."

I realize that I've got all I'm able to from Jimbo on this subject. China, hell could it be an assassination team into China. Christ, does anyone know the ramifications of this? I do not believe China would send troops into Vietnam as they had done when crossing the Yalu River in Korea almost twenty years ago. They do have advisors in North Vietnam. Hell, I've got to find out more about this one.

Entering the hut, I see Lancer pilots are laid out on the benches. It looks like they're tired from the short flight up to Quang Tri. This is a day of rest for them instead of the ten or twelve hours they would normally have flying for some brigade around Camp Eagle.

Jimbo goes into the back radio room searching for Captain Stanton to find out what the plans for today are. I sit down on one of the benches in the front row. Goose Baker from the 3rd platoon sits next to me. He's swapped today's flight with Lieutenant Cool Poole. His front seat is the newest W1 in the unit, Stockman, or Big Foot.

"Why the swap?" I ask, not knowing about it until I was preflighting Zero-Two-Seven in the revetment this morning.

"Jimbo and I are going to go down to 95th Evac Hospital tomorrow," he answers.

I have no idea how Goose got his nickname, but it's a carryover from his first tour when he was a warrant officer flying for the 335th Assault Helicopter Company down south. Not only is this his second tour, but he's on an extension. At twenty-three or four, he's made the commitment to the Army that he wants to be a career officer. Not married, he has a girl friend who is a nurse with the 95th Evac Hospital in Da Nang.

I used to watch E'Clair and him play one-on-one under the dilapidated basketball hoop in front of the 3rd platoon. He's good, at least E'Clair said so. In the volleyball games we have, he's usually the first chosen, not for his spiking ability, but for his tenacity at digging out a ball most of us would let go. His overhand serve is downright dangerous, especially if it doesn't make it over the net. More of his teammates have been hit without warning than care to mention it. If it gets over the net, the other side has their hands full trying to return it.

I think he has fixed Jimbo up with a nurse since this is the fourth or fifth time they've made the trip down to Da Nang together.

Though I haven't flown with him often, Rick says he's a damn good pilot, and yesterday proved it for me. I unzip my Nomex flight shirt as it's already getting warm. The sweat is pouring off me causing the shirt to stick to my skin. The Kid slithers up and hands us several cold sodas that he was able to scrounge from the team hut.

Jimbo walks into the room with a captain who is dressed in Nomex and has an ugly zig-zag scar running across his forehead. It's easy to tell the scar is fresh. Though no longer bandaged, the bright blue-red line is the new skin trying to mend the once large opening. I notice the Kid looking and then he turns to hide his laugh. Hell of a thing to do I think, as I elbow him in his ribs trying to stop his behavior. The Griffins know who can take what and who can't. But get caught fucking with a senior officer from another unit and Major Stafford won't be able to protect us.

"Here you go Jimbo," Klien says as he tosses the last unopened soda toward Jimbo. "We got anything going on?"

"One insertion today, but we are on a weather hold," Jimbo replies as he looks around for a church key.

The Kid throws a P-38 and Jimbo grabs it in midflight. After opening the can and handing back the most useful piece of military equipment designed since 1940, Klien rolls his eyes toward the door signaling me to go with him.

Stepping out the door, the Kid, who has grown on me like a son, bursts out laughing.

"What the fuck's so funny?" I ask, having seen nothing that would be taken as funny.

One of the Lancer pilots, a very young looking W1, comes over from the Huey parked in front of the Operations hut.

"Toby, I'd like you to meet the famous and dashing Sneaky White." Klien introduces us, though I've no idea why. Looking down to his name tag I read Allen.

Warrant Officer 1 Toby Allen is a bit chubby and several inches shorter than Klien and me. His complexion shows the marks left over from childhood acne which he probably recovered from within the past year. He has grown a moustache that consists of half a dozen thin and very straggly hairs across his upper lip. They're barely visible unless you are right up next to him. His sideburns are not razor trimmed but have been allowed to grow naturally and only end above his ear lobe. Taken aback by his appearance, I'm surprised that he could have made it through flight school. Maybe he could get through the flying end of it, but surely the TAC officers had a field day with him.

When I went through school, I was lucky in that most of our class was prior service. I roomed with a former E-8 1st Sergeant named Dick Korner who was looking for the day he could retire to his home on Lake Eufalua, Alabama. Once he got back to Vietnam, now as a new W1, he requested and got his old unit where he had served as First Sergeant. I had tried several times to get down to 1st Division's Big Red Pad at Phu Loi and go to the 1st of the 4th Cav, or Quarter Cav as they're called, to see him but was never able to schedule it. The last I heard, he was flying as an IP at Fort Walters.

Besides Dick, there were a dozen or so other Army ex-NCOs. Several of them came out of Special Forces and were heavily decorated from their tours in Vietnam. In flight school, you weren't allowed to wear any decorations or badges that you had earned in past service. It had to do with the Army's concept that we were all starting fresh. Though we knew, and they knew, that those with certain awards had proven themselves under fire and would surely do it again if the opportunity arose.

There were also several ex-crew-chiefs and a handful of aircraft maintenance specialists. We had two sailors, or squids as the Marines call Navy personnel, in the class and four Marines counting myself. So, for a flight class, we were fairly experienced in the ways of the military and the protocol needed to become an officer and gentleman.

"Toby, tell Sneaky what happened to your captain." Klien is excited with whatever this news is about.

"Well, the captain came to us from Battalion several weeks

ago and has made himself a royal pain in the ass, if you know what I mean," he comments with raised eyebrows. His accent is the thick New England, probably Boston, nasal type. The a's are the tell tale sign he's from the area.

"Get on with it!" Klien is trying to rush the warrant's story.

"Well, after giving our platoon the blues for the first week about the hootch not being clean enough to meet his standards, he made us rebuild our bunker." Then looking over to Klien as if asking for clearance to go on, he continues at my co-pilot's urging. "Well, we had a rocket attack last week."

"So." I answer, not knowing the direction this is leading.

"When the siren went off, he ran out of the hootch knocking over everyone in his path. When he got to the bunker, he forgot to stoop down and hit the galvanized tin roof full force with his forehead. That's why he's got that large jagged scar running across his forehead."

The young pilot and Klien break out in hysterical laughter. While they're laughing, I visualize this guy running full bore into the zig-zag shaped end of the bunker's roof. I can't help but start laughing at the thought of this idiot running into the bunker.

"You're serious?" I ask while trying to catch my breath.

"Yes Sir. There he was in his boxers pushing past us. When we got to the bunker he was laid out on his back on the steps going into the entrance. I thought he'd been hit by a piece of shrapnel. There was blood all over his face and chest and he was out cold." Then he starts laughing again. "He peed on himself."

With this revelation, Klien laughs even harder and is slapping his thigh with the thought of the captain laid out in his soiled shorts.

"By the time we got him to the Aid Station, the attack was over." Then looking around to make sure no one is overhearing him, he adds, "Several of the guys took photos while they were putting him in the jeep for the ride to get stitched up."

I now join in the uncontrollable laughter. This should have happened to some of the assholes I know, I think to myself.

Then to finish out his story Toby adds, "When he came back to the unit, his eyes were swollen shut and black and blue. Everyone is calling him Zipper Head now, ah . . . but not to his face."

"Well I've got to admit he's got one hell of a scar. I'd love to hear the war story on this one," I say after finishing the soda I've been holding.

"I've got to be cool, because he's my AC and he's scared shitless." Then after Klien's nod he continues, "In fact I'm scared with him at the controls just flying into POL, never mind if it's a hot fucking LZ."

This has put me in an awkward position. I personally don't know the captain. I've known assholes who were excellent pilots, especially under fire. I've known pilots that thought everyone else was scared shitless when in fact they were the problem.

"Well Toby, you've just got to lightly ride the controls in case something happens." Thinking about what I would do if what he says is true, "Can you get a transfer to another flight platoon?"

"I tried, but no way," he answers with a frustrated look on his face.

Changing the subject, I ask, "Where you from Toby?" Knowing he must be from my part of the country.

"Massachusetts on the Cape," he answers with the long nasal sound.

"Hell, I can hear that," I say, "Where on the Cape?"

"Well Mr. White, I'm really from Martha's Vineyard." He answers sheepishly.

"Yeah? I went to private school in East Pembroke. You know where that is?" I ask, knowing he must know the little town located off old state route 128.

He nods his head in affirmation, and I continue, "As a kid we use to go up to the Vineyard during the summer. We had a cottage there until my Dad sold it for a bigger one in Brewster."

He nods, knowing that Brewster is a small community half way out on the Cape when driving toward Provincetown. "We had a Navion. My Dad use to let me make the flight from Hartford to Martha's Vineyard without his touching the controls. I bet I can still land in zero-zero on runway six." Now both of the W1s are shaking their heads in agreement, although Klien has no idea what I'm talking about. Then I ask, "I bet you don't know the field elevation, do you?"

Toby looks surprised, not only at the question but he knows I will know the answer. Thinking for a minute, he finally says, "No, Sir," while shaking his head.

"Well I'll bet a case of beer, or a bottle of Scotch, that it's sixty-eight feet. I've landed there many a time."

The young Lancer W1 looks uncomfortable while standing in front of me, probably because he's not used to a senior warrant talking to him like he's a human being.

"How the hell did you two meet?" I ask them both.

"We went through flight school together and shared a room at Rucker. But, Buff got a Cobra transition and I thought I wouldn't see him again. So I wrote his mother and she told me he was with the Griffins." Then looking at Klien, he adds in a resentful tone, "Now he's almost an AC and I haven't made it yet."

"Give it time," I encourage him. "You know the only reason he got it is because we ran out of live bodies." I'm smiling as I can understand a young pilot's frustration of not being able to be in charge of a flight crew.

The eagerness of the young Army warrants has given the helicopter pilots in Vietnam a reputation for getting the job done in spite of sometimes overwhelming odds. True that once out of the aircraft, the Army usually had a youthful exuberant kid who didn't give a damn about protocol or had any military bearing. But strapped in the shaky green flying machine, he was just what the Army needed.

"Any idea when you're supposed to take your AC check ride?" I ask, hoping that he hasn't taken it already and failed. I don't know the procedures in B Company Lancers. Being in the 158th Assault Helicopter Battalion means they're under a different commander's policy than the Griffins.

"I'm supposed to take the check out this month. If Buff extends like he says he's going to . . . " then looking at Klien, ". . . I'll extend to come over to the Griffins."

I look at Klien. "What's this?" I ask louder than I mean to, "You're planning to extend, are you?"

"Yeah. Talked to the Old Man already, and he's going to get me the papers from Battalion."

Thinking that this might not be a wise decision for him I ask, "Does your mother know about this yet?"

"No, I figured I'd tell her while I was home on leave." Then, adding as if it would be vindication to his decision, "I'm sure she'll understand."

"Bullshit!" I say. Shaking my head, knowing that his mother would never understand.

Though Klien has matured and is no longer the Kid he was when given his nickname, he's not one who should stay over here in my country. The way the war is going now, only those who want to stay and who love this country should be here. The war is not for those trying to get an early out or one more oak leaf cluster to put on some blue and gold striped ribbon. This is not Klien's war, but mine. Mine and the one or two others of each unit who have fallen in love with the fragile country that has been raped with over thirty years of warfare. I have family here and will have another child just after the first of the year, so I have a vested interest at stake.

I leave the two warrants standing there and return to the Operations hut. In the hut, I decide that I don't want to be around anyone. So I stand with my back to the front door while watching Billy plot new information onto the large map. Captain America, standing next to Billy, is reading the grid coordinates from a handful of papers.

After finishing their marking of the map, both of the Green Berets turn and face the pilots, some of whom are seated, others lying prone and a couple standing over a card game. Billy calls attention by loudly clearing his throat. I'm not sure who is going to present this briefing. They both have papers in their hands and seem to be sharing the podium. I open the door and call the Kid and Toby in.

"Gentlemen! May we have your attention?" Billy's voice booms over the din of pilots occupied in their own projects. Shuffling continues while the pilots put away their distractions and sit up to prepare for a long day.

"Today we will be doing a flip-flop of teams into this area." He points to a newly black outlined grid area. "Going in will be a two American and four indigenous man team. Coming out is a three and three team."

A pair of Americans dressed in sterile uniforms with faces camouflaged steps from the radio room.

Stanton retrieves several glossy photos from a briefcase which are of the LZ for this mission. A flip-flop, or exchange of teams, on a CCN mission is rare, very dangerous, and only done when there's been good success in the mission so far and more intelligence is needed.

"The new team," looking over at the two men in their non-regulation uniforms that hopefully will deceive any NVA trail watchers that see them on their secret mission, "is Anaconda. The team coming out is Rattler. Both teams will be up three-five one-zero, call-sign," Looking down on a small piece of paper crumpled in his hand, "Fancy Alpine Indio for Rattler and Jaguar Melon Oscar for Anaconda." He then nods to Captain America.

The blond-headed Mission Launch Team Commander continues where Billy has left off. "The primary LZ is marked in this first series of photos you are being handed." Billy has now stepped forward and given the Lancer lead part of the stack of photos. "If you notice in the northeast corner of the clearing there appears to be several abandoned thatched huts. Rattler is going to be there for the pick-up. Those huts, we believe, were used by an NVA engineer group while working on the road just to the east of the LZ several months ago."

A moan is heard when the mention of the possible NVA living in the area is mentioned. The moans are coming from the slick pilots in the front of the room, loud enough that I'm able to hear it while standing back by the door.

Captain Stanton continues his briefing on the LZs. "We believe that there may be one or two men left for road security. Other than that, the area hasn't shown much activity in the past six weeks and Rattler says there has been no movement in the LZ or around the huts for the last forty-eight hours. What we would like is to get the flip-flop completed as close to the tree line . . . ah," then stepping forward he takes one of the photos and holds it in front of him, "lets see, ah . . . right here."

Though I can't see the specific location from my position, I'm able to gather that the slick pilots are not too happy with the pre-chosen location.

"On your photos, it's marked with the red grease pencil." Looking around at the pilots before him, he questions, "Everyone see the spot?"

Heads bob as the pilots, though not liking it, know where they have to land to complete this mission.

"We will also do two dummy inserts prior to landing. They will be in these two LZs," he says.

Billy hands out two more photos and the moans are repeated.

"I don't care where you land in these LZs, just hold on the ground for at least ten seconds."

"You can bet it will be the quickest ten seconds ever recorded," says one of the Lancer pilots, while the others chuckle.

"I understand your feelings, but we want to put some Nightingales out in these two LZs." Then looking at the radio room door as Blaster walks in dressed in a sterile uniform, he asks, "Got a weather check?"

Blaster is a gruff looking Green Beret that has more than once proven his ability to lead men under the most trying of conditions. He never talks about it, but he has won a

Distinguished Service Cross and a half dozen Silver Stars. Blaster answers the question so all can hear.

"Covey says the weather is clear with light winds." Then with his typical gung ho attitude he adds, "Rattler is ready for pickup, and the area seems cold. Let's get this show on the road."

"One last item," Stanton interjects as the pilots start to move around restlessly, "We also want one dummy insertion in an LZ after, ah . . . only after the new team is on the ground."

Billy now hands out the last photo he's been holding. "Once again," then looking over to Captain Stanton for approval, "we don't care where you land in this one, just hold for ten seconds."

Stanton nods his head affirmative with Billy's last comment.

Billy then continues. "Covey's on station and will give you a positive on the LZs, though we do not want to overfly any of the LZs. We want a straight in and straight out flight path. So, you men will have to rely on the Griffins for spotting."

If the slick pilots have any complaints, they would be blind inserts, bad weather, and the need to use strings. It appears the weather is good, and there's been no mention of strings. They will have to live with the blind inserts today.

Billy doesn't stop as he turns and points to the top of the map with the call-signs and frequencies written in black grease pencil.

"Covey's up on two-four-three two-zero UHF, call-sign Shiny-Tooth-Foxtrot One-Eight. As you heard, the weather's clear. Covey's got Spads and fast movers from Hillsborough on stand by, though I doubt we'll need them."

Looking directly at Jimbo, he says, "Griffins will be using Carpet Station for a call-sign, and the slicks will use Brown Cork." He scans the room as the pilots busily write down the information just given to them. As a majority of the bowed heads raise up, he asks, "Now, any questions?"

The Lancer captain raises his hand, apparently not used to the informal briefings we have here at CCN.

"Yes?" Captain Stanton replies.

"The last LZ, ah . . . the ah . . . dummy . . . ah is there going to be a Nightingale device left in there as well?"

I can tell, not only from the talk I had with W1 Allen, that this guy is a shithead, but he has asked a very good question. I look over and see Allen is busy writing notes as he sits behind the captain.

Before Stanton can answer, Blaster speaks up, "No." Stepping in front of both Billy and Stanton, Blaster continues, "I'll be in Chalk Three and will land in the first LZ and throw out a Nightingale. Chalk Four will land in the second dummy LZ and a *bac si* will throw out the Nightingale." Then directed at the Lancer captain, he continues, "Lead, you and Chalk Two will land in the primary LZ. Once Chalk Two is clear, he will call and Chalk Three will land in the last LZ. We'll hold for ten in the last LZ as well, then get the fuck home. Remember Three and Four, hold for ten seconds so the NVA think we're doing something."

Stanton adds, "Once all inserts are completed, Griffins will take the package over to Song Ba and hold 'til we get a team okay." Then looking across the room, "Any more questions?"

Allen speaks up without being recognized, "The team is split into One and Two, with you in Three and a *bac si* riding in Four, right?"

Billy nods his head in agreement, with the others standing before us, then adds, "Four will be the chase ship with the *bac si*, if there are any problems remember to use Four to extract any wounded."

The pilots mumble between themselves, but no hands are raised. It appears the briefing is over.

We all quickly, and surprisingly quietly, depart the room, each headed for his aircraft with the mission possibilities resting heavily in our minds. Missions like this can only go one of two ways. Smoothly or a goat fuck that turns worse as each minute passes. It comes down to luck. Any of the three dummy LZs can have an NVA trail watcher sitting in it waiting for some ungainly helicopter to land. The team being extracted may be under surveillance, and as the helicopters come in and make the swap things can get ugly in a hurry. If the shit hits the fan before the swap, we still have to go into the primary LZ and try to make the exchange or at least pick up the team on the ground. If, in the last LZ, the helicopter gets hit, we are now trying to pull an emergency extract with an aircraft loaded and a team that is tired from their week of hiding from the enemy, we're really pushing our luck. What I would give for one extra Huey.

If the whole swap goes off quickly and without a hitch, it's a beautiful sight. Surely the swap was well planned and run with the precision of the Rolex that I'm wearing on my right wrist. From the air, especially in a Covey, it's like a ballet. The green gangling helicopters swooping into the LZ and after a brief ten second interval, they hop back into the air and leapfrog to their next LZ. Timing is critical in these missions, as are the directions the Griffins will provide the Huey pilots as they fly blindly at ninety knots toward a small hole that will quickly devour them and, hopefully, release them unscathed. The primary LZ is like a flower, with a couple of awkward bumble bees lighting for a second then stumbling home.

Chapter 22

I climb into my aircraft and watch Thompson walk around to my left with the main rotor blade in his hand. I wave for him to swing it free. He does, then runs over to the nose of our Cobra to stow the blade tie-down strap. I quickly go through an abbreviated preflight check list. Thompson is sitting in the front seat writing the different frequencies on the left-hand canopy window. Thompson, like all the others, isn't as neat as Klien. When hung over, like this morning, I usually take it out on my front seater. Thompson's different, and though the black grease pencil writing is barely readable, I don't mind.

The flight to Laos is uneventful. After we repositioned to Quang Tri POL and then joined the flight of four Lancers over Camp J. J. Carroll, it has been more or less a sightseeing trip. The 175mm guns were firing when we flew past Carroll. We couldn't see or hear them, but the smoke rings left by the long barreled guns were clearly seen by our flight.

Jimbo has Leonard "The Lizard" Mock flying with him. Klien has Randy Hunt, which means they are the most inexperienced crew. After returning last night Rick gave Klien his check ride, then signed him off. No sooner had this happened then the Kid requests CCN in the morning. Flying in the third position, I have CWO 2 Dave Thompson with me. Goose Baker is on my wing with the W1 from Washington State, called Big Foot, in his front seat.

The flight to Quang Tri and now out to Laos has been a refresher course for Thompson. He just arrived in country from his tour as an instructor pilot at Fort Walters. His first tour, during

'67-68, was with the 1st Cav. He flew with the only other ARA unit in the Army, the 1st Cav's Blue Max of 2nd of the 20th ARA. During that tour, he flew Charlie model Huey gunships. He seems to be a competent pilot, and Rick said he did very well in his Cobra check ride.

The 2nd Platoon and, for that matter, all the Griffins have changed in the past few months. Whether it was Ripcord or just the normal rotation of old timers leaving and newbies coming into the unit, a flurry of new faces has been added. In the flight platoons, in the maintenance, and the support sections as well. The other day I stopped by Administration and found no one there I recognized. Special 4th Class Dozer has gone home. I'm sure that the new men are qualified, but it's not the same. Dozer answered my questions looking up from whatever he was doing at the time. His mop of long brown hair and unshaved face is missed in the hut. I'm sure the high standard of paper shuffling will also be missed.

I've watched boys come into the Griffins in their new crisp fatigues with the neat patches carefully sewed on, haircuts close to the skin and neatly trimmed, faces all clean shaven, without moustaches, and eyes that dart around alert to any new sight that they're eagerly soaking in as part of their Vietnam combat education. As time has eroded and faded the new look from the uniforms, it has washed away the young alert looks from the faces as well. Now they look tired, beaten and aged as if they were in the B movies, old faded B movies at that. With the monsoons coming, we'll get a rest in the number of hours we have to fly, but the stress of the missions being flown in less than ideal conditions will make up for the reduction in hours. It's a damned if you do, damned if you don't situation.

In less than ninety days, Jimbo will leave. Jimbo's orders are to Fort Leonard Wood. Jimbo is upset because his new assignment will not be a flying one. He'll be in a small ADA unit there. He's already tried to have the orders amended to get to Fort Bliss, or even Fort Rucker, so he can fly. Skip Verdine's orders are to report to Fort Bliss at the end of the month. He says he's not going to fly any more, but then he never flew any hot missions anyway. Killer's back in the States on leave and has sent me several postcards, all beautiful sunny beach scenes. Each had the message that he was bored and would be back in country early, because there was nothing for him to do at home.

Scoop Winston is no longer flying and, when I left this morning, he was stacking all the pocket books he had stuffed in his cubicle onto the platoon table. His remark as I passed him going out the door was, "Two and a wake up." Scoop's orders are to Hunter Army Airfield at Fort Stewart Georgia. He thinks he'll get into a Cobra unit there.

Doc Holiday is now completing his forty days make up, for time that he spent during his emergency leave home to see his father. The trip was longer than normal. The day before he was supposed to return his father died. At least he was able to see his father before he died. Since his return, he's taken on a different personality. He no longer goes down to the enlisted hootches late at night. I don't see or hear him leave the hootch in the dark hours to go smoke a joint. He goes to his cubicle and lies on his bed with his headphones on for hours at a time. We don't know if he's awake or asleep. Just the glow from the bright green hi-fi dials is all that's visible in the four-by-eight enclosure. Jimbo said he thinks he quit the marijuana though only time will prove this out. Frankly, I don't give a damn. He'll be out of Vietnam, and out of the Army soon, and I'll never see him again. He did get his registration for college completed, and he said that with two years left to complete, then law school, he should be a practicing attorney within five years. He came back with about twenty extra pounds that were quickly shed, and now, from a distance, he looks the same, just his actions are different.

Besides the ones gone, and going, the older pilots have now embraced Hunt and Klien. The Lizard will be the next AC, though he still doesn't act like he's ready to assume the responsibility to lead. Cool Poole is still waiting to take Jimbo's position, for the interim, though his afterhours activities are catching up with him. Cool has turned out to be more of a loner now that the realization of his upcoming command responsibility sinks in. Before Jimbo got his orders, Cool would only dispense bad news with the statement that "Jimbo said." Now the reality of the day that there will be no Jimbo to blame has hit home. Leadership is a lonely job, as one goes up the stairs, it gets lonelier and lonelier. I'm very happy being a warrant—this will never plague me. The unit is getting more commissioned officers worried about their careers rather than fighting the enemy. Not one of the new ones in the past month wants to fly CCN. It's a sign of the times. Over and over I hear, "I don't want to be the last son-of-a-bitch to die over here." Every time I hear it, I want to tell them to get the hell out of my country.

Klien has become what the Army wanted and his mother would never have dreamed of. He's a living, breathing, killing machine, moody when flights do not produce body counts, and irritable when targets are spotted and a FAC, or Command & Control bird, says to leave them alone. He's also daring to the point of dangerous when rolling in on targets. At some point, he'll need the shit scared out of him if he's to be snapped back into reality. He no longer writes his mother faithfully; in fact, she wrote the CO asking if he was okay. For several weeks, the Kid had to make the walk over to the CO's hut and deliver a letter addressed to his mother for the old man to see. His drinking has become worse than mine, and that's saying a lot. When not flying, he has a cigarette dangling out of his mouth and a beer can in one hand. Several nights, he passed out in the club only to be left there by the pilots rather than trying to manhandle him back to the hootch. His mother has no idea what is going to be arriving at her doorstep when the freedom bird opens it's doors and dumps him on the tarmac before her eyes. He may be too far gone now. Another wounded from the war, and this wound may not be the kind that can be healed with a few stitches and some gauze. This may be a bomb waiting to explode in a year or two. Wounds like this get no

Purple Hearts and will not be looked upon as honorable by others. His mean streak has developed from a youngster having good-natured fun to one of anger and viciousness. Jimbo talked to the old man expressing that the problem might exacerbate if he was allowed to extend for another six months. But like me, he'll find a way. As people leave, he'll be able to convince the replacements that he needs to stay. They will realize it would be better for the Army to leave him here than send someone who doesn't want to come to Vietnam to replace him.

Life goes on, yet it changes. I have found a way to extend; though I'm not going to until the first of February. I have a chance to go to the Condors of 2nd of the 17th Cav. I haven't told anyone but I know my plan will work. My friendship, though distant, with Captain Alfred Pratt down at Battalion has paid off. He has assured me, on several occasions, that he will get the paperwork signed without a hitch. He even agreed that it would not be wise to announce my intentions to other Griffins. So, when the day comes and my orders arrive, I'll just pack and be gone, with no fanfare. It's my style. Saying goodbye to men you have grown to trust and love is very difficult for me just as I'm sure it is for others. Usually during the last days, pilots promise to write once they get home and get settled, but I'm not going back to the US. Then the months go by and you never hear from them again. It will take years before they reunite. I saw it with my father after World War II. He didn't get in contact with his squadron mates until twenty years or so after the war. Then it was done by word of mouth, by accident, and by a few members of his unit that put in the time to try and locate the lost souls. After one or two reunions, Dad said the hell with it, he didn't have time to listen to war stories that now seem inflated and he didn't like remembering those that he lost. I'm sure in time we helicopter pilots will be like that.

"Well, what do you think of flying up in I Corps?" I ask my co-pilot, after I've shown him the locations of previous firebases on our trip to the border.

"When I was with the Cav, we came up here during Tet '68

for Operation Pegasus. So I've flown the area from Hue to Khe Sanh for several months. Though, we didn't get into A Shau as our battery was the first to return to An Khe after the operation. Plus there are many new bases, though most of them are smaller than before."

"Shiney Tooth Foxtrot One-Eight, this is Carpet Station Lead, over." Jimbo is making the initial contact to the Covey who is flying somewhere to our west.

The answer, though hard to understand because of the static, comes quickly. "Go Station Lead."

"Roger One-Eight we're at Lao Bao with the package, over."

All of us are now spread out to prevent any air bursts from the big guns from taking out more than one aircraft. We are now flying across the border and the veil of secrecy closes around us as we now become part of the secret war no one talks about, but many know of.

"Roger Station, continue up the blue. I'll meet you at the holding point."

With that transmission, we settle back for the next fifteen minutes of flying above the wide green valley that runs parallel and to the north of the Song Be. Though the river runs generally west to east through this section of Laos, it has many small twists and turns as it makes it trip toward the border. Once at the imaginary line, it will turn sharply south flowing at the base of Co Roc Ridge.

Just to the north and snaking along the center of the valley is the now abandoned QL9 that has been engulfed with growth because of the inactivity of any traffic since the closure of Khe Sanh village years ago. To our right, the northern panhandle of Southern Laos is deceiving with it's gently rolling hills until they rise up and reach the Plain of Jars in the heart of Laos. Though covered with lush green low scrub or single canopy trees, its base is limestone rock that was formed millennia ago and has provided a natural barrier for inhabitants to move in and farm. With the NVA using this area for their north to south transport of men, goods and materials, those that still eke out a life here are in varying degrees sympathetic to the Communists. If not because of ideology, for survival.

"Carpet Station, One-Eight has you in sight."

The Covey is not to our west, so I immediately scan the skies to the north hoping to see the small airplane. From our south comes a fixed-wing swooping up from the escapement. It's the newer model FAC, an OV-10 Bronco, which I didn't know the Coveys were now using.

"One-Eight's got a new ride," one of the slick pilots comments.

"Roger, we are starting to convert over to these high performance models."

As he passes before our flight he does an aileron roll with a quick snap back toward our flight after his roll out.

"It's agile and we've got more visibility."

He banks sharply to the west and gets down to business.

"Okay Station Lead, Fancy Alpine Indio is ready for pickup. We can let down here, and you can proceed north through the draw along the brown to our November."

Upon calling the let down, all of us start to reduce power, while starting a gradual turn to the north. The slicks are slowing, getting their needed separation for the insertions.

"Station Lead and Two will go ahead and get a positive on the LZs," Jimbo announces on UHF.

After a short pause, he comes up on VHF with, "Sneaky, you and Goose hold back and bring in the package. I'll try to get in position to lead them in."

I quickly answer with a double squelch break. I then reduce power so I'm beside the last two Hueys. I want to have a good view of the whole flight. I slide west of their staggering flight as Goose does the same on the other side.

Jimbo and the Kid have accelerated past the flight and are headed low level toward the point where we'll start the turn back to the west for the insertions. All the LZs in the XD584514 area are in a slightly off-line stagger to the north of a small gently rising mountain, intersecting the depression of an abandoned road traveling to the north. Somewhere I remember this track, which someone calls a road, to be labeled as 547 on some map. To the east of the road, on the rolling hill tops, are the first two dummy LZs. After leaving the second LZ, the flight will still fly westward crossing the barely visible track until we reach a tear-dropped LZ, where we will be doing the flip flop. This LZ's long axis runs to the northwest and from what I could make out on my map will be falling away from the exchange point, adding difficulty to an already difficult landing sight. I wonder why we didn't come in from the west in order to land into the wider part of the LZ. Once the swap is completed, the final LZ, where no Nightingale will be left, is a large field of fresh elephant grass growing through a previously blackened napalmed area. It's large and wide open, offering many enemy fields of fire. After overflying this LZ, each aircraft will proceed to a small stream before turning back to the south and flying over the southern small mountain that splits this valley into a small bowl with a pimple of a mountain in it's center. If there are any North Vietnamese Army trail watchers in this valley, some of them must be positioned on this pimple of a mountain. Though not tall, nor having any one site that can command an overall view of the valley, three well-positioned men could see any activity within a three-mile radius. We will be operating within this radius and as far as I can estimate, the NVA will be as well. This explains all the dummy inserts and the Nightingales.

"Station Lead, the first LZ is to your nine on top of the second hill." Then after squelch breaks from both Jimbo and the Kid, the Covey continues with, "At your ten, on the small hill, is LZ Two."

"Roger One-Eight, we've got a positive."

I look out to the horizon and see our two Cobras off to our two o'clock position now starting to make a turn to the east.

"Station Three bring the package over to the Echo now and get low level."

"Roger Lead," I answer, as I watch the lead Huey start its turn to the east and descend it's last four or five hundred feet to meet the rolling hills surrounding the valley.

"Cork flight, let's get into position with a forty-second separation," a heavy Boston accented voice calls.

Toby Allen is now exercising his control over the flight, either with or without the approval of the captain with the scarred forehead. After numerous squelch breaks, the first two Hueys slow while the last two fly past their wingman. In less than a minute, the four aircraft are in the proper order for the upcoming LZs. Their separation is not complete but once they turn back to the west, they will get what they think they'll need.

"Cork Three, start a left-hand one-twenty with a two-six-zero roll out."

Jimbo has now met us and is slightly above the flight so that he can direct the first two slicks in. From his position he can see all the aircraft, as well as the first two LZs.

I slow down trying to hold back further allowing the Huey flight to stretch it's formation and still be covered by one of the Griffins. The Kid has flown in behind the first aircraft and is off to it's five o'clock position. His position will allow him to pounce on any enemy willing to risk his life taking a shot at the plump green helicopter now flying at tree top level.

"Three start your flare. LZ's the top of this hill."

There is no verbal response from the slick crew just the noticeable change in attitude as it's talked into a never before seen field by the Cobra from behind.

"Turn five degrees to the north and bleed off more airspeed Three." Jimbo is still talking the ship down. "Cork Four ease to the right of Three's flight path, your LZ will be on a heading of two-eight-zero." Then before Four can reply. "Three, your on short final . . . it's at your one."

"Got it!" is the answer.

The first helicopter descends out of view. The long count down begins now as we all wait and hope for a quiet departure.

"Four, turn to your eleven and start your flare once you break the crest of this hill."

Jimbo is now leading the second aircraft toward it's landing, while the Kid has started a tight orbit over the Huey out of our sight. This one will be an easier LZ. Once Chalk Four flies over the occupied LZ, the pilot will be able to look down at the small knoll he'll be landing on.

Lastly, both Chalk One and Two pass over the Huey sitting in the LZ with Goose and I lagging in an extended trail position. The Kid is several hundred feet above us watching over Cork Three like a cat guarding its kitten's first excursion out in the wilds to play.

"Four, it's at your twelve on the knoll," Jimbo announces.

"Got it," the noise of the rotor blades is drowning out the pilot's response. "Four's on final."

Within seconds we hear, "Four's down."

Once again we all count as the slick waits for the Nightingale to be thrown from the aircraft and the ten second delay to be completed.

"Three's lifting . . . ah . . . all's quiet."

With just the noise of the rotor blades beating the air, the Huey suddenly appears on the knoll ahead of me. The Kid is in a tight left-hand turn to our ten o'clock as he circles around.

"Four's out!"

"Roger Four we have you" I call from my trailing position. In an operation like this, the number of radio calls can get confusing. Things must be said quickly, to the point, and with proper call-signs.

Jimbo now calls out to Chalk One, "Lead, take a heading of two-zero-five. Three, lag a bit or you'll overfly the insert."

At the same time, I hear The Lizard on FM calling to the team, "Alpine Indio, Carpet Station Lead is one out with the package."

A whispered voice returns his call, "Roger we're ready." Then, after a hesitation it adds, "We have the panels out and the

LZ is cold. Repeat cold!" Though this is the first contact the flight has made with the team, I'm sure the One-Zero of Anaconda's team has told him we're inbound, just as I'm sure he advised him of the dummy insert's progress.

Jimbo is now flying ahead of the flight of Hueys rushing to the main LZ so that he'll be in position to properly direct them into the tear drop shaped clearing on the western side of a small rise.

"Brown Cork Lead, turn to your twelve-thirty and the LZ is on the back of the hill before you." Jimbo is now slowing down letting the first of the squat green Hueys catch up to him.

"Roger." Allen responds.

"Start your flare Lead."

"Flaring!"

Then after what seems like an eternity, the transport helicopter slowly waddles and shakes as it flies over the narrow road used only by the enemy, then it settles out of my sight.

"Lead's down. Two watch your tail rotor, the LZ's slope is steeper then we thought."

"Roger Lead. Two's on short final."

Once again I'm able to watch the white blade tops giving an illusion of a translucent saucer holding the squatty green helicopter easily over the track.

"Lead's out with three."

Though not as close as they appear, from my angle behind them, the highlights seem to meld together, then separate as the second Huey is enveloped into the LZ.

"Two's down."

"Continue to the two-eight-five Lead," Covey calls out. "Chalk Three once over the LZ turn to two-eight-five. Your LZ will be in one-half of a klick."

Double squelch breaks are heard then, "Two's out with three."

"Roger," calls out Jimbo, "continue your heading two-eight-five. Three, you can start your flare at this time."

For the first time I can see the LZ where they have just

executed the flip-flop. It's a tight tear drop with a very narrow exit path to the northwest. Though now overgrown, it is obvious that at one time there were cultivated crops grown in here.

"Three, the Lima Zulu is at your eleven on the rise before you."

"Tally ho."

The mission is almost completed and we're all happy that so far there's been no gunfire.

"Three's on short final."

"Sneaky's got ya." Jimbo calls.

Staggered out before us is the flight of the three Hueys having completed their missions with the Kid flying off to their north trying to provide protection. Jimbo is closing in on the flight of three from their seven.

The time on the ground for the slick crew and Blaster must seem like years. Though it's supposed to be only ten seconds, I'm sure that Blaster will make sure that it's a bit longer. Blaster is not busy with a Nightingale in this LZ, so he's sitting on the floor with his rifle poised to return fire if they take one round.

"Three's coming out," is finally called out.

In my left orbit I watch the Huey spring off the ground and, rather than a max performance takeoff, the pilot is low leveling across the LZ quickly gaining speed. At what appears the last possible moment he executes a quick cyclic climb to clear the trees to the western side of the LZ, then settles back down, hugging the tree tops as the green machine rushes away from any possible danger.

I call up to the Covey, though I am sure he has observed this last dummy insert, "One-Eight, Three's clear and we're headed to the blue."

I look out and see the point ahead where the trees seem brighter and thicker. They grow in a narrow, snake-like meandering line before us. Hidden below these trees, is the stream that we are using to determine when we'll break to the south and hopefully escape this mission's possible deadly ending.

"Roger Carpet Station," then after a moment he adds, "Proceed to the holding point and we'll wait for a team okay."

"Roger, you copy that Cork Lead?" Jimbo asks.

The multiple squelch breaks let us all know that each has heard and knows that the mission is not over until we get the release from Covey. Usually the team on the ground will not release the Covey, or give a team okay, until ten to fifteen minutes after they have been on the ground and not only got a feel of the terrain, but have grasped the situation. The team certainly has already moved to a location not far from where they disembarked from the aircraft. They should have picked an area that offers them a defensive position with both concealment and the ability to view the surrounding area. If the NVA were close by, Anaconda team members will know quickly. If, after ten minutes or so, they feel comfortable enough to move, and there's no enemy activity, then they will come up on a pre-arranged frequency and break squelch twice. No talk, no ten count for a radio check. If they have to talk then there's trouble. The ten minute time frame has more to do with the amount of time we have left on station. If they are in trouble, we will have to do an immediate extraction because our fuel is running low. The waiting for the okay to start the insertion, the insertion, and now the wait, means we'll all have low level fuel lights blinking on our return to Quang Tri.

We have all come together over QL 9 in a large orbit. Not only are we far from being in a formation, but our altitudes vary from aircraft to aircraft. The Griffins are on alert, watching for any gunfire that may reach up to the slicks. These next few minutes are the toughest. If we're not released, it means a Prairie Fire and a hot extraction. In all my time working for CCN, only once have we ever been called back and it wasn't a shit sandwich. That day it turned out that as the team jumped from the hovering Huey one of the grunts broke his leg. So the emergency extraction was done in a cold LZ.

"Station Lead, One-Eight, over."

"Go ahead One-Eight." Jimbo's voice is relaxed and we are all expecting to be released for the trip back to the MLT.

"Get the package back over here right away. We have a Prairie Fire. Jaguar Melon is needing an immediate extract and they have casualties."

I've heard nothing on FM, so the team must have called its situation in via the secure radio. No telling what they've told Covey.

The news of the team being in trouble is like a bucket of cold water being thrown on us. First the shock of the news, then the feeling of dread overcoming us as adrenalin starts to rush into our bodies knowing that what we had all hoped would not have happened, has. This is a good news, bad news scenario. All four of us have full complements of rockets and turret ammo, which is good news. The bad news comes in two forms. First is the fuel situation of the aircraft. Though not critical right now, if the extraction doesn't go quickly then we have a serious problem. The second issue, and to me much more critical, is the condition of the team on the ground. If they already have injuries then they were not only observed during the insertion but their location has been compromised as well. The injuries will mean it will take longer to extract them as they will not be as mobile. CCN teams in Laos do not announce injuries and get an immediate extraction unless the injuries are mission debilitating. The multiple injuries indicate that they were hit hard and fast.

"We're on the way. Cork Three and Four will do the extraction." Jimbo is already giving out the orders for the flight.

Before he can continue, I squeeze the red communication button on the cyclic back past the intercom's first stop to send out the double squelch breaks for affirmative.

Jimbo continues his orders. "Lead, you and Two hold a high orbit to the Sierra-Echo from the Lima Zulu." Then before any of the slick pilots can respond, "One-Eight what's the situation?"

"Ah . . . it appears that a large enemy force has moved to the northwestern end of the LZ. The team has taken heavy automatic fire from at least two locations. I have them moving to the Echo, hopefully to extract them from the brown."

This must be serious if the team isn't going back to the landing LZ. The road is only one-hundred meters to the east, which may prove to be in our favor if they can get there before the NVA can reach the crest of the hill. If the NVA make the crest, they'll be able to shoot down on the Hueys trying to go in for the pickup. I can hear the slick pilots now. I surely wouldn't want to be landing on the road. This is getting worse and worse.

If we can catch the NVA in the abandoned LZ, we can nail them all and create an instant military cemetery minus the well-manicured lawns and the neat little line of white religious markers. We Griffins are hoping for this, catching NVA in the open will mean a turkey shoot for us, and relief for the team.

"Station Lead, hold the package to the south of the mountain. When I get the team to the road, you can bring the slicks in for a pickup. Ah . . . at this time they have four WIAs. Hold on . . . I've got Sandy calling."

The Covey has laid out his plan of attack. This was a pre-arranged alternate extraction point. Flying with the Covey is Valentino, so he has had long talks with the team in the pre-insertion briefing that the flight crews do not attend for security reasons. Valentino will be thinking the same as the One-Zero. This is one of the smartest moves the command structure has made. Allowing a fellow recon member to fly over the situation to act as an extra set of eyes and give insight on the planning of the team's ground movement.

"Roger, we'll hold."

"Station Lead, have your flight move to the Whiskey. I'll have a set of Sandys working from the eastern side of the hill to the road."

The Covey is now playing chess with all the pieces at his disposal. The pawns, though I would never tell it to their face, are the six men on the ground. The Covey is in effect the king with little offensive power but with the ability to call the other pieces into play. I like to think of the Cobras as the Queens of battle. Not because artillery is taught this, at least in the Army's view, but we are able to move any direction quickly and strike the enemy with killing precision. If needed, and Jimbo proved this months ago, we can land and pick someone up. There's a story of a Marine AH-1J, a Sea Cobra, that landed in an LZ southwest of Hill 55 near Da Nang and had a wounded Marine strapped to his ammo bay door in order to save the Marine's life. The Cav is known for landing a Cobra and flying fellow crew members out to safety hanging onto ammo bay doors. In another case, a Marine flew out of a fog shrouded hill with two Marine pilots riding on the stub wings. The Marines have glorified this story to add that the extra pilots were shooting their pistols as they left the LZ. Another Marine told me it was the same Marine aviator flying the mission each time. Knowing the Marines as well as I do, I believe it, but I'm alone among the Griffins.

The Bishops are the fast movers that we use when the anti-aircraft fire is too heavy. They can only move in one of two directions and usually are slow to react to the small changes within the battle plan. The Spads and Sandys flying the WW II A1-Es are the Rooks. Able to move in, hit the target and have the lateral freedom that the King, or Queen, enjoys. Last but not least are the Knights, or the Hueys. In more than one way, the odd shaped helicopter's movement is like a Knight. It moves along in one direction, with a last minute change, sometimes as much as ninety degrees, to get into their appointed LZ. This is the chess board, or at least the board from our point of view. Our goal is to check-mate the opposition, the NVA, and safely return home.

Covey has the pieces at his disposal. It now depends on the enemy and the team's ability to move quickly to ensure the extraction will be competed without further injuries.

"Station, keep your heads up, I've got Top Cat Three-Three and Three-Nine in position to roll in." The Air Force FAC says, then switching to FM. "Jaguar Melon you up?"

"Roger. Got you five by five," calls the raspy voice of one of the team members, who's no longer on the secure radio.

"Okay Melon, I want you to hold at the crest of the hill 'til I'm able to clean out any possible problems by the brown."

"Roger, we'll hold, but hurry up. We've got one with a sucking wound."

With that said we now know that the men were hit hard. A sucking chest wound means that they have to carry him which will slow them up.

"Heads down, Sandy's inbound."

From our location we are not able to see the Douglas aircraft enter into its ordnance run. While scanning the skies to the east of the hill, I see the first of the A1s fly into view. It's belly is all I can see as the aircraft is in a climbing left turn, but as usual they're low. They know their business and, after a tour of flying them in Laos, these guys could teach gunnery for any Air Force school.

Minutes seem to be ticking away as quickly as blood draining from a wounded body. We are getting to the point that lack of fuel will demand, our return to Quang Tri. If so, it will put the extraction back by at least an hour or so. That would only help the NVA gather more resources as well as set up their plan on how to stop the extraction. We've got to get this show on the road.

After four passes of the lumbering fixed-wing, we hear good news.

"Jaguar Melon I'm holding back the fixed-wing. Can you proceed down to the brown?"

"Roger, we are on the move. We'll be ready in less than ten."

Hell, if these guys can make it to the road in ten minutes they are moving. Hopefully, the wounded isn't an American. He'd be heavy. I wouldn't like to have to carry someone through all that brush, traveling the distance they must in a short period of time, and having the NVA all around just waiting to catch the team in a cross fire.

"Okay Station, come on over and let's help these guys get to the brown."

The Covey calls us over to provide a low level overhead cap

on the moving team. This will allow them to move faster because if anyone opens up on them, we'll be right there to take the enemy out of the picture.

"Roger we're on the way," Jimbo says on VHF, "Sneaky, hold back and escort the slicks over when I call."

"Roger." I answer.

The next six or seven minutes seem to take forever. We're in an orbit to the south of the hill to prevent the enemy from seeing we have the package nearby. It also prevents me, Goose, and the slick drivers, from seeing what is going on. But the scene is painted for us by the different radio calls. It's turning into a real shit sandwich, with Anaconda as the spread.

"Got dinks to the November!" comes Kid's voice. "Fuck it. I got 'em." He's found the enemy and, without waiting for approval, is dispatching them.

"Jaguar, this is Carpet Station. I've got you in sight. I'm bringing the package over—get ready. You're less than twenty mikes from the brown."

"Fucking dinks all over. Get the package over here!" It's the Kid again, this time more excited. But our newest AC has found his element, and it sounds like he's taken to it quite well.

"Let's do it Sneaky." Jimbo is on UHF, no time for VHF now. "Bring over the package in a long trail. Cork Four, try to hug the mountain. When you see the road, go low level to the western side. I'll call your flare."

The *Bac Si* in Chalk Four, a Wilson twin, must now be at the ready to receive the wounded, and to pump out a few rounds as well.

At the same time Mock calls on FM, "Jaguar package is inbound. Get smoke ready."

"Roger, smoke on your call."

"Lets go Three and Four. We've got you," I call as two Hueys break away from the large orbit turning to the northeast and the looming hill before them. "Goose, let's stay to the east of them. I'll have Four, you take Three."

"Sneaky, we'll have their Whiskey. It will be a straight November run in and straight out with an eastern break and low level to the hills. We'll come out the same place we started into the dummy LZs. Got it?" Jimbo says, knowing that if we had more time, we would have come in from the north, picked up the team, and headed south trying to get behind the hill as soon as possible for protection.

"Got it Griffin," the Lancer pilot calls, then adds, "You'll have to direct us through all this."

"You got it," Mock answers.

"We're at the trees," I call. The Huey is now racing at one hundred plus knots into an unseen LZ.

I cross the brown and turn sharply to the north. Out my left canopy, I see the Huey starting a left-hand bank following my lead. We are now past the mountain and he can surely see the other two Cobras to his ten o'clock. He is also thinking that with the wounded he'll have to take extra time in the LZ while the men are lifted into the ship. All the while he'll be sitting on a road with the enemy trying to climb over the crest of the small rise to his west. The mettle of this crew will be tested today.

"They're at your eleven . . . Ah . . . start . . . "

While on FM, Mock calls, "Jaguar Melon pop smoke! Repeat pop smoke."

". . . slowing down . . . Three, slow it down . . . Ah . . . "

"Smoke's out." At our eleven thirty, we see red smoke rising out of the scrub.

"Got bloody red at twelve," comes a call from one of the slick's crew with the slapping of the rotor blades loudly popping in the background.

"Roger, bloody red."

"Affirmative on that, Station," the team One-Zero seems to be calm though he has been wounded and is one step from a major disaster.

"Taking fire! Two o'clock! Shit!"

"Goddamn!"

The Huey lands in a large swirl of dust, small grass and the red smoke all coming together to obscure the rescue bird.

"Four's down. Plenty of fire from two and three o'clock."

The slick pilot is still excited. In a few more seconds, he'll have to lift out of the small dust bowl he's created and fly through a hail of gunfire all aimed at ending his flying career.

As we fly by the resting green helicopter, I am firing rockets along the east side of the road. Not aiming at specific targets, I'm putting down suppressive fire. Just before I make my break to the right, Jimbo calls that he's inbound. I abruptly yank the cyclic and grab a handful of collective trying to quickly regain altitude and get back into position so that I'll be able to cover the Huey's departure. During our rocket pass, Dave fired the nose turret only a few short bursts, so someone has taught him the need to conserve the turret ammo for emergencies.

"Three's on short," the second Huey AC calls out.

Before I'm able to get back into position I hear, "Four's out with three." As I hear this, though I do not have the altitude I want, I execute a tight cyclic turn while pushing as much right pedal as I can.

"Taking fire from three o'clock." A voice that I cannot distinguish as coming from Three or Four.

"We're hit! We're hit! Ah . . .   Going down!"

Though we're out of trim I'm able to roll out in front of Goose and watch the last Huey as it starts it's convulsive tremors just before setting down in the dissipating cloud of smoke. Is he the one hit, or is it Three? I'm not the only one who doesn't know.

"Who's taking fire?"

"Who's down?"

"Four's taking fire at three, . . . ah we're still up." In the background the rapid clatter of the M-60 machine guns is overshadowing the pilot's voice.

"Down! We're down. AC's hit. Help!" says another voice now screaming into the radios, which must be from Chalk Three.

I've overflown the LZ and am now catching up to Chalk

Four. Chalk Four has crossed the track and is gaining airspeed while heading for the relative safety of the eastern slopes that might be able to afford him some cover from all the NVA in the valley now shooting at the aircraft disturbing their peace and serenity. Jimbo is turning toward me and flying back to the LZ and to the aircraft in trouble.

"I'm breaking!" The Kid yells.

"Got ya. We're inbound." Goose calls.

"Lancer's down. Ah . . . its tail boom is bent to fuck." Hunt is advising the rest of the flight on VHF.

"Taking fire, eleven o'clock." Goose calls then adds, "Take that you fuckhead."

The mission is getting personal for everyone.

"One-Eight, Station Lead. We've got a bird down in the LZ." Jimbo's authority is taking control of the rapid fire remarks from the other two Griffin ACs. Then before the Covey can answer, Jimbo's switched over to FM. "Jaguar, what's going on?"

While on UHF, the Lizard is calling, "Brown Cork Three, over? Cork Three, can you transmit?"

"Christ, the aircraft's broke, but I can see guys around it," a voice calls.

"Station, get the other slicks over here and get us out." A voice that sounds like the One-Zero calls. Then he gives us the information we need. "We got the crew out, two hit but I think they'll make it, over."

"All right, get ready. Ah . . . We have the package on the way over." Jimbo then goes from the FM to UHF. "Cork Lead, bring your aircraft over. We'll pick you up at the brown. Be advised plenty of small arms."

A voice of indecision now answers, "Ah . . . Station, is the LZ still . . . "

Interrupting the transmission, a Boston twang overrides the weak voice. "Station we're on the way," then without changing to intercom, we all hear the change of controls from a scared captain to the young warrant, "I've got the goddamn thing, let's get over there and get 'em out. Ah . . . Station you'll have to direct us in."

"No problem, just get low and fast as you come up the brown. Expect fire from everywhere." Then Jimbo calls to our flight on VHF, "Alright, we'll need to get them in and out without any more losses. Sneaky, where are you?"

I've stayed with Chalk Four and we're now on the eastern side of the valley hugging the gently rolling hills while the Huey before me escapes any possible dangers by flying at one-hundred plus knots.

"We're southeast of your location."

"Okay, if the place is clear have the slick climb out and you come back over here." Adding to the rest of the flight, "Two and Four, go get Cork Lead and two."

I call to the multi-green colored Huey flying to my ten o'clock, "Cork Three, Station Four, over."

"Go Three."

"I've got to go back to the Lima Zulu. You need to climb out and I suggest orbit over the holding point."

"Ah . . . I'm coming up . . . give me a minute."

The Huey breaks into a steep cyclic climb leaving the comfort of the low fast envelope he's been using to escape any possible enemy gunfire.

On VHF I call, "Jimbo I'll be over there in a minute once this guy gets some altitude."

I can only watch as the Huey makes it's climb out of the valley to relative safety and then we'll return to what is proving to be a goat fuck.

After what has seems like hours, the silence is broken by the call from Mock to the other Lancers, "Cork flight, do a couple three-sixties until we're ready."

I know the slick pilots don't like killing time in Laos doing low level three-sixties. Even the Griffins would rather not kill time low level flying. Either we have a target or will search one out, but just to kill time waiting for a hot extraction doesn't set well with most pilots.

Simultaneously, on two different radios, the Lancer rogers Mock's request as Jimbo calls to the Covey, "One-Eight you need to get hold of White Dover Bravo and get more aircraft. We're low on fuel. If we don't get them out in this pass, we'll have to RTB."

"Station Lead, I've called in the situation, and there is a request for a launch at this time. Do you want to have the Sandys make some passes first?"

Jimbo's answer is anticipated. "No, it's all small arms and I think we can handle it. Our problem is fuel."

Seeing the Huey climb through two-thousand feet, I know he's as safe as he can be out here in Laos, so I call, "Cork Four, we're breaking away." There's no point in telling him where I'm going, he knows.

The intermingled squelch breaks acknowledge that everyone has heard me.

"Jaguar, Station Lead, over."

"Go Station," the whispered but confident voice replies instantly.

"Ah . . . Jaguar you ready for pick up?" Jimbo asks a question that I'd bet my life on the answer.

"Roger, we're ready. Call for smoke."

"Roger Jaguar, Ah . . . be advised you'll come out four and four."

"Roger, four and four, we're ready."

"Roger Station Lead, four and four," the Bostoner repeats then adds, "You got that Two?"

Squelch breaks are heard. Though I'm sure there will be communication between the slicks on their unit VHF with regards to specifics of the pick up and the LZ.

"All right, listen up!" Jimbo is now setting up his plan. "When Sneaky gets over here, here's what we're going to do. Cork Lead will come up the brown with me and the Kid covering. When you make your pick up, do a one-eighty and come out the same way. Lead will be picking up four. Understand, four!" He waits for acknowledgment then continues with, "Lead when you start your lift out call, then Two will start his approach in. Two will pick up the last four. Stay to the right of the brown as you fly the in and out. Sneaky and Goose will bring in Two. Any questions?"

None are asked.

Though not knowing what the next five to seven minutes will bring, we all know that asking a bunch of questions now will not stop what must be done. Now is the time to get it completed before the NVA can group together and turn this into something worse than it is. We've lost one plane and have wounded. We do not need any more losses. The Hueys will be hard pressed to land and take-off with the added weight of extra men. Fuel is running low. The enemy is getting their act together. Who needs bullshit talk now, it's about action. Or as an old unit's motto said: deeds above words.

Covey comes on the air with what may be good news, but at this point it's just information. "Station Lead, One-Eight. White Dover is launching a package, though do not expect them for another forty-five minutes."

"Roger, One-Eight. We're going to give it one more try, and then we'll have to check on the fuel situation. If you want, you can run the Sandys in east to west to our November."

"Roger, I copy your pattern. We'll hold off to see if we need to provide cover if you have to go refuel."

Covey sees the probable need of close air support if we don't get the men out during this pass. I can understand Jimbo though. He believes we will get them out on this pass. It's the way Griffins think. Why let them stay on the ground longer? Just go in, hang your balls out in the open fire, and hopefully get them out, fly home, and tell another wonderful war story in the club tonight.

"You ready, Cork?"

"Let's do it!"

Toby seems excited now, though it's the exuberance of youth and the lack of mature thinking that gives him the gusto. After all, we are all but mortal souls. The Army has exploited their over-exuberance when enlisting the young warrants to fly helicopters.

"We're on the way." Then after a moment on FM, "Jaguar, get ready. We'll have the first one to you in two." Jimbo has started the extraction process.

There are several moments of hesitation, then, coupled with the sound of heavy gunfire, comes an answer, "Roger, it's getting warm down here. Call when you want smoke and be advised we're taking automatic fire from the Whiskey, over."

"Roger, dinks to the Whiskey," the Kid calls. I bet the Kid is grinning as he said this.

I've now come up on the two Hueys flying low level in a non-descript pattern getting ready for the flight up the road to their north and hopefully home to safety.

"We've got you in sight Cork. Go ahead and start your run."

Jimbo and the other two Cobras are whisking toward me and then, in an unplanned starburst pattern, the Cobras turn different directions. Two of them start their convergence on the single Huey now turning away from me and heading north.

"Roger Griffin, ah, we're on the way." Then, adding half-consciously on UHF, "Get on the controls lightly. I've got the aircraft unless I'm hit. You got that!"

Toby Allen is showing his mettle today and the captain with the scar has surely made it difficult for him. I wonder what will happen after the flight? You can rest assured, he has my vote to become a Griffin.

On FM, the call goes out to Anaconda and the Lancer crew down on the ground. "Jaguar, pop smoke."

This time an instant response, though the gunfire in the background is still heard by us all. "Roger, smoke's out!"

From my position, I can see smoke, purple I think, rising to the north and the two Griffins several hundred feet off the ground flying at over one-hundred fifty knots. The ship with the young Bostonian at the controls is no longer visible. He's at or below tree level. At this point, I would be too. The only thing that would bring me down is some dink throwing a grenade up into my flight path. I'd be that low.

"Tally Ho, goofy grape at eleven," Toby, on FM, calls.

"Roger, I've got goofy grape," Mock replies on FM.

"That's an affirmative," the team One-Zero answers.

"On final, ah . . . get ready." The young warrior is now in his element. "Ah . . . taking fire at two . . . three . . . Shit! Taking fire in the LZ. Get off the controls." Then, after a moment of dead silence, we hear, "Lead's down."

I hear the background noise of gunfire and have no way of knowing if it's incoming, outgoing, or both. But I'd bet it's both.

Then the wait. Everyone hears it because someone has a hot mike in the lead Huey.

"We've got four and are coming out."

Toby seems to have calmed down as the fire has grown more intense, it's like entering a hypnotic state where you do things without planning or thinking of the consequences. It helps that adrenalin has charged the body.

"Two, when you come in, make a one-eighty over Three's aircraft then land back at the tail. They're hunkered down next to the road in a small depression."

The young man from Boston would surely make his parents proud today. Though he ran the gauntlet of enemy fire going into the LZ, he never let his voice raise to an excited level. Can this be the same warrant I was talking to several hours ago about not being allowed to become an AC? Surely strapping oneself into a helicopter, changes some of these men from one-hundred and fifty pound teenagers into two-hundred and twenty pound John Waynes and Aldo Rays. Our country doesn't appreciate the one true resource we have. It's not oil, trees, coal, steel or, the miles of golden grain growing on the plains. No, it's the young men who display traits every day that can't be learned on the playground, in a small one-roomed classroom, or on Friday nights with the boys drinking beer and talking about Susie Q in the tight sweater. No, America's greatest resource is it's people and days like this prove it to me. It's a shame that the politicians, and generals that are really no longer soldiers but politicians in uniform, don't understand this. The few that do are shuffled off to some obscure assignment, or even retired early because their concern and care for their men is taken as a sign of weakness. And in a cold war, which Kennedy and the others have said we're in, there is no room for weakness, even for one of your best resources.

"Roger Lead, we're on the way in."

The slick I'm flying above turns abruptly to the north. This slick has two warrants in it, and there will not be the confusion of a hot mike on this ship, nor will there be the problems with the controls either. As a warrant you either fly CCN because you want to or you don't fly it. For the lieutenants and captains, it's a macho thing. They have to prove to the warrants that, as platoon leaders, the RLOs cannot only fly the missions but they can also lead them. This is done even though some of these guys couldn't find their asses with both hands and a map to work from.

"I'm on your four," I announce.

"Got your seven," Goose adds, though I'm sure the door gunners have kept the pilots informed of the location of the two Cobras flying above him.

"Taking fire! We're hit!"

"Shit! We're fucked!"

"Get off the controls."

The Huey coming out, is taking fire and it sounds like there may be a fight in the cockpit as well. Hopefully Toby will win.

"Kid, get in behind me. Fifty to the two o'clock!" Jimbo yells.

"I'm on you! Break left!"

The Kid yells as he's ready to fire rockets into the fifty's location.

"Two, there's a fifty at your eleven just before the Lima Zulu." Young Warrant Officer Allen is still weaving his magic, controlling the aircraft and directing the slicks.

"Got it. Go ahead with the smoke." The AC from the Huey

in front of me has lowered his aircraft right into the brush tops and he's racing up the road.

"Jaguar, pop smoke. We're inbound." I announce on FM as I listen on VHF to Jimbo and Klien working over the fifty.

"Smokes out!"

"Mellow yellow!" is called out.

"Roger, lemon is out." The sound of gunfire has picked up on the background of the recon team's radio.

"Break away and cover Lead's exit," Jimbo calls, knowing that it would be easy to get hung up trying to take out an NVA fifty-one and forget the primary mission of covering the escape of the overloaded and vulnerable Huey skimming it's way along the road headed south.

Our planes pass without comment. I remind Thompson that he's free to shoot the turret if he sees any targets of opportunity. He looks up at me through his clear visor and nods his head in agreement. This will be a hot extract and it must bring back memories of his first tour with the Blue Max.

I watch the Huey start his flare. Then, as we pass him, I start a tight left-hand turn trying to keep the nose of our aircraft aimed near the downed plane so that Dave will be able to take out any fire close to the LZ. The Huey AC slows to twenty knots or so and though very nose high he executes a right-hand pedal turn. Throughout this unexpected move, the helicopter looks like it's going to fall out of the sky. For an instant, it hangs suspended shaking above the now dead Huey that was formerly Chalk Three. Then, with the ease and gentle hand of someone handling a Faberge Egg, the pilot sets the Huey down in the center of the bright yellow smoke. The blades grab the yellow tinted air and send it swirling back into a protective cloud.

"Two's down. Ah . . . we're taking fire. Four o'clock. Ah . . . we're hit . . . ah, taking hits."

With his call of fire, we're not in position to return, but Goose yells, "We're inbound!"

Before I'm able to swing around to get behind Goose, the

Huey starts it's lift out. Though really not lifting, it is actually sliding down the road. Hell, a running take-off down a road deep in Laos under fire. This warrior is good! He's overloaded and he's using every trick he's learned to get out of there. "Two's out with four. Repeat four! LZ's clear."

For the first time in the past ten minutes Covey calls down to confirm the last radio transmission. "Cork flight, this is One-Eight. Repeat count, over."

"Four in Lead."

"I've got four."

The Huey in front of me is flying across the road to the southeast now, which was not the planned egress route.

"You got problems, Two?" I ask.

"Negative just trying to miss the fifty."

Just then the fifty opens up with it's glowing tracers reaching toward our flight path. Thankfully, they fell short at the last possible moment.

"Let's give him a taste of Griffin medicine!" I call to Goose who's slightly ahead of me but off to the east of the road.

"Let's do it!"

"Make one pass then get back onto Two's ass."

Goose's answer is a double squelch break while turning in toward the active fifty-one location. I pull back on the cyclic and, while lowering the collective, push in the left pedal trying to lose airspeed but maintain my altitude, letting Goose roll in front of me.

"We're in hot!" Goose calls as his aircraft slices in front of us. I watch pair after pair leave Goose's aircraft. Then he calls, "Breaking left!"

"Inbound!" I call and pull in collective while pushing the right pedal to force the glowing pipper onto the still firing fifty. Once on target I start firing at the gun emplacement as it still tracks Goose.

"We're hit! We're hit!" Goose yells. "Taking fire!"

With his call, I gently massage the red button with my right thumb until it becomes a furious pounding to send out the rockets from my pods to the target.

"Ah . . . We've taken hits in the cockpit. Ah . . . I don't know about my front seater." Goose, his voice several octaves higher than normal, is rushing to get the words out.

Jimbo comes up immediately, "Goose, get altitude if you can."

"Ah . . . everything's in the green but we're hit bad."

I've broken off my rocket pass and am now gaining on my wounded wingman. The fifty-one is still firing but with Goose out of range he's sending his multi-colored glow of tracers toward me. Looking out to the rear of my right canopy I see they're missing the mark as I've not allowed him the time to get a good fix on my range. I slam the collective down and we plummet the last few hundred feet to the brush, then, at the last second I yank up on the collective shoving in right pedal to compensate for the torque I've demanded from the Lycoming engine and shove the cyclic further forward. I'm now, hopefully, totally out of the NVA's field of vision, therefore, his field of fire. The NVA don't fire at targets they can't see, ammo's too precious.

Looking to the south, we can see that the Huey we were escorting has started its climb out, hopefully to safety, to join the two other heavily laden orbiting birds. I can also see our two Cobras flying toward us.

We are gaining on Goose who has slowed down and remained close to the ground. Flying like this wasn't taught at flight school. In fact, it was discouraged by those who had no idea what heavy combat was about. But then, I've never met an IP who had flown into Laos and had the opportunity to attack 23 and 37mm anti-aircraft weapons or have them attack him. I wonder what CWO-4 Chambers would say if he knew that his star pupil had thrown all the valuable instruction time away and now flew under a new set of rules. Chambers probably doesn't even remember me and I've heard he's retired. Someone wrote me that he moved back to Texas to live on the shores of Lake Breckenridge to pursue his favorite pastimes—fishing and sipping a cold Lone

Star beer.

"Station Lead, One-Eight, over."

"Go ahead One-Eight," Jimbo answers. At this point he's more worried about Goose than getting the release from the Covey for us to return back to the MLT.

"Your package is cleared to return to White Dover Bravo. I'll have Sandys take care of the fifty-one problem."

"Ah . . . Roger One-Eight. Ah . . . do you need a mark on it."

Shit, Jimbo can't be serious. If Covey want's someone to go back over there and lure the fifty-one into firing, then why not him and his new high-tech - with the great visibility from the cockpit OV-10?

"Negative Station, I've got a good mark on it and both the Sandys were watching when it opened up. Ah . . . a little nape on the area should do the trick."

"Got that right," says Goose.

"All right we'll head back. How you doing Goose?"

By now we've all caught up to Goose and have started the curious rite of flying close to the wounded aircraft to see if we can see any battle damage that is not known to Goose or Stockman. Goose's plane, one of the last with the old style non-tractor tail rotors is showing the effects of the hits. There are several holes going into the ammo bay doors, very high up, so it's lucky that no one was hit in the legs. The next hit is in the front canopies and has not only blown part of it away, but has peeled some of the plexiglass back. Now, with the added force of the wind blowing at seventy knots into the cockpit, the jagged plexiglass is flapping dangerously at the bodies trying to fly the wounded helicopter back to safety.

Moving in close, I'm able to see W1 Stockman sitting, in the now open air cockpit much like Wilbur and Orville Wright must have done almost seventy years ago. Stockman's tinted visor is pulled down and he looks like he's being buffeted back against the seat, though his head is slightly tilted into the wind.

Calling, I ask, "Looks like your front seater had a scare. He okay?"

Stockman's hand raises with a slight wave to acknowledge the transmission before Goose is able to answer.

"Yeah, I'd call this air-conditioning to the max. I can only get this thing up to sixty or seventy knots, then it starts to nose over, so it will be a long flight back. Big Foot's okay, though he can't talk because of all the wind — can't hear him."

Once again the young warrant from Washington State gives a slight wave as a co-sign to Goose's last transmission.

"All right flight, let's head back. How's the fuel, Cork Lead?"

Jimbo knows that we're through out here and all we can do is limp home. Hopefully, and we'll know within twenty minutes, everyone has enough fuel and there are no hidden mechanical problems.

After a minute or so the warrant, who's no doubt the unofficial leader of the Lancer's flight today, answers, "We all have enough but we need to get to the Surg."

On VHF each of the Griffins state their fuel loads and Jimbo has advised us that the Kid and I will escort the package directly back to Quang Tri. Jimbo will lay back with Goose and nurse him into friendly territory.

I call to the Lancers and tell them to start the flight back to Quang Tri. They have wounded on board. The grunt with the chest wound is on borrowed time unless the Wilson twin can weave his magic. The word I've heard is either one can, so these team members should be in good shape.

"Cork flight, this is Sneaky, start back and I'll be joining you along the blue." Then, as an afterthought, though I know he will do it anyway, "Jimbo, stay up this uniform."

He acknowledges quickly.

I start my climb out as we need to join up on the flight of three Hueys headed down the Song Be on their trip back into South Vietnam, past Khe Sanh and finally onto Quang Tri.

The flight back passes quickly. When the twenty-minute

fuel light starts its maddening blinking, we're approaching Vandy. Just before crossing the Rockpile, I call to Jimbo who's now over Khe Sanh with Goose in tow. I report our location, and we start our let down to the plains that stretch east from the mountains. The rolling hills surrounding the now silent artillery guns of Camp Carroll are quickly passed.

"Flight, let's go up Quang Tri," I announce.

Before I hear the replies I've made the change on the UHF radio and then call, "Quang Tri Tower, Sneaky White, over."

"Sneaky White, Quang Tri. Go."

"Quang Tri, Sneaky White with a flight of three UH-1s and two snakes to the west for landing. Ah . . . two Huey's will be going directly to 18th Surg. One slick to CCN and the two snakes to re-arm, over."

"Roger Sneaky, your flight of two is cleared directly to the Surg. What's their call-signs?"

The Lancer lead aircraft with the Bostonian at the controls is racing low level with a wingman close on his flank toward the northwestern side of the runway. 18th Surg's PSP pad, with the large painted white box and bright red cross centered inside of it, is just west of QL 1. Sometimes, when several medevacs are landing at the pad, the military vehicles on QL 1 will pull over to watch the gut wrenching sight. Bodies of young men being dragged across the helicopter floors leaving trails of red blood. They're slid onto a stretcher for the mad thirty-foot dash through the triage double doors and into the skilled hands of doctors who now hold their ticket to life.

"Tower, this is Lancer Two-One. A flight of two with Sneaky White for a direct to Surg. This is an emergency."

"Roger, Two-One you're cleared direct to Surg. We've notified them you're inbound. Altimeter three-zero zero-six. Winds zero-two-zero at four. Call on final."

"Roger, Two-One's on short final."

"Tower, Sneaky White with two snakes entering downwind, weapons cold. We have the numbers."

"Roger Sneaky, call base."

"Quang Tri, Lancer Two-Seven on final to CCN with the numbers."

"Roger Seven, you're cleared to land."

"Sneaky's on base with the numbers."

"Roger, Sneaky you're cleared to land the active, altimeter three-zero zero-six. Winds ah . . . zero-two-zero at six."

"Roger Quang Tri."

We land and hover over to the northeastern taxi-way to the re-arm point. Passing the fuel pits with a half dozen aircraft nosed up to the points. Each with a large black hose snaking out from the sand-bagged encircled fuel bladders.

Nosing into the re-arm point, I, for the first time in over an hour, relax. My back is tight from the tension of the flight and I'm drenched in sweat. In ten or fifteen minutes I'll be able to unstrap and climb out of this aircraft and hopefully be able to gulp down something cold. My stomach is still in knots from the effects of the adrenalin being pumped into my body. My tongue fills my mouth as it's expanded to twice its size. My dry mouth makes it hard to swallow.

"White Dover, this is Sneaky, over."

"Go Sneaky."

The voice is not one I recognize, but then I expect Stanton, Billy, Blaster, and whoever else can go, to be over to 18th Surg to check on the team and flight crew members.

"We're at re-arm and will be over to the pad in ten. Have you called for replacement aircraft?"

"Roger, Six did and we should have them up here any time now."

"Roger, I'll call on final."

"Roger Sneaky, over and out."

After Dave has helped with the re-arming he takes a quick walk around the aircraft then comes back to my open canopy.

"Sneaky," he yells.

I pull the side of my helmet away from my head, pulling

away the ear piece that is stuck to my ear from the sweat.

"We got a couple holes in the tail boom, but other than that it looks okay. Holes are AK." Then, without waiting for a response, he climbs back down and goes around to the front and climbs in. We reposition for a partial load of fuel.

I make the call, and we hover out to the active with a north take-off. After a straight climb out to five hundred feet, we turn to the west and fly past the sprawling 5th Mech areas before turning back east. After completing the easterly turn, I once again call the tower, now requesting clearance to land at CCN, while The Kid calls the MLT telling them we are on short final.

The landing area is vacant, since the one undamaged Huey has unloaded its team members and has now gone over to POL. The compound looks vacant because the exodus has made its way to the Surg checking on team members, ensuring proper security measures are taken, and the collecting of gear from those staying at the Surg.

After shutdown and a close inspection of the aircraft, we all walk into the Operations hut. An open merimite can is sitting on a bench with sodas floating in the cold water. After taking one, I continue back to the radio room and flop into one of the chairs.

The Sergeant turns and reading my expression says, "A tough one."

It's not a question, more of a statement. He wasn't there this time but he knows, he's been there in the past.

"A fucking bitch," is all I'm able to reply. It's not out of anger or disrespect to the Special Forces NCO but out of frustration and being drained from the mission. "Did Billy and Stanton listen to the mission?"

"Well, we couldn't hear everything but Covey kept us informed."

"That Lancer W1 needs a fucking medal."

"Stanton knows about it."

I get up without further comment. What's there to say? Another mission, another day patrolling the Laotian Highway.

Tomorrow will bring another flight, another insertion, and another extract. The faces, the teams, the LZs, all come together in a fuzzy haze. A year from now, two years from now, the specifics of this flight, like all the rest, will be forgotten by the brass. But not us. Not the ones that had to endure. Not the members of the Laotian Highway Patrol. A year from now, two years, the highway will still be there. It still will have NVA who need to be eliminated, and Griffins flying the Laotian Highway Patrol will be in the air, just as we have today.

Chapter 23

After a few days, I was able to ferret out what happened with Rick's late night flight for CCN. I wasn't able to get anyone up at CCN to talk about it. This was one mission that they were going to hold close to the vest. I'm not sure if this is because it wasn't their mission, or it's just the nature of CCN personnel. Knowing Billy, and probably Captain Stanton as well, the word at the MLT was put out to forget it, and so as far as MLT personnel were concerned, they have.

The fact is, if I hadn't caught 'Bones' Collier in the club one afternoon, I would never have found out. He was drinking a soda and writing to his wife. Dale Collier was our resident former Air Force member. Though twenty-four years old, he gives the appearance of being much older. We called him 'Bones' as his prior service had been as a medic, though I'm not sure an Air Force medic could compare to an Army medic or a Navy corpsman assigned to the Marines. At first, some called him Doc, but we already had a real medic, well two of them, so I started calling him Bones and it stuck. Anyway, he's married to a girl who's attending the University of Maryland. She's a top student, studying nursing, and from the scuttle-butt I've heard, they met while they were both stationed together. So, he got out and came to the Army and she got out and is attending school. But Dale Collier is loyal to his wife. There is not a day that has gone by when he wasn't found writing a letter to her. At the Club, in his hootch, or even in the Hot Shack while on Hot Status.

After sitting down with him and making some small talk, I

asked him about his flight with Rick. He put down his pen, and after downing the rest of a soda, he told me the story in very hushed and solemn tones. Once he started, he was almost transfixed back in the mission. It took only a couple moments when I realized that there was no way I could stop him even if I wanted to, which of course I didn't. Dale laid it out, reliving each minute, not in terror, not in anger, but almost like a third party observer, which wasn't true as he had flown as Rick's front seater that night.

Rick had gathered a flight crew of eight including himself. Most of his crew was in the hootch, not at the Club where I was, when he was called for the mission by Jolly Roger. After assigning the crews, and having the co-pilots head down to preflight the aircraft, Rick and his three ACs went to our TOC. Jolly Roger couldn't tell them anything other than Battalion had fragged the mission with orders that Rick be sent as the Section Leader. They were driven, by Jolly Roger no less, down to the Pit and they quickly took off to the North and MLT-2.

What waited for them came as a surprise. It wasn't a briefing conducted by Captain Stanton, or Sgt. Maj. Washburn. No, it was held by one man in civilian clothes, khaki, but it was obvious he was a civilian. There were two others in the room, but neither of them had muttered a word, just observed. Several times, the civilian stopped and repeated that this was a highly classified mission and that it, the fact they were up there, and that they had ever seen him should never be talked about, mentioned, or even thought about — ever again.

Their mission was to take off and fly north, due north, until they came to a set of grid coordinates. There, at those coordinates, would be a 'package' for them to pick up. The flight would consist of four Griffins, who were told to exchange their regular rockets with an all flechette load when they refueled. Also there were a couple of Hueys, and an Air Force FAC. They would have fast mover support, if they needed it. There were no papers to sign, but then why would there be, this night didn't exist. They were all told that all the flight time was to be logged as a night instrument training flight. When asked if all understood, he waited till each air crewman verbally said yes. They were told if the package wasn't ready when they got there, they were to abort the mission and return to Camp Evans. They were told if anyone was shot down, to stay near the aircraft for one hour then head to the east, to the shore, and then south till they got back to South Vietnam. They were told this and that, but each man sitting there, in the dim lit room that night knew this wasn't a regular mission. This wasn't a CCN mission, this wasn't an MLT-2 mission. This was something that they would never, never ever again experience. Then just before the mission briefing seemed over, the little man in the civilian clothes, neatly starched and pressed, gave the call signs and frequencies. The team, because by this time everyone knew it had to be a CIA team, was called Five Fingers. But all knew this was probably a cover name.

The team consisted of five men. One was an Australian, who would be the man they would be talking to on the radio. There were several Americans, and some other nationalities. Dale though he heard French mentioned, but he couldn't remember. They already had wounded and dead. This struck all the pilots in the heart. How could these five, well less than five alive now, be so far north, in trouble, still fighting, and believing that the sixteen men in this room were on the way to pick them up? As typical with MAG-V-SOG missions, though this one surely wasn't, no mention was made of where they had been, how long they had been in Indian Country, or what they were doing there. It was for this crew, this night, a flight deep into North Vietnam, with the intention to go in, pick up a team, and return back to Quang Tri, South Vietnam. As he finished what appeared to be the end of the briefing, the rear door opened and two men entered the room — the Wilson twins, dressed in sterile gear and loaded down. With the dimly lit room, and the heavy camouflaged faces, most would have never recognized them. They never spoke, just stood and listened. Then, and only then, did the civilian add that, by the way, "Five Fingers is in heavy contact as we speak now." Collier felt that his remark was almost funny, using the word we, as if this had been an indepth conversation, since they had entered the room. Only he had spoken except for the yes that he had required out of each man about the mission not existing. Once heavy contact was mentioned, no one made further comment. It was like they had all expected it, after all this really wasn't happening, was it?

When dismissed from the briefing, and after issuing the Huey crews STABO rigs, the civilian headed out the door. He returned after a minute, and said that the map had the latest AA positions marked on it, just for them, and they should be ready to take off within fifteen minutes. There was not the standard, "any questions?" Not tonight. They were given all they needed to know, or at least what the little man thought they should know.

Rick quickly went up to check out the large, open, map. He now was looking at an area we never flew into. Rick, who's mission preparedness is legendary, and this night, though only with a fifteen minute window of time, was another one of his typical mission reviews. He went over the route they would fly, the altitude, the orbit areas, the egress path after the pickup, and everything that pilots really need to know. Rick completed this in less than ten minutes, as well as pointing out the route on the large map, taking care to show each of the known large, 23mm or larger, AA gun emplacements. After this, Rick asked if there were any questions. The few that were asked were quickly discussed and answered. Then Rick gave the word, strap in and top off at Quang Tri. As Rick lead the pilots from the hootch, the two *Bac Si* - the Wilson twins - filed in behind them. After getting outside, the *Bac Si* split up with no visible acknowledgement, and climbed into the waiting Hueys.

According to Collier, Rick had all six of the helicopters up the same pushes, on all three radios. Good move, as there really was no need for the Hueys and the Griffins to talk without the rest of the package knowing what was going on. Collier went through the rearming and refueling done at Quang Tri as if I had no idea how it would have taken place. He did say that Rick was not to talkative, but then Rick isn't, so this didn't surprise me. He did ask for and received, just before they finely took off, a verbal ready from each AC, not the customary squelch breaks most pilots use. Rick then lead the flight to takeoff, but never told the Quang Tri Tower that this was a scramble mission. As they took off on runway 36, Rick had the flight fly to the north toward the South China Sea.

They headed up QL-1, on its eastern side, past Dong Ha Combat Base. When they passed by Qua Viet, they broke toward the South China Sea, while Rick made the call to the Air Force FAC. The FAC didn't answer. Instead King, the high flying C-130 Airborne Command Center, answered and said they were to proceed North and call when they headed inland. The night was overcast, but not stormy. No moon to give them away tonight. But helicopters flying in North Vietnam would be heard, and this would mean the radar tracking stations of the NVA would light up after a few minutes into North Vietnam. When the flight, according to Rick, passed the visible line that separates the two warring countries, which runs through the middle of the Ben Hai River, Rick again called King to advise them they were no longer in South Vietnam.

Collier said there was not communications between the crews, well at least none outside the aircraft. He was sure, and so am I, that within each cockpit there was some talk, but other than Rick's calls it was radio silence for twenty minutes. Collier also said that at first his stomach was tied in a knot, then he felt like he had the runs. All the time, he had his map folded in front of him. He could see where he was, and it scared the hell out of him.

Collier stopped his story for a minute, got up and walked over to the first refrigerator and took out a couple sodas, threw some paper money in the box and walked back. He sat down, quickly opened the can, drank it down without stopping till it was empty, and tossed the can into the trash can. This action was totally uncharacteristic of Collier. Then after a deep breath he continued.

Rick all of a sudden told the flight to reduce altitude to three hundred feet, which was pushing the envelope but Rick was trying to protect the flight. They lowered, all the while each crew went on the alert knowing they could easily crash into the South China Sea without any chance of being rescued. Collier rambled on some more about how he felt about flying at night three hundred feet above the South China Sea, and to top it off being a mile or so off the coast of North Vietnam. Collier told me how he prayed. Prayed that he would survive. That he would be alive to be with his wife when this tour was over. Collier had seen the light, or at least this is what he relayed to me. Whatever, that flight scared the hell out of him.

He went on to say that when Rick decided they were at the point to cross over land into North Vietnam, that his voice was calm, reassuring. Not only did he tell the Huey to come about to a new heading, two-eight-five, as Collier remembered somberly, but he called to King to tell him that their feet were dry. Collier said as they crossed over North Vietnamese soil, he felt like he was going to have the dry heaves. His stomach was totally out of control. But all the while Rick was rock steady. Then, and it damn near scared him out of his skin, a FAC radioed and it was much too loud of a call. His message was brief. The team was on it's last legs, they had two KIAs and the other three were wounded seriously. Asked how long before getting to the area, Rick still calm, told the FAC they had just left the Sea and were cruising at one-hundred and twenty knots. They could be expected in fifteen minutes. Then Rick advised the Hueys to climb up to five hundred feet. Over and over Collier remarked how Rick was so calm, almost cold in nature. Rick was in his zone, he was now detached from his emotions. But he also said that Rick surely calmed the others and without him they would never have made it that far.

The FAC, several times in the next fifteen minutes, requested Rick to give him a long count so that he could get a radio fix on the flight. Each time, the steady voice complied. Then the FAC told them to pick up and orbit as they were just south of the team. The lead Huey started a right hand orbit, with the Griffin flight a bit higher, and further out than the Hueys. After what seemed like an eternity, the FAC said they were ready to be picked up, and be advised they were still in heavy contact. Rick then asked the FAC where he was, and was told to look to the north for a set of navigation lights flashing starting now. Rick immediately spotted them and advised the flight. They quickly were turned off, and Rick flashed his landing lights once, which Collier said at that moment he knew he was dead. Flashing one's landing light six hundred feet above North Vietnam was surely signing one's death warrant. Rick contacted the team, and a thick Australian accent came up, and calmly asked where the hell had he been. But the background noise told another story. It was decided that only one Huey would go in for the pickup, and that he should pickup the three survivors and if time, and more importantly, if enemy gunfire allowed it, to go ahead and try to bring out the two bodies. I'm sure this was not a choice Rick made easily, as he believes we should always try to bring our own home, dead or alive. But understandable, in North Vietnam, and in a shit sandwich at night, I know he didn't want to lose an aircraft and possibly a crew.

The next few minutes the pickup was discussed between Rick and the Aussie. The hardest problem would be getting into the right location to do the pickup. Smoke grenades would never work, after all it was dark. Finely the Aussie said he would pop up a couple of pen flares, Rick would make the call on the color, and the Huey AC would then turn and shoot an approach to the site.

That was it, I asked Collier? No decision on which way to fly into the area, what to look out for? Bones, by now pale and spent from reliving the flight thought for a while before answering.

"Sneaky," he said solemnly, and clearly with a lot of thought behind it now that he thought about it, "there really wasn't enough time to do all this."

It was get in, pick them up, and get the hell out of there.

Though they had not been fired upon as of yet, at least to their knowledge, several times their FM radio sets had come alive with the humming of some sort of radar painting them. He went on to explain that the Huey AC had also become very calm and matter of fact when he saw the first flare, a green one, rise into the air. He said he had it in sight and was shooting a straight in. That's it!

Collier when on to say that by now any illness he had felt was gone as the adrenalin had done its job and though not in a stupor, things sort of flowed slowly from there on out, without any feelings of fear or death. After all, he was in Rick's hands. When he said this, I felt I understood his feelings, as a couple of times I too have felt this way when flying with Rick.

Rick had turned all four Griffins into the area of the first flare, and then as the Huey, though only visible because of its dimly lit navigation lights, started its approach, another flare rose in the air. Once again it was a green one, and all eyes had seen where it came from. As Rick called to the Aussie that they were headed for the green flare, two streams of tracers sprayed into the air from the same location. The bright red sprays were one-hundred and eighty degrees apart, and in a fan like pattern. Though only a short burst, the Aussie called that they were in the middle of the tracers, and without a trace of fear, that they were damn near in hand to hand again, yes again, and would the Yanks hurry up.

The Huey started taking fire, from all around him, as he slowed to sixty knots.

I looked strangely at Bones. How did he know they were at sixty knots? Turning his head off to the left, looking through the screen covered windows up at our TOC, he waited before answering, as if to retrace his story to see if he had already told me this. Minutes went by, then with what seemed like new vigor, he rapidly started in again.

When the Huey started making its approach, the AC went to hot mike, so everyone would know what was going on. Normally, I would not have liked this, but thinking about this kind of mission,

I can understand it. Having flown Aero-Scout LOHs, I know how we used to fly with a hot mike when working an area. Everyone knew what the little bird was seeing, doing and going to do. Good idea Huey AC, good idea.

As the Huey started to receive fire, Rick had the Griffins put down rockets. No certain spots, and really with no intention other than trying to get the NVA to get their heads down. Once the Griffins opened up with their rockets, then the ground fire was directed up at them. Flying without external lights meant a bit of stealth, but once firing the rockets, the enemy as well as the FAC, could see where the Cobras were. Collier went on to say that though they took a few hits, it was all small shit, and the fifty cals that were firing up at them, with their basketball-like rounds arcing up at them, never seemed to get a good position on them. Reflecting back, Collier felt it was because they were not used to firing at such a slow moving target. Saying that brought a smile to his face for the first time in the twenty minutes or so he had been telling his story.

The Huey, though taking hits, had to hover around, all the while being guided in by the Aussie, until landing on top of them. They climbed in and instead of a normal climb out, did a high hover until airborne at a very low level. The AC called his heading, via radio compass, and for a time was heading deeper into North Vietnam. Then , when his airspeed was over a hundred knots, and he finally had control of the aircraft, he turned east and headed for the big blue sea, that would provide safety for them. Rick, according to Bones, kept asking the slick to come up to at least three or four hundred feet in altitude. But the Huey AC was steadfast in his replies of just getting the hell out of there. Rick had to herd the other Huey over to the egress route, as he was flying about seven hundred feet and no one knew exactly where he was. But just before they crossed back over the South China Sea, the link up was made, though each aircraft was at a different altitude. Once they all were free of the shores of North Vietnam, and immediately after Rick called 'feet wet', Collier said that King came up on their push and give them a well done, with a mission complete and a return to base okay. Then, only after King give his okay, did the Air Force FAC acknowledge Rick's call of 'feet wet' and that we had pulled out three WIAs.

Bones said they really didn't feel safe, even after getting over a mile from shore, until they knew beyond a shadow of a doubt that they were off the coast of Quang Tri. Rick at this time requested all to turn on their navigation lights to bright, and to form up, while he made the call to Quang Tri Tower for landing instructions. Then he called the MLT. Though I do not know if Collier knows all the voices that might answer the MLT radio, he said that he had never ever heard the voice that responded to them. All it said was to land at the airfield, next to a C-130 Blackbird and unload the team, then rearm and refuel. This, to be very honest was not only unusual, but Collier said that Rick commented to him that he had never done this before, which surprises me.

After landing, discharging the team, or what was left of it, and rearming, refueling, all six aircraft repositioned to the MLT pad. As they were shutting down, the small compound was alive like normally. Not at all like their departure, when no one was out around the aircraft. Rick made an aside to the pilots as they were walking to the operations hootch, that maybe everyone had been confined to quarters while the 'spooks were here'. Rick went, once he grabbed a cold beer, into the radio room with Captain Stanton, and talked for about a half hour. Then he came out and said they were released and could go back home. With that the Huey crews quickly vacated the hootch and turned up their birds and took off. As the Griffins headed out to their aircraft, Rick held a mini briefing in which he gave them what he was able to gather in his meeting with Captain Stanton.

What Rick told them seemed impossible, but then within MAC-V-SOG's missions, maybe not that impossible at all. Rick said the team members they picked up, and the two dead ones left, were a team that had been inserted over a month ago. That bit of information, in the darkened area, drew gasps, as just the thought of being in North Vietnam on the ground for a day was frightful enough, never mind running around in the bush for over a month. They had been inserted up on the Plains of Jars, in Laos, and worked their way into North Vietnam and then north along the Red River Valley until, as Rick said in very hushed tones, they crossed into China. Bones admitted to me when Rick said China, he repeated the word China loudly, which caused Rick to hush him up. Rick said yes, China is where they went. Some sort of an assassination team, with the Aussie running the show. Anyway, the CIA and whoever called the mission off, and told them to come on back. But along the way, besides being compromised, the CIA, and whoever else was in charge, seemed to forget to rush and get them out. If anything, the mission was given up, but somehow, and Rick was awe struck by this as well, the team kept fighting its way south until they were within range for a CCN flight to go up and get them.

Before they broke up for the fifteen minute flight back to Camp Evans, and a very short night's sleep, Rick reminded them not to talk about it to anyone, even in the platoon. With that Rick had them saddle up and fly back home.

Dale 'Bones' Collier had not told me some old war story. As he completed his debriefing of that night's flight, I could tell that he had just relived it as well. He was worn out and tired, and his clothes were suddenly sweat stained even though we had three large fans blowing on us. He had told me the story without emotion and really without any thought, except for the time where he thought about Rick sending in the Huey without any predetermined route in or out. Then, Dale, now looking down at the five by seven color picture of his wife, said, as if not talking to me but to her, that he didn't think he would fly CCN anymore. The minutes dragged by in utter silence. There was no way I could respond to him. Yes, there was a gung ho side of me that usually would make some remark about being gutless. But this decision wasn't made because of this, it was something else. Bones look disillusioned sitting there. If there was ever a time I have seen someone with the wind knocked out of his sails, it was here. Looking at Bones, I didn't know what to say. In my heart I couldn't agree with him, but then if I was in his shoes maybe, just a slim maybe, I'd look at life differently. The time, whether it was few minutes or ten minutes, didn't seem to pass but instead just stood still. Even the air from the fans seemed to stop, and the normal din of helicopters flying overhead or in the revetments turning up for some maintenance function seemed to disappear.

I sat there, it was for Bones to say something, move, or just raise his head and look at me. When he did, I saw it is his eyes. Before I could avert my stare, he said, as if he read my inner thoughts, that maybe he'd just quit flying CCN until after his R&R with his wife in Hawaii next month. If there was a chance for him to spend some time with his wife to sort things out, then he was sure he could get back into CCN flights.

My thoughts were how I treated my wife, my mother, and father, hell my whole family, about CCN flights. They didn't know what I do. Not so much because of the papers I had signed assuring me I would see Fort Levenworth if I did say anything, but because I really never talked about any of my flying to them. None of them knew what I do, what I flew, where I had been and what I had done. It just was impossible for me to sit down and talk about what I do. Not even with Twit. Though she knows I fly Cobras. I don't think she has any idea about me flying for CCN. Maybe someday, some time far and away from now in a different climate I can open up to someone who isn't part of the missions and bare my soul. But to do this would mean there is something wrong with me, and I know that there's nothing wrong with me or what I do. But how can Collier talk to his wife about what he does? What kind of relationship does he have that he can sit down and do this? What kind of woman is this who will listen, and try to understand what we Griffins do for a living? It's our secret, ours and the men of MLT-2, CCN, and MAC-V-SOG.

I got up, there is no use reminding him that he's signed

papers never to reveal what he's been involved in. His mind is made up and no matter what I say it will not change. He needs to come face to face with the demons that seem to be plaguing him. If his wife can help him through this, well good for them. Yes them, for if their marriage is to last and he stays with us flying CCN, then she will have to bring him around. I'll talk to Rick, but I'm sure he'll agree. If you can handle it, then go for it. If you can't get the hell out of the way, we can't afford to have indecisiveness when flying for the Laotian Highway Patrol.

Yeah, I'll talk to Rick, and then get ready. I'm going to Hue and spend a few days with Twit. The rains are starting and we'll not be flying much. The old man said I could go down to Battalion and I'm going. Bones is going to have to sort this out without me, I need to be with Twit.

Chapter 24

The rain has been driving against the hootch since I've been back. My last two days were spent with Twit in her small house just north of Hue on the eastern edge of QL-1. When I left this morning, I looked at the flatlands toward the ocean and could see the rice paddies flooding from all the rain we've had. The low clouds were dark and ominous, full of water and threatening. Now, it's getting colder and, though in Vietnam where one would think that you could never get a cold, I've got one. The monsoons have arrived early. In fact they didn't come in gradually like last year, but rushed in without warning last week.

Once I knew we'd be flying a reduced number of missions, I received permission to go to Battalion to spend some time with Captain Pratt. Our friendship has deepened over the past few months. After I arrived, he showed me all the completed paperwork for my six-month extension. He then quoted a rumor that's been circulating up at Camp Evans that there might be an operation coming up in the Khe Sanh area. He asked me to decide if I wanted to submit the extension paperwork prior to the operation or wait until after it. If I submitted now, I might miss flying in the valley I had lived in four years ago. My decision was to hold the paper work until Pratt could find out more about the operation. Rumors have been floating around a lot lately, but most dealt with us going home without finishing the war. I need to get the extension approved quickly. If they do send some 101st troops home, I'll be one of the last because of the extension.

Pratt took me to his hootch for a few beers before finding

one of the battalion drivers to drive me from Camp Eagle to Houng Ca. While I was stuffing bags with Tide soap power and three bottles of cognac into the back seat of the jeep, Pratt reminded me to be ready to come back in two days. It was all the time he could cover for me. As we pulled away from him, I yelled that I'd be ready, but I didn't know about Twit. Pratt gave a wave and yelled back something.

The jeep driver, a PFC, made note of where I was going. He didn't ask me about what I was going to do there, though his looks over to me during the trip betrayed his curiosity. The PFC was startled after getting directions to pull off to the side of the road in front of the small concrete house as we entered the village of Houng Ca. A little black haired boy ran out to us yelling for Daddy. At first, the driver started to pull away, until I told him I'd be getting off here and he could return to Eagle. He watched suspiciously as I grabbed my son and hoisted him onto my shoulders. Then, with a free hand, I leaned over and took out the two bags of goodies I had brought for my family. As I walked to the house, I looked back over as the PFC eyed me, not knowing for sure if he was really supposed to leave. Pratt had given him orders to take me where I wanted to go. When he gets back to battalion, he'll have a story to tell about his activities during the day and the crazy warrant officer he let off in the middle of forty or fifty houses spotted along the road to Hue.

Even though it rained heavily the whole time I was in Houng Ca, I was able to spend some playful time with my blue-eyed black-haired son, and later each night with his beautiful mother. This time has taken the sharp edge off and relaxes me like nothing else can. Though I've never been a good father to my children in the States because I was always too busy going off to play military games, I have grown to enjoy my Vietnamese son. Loc came into my life when I finally understood the joys of fatherhood. Twit's nurturing me into the role of fatherhood has helped tremendously with this newfound relationship. With the thought of another child due soon, at least from looking at Twit's bulging stomach, I'm now starting to look forward to taking more time off to spend with them. I'll have to carefully select my next unit. I really want to fly for the 2nd of the 17th Cav and my extension papers are made out for C Troop. But with the Cav, it will be hard to get several days off at a time. If they relocate up to Quang Tri like I've heard, then I'll move Twit up to Quang Tri City and at least see her every couple of days.

The biggest change in me, as far as fatherhood goes, is patience. This, I am now learning, is the most enduring part of being a parent. The times when Loc wants to play are at his demand and not whether I want to sit and relax, curl up next to Twit, or have a drink with the few elders of Houng Ca. Loc is also at the inquisitive stage of his life. Some may call it the terrible twos, but I really think its all the curiosity that seems to come to a head about this time in their life. Children have mobility and speed now that they no longer have to crawl to get where they are going. They have wide eyes, looking for things new to challenge their minds. Then you have and, for me the first time, a father who enjoys seeing this time. Also, I'm only able to get down here at best a couple of times a month and then for only a few days, I want to share in his new adventures as much as possible. I missed his first steps, but then I also missed Robert's and Muffy's as well in the States. I know that I am missing out on a lot, and these times cannot be replaced or duplicated. The day will come, if an NVA bullet doesn't prevent it, that I'll be sitting on a porch reflecting back to my children's early years. This will probably come after I'm a grandfather and when what I have missed and lost hits me full force. This reflection hopefully will be able to include some of these times that Loc is sharing with me. Yes, he's sharing them with me. For if I was not able to be here, either because of my or the Army's choice, Loc would do things anyway. He, nor any of my other children, waited on me to get my act together. I blew it with my children in the States and I'll not blow it with these two.

Twit and I went to Hue for dinner and, although the winds blew cold and sharp off the Perfume River, we were able to enjoy ourselves. I had decided that we would go to one of the only two snake restaurants in Hue. In fact, I think these might be the only two north of the Hai Van Pass and Da Nang. I've been to a couple in Da Nang, in fact, this is where I first learned the art of dining this way.

The restaurant was located off the beaten path, so to speak. If you know where it is, meaning you've been there before, its still difficult to locate. One night, I spent at least fifteen or twenty minutes driving up and down the street looking for the building. It wasn't that I had a few beers before coming, but because it was set back off the street and looked like every other building on the street. In fact, had not a couple Vietnamese soldiers exited the place, I probably would have never made it that night. Now, I count the number of buildings from the intersection up the street, thirty-one on the right, and I know I'm there.

The building, a single floored white stucco building with what appears to be a flat tile roof, has no outward signs of being an eating establishment. It was once a home, that has been converted, by changing the furniture to make it into a small six room restaurant. You have to park in the driveway or on the front if there are more than two vehicles there. The front door is open, meaning the place is open. When entering you go through a very short hallway lit by a string of one-hundred-watt bulbs, half of which are burned out all of the time. After the quick walk, you're dumped into a courtyard which serves as the meeting place, the holding pen, and the passageway to and from the kitchen. On the wall are cages, which seem to be empty because of the darkened area. Even upon closer inspection, you do not see life in them as everything is still. I know what lurks in the cages.

The first time in the courtyard I was struck with fear when I saw many snakes slithering about on the broken tile floor. Hell, I thought they let the damn snakes run loose on the floor. On Twit's and my first visit, she quickly explained that these were the nonpoisonous variety. What a relief, if she was telling the truth. Though not afraid of snakes, I'd rather not sit down and have dinner with them freely going between my legs, especially the killers. This place was not at all like the one in Da Nang, which was an upscale establishment. This would be labeled a country-style affair. But once you threw away all the higher priced trappings, the food and service were equal to, if not heads above, the Da Nang restaurants.

Immediately an old grandmotherly lady dressed in a beautiful hand stitched and embroidered *Ao Dai* came up to us. As Twit talked to her in their native tongue, I examined the handwork done on the dark purple *Ao Dai* and it was as well done as Twit's.

She then smiled broadly, showing the loss of several front teeth, and slightly bowed her head. Then with a staccato of orders, she had two waiters, in clean but threadbare dark clothes, rushing to one of the rooms off to our left. The curtain was quickly pulled back, a couple of faint lights turned on, and a great display of candles in the center of the table was lit. With the same speed they had arrived and prepared the room, they returned to some recess where they waited for more directions from the lady. She then, by waving her hand in a large sweeping motion, presented the room to us. As I went in, Twit was speaking quickly though I knew she was not ordering.

As we sat down, the lady stepped back and reached up and jerked the purple curtain closed. We were now in a private, dining room, big enough for four, but it would have been very tight if they were all Americans. It was then I noticed the sounds of a stereo system playing the traditional Vietnamese music, and the wonderful high pitched singing. Before I had a chance to ask Twit what she had said, the curtain was once again yanked back revealing one of the waiters. He held a bottle of Cognac, two glasses, and a bottle of 33 beer in one hand. Without acknowledging me, he placed the beer, which was cold enough to have small chips of ice still stuck to the wet outside, in front of me, and then placed the Cognac between Twit and me with a glass to our left. He had this large smile on his face, though it looked forced. His shirt, as his hand crossed in front of me with the Cognac, was ironed and clean, but large. Maybe two or three sizes too large, on his slender frame. After this, he stepped back. But before closing the curtain again, he asked Twit something.

Twit asked me what we were going to have, though she knew that all they served was snake. I'm sure this talk with me was done more out of respect to me than the need to know what was for dinner. I replied, looking up at the waiter, that we were going to have cobra tonight and to treat this night like a celebration as I had a surprise to tell her. I'm sure the man understood every word I said, but not once did he reveal it. Instead, he waited patiently while Twit relayed what I said, but leaving out the possible surprise. All this time his broad smile never left his face. He, like so many Vietnamese, had serious dental problems, but tonight his job was to serve, and he was going to do this to the best of his ability. After he closed the curtain, I wondered to myself why a man his age, he appeared to be in his twenties, was not in the military. Then, a flash across my mind, maybe he is, but not in the ARVN military. There were many rumors, primarily spread by overzealous intelligence types, that Hue was full of NVA. I do not believe this, for I know the truth about Hue. While the Americans during Tet '68 were trying to stay alive at Khe Sanh, Hue was captured by the NVA forces. What was never reported was the thousands upon thousands killed by the NVA and hidden in mass graves. If Hue was an NVA stronghold, why the destruction of so many of its people? But in the rush to sell the American people that we were losing the war, our free, open, unrestricted press forgot to make mention of this. A typical press lie by omission. So, Mr. Waiter, are you or are you not an NVA sympathizer? Will the day come when you and I are in each other's sights?

Twit interrupts my sick train of thought by taking our glasses and pouring Cognac into them. While doing this, there is a rustle outside our room, then the curtain is slid back and after a moment a youthful man stepped in. In his hand, though extended out at arm's length is a four and a half foot snake being held by the head. The snake is a cobra. This snake, was plucked out of one of the cages that were on our right when we entered the courtyard. During all my visits to this type of restaurant, I've never seen anyone refuse one or request to see what others they might have to offer. What is brought before the table, is what is accepted. The size, I've seen them up to six feet and very agitated, is dependent, I think, on the number of diners at the table. For the sake of the holder of the writhing reptile, I make it a point to carefully inspect it. Though knowing some about snakes, I could not tell you if one would taste better than the other.

After a few moments, I smile and nod my head up and down, knowing that if anything, he'll understand this. I then say to Twit, thinking that the snake handler might understand, what a good looking cobra this one is. Like I thought, upon hearing this he nods his head. Though they might not talk to me directly in English, they know what I am saying. Could he too be an NVA ordered here to spy on guests and to be ready to take up arms for any nocturnal excursion order from the higher ups?

I have learned, from a previous visit, that this restaurant has been here for years and the old woman who greeted me was the daughter of the first owner. Like many Vietnamese businesses, they are passed down through the family tree, with some operating for several hundred years under the same family name. Tradition and honor run deep in the oriental culture and the Vietnamese are deeply rooted with this. But whether this man, or any of the others that seem to be working here, are family or not will never be learned by me. And if they are relatives, this does not mean that I can take it for granted that they, in toto or individually, aren't pro-NVA. He eases back out the door, still holding the snake out in front of him.

For us, this night, the restaurant is not at all crowded. It's not a payday or the end of the month where some might take a night out to spend the high, at least by Vietnamese standards, cost for a meal. There are no large groups enjoying their meal, which is usually the case. Nor is there any excessive noise coming from adjoining rooms that would signal a festive event of some sort. No, tonight Twit and I are here for something rare, a romantic meal. But I'm sure in the background, in the kitchen, they are talking in whispers that the American in the small room with a French-Vietnamese woman is here to eat snake because of its aphrodisiac gifts. The snickers must be pointed, as they talk about how young the American is and why he would need something to help with his sexual prowess. The remarks are way off the mark.

After some small talk, mostly about Loc and how he's growing, our waiter returns again with a small pot, cracked years ago and now stained along the airily thin lines, full of light green tea. The cups, already set on our table are turned over, but Twit waves him away and quickly says something to him. I know it's that she will take care of me, as she has not only been raised to do this, she genuinely enjoys pampering me. I've grown to not only enjoy this part of our relationship, but look forward to it.

As the waiter backs out, the snake handler re-enters with what appears to be the same cobra hanging down. First, a slight bow of his head, then after my return of a nod, he makes an incision into the underside of the twisting dinner. Then, very deftly, pulls out a small piece. This I know is the heart. He quickly hands it to me, as the case for tonight is that I'm the honored guest. I quickly take if from him, and without looking at it, pop it into my mouth. I learned some time ago to make an effort to chew it, rather than my natural desire to swallow it whole and get on with the rest of the meal. So, more for the snake handler's sake than Twit's or for my need to chew the morsel properly, I chew slowly. After I think he's got the message, I swallow and he backs out with great fanfare. He'll report that the American not only took and ate the heart, but that he never batted an eye when the knife was thrust into the snake and the heart cut out. Thinking back to the times I've been here before, the staff should know me by now. After all, this place isn't the busiest in Hue, and any American coming in here will gather attention. After several times, though they don't show it, they know I'm a regular.

Twit and I, for the next hour or so (well really longer as we take our time because I don't have to make any curfew tonight), enjoy the many courses served in less than grand style, but of excellent taste. I've looked forward to tonight, not only the food, but my time with Twit, both here and when we get home. For me, if I was going to explain this meal to someone, I'd say the eating of the freshly severed heart from the cobra might be called an appetizer. I can just imagine my folks if they knew what I had for an appetizer tonight. Hell, this would set the White household, in Granby, Connecticut, back one-hundred years. But then just the thought of snake, for any reason, being in the White household is beyond belief.

Quickly the waiter has returned with a tray with plates and bowls loaded on it. He sets before us the large bowls and plates toward the center of the table then several small bowls and a plate before Twit and me. The meal has begun!

First is soup. It's light colored, almost a faint yellow and it's loaded with surprises. I ask Twit what's in this soup and she gets a quick explanation from the waiter, though she never asked him. Yes, he understands English. The rapid fire Vietnamese is quickly spit out with it's melodic sing-song tones. Vietnamese words can be spelled the same, and with a very slight change in the tone of part of the word it changes the meaning completely. What a complicated but beautiful language. Anyway, she explains, while picking up each piece with a chopstick in her slender and delicate fingers, that there are small morsels of cobra neatly folded in the soup. Floating along are shreds of cilantro, mushrooms, and lemon grass. Before I start to eat it, I see gently floating on top what appears to be pepper. As a side dish to the soup, is a small tray piled high with fresh veggies. Though I don't know the name for most, some of it I've had while at home with Twit. But some, like the cucumbers and figs, are familiar to me as a kid. I drink the soup with the flat shaped spoon that is uncommon in the States except in the Oriental restaurants that I've seen. I take turns, with the chop sticks, and pick pieces of the green and dunk them into the soup before shoveling them into my mouth. It's past good, it's tantalizing.

As I finish the soup, the curtain is pulled back. I've got no idea how the waiter knew I had just put my spoon down for the last time, but it hit the table and the curtain started moving. Quickly he takes the empty bowls and dishes from the table and, as he returns, brings another course. This one I know, it's fried snake, served ground and fried in chili powder. There are other spices mixed in that I am not able to recognize, but I do taste the faint ginger that was also used. Twit, after finding out that I like ginger, has begun to use it whenever she is cooking something that will allow it. But, I've told her this several times, I'm not too fond of chili powder. In fact, this is one reason I do not like Thai food, it's loaded with powders, both chili and curry. It's probably the curry powder that gets to me the most, but here in Vietnam I do not have to worry about it. Along with this are rice crackers, which I use to scoop up the fried snake meat. These small crackers are the most tasteless things I've ever eaten. It's an exercise to eat them alone, just chew with absolutely no flavor. But without saltines that my mother would have had on the table, these more than fill the bill. Maybe they are served like this so they don't take away from the flavor of the meat.

As I finish this, which Twit has playfully made a show of feeding me, the curtain once again is pulled back. This time our waiter is taken aback by the sight of Twit having moved next to me to feed me. When I tried to take some crackers, she pushed my hands down and told me, "No, no." I'm sure this has been heard by whoever is standing outside the door to cue the waiter when we're almost ready for the next course. Quickly Twit moves back away from me, giving the appearance that we were doing something wrong or illicit. The ritual has started again. The removal of the used plates. The new course, steaming hot, being brought to the table.

This I know, from its appearance, is stir-fried cobra. Not that I can tell stir-fried snake from cobra, but it's the addition of the scallions, heaped on top, that gives it away. How I love scallions. Mixed with garlic and ginger and then with the cobra, overlaid by the salty tange of soy sauce, it's wonderful to smell. The meat tastes like frog legs and, in a way looks like it, or maybe squid. It's the translucent appearance that first makes you think it's anything but cobra, but the texture is a lot stronger, or maybe tougher.

I eat this course on my own and, in fact, take a few chop stick loads from Twit's little dish. Though we each take some off the larger plate, once it's empty, I decide that Twit can share hers. She smiles and doesn't complain. She knows my enjoyment for this course. She's even started cooking several of our meals in this stir-fried method with the scallions heaped on. I taught her to cook the scallions like my mother does. So now, not only are they quickly cooked, but she takes them out of the wok as soon as they turn translucent and are glistening. She has even, several times, made a side dish of scallions that had been quickly cooked in the wok at the last minute.

Once again as we both finish, the curtain is moved aside and the exchange takes place. This time comes the course that separates the Americans from the Vietnamese. Few, very few, Amercians can eat Vietnamese food with the native fish sauce, *nuoc mam* either poured on or as a side dish for dipping. For most, the smell gets to them. For me, it's an excellent sauce. Where an American would use Lea & Perrins or ketchup, the Vietnamese use *nuoc mam*. Along with the large bowl of *nuoc mam* is a plate with Cobra *mem* stacked on it. *Mem* is what the normal American would get at his local oriental restaurant when he ordered a #3 or #7, spring paper, but tonight it's Cobra wrapped in the thin rice paper. The cobra *mem* is heavily laced with un-named herbs, when I ask Twit about them, she raises her shoulders and gives me a slight swinging of her head. Then, she says that if I like then, she'll find out what they are so she can please me. In some future meal, I'll taste this again, though not with cobra, but probably pork for the filler. Though this is about the eighth course, I'm not full yet. Looking down at my Rolex, I notice we've been here for over an hour already. My beer is finished and I've had a couple glasses of Cognac, but I feel none of the alcohol and I'm really just getting started with the meal.

After the next exchange of dishes, dirty removed and newly arriving heaped with more treasures, I settle into the rhythm of starting the new course and quickly attacking it, then finishing it and, before I can relax, getting a new course laid out before me. Then it starts all over again. This goes on, over and over again, and I love every minute of it. Though expensive by common Vietnamese family standards, for Twit and me it's almost nothing. Anyway, the next course, or maybe courses as I'm losing track, contains a large plate with roasted cobra mixed with tasty spices and a very large plate of steaming rice with little yellow beans mixed in. I've checked out the beans before, thinking they might be like our yellow wax beans that I was raised on, but no. To me, they're just as good, especially when mixed with rice. There is also a batter-dipped meat, which must be snake meat of some sort, that one might find in Cajun country of lower Louisiana with a large colorful Creole woman bent over a grease-filled pot with some batter-dipped catfish. It's like the corn fritters my grandmother used to make and my mother used to threaten to make so that my father would give her his look when she mentioned it. So, I wonder how deep-fried snake fritters would be received in Granby. Very interesting thought and I smile thinking about it . Twit's eyebrows raise. The questioning look demands an answer and I tell her how in some parts of America, the Deep South, a food called fritters are made, and how these are so much like them. She asked, though I knew she knew the answer, if they would like snake meat. As I shook my head no, we both giggled, knowing this time was ours and shared with no one.

Also with this course is a small plate of chips, or pork rinds, but I don't take any. Twit, sensing something is wrong, as I've not missed a plate or bowl tonight, asks. I tell her I'd rather not have any pork. She then explains, using mostly her hands, that this is snake skin. So I try one, not too bad, but not filling. It's another new experience that relates back to my childhood, rinds, though these are snake, and another dish that would not be well received in Granby. I save the half dozen snake pate that are wrapped in pale green leaves for the last. I dunk them into the *nuoc man* and each time drop them to allow them to soak the flavors before I fish them out with the thin wooden sticks. Over the years I've gotten where I can eat better with the chop sticks than I can with regular tableware. Plus, it causes me to eat slower, thereby allowing me to enjoy what I'm eating. This, at least everyone in my personal life, would be glad to see. I eat far too fast and so far only chop sticks seem to slow me down.

Once the plates are cleaned away, one large bowl and two smaller ones are put in front of Twit and myself. Our waiter explains it to Twit. He stops several times so she can relay to me that the cook has sent out this to us as a special surprise. Its not cobra, but a snake stew. I eagerly scoop some into my small bowl, all the while being supervised by the waiter. He stands, almost hovering over me, waiting for my reaction. Truthfully, had no one told me it was snake, I'd never have known. It's a typical Vietnamese stew, which in itself is not a typical Vietnamese meal. But it's got a tangy taste from all the herbs and spices added, but it's good. I turn to him and smile and thank him and tell him to thank the cook. Though Twit is translating this to him, his sparkling eyes reveal that he understands what I've said. He quickly backs out and closes the curtain, and I can hear him tell someone out of sight something in Vietnamese. Twit rolls her eyes, then leans over to me and whispers that the cook was just outside the door and is now very pleased that I liked his surprise. She then explains, in very hushed tones, almost whispering again, that the snake stew is probably what the help eats every night and they just dished some up for me. It's not that special of a course. It takes over ten minutes to finish this, not because I'm disappointed in it, but all of a sudden I'm really getting full. Plus the Cognac has hit me a bit. I'm not drunk, but I feel very relaxed. Here, after ten o'clock in a back alley of Hue, not too many Americans would feel relaxed with no known friendlies around them. For me, I feel totally at home and safe.

The last course is served and, like the start of the meal, it's a soup. This is a light broth. This has been explained to me as an ending of a cobra meal. The cook has taken the stripped cobra, with only its backbone left, and thrown it into a pot. As it was boiled, he added cilantro and the ginger that I love and, of course, pepper can be seen floating on top. Twit and I leisurely enjoy the end of an eleven to thirteen course meal, depending how you count the courses. The waiter, who now is beaming with pride at not only providing great service but seeing that I ate everything brought to me, cleans the table off. I ask for another bottle of Cognac. Though we have no intention of staying much longer, I'll share the bottle with the staff in a show of appreciation for another fine meal prepared and delivered. This is not the first time I've done this, in fact the first time I did it here, Twit had difficulty explaining this to the old lady. It's after I take a couple of small glasses of Cognac that I request a check and ask for extra glasses. They know me and quickly the waiter arrives with what I'm sure was a prepared tray with a half dozen glasses on it. Twit asks for the cook, so that her husband can thank the staff. Twit usually uses the statement of me being her husband, she even wears a thin gold ring.

The paying of the check, though not expensive for me, is done quickly. I also add a tip, a rather large one Twit tells me on the way home, for each of the staff, the cook, the waiter, his helper who other than getting the room ready when we first arrived I've not seen, and the old lady. The goodbyes are said after the old Mercedes taxi that Twit called had arrived. I feel totally relaxed as I climb in the back with Twit in her *Ao Dai* gathered up in her hand to prevent it from being dragged through the puddles. It's rained, at times hard, while we were dining. If anything, it's getting downright cold. Twit snuggles up next to me as the driver rushes us back up QL-1 a few miles to Houng Ca. Before getting out I pay the driver, who wants to argue over the price because he had to drive in VC country. He may be right, but he picked us up and drove up here without a complaint until he saw my roll of bills. I split the difference with him and Twit and I rush to the house.

Time is too valuable to us for me to argue with a money hungry cabbie. I don't have the time off that I used to have in my prior tours. With the joys of family life, each time away is more painful than it was with my family in the States. For some reason, I don't feel the pain of separation with those in the States as I do with Twit. One night Rick told me he felt I should never return to the States. He said, with no rancor, that I had gone Asiatic. I didn't think so and defended my reasons for staying in Vietnam, but later that night in the cubicle with Fred laying on my legs, I thought about it. Had I become like some of the old China hands that were a legend in the Marine Corps? Who knows, but if Rick thinks I've gone native, then I'm sure it's been talked about behind my back. I need to hurry up and get my extension papers approved.

Chapter 25

When I was picked up , the same PFC arrived during a heavy downpour and beeped the horn several times. Though I was about ready, Twit said to have him come in out of the rain. When I waved him in, he hesitated, than looking around for god-knows-what, turned off the jeep and dashed to the door. I immediately took his poncho and told him to sit down next to the heater. I went back into the bedroom to gather my stuff, while Twit served him a cup of hot tea. When I came back into the room, he was standing up looking at the pictures on the wall. Surely he was trying to piece together why this warrant would come here to this house, and stay for several days, and have a Vietnamese boy run out to meet him calling him Daddy. When Loc came into the room the PFC studied him closely. It had to put his mind in high gear. After seeing Twit, who clearly was Euro-Asian, and Loc, who looked a lot more like an American child than an oriental, and Twit's pure Vietnamese mother come in kiss me goodbye just before we left, his young mind was spinning.

The house, at least from what he could make of it, was a lot nicer than the few whore houses he'd been in for his fifteen minute quickies while a friend stood outside next to the jeep pretending to be looking for something under the hood. It had to be obvious that I had spent money to spruce the place up. Not only the Japanese electronics, but the place in general. Plus, I'm in several of the photos on the wall and so was Twit's father, dressed in his French uniform.

After I kissed Twit, several times, and gave Loc a good strong hug, I left with the PFC. He quickly sped off and joined the traffic headed north toward Camp Eagle. After a few minutes, and for the first time using the word Sir, he asked how long I'd been in Vietnam. When I told him, he said softly, as not to embarrass me, if I had known the girl for long. I told him it was a yes and no answer. Yes, it had been a while, but no I had not known her long enough. He accepted the answer, but made no other comment till he stopped in front of Captain Pratt's office. Then he said, loudly now, that anytime I was down at Eagle he'd give me a lift anywhere I needed to go.

I went in and caught Pratt milling over some paperwork. He dropped everything and invited me over to his hootch for a beer. The battalion log bird would be headed up to the Griffin pad later in the afternoon. He told me that it appeared that the Condors of 2nd/17th CAV, would be moving up to Quang Tri for a new operation. But he had the papers all ready for me to sign. Plus, he could work it so after I signed them, I would be transferred within ten days or so. It didn't take me any time to grab a pen and scribble my name onto the bottom of the three sets of papers. Twenty minutes later I was on the LOG Huey, on the way to the Griffin pad.

Hell, I'm going to be able to stay for another six months for sure. The other night, after the Cobra dinner, I explained to Twit how I planned to stay in Vietnam. Now, once this is processed I'll be able to stay with her. I even went over the option of going back into maintenance. She didn't seem to understand what I meant that if I went back into maintenance, and somehow got assigned to a general support aviation maintenance, we could spend more time together. The problem with a maintenance assignment is that I must give up my first love — flying combat. Twit still doesn't understand what I do. Other than being a helicopter pilot, my whole talk was Greek to her.

It's not the hours in the air that has become addictive for me. It's the combination of the power of the aircraft you're strapped into and its deadly weapons systems. Add to this the ability to make life and death decisions and I quickly became romanced into this love affair with armed helicopters. The rush of adrenalin pumped me up as well. It also helps not having an RLO sitting over your shoulder telling you that he knows it all because he learned it in ROTC or some ninety-day shake-n-bake school. We all know better. The freedom of soaring into the air is something that has drawn me like a magnet since I was a little boy. Pedaling my English made three-speed Raleigh bicycle the six miles to the grass strip in the neighboring town, Simsbury, and laying on the freshly mowed grass on the approach apron watching the small tail dragger aircraft do their touch and goes all day was a treat. On many a night, I completed the trip home as it turned dusk, while dreaming of being up there with them. Then, when my Father could take the time off, we'd go up in the Navion and he eventually let me steer the aircraft. I thought that if I could steer an aircraft, I could fly one. As the hours added up, I learned that there was a bit more to it than that. As time went on, I learned more and more. As the fumes of the AV gas snaked up into my nostrils and through the membranes of my lungs, the love for aviation entered my blood stream. I became addicted, just like the heroin users who go down to cabbage patch in Da Nang with the excuse that they got lost going to the Freedom Hill PX. It tugs at your spirit. Frank Sinatra sings a song, "Come Fly With Me," that describes how I feel the aircraft's beckoning. The sound of the engines running, the noise of the blades turning, the smell of the burned fuel has captured me. I can't, no, I won't give it up.

It was destiny for me to arrive here. Just as it was destiny to be in Marine aviation, then to transfer to the Army to fly. What will the future bring? I'll be flying, but where? For who? Doing what? If the war is really winding down, depending on whose news reports you listen to, what will happen to all of us that want to stay in Vietnam? We can't believe Nixon. Not after watching him repeatedly deny that U.S. troops are operating, flying, or are near neutral Laos. His brief television appearances come usually right after I've spent a day of flying CCN. And what about the guys flying CCC or CCS or those flying out of NKP in Thailand? Yeah, right, we're not in Laos and we're going to reduce our troop strength. I've got some land for sale in southern Florida, so step right up. We haven't lost this war and America has never, repeat never, lost a fucking war. Though some historians think that our Civil War was a loss, not only for the south but for the nation as a whole.

"Sneaky, you going up to CCN for the party?" Jimbo hollers from his cubicle in the front of the hootch. Hell I'm here at Camp Evans and not where I've been day dreaming — in Houng Ca with Twit and Loc, like I was last night.

Though this is the first I've heard of a party and I've got a head cold, I would never miss a chance to have a few beers with Billy and company. "Shit Yeah!"

While setting up my Teac with a new tape of Rachmaninov's Piano concerto No. 2 in C Minor, I hear the other pilots coming into the hootch complaining about the cold and the rain.

Jimbo yells once more, "We'll be flying up with Phoenix. They have a slick leaving in an hour. Supposed to land up at the Hot Spot so be ready, cause he isn't going to wait."

"That you, Sneaky?"

"Yeah, it's me." I answer Klien who moved into the cubicle next to mine a few weeks ago.

He's becoming more and more of a recluse and only talks to the other ACs about missions and tactics. Several times I've had crew-chiefs and mechanics bitch about his attitude toward them. The war has produced another wounded soldier. Maybe not with a Purple Heart, but still wounded.

I've tried on several occasions to talk with him. First as a friend, which didn't last five minutes before he told me to fuck off. Then I used a father-son approach. He told me that his father was dead. He didn't need one ten years ago and sure in the fuck didn't need one now. The last time I tried I used my rank, though going in I knew it wasn't going to work. I wasn't comfortable with it and it showed. In the first minutes of our conversation, he looked at me with his mouth agape and anger growing in his expression. Then, he stood up and told me that I had turned over and was like all the other lifers in the Army. As he walked away, he told me not to talk to him again. Since then we have hardly talked, though it's as much my fault as his. I'm loyal, and probably to a fault, but once I'm pissed, I'm vindictive as hell. I do get even and nothing's above me to make my point. Hell, I don't need this. Klien's not my kid. Never was and never will be.

"You owe me five bucks," Klien says as he comes up to my door and pulls back the camouflaged poncho liner I have hanging to slow down the cold wind blowing into my cubicle.

"What?" I answer bothered with his request, or demand, for money.

"I had to spend five fucking bucks for Spam so I could feed your fucking mutt while you were gone, that's what!" He's holding back the liner peering in my cubicle.

"Shithead, you know damn well he'll eat anything. You didn't have to spend money for food." I yell at him, not because he spent the money but, because he knows better.

He lets the poncho liner go, then walks back to his cubicle. After slamming his chair against our adjoining wall he asks, "You going up to Quang Tri tonight?"

"Yeah, if I can afford it," I answer, as if whether I go or not will have any bearing on what he will be doing tonight.

"Forget about the five. Hell, I like the fucking dog."

"His name is Fred, not 'the fucking dog'," I yell at the wall.

I can't be mad at Klien for too long. Though his nickname "The Kid" has stuck and he's still got the baby face, he's far from being a kid now. The months of combat have aged him. I've been thinking about trying to talk him into taking an early out rather than staying in Vietnam. I would hate to hear of him getting killed and he's acting at times like he doesn't know the dangers out there. For me, it would be like losing a younger, much younger, brother. One minute you're mad as hell at him, then the next you worry deeply about him. Then I've never had a real brother, just

Jimmy, who was like a brother, but he died while flying around Khe Sanh in '67.

Putting on my headphones, I flop down in my custom chair. I haven't opened a beer, but I'm able to relax.

The Kid is standing over me and kicking at my feet. I must have dozed off. I lift off one of the earphones to listen to what he's saying.

"If you're going to the party, better get moving. Slick's on the way to the hot spot." Klien turns and walks away without waiting for a reply.

Getting up I quickly turn the reel-to-reel off and reach under my bed to the refrigerator. Opening it, I see the small brown bag that one of the cooks gave me last week. Inside it are pieces of overcooked and now very cold hamburger. I pull two patties out of the bag before kicking the door shut. Fred, who's sitting perched up on the foot of the bunk, cocks his head in a manner as if asking me what I have. He knows. His nose is sensitive as hell when it comes to ferreting out food.

"This is all you get tonight Fred."

I throw him the two dark brown disks.

He catches one in mid air and with his head tilted up, I guess to allow a straight shot down to his stomach, he inhales the first disk in three bites without dropping any. Then he picks up the other piece that's resting on the side of the bed.

I grab my flight jacket and walk through the hootch toward the front door. With the changing weather, the hootch takes on a different personality. The outgoing personalities of the young warriors are more subdued and at times they are even belligerent to one another. Getting out of here and going up to CCN will be relaxing, though only three of us from our platoon are making the trip. With three newbies in the platoon, the drunken, let's party till we drop, attitude has left. Fuck 'em! In less than an hour I'll be with my kind. These newbies can worry about dying without me hearing about it.

Stepping out the door, the force of the monsoon wind, with

its thick piercing rain drops, hits me in the face. Head cold or not, I'm going to Quang Tri. Walking up the hill to the hot spot, I notice some men milling about in front of the hot shack. I wonder who all's going up with us? No telling who's hiding from the weather in the converted hut that serves as a two-minute alert shack. Many is the night when I had the two-minute hot status and I would spend time in the dirty run down shack on one of the broken down cots. I've re-read all the old crumpled up magazines or some of the pocket books that had not only been skimmed by every pilot of the battery at least once, but now each has pages ripped, folded, or missing. You can't find a complete story among the stacks of literature piled on the broken table in the hut.

"Wondered if you were going to make it," Rick says, standing with a rain jacket draped over his flight jacket. He's the only one that's had the sense to dress appropriately for the weather. With the hood over his head, he will probably be the only one not sick with a cold in the morning.

"Yeah, got back late this afternoon."

I stop in front of him and peer over his shoulder to see who's in the hot shack. Although it's 3rd Platoon's twenty-four hour duty, Rick has opted not to fly in order to go up to the MLT and party.

The Phoenix slick lands and, luckily for us, it is one that still has a set of cargo doors installed. Our ride up is dry but cold. Besides the four regular flight crew members, there are five other Phoenix pilots on board. With them and the six Griffins on board the plane was full. I sit on the floor with my back leaning against the center console. Squeezed to my right are Crusty and the Kid. On my left, Goose and Rick. Jimbo uses his officer status to steal the seat between a couple of the Phoenix pilots. When I climbed in, I am surprised to see Toby Allen sitting there smiling at me. I wonder how he got up here with the Phoenix crew. As the doors are closed, Toby pulls out several beers and passes them around, then leans over in the noisy cabin and whispers something to the Kid. The Kid then yells over the whine of the helicopter's operating noise that Toby had the day off and has hitched a ride up to Quang Tri. He didn't even know about the party until an hour or so ago.

After landing at the MLT, we immediately jump out and make a dash across the soggy semi-flooded PSP pad for the hut that has been converted into a lounge and club. The Phoenix aircraft then lifts to a hover and after executing a left pedal turn, takes off to the south. Apparently the Phoenix flight crew isn't going to stay with us tonight.

Entering the hut, we realize that we're the last to show up as the party is in progress. The room is noisy and full. After stopping for a beer at the bar, I walk into one of the back rooms and throw my flight jacket onto a cot that is now stacked with flight jackets from the Coveys, Phoenixes, and other Griffins. In the corner I see Rick had the sense to throw his wet rain jacket against the wall rather than adding to the pile on the cot.

The booze is flowing and the party is in full swing with the newest arrivals immediately joining in and trying to catch up to the others. Stories are being exaggerated at each of the five tables and the laughter is contagious. The time passes quickly with booze flowing like water over a burst dam. The music is loud but is still drowned out by the laughter at each table.

Captain America, or maybe it was Billy, has ensured that one of the Vietnamese girls from Da Nang is up here to provide entertainment. She is what we in Nam call a blow girl. Ugly as sin, half her teeth missing and pock marks she'd been carrying for the last thirty or forty years scarring her face. Without these noticeable features she would still be considered ugly. She is very thin, even by Vietnamese standards. Several of the guys said all she'd do was blow jobs, but each then commented how well she completed what she considered the perfect form of birth control. After the Kid came back, he said he tried to feel her tits and there were none.

As the party went on, time seems to escape me. I, like the others, am more worried about getting drunk as quickly as possible than about any possible hangover I might have in the morning. At some point one of the medics brought in a plate stacked high with steaks. Looking at them, I knew they were not government issue Australian or United States Grade A beef. They were probably the red deer that roamed freely in the valleys to our west. The poor deer, though only the size of a large calf, must have been spotted by a door gunner on a return flight from a mission and then didn't break and run quickly enough to escape the 7.62 rounds pumped into its hide. The meat is good and tasted like caribou and just as grainy, though a bit too well done for me. After quickly devouring it, another heaping platter appears and the pieces in this group are cooked more to my liking.

"Attention! Attention!"

Billy is yelling over the loud noise of the fifteen or twenty drunken men sitting around the several tables with empty beer cans stacked as monuments, and the paper plates with no leftovers shoved to one side. Billy walks over to the hi-fi and turns it off then returns to the front of the bar. It still takes a few moments but he finally gets the attention of everyone.

From out of the back hallway enters Captain America with some plaques. Flying for CCN has its rewards. It's not the medals awarded like the other units flying conventional flights are given. These rewards, to me, are much more valuable. The friends and respect gained flying Prairie Fire missions is something that money can't buy. Those that need to walk around with their medals at their next assignment are part of the Army's problem and have been seduced into the ticket punching mentality. When I finally hang up flying, I'll be able to sit on my front porch and know that I not only flew with the best, but I worked for the finest unit in Vietnam. The standards are high, especially with Billy and Captain Stanton overseeing things, and one quickly finds out if he can make it. Though it's not a dishonor not being able to do this kind of mission, those that can't, envy those of us that can. It's not something they would sit around in a club and talk about. In fact, it's the opposite. Those that can't hang in this type of flying environment will put us down. They'll say we're crazy, dumb, glory hounds, and whatever else they can think of. There is no way a group of pilots would sit around a table and say they wish they had the balls to go out and fly CCN missions. If you want to fly for SOG, volunteer. Simple as that.

I've learned from watching men that I consider gutless, that the way they mask their fears and inadequacies is to talk about someone else's deeds in a negative way. Those that can't cut it, think of us as lower species of men.

Once in a while, we who fly for CCN, receive formal recognition for our actions. Though it's really once in a great while. Jimbo never got a thing for picking up the 'yard while flying deep in Laos. Had he picked up an American, they would have been forced to give him something, but because of the nature of the mission and the fact it was only a 'yard, the higher-ups didn't want anything in writing. Rick has received several awards, but the wording was such that you would have to know what CCN is to figure out the buzz words. Young Toby Allen will probably get a Distinguished Flying Cross, though CCN Headquarters is pushing for a Silver Star for his flight several months ago when he went in and picked up the rest of Anaconda. Though like other CCN earned awards, the wording will contain the non-committal phrases such as, "while flying in denied territory, or deep in enemy held territory." The word Laos will not show up on any citation or supporting document. It will be whispered to the approving members by word of mouth that can be easily denied for the interest of national security, if someone asks formally years from now. The pinpointing of locations such as west of A Loui or northeast of Techrone, will not show up. The phrases like Special Operations, Command and Control, MAC-V-SOG, or Mission Launch Team 2 will never be printed. Recon teams will not be named, just the words "reconnaissance team" or once in a great while I've heard the use of "long range reconnaissance team."

Years ago, I received a single mission Air Medal, and the citation stated we rescued a long range reconnaissance team. What they considered long range on that action years ago would be passed over during CCN flights now. Our flights across the Laotian border are daily. Years ago, just the thought of being close to it would have given flight crews the jitters. But years ago, before operations Shining Brass and Nickel Steel were combined into Prairie Fire, very few units flew the MAC-V-SOG missions.

The only physical awards one can possibly get are the few patches that we wear. To most of us, the Laotian Highway Patrol patch says it all. Though copied from a stateside law enforcement unit, it represents a lot more to us. We don't ticket speeders or those making U-turns, we kill them. The Ho Chi Minh trail is really the most dangerous highway in the world. And we, the aerial law enforcement, have the toughest beat of all. We do not throw out slips of paper. No, instead we send 2.75 mm folding fin aerial rockets raining down on the law breakers. As one of the patrollers of the highway, I wear the patch on my right shoulder. This is my reward. Along with the patch is the privilege to wear the MLT-2 patch on the right breast pocket of my flight suit. Those who see it know that we earn our flight pay.

The other award that some, and really very few pilots earn, is one of the plaques that CCN or one of the MLTs will give out. These plaques are given to those who have repeatedly flown Prairie Fire operations and have become part of the CCN family.

Because of the rotation among the slick units I've only known one slick pilot who received a plaque. It probably had to do with his being an ex-Special Forces NCO who went on to flight school. I'm not sure if this is fair to the slick pilots, but it surely makes the plaques more coveted to those of us that do receive them.

Most of the Covey pilots receive them as their flights are daily and the relationship between the Air Force aviator and the recon team members is special. One might say they are the umbilical cord between those men fifty miles out in Indian country and the mother unit. It's the Coveys that watch over the teams as they move throughout Laos. No matter what the weather is, a Covey will be out flying somewhere in southern Laos. When the

Cobras are grounded because of weather, the Coveys will be orbiting above the team maintaining radio contact with them and charting their course for Headquarters.

Griffins have been fortunate because we've been the primary Cobra unit assigned to MAC-V-SOG flights for the past several years. This allows some of us to become close to the Special Forces men we work for. An example is Billy becoming a surrogate father to me. I'm sure Rick and Stanton's relationship is closer than most know about. The friendship is not only based on the days we are flying CCN missions but also during our off time. Several of the Griffins have been to NKP to spend time with the MLT based there, or have taken a Blackbird C-130 down to Na Trang for a few days in-country R&R. It's common to have one of our pilots holed up drunk at CCN Headquarters in Da Nang or stopping over while waiting for a flight to or from R&R.

I've been to the Coogie Beach Hotel, just south of Sidney Australia, which caters to Special Operations personnel. On the upper floor is a private bar with the different plaques of the units within MAC-V-SOG's secret war. When I checked in, I was given an unexplainable examination by the manager until he asked me what unit I was with in Vietnam. I told him I was a Griffin flying for MLT-2. He immediately called the owner from some hidden back office and after whispering in his ear, I was given the red carpet treatment which lasted my entire stay. GIs from regular line units that were staying in rooms on the lower floors couldn't comprehend why this GI was treated so special, but I knew why. The owner's brother had been an Australian SAS member who had been killed in Vietnam, and his commitment to his dead brother had been to give all MAC-V-SOG personnel the royal treatment. It was a phenomenal stay. Nothing like the noisy clamor and hubbub of Kings Cross that the regular GIs see.

Several of the Griffins have received plaques and each one of us has considered it the highest award we'll ever receive in this war. The wooden plaque with the brass multi-colored CCN patch resting in its center has below the emblem a small brass plate with a personal message. All the messages I've read revealed to me the serious thought that went into it. Nothing like normal units where the name, rank, and then specific dates of service were all that was engraved on it. No, CCN went out of their way to be distinctive and classy.

I've received two of the much honored plaques. The first, from CCN Headquarters, had engraved on the brass plate:

To Chief Warrant Officer
Robert White
for a job only Sneaky could do

The second one was given to me by Billy Washburn several months ago. It was from Mission Launch Team - 2 and its engraving said.

To SNEAKY WHITE
with LUV

Rick said when I received it, it was the only time he's ever seen me lost for words. I remember that it did take me by surprise even though I was well on my way to being drunk. But I also knew it was given with love. Love from men who not only know the value of freedom but know the costs to obtain and then keep it. To be considered a member of their team is the highest honor I'll ever receive. And though I won't wear a small multi-colored ribbon, or some badge to show that I was part of the best, I know and cherish the fact that I've received a plaque. I know that wherever I am in the Army, on my flight jacket will be either a CCN, MLT-2 or Laotian Highway Patrol patch. Damn what the regulations say, these are my awards, and I'll wear them with pride just as any other military man would wear his medals.

The presentation of plaques to the two Covey pilots getting ready to go back to the States goes off smoothly. Then, to our surprise, Billy calls Goose up to the bar and Stanton presents him with a much deserved plaque. Though none of us knows who will get a plaque or when, it's obvious that Rick had the duty to make sure Goose was present. Billy read the engraving out loud for us all.

"To First Lieutenant Daniel 'Goose' Baker
who was always ready to shoot one more shot."

Goose was drunk enough to not go into a long list of thank yous, and was quickly sent back to his seat after we all sang a few "hims." That's "hims" as in, "Him, him, fuck him."

Billy played the part of Master of Ceremonies in his grand style. After the fifteen minutes of formalities, we were all back to getting drunker.

Billy and several of the MLT members came over to our table to individually wish Goose best wishes on his trip home. Goose will be leaving in a few days. He has orders to Fort Rucker as Instructor Pilot. The Special Forces men are very guarded with their awards. They take it personal and not like the regular Army where everyone gets something for just being here.

"Sneaky, if you ever get another plaque it will read, never forget to check the tourniquet." Billy hasn't let me forget getting shot in the foot.

After all these months I still haven't been able to shake him off his harassment. But I have a weapon and I've been waiting for the proper time to use it. Tonight is that time so I stand up and yell, "Attention. Everybody shut the fuck up. I've got a very important announcement to make." The din of the conversations starts to die down as everyone looks my way. Though definitely not because of my commanding nature but more because of my hollering so loudly.

"As you all know," then looking at Billy and pointing, "thanks to Sergeant Major Washburn, I've been harassed for months regarding some serious injuries I received while flying a mission for him."

Chuckles are heard and Captain Stanton pounds on the bar to get the attention of everyone.

I look around until it's quiet again. "Thank you *Dai Uy*." I then make a sweeping bow to Captain America and turn back to face Billy.

"During the past several months I have become friends with an NCO who is attached to the MAC-V Advisory Team located at the Citadel down in Hue. During one of our talks over a few beers, one name came up several times by us both." Then, snapping my arm out and aiming my index finger at Billy, I gaze around the room to see if everyone is watching.

"It seems that my injuries to my right foot have been of some great concern to our Sergeant Major here. For a long time I thought it was out of concern. Maybe worry? Or if I dare use the word . . . ah . . . love."

Several snickers are heard from around the room.

I continue over the laughing men, "Love for an old Marine who has successfully integrated into the Army in spite of all the goat fuck rules and regulations."

"Here, here," one of the Air Force pilots says while the other Covey's tap their beer cans in unison.

Looking to my left I respond to the Covey's agreement of the Army's rules, "Thank you gentlemen. I'm sure that you understand the problems one has to endure making this change." I then glance back at Billy. "It seems that my thoughts of why he was distressed about my being wounded in the foot were not accurate."

"Nnnooooo." A voice from my table says. Again, chuckles are heard.

I continue once the noise has abated. "It seems that once upon a time there was a Special Forces Master Sergeant who was assigned to the 883rd Vietnamese Regional Forces Company. Now, I may be wrong on the unit but I'm sure that our most knowledgeable Sergeant Major can correct me if there is an error on any specific facts. Though I know it was years ago."

Billy has been looking questioning at me, but now a smile starts to emerge on the open round face.

"It seems that this certain Master Sergeant was attached to this unit in Binh Dinh Province of II Corps during June or July of 1965." Looking around the room, I go back to Billy's chuckling face.

"Anyway, if I may continue, this Master Sergeant got caught out in the middle of a rice paddy during an ambush. After being hit the first time in . . . " I point my finger to my right foot, then continue, " . . . guess where?" I ask the group, now listening intently after noticing Billy's reaction. They know I have something on him.

"His foot."

"The leg."

"Nah . . . had to be the foot."

"Couldn't be the ass cause Sneaky's the only one to shoot him there."

Laughter and shouting throughout the room as each of the men add their thoughts of possible injuries.

I raise my hand for silence. "Well for those of you that said the foot you win the $64,000 question. But there's more."

Laughter is starting to build up and I almost have to scream my next few sentences. "While laying out in the rice paddy, the wise old Master Sergeant was shot three more times . . . all . . . yes . . . all in the same right foot."

Everyone is hysterical and the noise from the pounding of the table with cans of beer, hands, and a couple of bottles of red rosa Mateuse wine, is the loudest yet.

Billy rolls up his huge fist into a tight ball and shakes it at me in a threatening manner. My only defense is the best smile I can put on my face and nod my head up and down enjoying my moment of glory. I've got him and he knows it. I've waited like a sly fox waiting for a chance at the hen house. The man who always gets you first, and never leaves you a comeback is in for a surprise tonight. It's my night to revel in this glory, which I'm sure will be reported to CCN Headquarters by several of those here tonight.

"Gentleman, it should be noted that one fine captain, named Davis I think, tried several times to go out and rescue this Master Sergeant. Each time he got to the wounded NCO, he found he couldn't lift the lard ass off the ground."

The roar of laughter is out of control. Everyone knows I've got Billy and there's nothing he can do. After months of ribbing me about my small injury I now have the goods on him and I'm going to play this like a harp.

"It took almost an hour before they were finally able to have a medevac come in and several, . . . yes I'm sure it had to be several . . . men carried the Master Sergeant to the helicopter for his trip to the hospital. Now before I name the Master Sergeant I want you all to know that I have checked my sources. The story was told to me by an NCO named Morgan who I met in Hue. I have since double checked it with the past Deputy Commander for the Rough Puffs, a Colonel . . . full Colonel that is, Colonel Ranck who's presently stationed at the Pentagon."

Everyone is laughing, knowing Billy has finally been on the receiving end of a joke.

"Sergeant Major Washburn, by any chance would you know who this Master Sergeant was, and if you do, could you enlighten us on his name?"

Billy, for the first time has a chance to reply. "Sneaky, don't go to sleep tonight." Then he steps over and hugs me.

Though most would consider hugging another man not the manly thing to do, who the fuck is going to tell a Special Forces Sergeant Major he was acting unmanly. After my little speech, everyone goes back to their conversations and the night wears on. Every so often the subject of getting shot in the foot is mentioned and everyone laughs.

Deep into the wee morning, after what seems like hours, I leave the few surviving men at the last occupied table. Leaving them, I hear the remarks regarding my inability to stay with them and finish drinking whatever may be left behind the bar. But not tonight, I'm too tired and now too drunk to continue. Staggering against the narrow walls of the hallway, I enter the large back room with its cots laid out in typical military fashion. Though dark, I'm able to avoid the cots with the snoring forms until I'm able to maneuver to the back wall and find an unoccupied one. I fall down on it. Then sitting back up I unzip my nomex shirt but because of the cold decide to leave it on. I unfold the poncho liner that was on the foot of the OD green and aluminum cot, hoping for some protection against the cold night air. I wrap it tightly around me and fade quickly into a sleep that shelters me from the thoughts of tomorrow's hangover.

Tomorrow will be another day. Another day of CCN recon teams going out where others dare not. It will be another day for the Huey crews. Both the crew-chiefs and door gunners depending on their pilots to guide them safely to and from the LZs that have been carefully selected. The Huey pilots also will depend on others. Not only the safe maintenance practices of their crew-chiefs and mechanics but the sure shooting of the men manning the M-60 machine guns mounted on each side of the aircraft.

It will also be another day for the Griffins. We will once again go out and lead a flock of over-extended birds laden down with their precious cargo, hoping to insert or extract them safely. For me, until I transfer to the Condors in the next few weeks or so, I'll be a Griffin. An honor that commands respect within the aviation and Special Forces community. It also burdens me with a responsibility to those we fly to the west of South Vietnam. The Griffins will be on patrol tomorrow as they were yesterday. They will be on patrol next week as they were last week, and they will be on patrol in the future as in the past. Griffins will be patrolling the highway, as members of the Laotian Highway Patrol.

My last thought is of Twit, of her expanding belly. Will it be a girl, or another boy to grow with our son? I do not want to think of the day that I might have to go home permanently. I don't want that. Not now, not tomorrow, not ever. Leave me alone. Here with my mistress, Vietnam. The land I love.

Good night Twit.
Good night Vietnam.

THE END

Glossary

AA/AAA	(Triple A) Anti-aircraft fire, usually 50 cal or larger in size.
AC	Aircraft Command
ADA	Air Defense Artillery. In the Army usually a missle unit.
ADF	Automatic Direction Finder. A radio in an aircraft/helicopter.
AFVN	Armed Forces Radio - Vietnam. A U. S. military operated radio station in Vietnam.
AGL	Above Ground Level.
AHIG	Attack Helicopter - Model G (Cobra)
Air America	A civilian air line, operated by and for the CIA, that flew throughout Southeast Asia.
AK(AK-47)	Standard issue, communist, 7.62 mm, automatic, assault rifle.
ALO	Air Liaison Officer.

AMOC	Aircraft Maintenance Officers Course, an Army school located at Fort Evstes, VA, to train Army officers to become Aircraft Maintenance Officers.
AO	Area of Operation or Aerial Observer. The Aerial Observer was usually an enlisted man who flew in a LOH, while in the Aero-Scout mode.
Ao dai	Long Dress, slit up the sides with long sleeves. Worn by Vietnamese women with pajama like pants underneath.
ARA	Aerial Rocket Artillery. An Army Cobra unit that flew only Heavy Hogs and was set up like an Artillery unit. Only two such units in the history of the Army — both only in Vietnam; 2nd of the 20th ARA attached to the 1st CAV, 4th of the 77th ARA attached to the 101st Airborne Division.
Arc Light	A B-52 bombing raid, usually with at least three B-52s in the flight (or cell as the Air Force calls it).
Article 15	Nonjudicial punishment for minor offenses.
ARVN	Army of the Republic of Vietnam. South Vietnamese soldiers.
ATR	Airline Transport Rating. Highest FAA pilots rating in US.
Bac si	Vietnamese for medic/corpsman.

Battery	An Artillery unit that consists of several sections, and with usually four Batteries to a Battalion.
BDA	Bomb Damage Assessment. An examination of an area after bombing. rockets, or artillery fire. Could be completed by ground troops, fixed wing observation or low flying helicopters.
C4	Plastic explosive used extensively in Vietnam.
CA	Combat Assault. Usually from helicopters.
CAR-15	A smaller version of the M-16.
CAV	A division of Army units divided into a cavalry troops(s). 2nd of the 17th CAV was the 101st Airborne Division.
C&C	Command & Control helicopter. Usually with staff officers either overseeing or directing operations (either air, ground or both).
CBU	Canister Bomblet Unit or Canister Bomb Unit. After being dropped by aircraft, the canister opens and hundred of smaller bombs fall to the earth. This gives a larger dispersal and is very effective against enemy troops in the open.

C/C	Crew Chief. Usually flew with helicopter and worked a side mounted machine gun. In Cobras, crew chiefs didn't fly and a co-pilot flew in the gunner's seat.
CCC	Command & Control - Central. A unit of MAC-V-SOG. AO was Northern Cambodia and Southern Laos.
CCN	Command & Control - North. A unit of MAC-V-SOG. AO was Laos, North Vietnam and the five southern provinces of China.
CCS	Command & Control - South. A unit of MAC-V-SOG. AO was Cambodia. This unit had of lot of Navy Seals assigned to it.
Chalk	Position of a helicopter in a flight. Chalk 4 would be the 4th helicopter in a formation.
Charlie	Vietnamese Enemy.
Chicken Plate	A bullet resistant plate worn by flight crews that slowed, if it didn't stop, enemy small arms fire.
Chinook	Boeing-Vertol CH-47. A heavy lift helicopter used by the Army. Sometimes called "shithook".
Claymore	Anti-personnel mine used by allied troops. Its deadly killing zone could be triggered by several methods.
CO	Commanding Officer.

Cobra	Bell's AH-1G helicopter gunship, used a flight crew of two - in tandem.
Concertina	A barbed wire roll used extensively in defensive positions by allied troops.
CONUS	Continental United States.
CWO	Chief Warrant Officer. A rank that is a cross between an NCO and Officer. Usually did not command troops, but was a technician in a specific job. The Army used them extensively as helicopter pilots. Above Warrant Officer were three further levels of CWO: CWO-2, CWO-3, CWO-4. All CWOs are junior to 2nd Lieutenants.
DA	Density Altitude. A figure based on air temperature, humidity and barometric pressure. This measurement provided a good indication of the expected performance of a helicopter.
Dai Uy	Vietnamese for Captain
DEROS	Date of Estimated Return from Overseas. Usually 12 months from date left CONUS for the Army and 12 months and 20 days for Marines.
DFC	Distinguished Flying Cross
Di di	Vietnamese slang - Leave.

Dink	Disrespectful name given to orientals by U.S. troops.
DMZ	Demilitarized Zone. An area along the 17th parallel, dividing North and South Vietnam.
Dustoff	Call sign for medical evacuation helicopters that was usually used with another call sign to signify the specific unit.
EGT	Exhaust Gas Temperature. On a turbine engine a major limiting factor on the amount of power it will produce.
FAC	Forward Air Controller. A man usually flying in a small fixed wing directing artillery, bombers or both.
FAM	Familiarization
Fast Mover	A jet plane, usually a fighter or light bomber.
FFAR	Folding Fin Aerial Rocket
Flack	Shrapnel given off from exploding shells at altitude.
Fleschette	Small dart shaped pieces of metal packed into a rocket. Once fired these small darts (nails) cover a large area and are very effective as an anti-personnel weapon.

FNG	Fucking New Guy. A term given to the new man in a unit. Usually carried for 60-90 days or until he earns an appropriate nickname.
FOB	Forward Operating Base, replaced by MLT in Summer/Fall 1968.
Fox Mike	FM (Frequency Modulated) radio
FSB	Fire Support Base. A major combat base in Vietnam, with artillery and sometimne helicopters present.
Gook	See Dink.
Ground Effect	A cushion of air from a helicopter's rotating blades that aides in hovering. Usually lost after airspeed reaches 10/15 knots.
Grunt	Infantryman.
Guard	One of two frequencies used for emergency radio calls. UHF-243.0, VHF-121.5.
Gunship	Either helicopter of fixed wing that was heavily armed with a primary mission to provide close air support. Fixed wing included AC-47, AC-119 and AC-130. Helicopter types included UH-1C, UH-1E (used by USMC) and AH-1G (Cobra).

Harassment & Interdiction or H&I	Artillery units firing at a pre-set time into pre-set known enemy areas to upset moral and movement.
HE	High Explosive
HEI	High Explosive Incendiary
Heavy Hog	Cobras of the two ARA Battalions in Vietnam. They carried four XM-159, 19 tube, rocket pods in their wing stores. All other Cobras carried only two at the most. This gave ARA Cobras the ability to carry 76 rockets.
Huey	Bell's UH-1 series helicopter.
Hunter-Killer	Teams of helicopters that included at least one LOH and one gunship. Usually were in CAV units. The LOH would hunt the enemy and then the gunship would roll in and kill them.
HMH-	Helicopter, Marine Heavy lift squadron. CH-37s were used until replaced in 1966/67 by the Sea Stallion (CH-53).
HMM-	Helicopter, Marine Medium lift squadron. UH-34s were used until replaced in 1966/67 by Sea Knights (CH-46).
ICS	Intercommunication System for aircraft.
IFR	Instrument Flight Regulations

Incoming	Enemy fire, usually artillery, rockets or mortars.
In-Country	In Vietnam.
Jolly Green	Call sign for Air Force Sea Stallions. See also Sea Stallion.
Kiowa Scout	A LOH made by Bell Helicopter (OH-58) that arrived in Vietnam in late fall 1969. Called Bell Jet Ranger.
Klick	Kilometer, 1000 meters.
KY-38	An add-on to the PRE-77 Radio, used to scramble the radio signal.
Land of the Big PX	United States.
Lifer	Derogatory term for career military personnel.
LLRP	Long Range Reconnaissance Patrol
Loach (LOH)	Small helicopter, either OH-6 or OH-58. Rumor is it comes from "Little Ole Helicopter," not "Light Observation Helicopter."
LURPS	Comes from LLRP (Long Range Reconnaissance Patrol). Here, it would be the specially prepared and packaged foods used on such trips.

LZ	Landing Zone. Anyplace where helicopters could land/hover and load/unload their cargo.
M-14	United States 7.62 mm rifle which was replaced with much media attention by the M-16.
M-16	Colt Firearms's 5.56 mm rifle, nicknamed "Mattel Toy" by grunts because of its plastic stock.
M-60	A 7.62 mm machine gun used by allied troops.
M-79	A single shot, hand held, 40 mm, grenade launcher used by allied troops.
MAC-V	Military Assistance Command - Vietnam.
MAC-V-SOG	Military Assistance Command - Vietnam - Studies and Observation Group. A highly secret unit that among other things controlled, under CIA's guidance, operations in Laos, North Vietnam and China. All operations were highly classified.
MAG	Marine Air Group. Usually consisted of a Headquarters & Maintenance Squadron and a number of aircraft squadrons. A helicopter MAG generally had one observation, one HMH, and five HMM squadrons.

Minigun	GE manufactured, six barreled, 7.62 mm, gatling gun, capable of firing 2000 or 4000 rounds per minute. Mounted in nose turret of heavy hog Cobras and in wing stores in non heavy hog Cobras.
Mini-Grenade	A Dutch made NWMV-40, 3 1/2 ounce hand grenade used only by SOG personnel.
Mikes	Short for millimeter
MLT	Mission Launch Team. Small units under CCS, CCC or CCN. At any given time a Command & Control would have three or more in operation. It replaced the FOBs in the Summer/Fall of 1968.
MOS	Military Occupational Speciality. A number letter series that states the holder's job description and sometimes extra qualifications, i.e., 11B40P - parachute qualified infantryman; 671CP - parachute qualified rotary-winged qualified maintenance officer.
Montagnards	A tribe of indigenous people who disliked and were in turn hated by the Vietnamese, but loved by Special Forces.
MPC	Military Payment Certificates used in Vietnam in lieu of U. S. currency to try and prevent black marketing.
Nails	See Fleschette.

Nape	Napalm bomb, a highly volatile jelly like substance that burned everything it landed on.
NKP	A small base in Thailand. A lot of secret operations were based out of there.
NVA	North Vietnamese Army soldier.
O-2	Cessna's military version of their 337 model. A twin engine model set up as a pusher/puller and used by the Air Force.
Old Man	Commanding Officer.
One-one	Call sign for a MAC-V-SOG Recon Team's assistant team leader.
One-zero	Call sign for a MAC-V-SOG Recon Team's team leader.
OV-10	North American Co.'s FAC aircraft, nicknamed the "Bronco" and flown by USAF and Marine units after 1969.
PBY	A WW II amphibous aircraft, used as a patrol plane looking for U-boats.
Phantom	McDonnell-Douglas made fighter/bomber (F4).

Pink Team	A combination of LOH and Cobra flying in a hunter-killer mode. A Heavy Pink Team could have an extra LOH or Cobra. Sometimes called a Red Team or Heavy Red Team.
Pipper	A red dot on the Cobra's Rocket Sighting System.
POL	Petroleum, Oils, & Lubricants. A refueling point.
Pooper	Infantryman's M-79 grenade launcher or a helicopter gunship's automatic 40 mm grenade launcher.
Prairie Fire	A code word used to signify an "emergency extraction" as well as missions operated out of South Vietnam.
PSP	Perforated Steel Parking. A material used in runway/helicopter pad construction.
Push	A radio's operating frequency.
Quad-Fifty	Four 50 cal machine guns generally mounted on the bed of a 2 1/2 ton truck.
QSY	An unofficial term to mean that you are going off that frequency.
R & R	Rest and Recuperation.
Red Team	See Pink Team.

REMF	Rear Echelon Mother Fucker.
RLO	Slang term meaning a Real Live Officer, usually meant in a derogtory way.
RPG	Rocket Propelled Grenade (Gun). A NVA weapon that was deadly to helicopters.
RT	Recon Team.
RTB	Return to Base.
RTO	Radio Telephone Operator. Radio operator in an infantry unit.
Ruck	Rucksack - Infantryman's backpack.
Sandy	Call sign for an Air Force unit flying Douglas Sky Raiders (A1). They were propeller driven, highly effective, close air support aircraft.
Sea Knight	Boeing-Vertol helicopter (CH-46) used by the Marines as a medium lift helicopter.
Sea Stallion	A Sikorsky helicopter (CH-53) used by both the Marines and the Air Force. The Marines used it as a heavy lift helicopter. The Air Force used it as a rescue helicopter, nicknamed Jolly Green or BUFF (Big Ugly Flying Fucker)
Section	A unit of four ARA Cobras. The smallest unit in an artillery unit.
SF	Special Forces

Shadow	Call sign for the Air Force AC-119 gunship.
Short Timer	Personnel with less than 60 days until DEROS.
Sit Rep	Situation Report.
Sky Crane	A Sikorsky helicopter (CH-54), used for hauling heavy equipment. The largest helicopter used in Vietnam.
Slick	A Huey.
Snake	A Cobra.
Snake & Nape	A combination of bombs that include slow drag and napalm.
Soap bubble	A MAC-V-SOG term meaning indigenous personnel
SOI	Signal Operating Instructions. A small booklet with the latest units and their call-signs.
Spad	Douglas Sky Raiders. See Sandy.
Spectre	Nickname for Air Force AC-130 gunship. Still in active service today.
Spooky	Call sign for Air Force C-47 gunship. Sometimes called Puff for "Puff the Magic Dragon".

Stabo Rig   A harness worn by flight crews on CCN
             missions to allow for a quick extraction with
             strings if needed.

Strings   120 foot ropes that could be lowered out of
             a helicopter to allow personnel on the
             ground to be lifted out.

TacAir   Tactical Air support. Could be any type of
             fixed wing that was on station at the time.

TOC   Tactical Operations Center. A unit's nerve
             center

Torque   Used to measure power in helicopters,
             taken from the oil pressure in the main
             transmission.

TOT   Turbine Outlet Temperature. A limiting
             factor in LOH helicopters.

UHF   Ultra High Frequency. A band of radio
             frequencies used.

Uniform   UHF Radio.

USARV   United State Army - Republic of Vietnam.

VC   Viet Cong. South Vietnamese guerilla
             soldier.

VHF   Very High Frequency. A band of radio
             frequencies used.

Victor	VHF Radio.
Victor Charlie	V. C.
Viet Minh	Pre Viet Cong name for communist soldiers.
VNAF	Vietnamese Air Force.
White Team	A combination of two or more LOHs in a Aero-Scout mode.
Willy Pete	White Phosphorous. Grenades, rockets or artillery.
Wing	Largest Marine Aviation Group. Three active during Vietnam.
WO	Warrant Officer. Lowest ranking officer in the Army. After one year is promoted to Warrant Officer 2. See also CWO.
World	Anyplace except Vietnam, usually means the U. S.
WP	Willy Pete.
XO	Executive Officer. The #2 man in a unit.
ZPU	A communist gun (23 mm) that came in several models. ZPU-2 had 2 barrels and the ZPU-4 had four. It could be mounted on a truck. Some advanced models had a high rate of fire and were used in AA gun emplacements.

Made in the USA
Las Vegas, NV
29 February 2024

86351792R00308